"EARTH ANGEL"

When the band began to play the first song, Laura's eyes widened. " 'Earth Angel,' " she said, sighing. "Oh, Steve, did you know this was a fifties band?"

He grinned and reached across the table to take her hand. "It brings back memories, doesn't it?"

Laura didn't bother to answer. Wordlessly she rose to her feet and walked into Steve's arms. They made their way to the postage-stamp dance floor. Other couples were already dancing, but to Laura it was as if she and Steve were alone on a private island.

His arms encircled her with an easy familiarity, as though the thirty-three years they'd been apart had never been. Laura closed her eyes and leaned into him. She was sixteen again; there were no grown children with marital problems, no crying grandchildren, just Steve and the magical music of their youth. They leaned closer to each other and touched their lips together lightly.

"I feel like a kid again," Steve murmured.

"Me, too," Laura said softly. "Me, too."

REMEMBER LOVE

STACEY DENNIS

ZEBRA BOOKS
KENSINGTON PUBLISHING CORP.

In loving memory of my mother,
Esther Laws, the world's best Mom
and "Granny."
This one is for you, Mom.

ZEBRA BOOKS

are published by

Kensington Publishing Corp.
475 Park Avenue South
New York, NY 10016

First Printing: December, 1992

Printed in the United States of America

Prologue

Laura Kinsey closed her eyes and groaned. There were gray hairs streaking her auburn hair, tiny laugh lines around her mouth, crow's-feet edging her gray eyes, and the merest hint of a spare tire around her middle. How had it happened? When had it happened?

Staring back at Laura from the full-length mirror on her closet door was a middle-aged woman. A woman who had already experienced the best years of her life. A woman who was precariously perched on the edge. The slightest nudge and she would topple right off the edge and into the "golden years."

"The devil you will, Laura Kinsey!" The mirrored image challenged her. "You've got a lot of living left to do, even if gravity is taking over."

Turning from side to side, Laura examined herself critically. She'd been lazy since Paul's death and it showed. She'd always prided herself on having kept her slender, youthful figure, but somewhere along the line, somewhere in the maze of grief and confusion following her husband's death, she'd gotten off track. "You'd be disgusted if you could see me now, Paul," Laura muttered.

Suddenly the all-too-familiar fatigue and lassitude rolled over Laura and she sat down on the edge of her king-sized bed. Maybe it was crazy to worry about her figure, crazy to think there was anything left. After all, she'd done everything she'd set out to do, hadn't she? She'd been a good and faithful wife to Paul, a devoted mother to her three children, Vicki, Valerie and Greg. She'd kept a clean house, attended PTA meetings religiously, baked tons of cookies for Brownies and cub scouts. She'd taken care of her mother during her last illness, and she'd cared for Paul after the stroke that eventually took his life. Now what?

Buttons, Laura's fluffy white mutt, hopped up on her lap and peered at her with his big, shoe-button eyes.

"And what do you want, brat?" Laura asked, smiling at the dog's comical expression. Buttons always looked as though he was trying to figure life out. Laura chuckled. "Join the club, little friend," she said, scratching Buttons behind his ears. "I don't have the answers either."

Somehow Buttons's appearance jolted Laura out of her temporary doldrums. She'd always been an upbeat person, quicker to smile than cry. It was just that this past year, since Paul's death, she'd felt scared and uncertain, and very much alone.

"Don't worry, little pal," Laura assured the pup. "I'm not going to leave you all alone to shift for yourself. I'll take care of you the same way I took care of everyone else."

An hour later, after feeding Buttons and dialing in her favorite late-afternoon talk show, Laura fixed herself a salad and made a small pot of decaf. It had never bothered her when she was young, but lately regular coffee made her jittery and kept her awake at night. She watched the show without much interest. It was hard to care about a woman who was feuding with her sister-in-law over a borrowed dress.

When she finished eating, Laura turned off the television and loaded her few dishes into the dishwasher. She frowned, knowing it would be at least a couple of days until she had enough dishes to run the machine. There was a time when the dishwasher ran three times a day, but that was when the kids were at home, when Paul was alive and well, when Laura was still needed.

Laura's salad dish nearly slipped from her fingers as a new, and completely foreign thought occurred to her. After years of putting others first, of pushing her own needs and desires behind everyone else's, she was free. She was free to do whatever she wanted, whenever she wanted.

A strange tingling sensation began in Laura's fingers as she quickly finished loading the dishwasher. Her years with Paul and the children had been wonderful. Her life had been full and satisfying, and she wouldn't have traded a minute of it, but all that was over now, and maybe there was still time for Laura to do some of the things she'd always dreamed of.

Maybe there really was a lot of living left to do.

One

Laura stripped off her damp sweat suit and stepped into the shower. It was great to feel so alive again, exciting to be exercising and eating right again. To be thinking of the future instead of dwelling on the past.

As she soaped up, Laura scrutinized her newly slender body. Pretty good for fifty-one, she thought proudly. The slight spare tire she'd picked up after Paul's death was gone, and her legs were tight and trim. Was this how other women felt when they began to come out of their first raw grief after the loss of a mate? Like life was starting all over? Was it wrong to feel such optimism, such glory in her newfound freedom?

Toweling herself dry a few minutes later, Laura dusted herself with perfumed powder, then dressed in khaki slacks and a beige T-shirt. She finger-combed her hair and headed for the kitchen to get her half-grapefruit and a glass of mineral water.

Such luxury, Laura thought, opening the morning newspaper as she nibbled the slightly tart fruit. No one to disturb her, nothing she absolutely had to do. She'd been scanning the want ads for several weeks now, but so far she hadn't found the perfect job, and until she did she was going to keep right on looking. When she finished reading the paper, Laura looked around her squeaky clean kitchen. The small breakfast area with its cute round table and two chairs where she now sat, the gleaming stainless steel sinks, the pale green formica countertop. They'd barely finished remodeling the kitchen when Paul suffered his fatal stroke. Laura closed her eyes, remembering the fun she and Paul had, picking out wallpaper and new cabinets. Even the occasional argument over color or style had been fun. Paul hardly had a chance to enjoy the fruits of his labors before he died. At least, Laura thought, Paul had known he was loved right up to the last moment of his life. Both girls adored him. He'd always been their hero. And Greg had modeled himself after his beloved Dad.

Paul had provided well for his family during his lifetime. They hadn't been rich, but they were always comfortable and now, after his death, Laura was fortunate enough to be free from any serious financial worries. No, she didn't have to go to work if she didn't want to, but she'd decided that a job would keep her focused. It would also help her meet new people and develop new interests.

The telephone rang and Laura picked up her portable receiver.

"Morning," she said, her eyes still scanning the want ads.

"Laura? Is that you? Goodness, you sound so perky. What have you been doing with yourself? I was telling Jim yesterday that we haven't seen you for weeks."

Laura neatly folded the newspaper and shifted the telephone receiver to a more comfortable position. "Hello, Blanche," she said, her voice taking on a more sober tone. "It has been a while, hasn't it?"

Paul's older sister, Blanche, lived only blocks away from Laura, but the two women had never been close; they had nothing in common except their devotion to Paul. Blanche had a gloom-and-doom personality that was completely at odds with Laura's optimism.

"I'm sorry I haven't been around lately, Blanche," Laura said, "but I've been trying to get my life back in order."

"Oh, of course! You poor darling! Your life will never be the same without our dear Paul, but you must go on, if only for the sake of your children."

Laura managed a small laugh. "The children really aren't children anymore, Blanche. They're all doing quite well on their own. You heard that Greg is working in the obstetric and gynecology division of his hospital, didn't you?"

"Yes, of course. That darling son of yours sent us the sweetest letter. He is so like Paul, isn't he?"

Laura nodded into the telephone. "He does have a lot of Paul's characteristics, yes."

"Well, of course I realize your brood is all grown up, but children always need their mothers, you know."

"How are you and Jim doing?" Laura asked. She pushed her empty plate away and grimaced, preparing herself for a long discourse on the state of Blanche's health.

By the time Laura said good-bye to her sister-in-law her ears were ringing. The doorbell was a welcome diversion.

Pushing a thick strand of hair out of her eyes, Laura opened the front door. Instantly, she was flung back into the past. Her breath caught in her throat, and her blood galloped through her veins. She was sixteen again. She was young and vibrant and wildly, crazily in love with the high-school football star, Steve Walker.

The feeling only lasted for a few seconds, then her heartbeat returned to normal, and her thoughts once again became rational and sane. A coincidence. Just a coincidence. The young man standing on her doorstep was about the same age as her son, Greg, but he looked like a replica of Laura's long-lost high-school sweetheart. A crazy coincidence.

Then the young man spoke. "Mrs. Kinsey? Laura Cramer Kinsey?"

Laura's hand fluttered at her throat. It was eerie. He even sounded like Steve.

"Yes. That's my name. Who . . . are you?"

Now the apparition grinned, and Laura's heart did a funny little skip-dance in her chest. Blanche's depressing phone call had unhinged her mind. There was simply no other explanation!

"My name is Steve Walker, Jr. I believe you went to school with my dad?"

"You're Steve's Walker's son? Oh thank God! You look so much like him—I was afraid I was hallucinating."

The young man laughed. "May I come in? I'm here in town on business and Dad asked me to look you up and extend his sympathy on the recent loss of your husband."

"Please, do come in," Laura said. "You must think I'm crazy, the way I was staring at you. It's just that you resemble your father so strongly."

"I know," Steve said, following Laura into the living room. "Everyone says I'm the image of my dad."

"How is he?" Laura asked. After high school she'd lost track of most of her old school friends, and Steve had dropped off the face of the earth after enlisting in the Army. *After making love to Laura and promising to love her for all eternity.*

Five years ago she and Paul had attended a high school reunion. She'd learned then that Steve and his family were living in Arizona.

"Dad's doing okay, I think," Steve said, sobering. "My mom died of cancer two years ago, you know. She was sick for a long time, and it took a heavy toll on both of us. Dad's bouncing back now. I think he's going to be okay."

Laura motioned for Steve to take a seat on the floral upholstered sofa. "I'm sorry," she said. "I didn't know about your mother. I never met her. Your dad never made any of our school reunions." She'd always wondered about that, always wondered if Steve was ashamed or embarrassed to meet her again.

Laura made a pot of coffee, and she and young Steve talked for nearly an hour, then the young man explained that he had a sales convention to attend. "I sell pharmaceutical supplies," he said. Then he grinned. "Dad's coming to

Florida to visit some cousins in a few weeks. He wanted me to ask if it's okay for him to stop and say hello."

Laura felt her face bloom into a smile. "Okay? Why, it will be wonderful to see Steve again. You tell him that I'll be highly insulted if he doesn't come by."

After seeing Steve to the door, Laura went back to the living room and sat down, letting the faded memories spring back to life. All at once she could smell the flowers that had banked the walls of the school gymnasium the night of her senior prom. She could feel the crisp scratchiness of her pink tulle formal, and she could remember what it was like to have her whole life spread before her, a virtual smorgasbord of pleasures just waiting to be sampled. Most of all she remembered her first real love—a tall, dark-haired, broad-shouldered football player.

And what a love it was! Steve had been her first serious boyfriend, and she had lusted after him for months before he finally noticed her. Then he did, and she was transported into the magic known as first love. Laura squirmed uncomfortably on her sofa. She could still remember the wonder of those first, tentative kisses, she could still feel the heat of Steve's hands as he hungrily explored her body. Lord, but they had sure steamed up the windows of his old Ford!

Laura shuddered as the familiar longings swept over her. Paul had been gone for a year, and for months before his death they had been forced to live without sexual fulfillment. Paul had simply been too weak and sick.

"You're definitely a love-starved old broad, Laura Kinsey," she chided herself. "Aren't you ashamed?" She smiled ruefully. She wasn't ashamed at all. She'd loved Steve, and after him, Paul. And she'd given each man everything she had to give at that particular stage of her life. And now she was beginning to feel hungry for a man again. Not just any man, but someone special, someone who would be just right for this time of her life. And she'd be damned if she'd feel guilty!

Exactly three weeks later Laura's doorbell rang again, and this time it was Steve, Sr.

"Steve."

"Laura."

They gawked at each other like second-rate actors in a soap opera. Then they both grinned.

"Are we nuts or what?" Steve asked, opening his arms.

It was perfectly natural to move into the sheltering warmth, absolutely right to nuzzle her head against his shoulder and breathe in the male essence of him. Time stood still and everything was as it had been all those many years ago.

"This is astonishing," Laura finally managed, moving away and feeling just slightly self-conscious. "After all these years."

"Yeah. This would make a great television movie, wouldn't it? High-school sweethearts sharing a hug after more than thirty years."

"Well, I'm not sure . . ." Laura shook her head uncertainly. Wasn't this just a casual meeting, a fleeting moment in time, a glimpse back at the past?

"Don't try to analyze it, Laura," Steve said, shaking his head. He reached out and grasped her hand, and as they walked into the living room, he swung their hands between them, the same way he had when they were seventeen. "You always did like to figure everything out, didn't you?"

Laura felt her head swim. She was suddenly overcome with the sight and sound and smell of her youth. Steve was older, of course, just as she was, but there was much about him that was the same. His shoulders were still wide and strong, and his smile still took over his face. It started at his lips and traveled to his eyes, those beautiful, unforgettable chocolate eyes. And his voice. It was just as deep and strong as it had been so long ago.

"You look as beautiful as you did the night we went to the prom," Steve said softly.

Yes, his smile was the same, yet different, Laura thought. Now it was tempered by time and the experiences of a lifetime.

"I remember your dress," Steve said. "It was pink, and every time I got close to you it scratched me."

They both spoke at the same time.

"I'm sorry about your wife."

"I'm sorry about your husband."

Silence, awkward and strained, then a mutual smile, softened by loss.

"Sit down," Laura invited. "I'll make coffee."

"Three grandchildren! I can't believe it," Steve said later, shaking his head. "You don't look much older than you did at our senior prom."

Laura laughed. She felt lighter and freer than she had since Paul's death. Steve was exaggerating, of course, but it was still delightful to hear. "You're pretty well preserved yourself," she teased. And he was. His jaw was still firm and strong. He still walked with a sure, steady step.

She turned the page in the photo album she kept on the coffee table. It contained her life, starting with her marriage to Paul.

"You were a beautiful bride, Laura," Steve said. "Paul was a lucky guy."

"We were both lucky," Laura corrected. "Paul was a wonderful husband and a devoted father." Her blue eyes dropped to the photo taken at their thirtieth wedding anniversary.

"Marcie and I had a good life too," Steve said. "Our only disappointment was that there were no other children after young Steve. We thought about adopting, but I guess we never really gave up hoping that Marcie would get pregnant again, and then one day it was too late."

"Well, if you could only have one child, you did well with your son. He seems like a remarkable young man."

Steve smiled and lifted his coffee cup. "He is that. Did he tell you that he and his wife, Joyce, are about to make me a grandfather?"

"No! Really? That's wonderful You'll make a great grandpa."

It was as if they'd never been apart. The first brief awkwardness had disappeared and Laura felt perfectly comfortable sitting next to the man she had once loved so passionately.

"How long will you be in town?" she asked, wondering if she would have a chance to introduce Steve to her children.

Steve leaned back against the sofa cushions and smiled. "I'm thinking of moving here," he announced.

Laura's breath caught in her throat. All at

once the awkwardness was back tenfold. Steve living in the same town? "Are you serious? Moving to Miami?"

Steve's expression changed, became serious and intent. He put down his coffee cup and leaned forward. "Why not, Laura? There's nothing left for me in Arizona. Marcie loved it there, but she's gone now, and I've always missed being near the water. You remember my cousin Robert, don't you? Well, he's opening an auto rental agency and he wants me to manage it. Young Steve will be traveling through here on a regular basis, so . . ."

"What about your home in Arizona?" Laura asked. Her own house had always been so important to her. Although she was rattling around in it all by herself she still couldn't imagine selling it.

Now Steve stood up and walked to the window to look out at the graceful palm trees. He shrugged his broad shoulders and grinned. "It's just a house now," he said. "Marcie made it a home, but with Steve married and gone, I figure I don't need much space, you know?"

Laura glanced around her comfortable, lovingly decorated living room. She supposed men looked at things differently. Just after Paul's death, his attorney had suggested she might want to put the house up for sale, but she had vetoed his suggestion immediately. Selling her home would be like erasing her life with Paul and the children. She'd brought all the children to this house as newborns. She could close her eyes and experience all the wonderful Christmas mornings this house had seen, the children's birthdays, the graduations, the anniversary parties and finally, the last days of Paul's life. She had set his hospital bed up beside that front window where she and Steve sat now. She'd read to Paul by the hour as he stared out the window at the gently rustling palm fronds.

Two fat tears slid down Laura's cheeks as she remembered.

Then Steve moved closer. He bent down and pulled a snowy handkerchief from his shirt pocket. Gently, his lips curved into a sympathetic smile, he wiped the tears away, then he grasped Laura's hands and pulled her to her feet and into his arms. "It's all right," he said softly. "It's going to be all right."

He stayed for dinner. He tossed a salad while she broiled a thick juicy sirloin. For dessert they nibbled cheese and chunks of sweet apples and pears and drank strong hot coffee laced with a dash of Irish whiskey. Afterward they listened to Laura's collection of records from the fifties, but they didn't dance. Laura wanted to. From a place deep inside her, she wanted to feel Steve's arms around her again. She wanted to press close against him, feel his warm breath against her cheek and smell the earthy, male scent of him. She wanted, however briefly, to be young again. But it was too soon. Or maybe it was too late.

That night, Laura tossed from one side of her king-sized bed to the other. She saw herself at sixteen, going out with Steve for the first time. She'd been too thin in those days, all angles instead of curves. She was shy and scared, convinced that Steve would dump her off on her doorstep after the movies and never speak to her again. But when he walked her to her door he asked for a second date, and that was the beginning.

Then Laura's dreams shifted her to that last night, before Steve left to go in the Army. They'd climbed into the back seat of his Ford and wrapped themselves around each other.

Between fevered kisses, they'd made promises, promises that were destined to be broken. They kissed, and Steve's hands, so young and strong and manly, moved over Laura's body with shy determination. They'd kissed and petted for more than a year, but they'd never crossed the line, never taken that final, irrevocable step. That night everything was different. There was an air of fear and uncertainty in their kisses, a tinge of desperation in their frantic, adolescent caresses.

Laura felt again that sudden stab of pain when Steve entered her. She remembered the fear, and then the sweet, melting ecstasy as her body learned how to please a man.

They both cried afterward and vowed that they would always be true to one another. She didn't see him again for thirty-three years.

He came back the next day, for a breakfast of croissants and coffee. He tried to talk her into going shopping at Bayside, and then for a sunset boat ride, but something held Laura back. It was too soon. It had only been a year since Paul's death. She was still a widow, not a woman free to date and feel pleasure with another man. She tried to explain her feelings to Steve.

"I am glad to see you again," she said slowly, "but I can't just . . . what I mean is . . ."

In truth, she wasn't exactly sure what she meant. Her body was clamoring, and even though her gynecologist claimed her hormone levels were low, Laura knew different. Her femininity was wide awake and alert. But Steve? She reminded herself that this was the nineties, not the fifties, and a single woman was perfectly free to enjoy a satisfying physical relationship with a man she cared about. And it didn't necessarily have to be the love affair of the century. But would she dare?

Steve lifted her hand, held it gently to his lips, then released it. "I understand, Laura. I'm not here to pressure you. It's just so wonderful to see you again, and I've been lonely since Marcie died. When you've been married for so long it's hard to live the single life again."

"Yes, it is." Laura's hand felt the imprint of his lips. She was vulnerable. They both were. It would be a terrible mistake to rush into anything. They were different people now. They were no longer frantic teenagers. They were mature adults with family responsibilities. For heaven's sake, she was a grandmother three times over!

"Well, thanks for the coffee and conversation, Laura," Steve said. "If I can't change your mind about spending the day with me I'd better be on my way." Then he smiled that crooked, wonderful smile of his. "But I will be back."

"I hope so," Laura whispered after him. "I really hope you do come back this time."

But after Steve pulled away from the front of the house, Laura sank down with a million questions swirling in her head. What kind of relationship could she and Steve have after all the years that had separated them? They couldn't possibly go back to what they had been, and Laura wasn't sure what they could be as mature, experienced adults. Friends? Lovers?

The thought of having a lover scared Laura skirtless. How could she go to bed with a man at her age? With her belly still bearing the stretch marks from her three offspring, with her breasts not as firm and high as they'd once been . . . with her, or so her gynecologist claimed, lowered libido.

Yet how could she not be tempted when after only one meeting her hormones were already on overdrive? It was amazing that after all these years she was still physically attracted to him. Laura fell asleep that night clutching her pillow against her middle, wishing it was a warm, live male body.

"Mother, I'm desperate. Please! You've got to help me out!"

Vicki was Laura's oldest daughter. Her urgent plea vibrated over the telephone wires the next morning, and Laura's heart plummeted to her toes. So much for not being needed any more.

"You know I'll do whatever I can to help, honey," she said, "but are you sure leaving Tim is the right thing to do?"

"It's the only option I have, Mother," Vicki de-

25

clared flatly. "He refuses to talk about our problems and this is the only way I can think of to make him realize I mean business."

"But the children . . . Andrea is old enough to realize that something is wrong, and you know how sensitive she is."

"Of course I do," Vicki replied shortly. "After all, I am her mother. I've taken care of all that. Andrea understands that sometimes grown-ups have problems. She'll be fine."

Laura sighed. She had been using Paul's den as a storage room, and the room that Vicki had slept in before her marriage was hardly large enough for a mother and three children. Of course there was always Greg's old room, but there was only a single bed in there.

"All right. You and the girls can have my room," she said. "I'll sleep in your old room, and Bobby can have Greg's room."

"Oh, Mom, thank you! I knew I could count on you. And you'll see, once Tim realizes I mean business he'll beg me to come home. You'll see!"

Laura spent the rest of the day rearranging furniture and making up beds. Twice she called Vicki to remind her daughter to bring plenty of disposable diapers for the baby. She climbed up in the attic and found some old toys to keep Andrea and Kelly occupied. The girls were adorable, miniature copies of their mommy at the same age, but it had been a long time since Laura had had small children living in her house. She was used to having things stay where she put them, used to a quiet, peaceful house. She'd gotten used to being alone, and she liked it. And Vicki had always been a little difficult. She'd been a good girl, and as bright as a new copper penny, but she was very emotional, and she tended to be a little self-centered.

Laura helped Vicki get settled the next day, with one ear straining to listen for the telephone. If only Tim would call!

"He's absolutely impossible, Mother," Vicki said that afternoon. All three of the children were napping and the house was blessedly quiet. Laura and Vicki sat in the back yard under an old banyan tree.

Laura sipped her tea thoughtfully, then she shook her head. "I always thought Tim was just about the most reasonable young man I've ever known. It's difficult to imagine him being hard to get along with."

"Don't you believe me?" Vicki demanded, her voice rising. "Do you really think I'd make something like this up?"

Laura felt the start of a tension headache. Her neck felt tight and she wished she could crawl into bed and pull the covers over her head. Vicki was a beautiful young woman. As far as Laura knew, she had matured into a good wife and an excellent mother, but she had always been high-strung and excitable, and quick to go on the defensive. And she demanded a lot of attention. She always had.

"Of course not, honey," Laura said soothingly. "You know better than that, but I was just wondering if you and Tim have somehow gotten your signals mixed. Tim's an ambitious young man, but you knew that when you married him. In fact, isn't that part of the reason you were so attracted to him in the first place?"

"Sure, but I never expected something like this to happen. Does he really think I should pack up three kids, give up our beautiful home and just fly off into the sunset with him?"

Laura couldn't help laughing. Vicki was also the most dramatic of all her children. Fly off into the sunset, indeed! Hardly the way she'd describe relocating to further a man's career.

"Do you think it's fair to expect Tim to give up this opportunity, just because you don't want to move out of the state, honey? You know, it would be different if you had a successful career of your own to consider, but as it is . . ."

"I cannot believe you're taking Tim's side this way," Vicki cried, her blue eyes filling with tears. "I thought you'd understand!"

"Honey, I do. I'm just trying to get you to look at all sides of this situation. I know it would be hard for you to uproot the children and move to the other side of the country, but on the other hand, wouldn't it be fun to see something different? To experience a different lifestyle?"

Vicki huddled in a ball of misery on the sofa. "You don't understand at all! I don't want anything different. I like my life just the way it is!"

Laura smoothed her daughter's dark, silky hair. And that was the problem, she thought. Vicki was thinking of it as her life, but it wasn't. It was Tim's life too. Her headache was in full bloom now, and she didn't even dare contemplate the outcome of this latest development in Vicki's life.

By dinner time Vicki was in her room, pleading an upset stomach. Laura did her best to keep an eye on the two little girls, while the baby played in the playpen. Her nice, neat house was a shambles. Not dirty, just incredibly messy. Funny, Laura thought, how quickly parents forget about the messes small children can make with hardly any effort at all. There were toys scattered all over the living room carpet, and Kelly had somehow gotten hold of Andrea's crayons and started drawing a mural on the kitchen wall. Fortunately, the wallpaper was vinyl and could be washed.

The thing was, Laura thought, as she helped Kelly build a house with Lego bricks, the kids weren't really doing anything wrong. They were just being kids. And she was just being an older woman who wasn't used to having toys underfoot all the time.

Satisfied that the girls would be okay by themselves for a short time, Laura wandered out to the kitchen to figure out what she could fix for dinner. She'd been eating a lot of salads lately, but she knew the children wouldn't touch anything that was green or crisp. Sighing, she set the table with her everyday dishes and thawed some ground beef. Hamburgers and baked beans. Not the best thing for her figure, but something she knew the girls would eat without complaint.

By the time she had Bobby strapped in his high chair, Laura knew it didn't matter what she'd cooked. Her appetite was gone. It had dissolved in a flood of Vicki's self-pitying tears and her own maternal worries. And the damned telephone stubbornly refused to ring!

What were they going to do if Tim refused to call, and Vicki continued to be so stubborn? What if Tim got fed up and "flew off into the sunset" without his wife and children? Would Vicki expect to stay on in her childhood home?

Laura's headache was accompanied by a sick

stomach by the time she got all three of the children settled in bed. She took an Alka-Seltzer and climbed in the narrow twin bed, and did what she'd been wanting to do since Vicki moved in. She pulled the covers up over her head.

Two

"Wake up, honey," Laura told Vicki the next morning. "I'm going for my run, and the kids are all awake."

Vicki groaned. "So early?" She struggled to sit up. "Don't you think you're too old for this kind of thing, Mother? Why, you could have a heart attack!"

Laura shook her head and adjusted the sweat band on her forehead. "No, you've got it backwards. I'll have a heart attack if I don't do this. I'm keeping my arteries nice and clear and my blood pressure right where it's supposed to be, not to mention the fact that weight-bearing exercise is good for my bones."

"All right, all right, I'm getting up," Vicki said. She shot Laura an accusing look. "I would have thought you'd be glad to spend some time with your grandchildren. You don't see them that often."

"I spent several hours with them last night, dear," Laura reminded her daughter. "I gave them their dinner, bathed them and played with them before I put them all to bed. You were sick, remember?"

"I was, Mother," Vicki said, her lower lip thrusting out the way it had when she was little and didn't get her way. "Do you think I was faking?"

Laura shook her head. "No, not at all. I'm sure you were feeling rotten. Now I've got to go, honey. I'll see you later."

Vicki managed to get in one parting shot. "Don't you think those spandex tights are a little youthful, Mother?" Her normally wide blue eyes were narrowed as she scrutinized her mother's attire.

Laura bit back a sharp retort. Vicki was upset and unhappy. She didn't mean to be cruel.

Vicki didn't say anything else, and Laura knew she'd caught the angry warning in her mother's eyes. A glance over her shoulder as Laura left the room showed Vicki in front of the full-length mirror, studying her own figure.

Laura followed her regular route through the park, her head spinning with a hodgepodge of crazy thoughts. What in the world would she do if Vicki and Tim failed to make up? Selfish or not, she couldn't imagine having her quiet, orderly life disrupted permanently. Toys scattered all over the living room, her lovely bedroom taken over by a sobbing woman and two sweet but noisy little girls. Even Buttons had gone into hiding. The minute the children had arrived, the little dog had crawled under the sofa, and now she practically had to drag him out when she wanted to walk him.

"It's only temporary," she muttered. "It's only temporary!"

But what, Laura wondered, was going to happen when Steve came back to town? How could she manage a love affair with her adult daughter and three young grandchildren in the house?

Laura quickly swallowed two aspirins as her daughter slumped into the kitchen the next morning.

"Coffee made?" Vicki asked, raking her fingers through her long dark hair. She flopped down on a kitchen chair. "Andrea wet the bed again last night. If this keeps up I'll have to buy you a new mattress."

Laura resisted the urge to ask Vicki what she had expected. Seven-year-old Andrea was an extremely sensitive child, and she adored her daddy.

"Maybe if Tim came over and talked to her it would help," she suggested.

Vicki accepted the cup of coffee Laura handed her and shook her head. "Don't be silly, Mom. How am I ever going to get Tim to see that I'm serious if I keep running back and forth, or if I call him and beg him to come to us? No. This time I'm staying right here until he comes to his senses. Andrea will be fine. She'll adjust."

Under her breath, Laura groaned. Maybe Andrea will adjust, she thought, but will I? She loved all her children dearly, but she firmly believed that they were all better off in their own homes.

"I just want to help, Vicki," she said, adding skim milk to her coffee, "and I can't help being concerned about Andrea. She's always been such a serious, solemn little mite."

"That's just because she's so intelligent, Mother," Vicki said shortly. "You know what the school psychologist said about her. She understands more than most other children her age."

Kelly came racing into the kitchen just then, dragging her beloved "Boo bear" behind her. "Andrea is crying, Mommy," she informed Vicki, "and Bobby is trying to climb out of the playpen again."

"Come over here, sweetheart, and Grandma will fix you some breakfast," Laura said to Kelly. Resisting the urge to go comfort Andrea was hard, but Laura knew she had to let Vicki handle things in her own way. After all, Vicki would be thirty years old on her next birthday.

Laura poured juice for the three children and fixed a plate of scrambled eggs and toast. Kelly ate hungrily, but Laura's stomach churned at the mere thought of food.

The eggs had congealed on the plate by the time Vicki returned carrying Bobby and herding Andrea ahead of her.

"Hello, sweetheart," Laura said, smiling at her oldest grandchild. She loved all the children, but she had a soft spot for Andrea. The child was so sweet and gentle, so loving. Sometimes it almost hurt to look at her.

"Are you hungry?"

Andrea nodded and slid onto a chair. "I'm sorry I wet your bed, Grandma," she said shyly. "I'll try not to do it again."

"It's all right, honey," Laura reassured the child. "We all have accidents once in a while."

"But she does it all the time," Kelly taunted. "Every time Mommy and Daddy have a fight she pees all over our bed!"

"Kelly! Do you want to stay in your room all day? Why do you try and hurt your sister?"

Vicki looked completely frazzled. She strapped Bobby into his high chair, and Laura thought that the fat, rosy baby boy was probably the only one in the house who wasn't suffering stress of some sort.

Laura slid a plate of rewarmed eggs in front of Andrea and a smaller plastic plate to her little grandson. "I'm going upstairs to get dressed," she told her daughter. "Just load the dirty dishes into the dishwasher and I'll take care of it when I come down."

In the sanctity of her daughter's old bedroom, Laura sat down on the bed and put her head in her hands. Please Lord, she prayed silently, let Tim come to his senses quickly. I'm too old for all this! The minute she had the thought, she whooshed it away. She wasn't too old. She simply didn't want to raise another family. Being a mother had been the joy of her life, right up there with being Paul's adoring wife. She had loved each and every minute of raising her two daughters and her son, but all that was in the past now. The years of crying babies and soggy diapers were behind her, and she wanted to keep it that way. Did that make her selfish? An uncaring Mom? Was she failing Vicki in some terrible way?

She was just combing her hair when the telephone rang. She picked up the receiver and heard Vicki on the downstairs line.

"I've got it, honey," Laura said when she recognized Steve's voice. "It's for me."

"Oh," Vicki answered in disappointment. "Well, don't tie up the phone too long, will you, Mom? Tim may be trying to reach me."

"Do you have houseguests?" Steve asked, after Vicki hung up.

"In a way," Laura said. "It's a long, complicated story. My daughter and grandchildren are staying with me for a while. A little domestic squabble."

"Oh. I'm sorry to hear that. I got back in town last night and I was wondering if I could take you to lunch, but I suppose this isn't a good time."

Laura laughed. "On the contrary, your timing is perfect. I'd love to have lunch with you. Will you pick me up or shall I meet you somewhere?"

"Hey, great. I'll pick you up. At noon?"

"Perfect," Laura said. "I'll be ready and waiting."

"You're having a date?" Vicki asked incredulously, when Laura went downstairs dressed to go out in a soft blue sundress. "With an old boyfriend?"

"It's not like that, honey. Steve lost his wife two years ago, and he's planning to relocate here in Miami. It's the least I can do to show him around."

"But what will people think?" Vicki insisted. "Daddy's only been gone a year. Should you be doing social things like this?"

"Vicki, I told you this isn't a date, and even if it was there wouldn't be anything wrong in it. Your father would be the first one to tell me to get on with my life."

"But it's . . . well, it seems disrespectful to Daddy's memory," Vicki protested. A suspicious gleam entered her eyes. "Does this guy think you have money or something?"

Laura's blood bubbled with rage, but she managed to keep her voice quiet and calm. Vicki was distraught. Her life was in turmoil. She hadn't meant that the way it sounded.

"I won't dignify that with an answer," she said. "Maybe I'd better just meet Steve outside."

Vicki had the sense to realize she'd gone too far. Even as a little girl she'd had a knack of knowing when she'd overstepped the bounds.

"I'm sorry, Mom. That was a rotten thing to say. I don't even know this guy. And I'm sure any man in his right mind would love to take you out. I guess I just can't imagine anyone taking Daddy's place." Vicki's eyes filled with tears, and Laura softened and gave her daughter a quick hug.

"No one is going to take your father's place, dear," she promised. "I would never allow that to happen."

Vicki's tears dried quickly. "I may have to look for a job," she said thoughtfully. "I mean, just in case things don't work out for me and Tim. You'd be willing to look after Bobby and the girls, wouldn't you, Mom?"

"You mean babysit while you go out to work?" Laura asked. She felt like every hair on her head was standing on end, and she was sure her eyes were as round and shocked as someone who's suddenly seen her life flash before her. "On a steady basis?" she squeaked.

"You wouldn't want to?" Vicki asked incredulously. "I thought you loved the children."

"I do. You know I do, honey, but to look after them full time . . . well, I've been thinking of getting a job myself. You know, so I can meet people and keep active."

"Meet men, you mean," Vicki said sharply. "Really, Mom, at your age! You had a perfectly wonderful husband for over thirty years. Wasn't that enough? I thought women your age liked to spend time with their grandchildren."

"I do, sometimes. I'm just not sure I could handle it on a regular basis, or"—here Laura stiffened her spine—"if I even want to try. The children are your responsibility, Vicki, and if you feel you need to go out and get a job, I think you'll have to make arrangements for daycare."

Vicki's eyes widened. She looked a lot like her father had at thirty, Laura thought. Vicki was a feminine version of Paul. Now those striking blue eyes stared at Laura accusingly.

"You really want me to put your grandchildren in daycare?"

Laura felt herself weakening. She had read all the horror stories about abusive daycare centers. Her scalp prickled with horror. Of course she didn't want to see her grandchildren in daycare. What she really wanted was for her daughter to go back to her perfectly acceptable husband and work at her marriage. So Tim didn't always listen to Vicki the way he should. And maybe it would be hard for Vicki to leave everything familiar behind and follow Tim halfway across the country, but was that reason enough to break up a family? Much as she hated to admit it, Laura knew that her daughter was acting like a spoiled child.

"No, I don't want to see the children go into daycare, Vicki, but I don't want to spend my days taking care of them either. I spent quite a few years doing child care, and now I'd like to have some time for myself. What I think you should do is talk to Tim and . . ."

"Don't tell me to go back and work things out with Tim, Mom. This time he has to come to me. He has to realize he's not giving me the respect I deserve. I should have some say in how we live our lives, shouldn't I?"

Laura sighed. Laura knew that if she tried to nudge Vicki into going back to Tim, she might do something really stupid. "All right, have it your way," she said. "Oh, there's Steve. I'll bring him in to meet you some other time. Have a good day, honey. I'm not sure what time I'll be home."

Sliding into the seat of Steve's well-polished blue Bronco, Laura willed the morning's tensions away. She sighed, and met Steve's knowing, sympathetic eyes.

"Rough morning, huh?"

"The worst," Laura said, nodding. "Vicki's a doll most of the time, but she can try one's patience. And I'm not used to having children underfoot all day. The kids are feeling the strain and . . ."

Steve slid behind the wheel and started the engine. "Come on, let's run away," he said, grinning wickedly. He winked and tried to look like a rogue.

Laura couldn't help laughing. "Let's," she agreed.

An hour later Laura sat across from Steve at

a waterfront restaurant that had been a favorite of Paul's. At first, when she realized where Steve was taking her, she'd felt a pang of sadness. Then she raised her head and saw Steve's smile. She'd loved this man once, with all the passion and fire of youth, and after that she had loved Paul, with a deep, steady devotion. It was good to be here with Steve. It felt right.

"So, do you think your daughter will work things out with her husband?" Steve asked, after ordering shrimp cocktails and white wine for starters. "This isn't serious, is it?"

Laura shook her head. "I doubt it. Tim is a doll, the perfect son-in-law as far as I'm concerned. He adores Vicki and the children. He's a good provider, and he doesn't run around or drink to excess. He's even," she grinned crookedly, "good looking. I'm not exactly sure what it is that Vicki feels is lacking in her marriage. She's always demanded a lot of attention. The only thing I can figure is that Tim doesn't pamper her enough. And of course, she's unhappy about having to sell their home and move to Indianapolis."

Steve shook his head. "What do you think will happen if Tim doesn't come running to her side?"

Laura took a sip of her wine and shuddered. "I'm afraid to think about that," she said. She played with the stem of her wine glass. "Do you think I'm an unnatural mother not to want my children and grandchildren living with me? Am I being selfish?"

"You? Selfish? I doubt it." Steve smiled, remembering. "I see a young girl who would lend her last dime to a stranger, a girl who would give up her chance to be on the cheerleading team to keep her friend from having hurt feelings, a girl who . . ."

"Stop! That was a lifetime ago, and this is my daughter I'm talking about. What if she can't make her marriage work? Maybe Tim isn't as great as I think he is. Maybe he leaves the cap off the toothpaste and drops his underwear on the bathroom floor. Maybe he snores!"

Steve refilled Laura's wine glass and laughed. When he put the wine bottle down he covered Laura's hand with his own.

Such a large, strong hand, Laura thought. Why did Steve's touch make her feel so confused and unsettled? Why was she worrying? They were only friends, weren't they? There was no need to rush into anything.

"I haven't had to cope with anything like this yet," he said. "Steve has only been married for three years and so far everything is rosy. God, I hope it stays that way!"

"Vicki and Tim have had their squabbles off

and on from the very beginning," Laura said, "but there's never been anything serious. This time, though, I really think they need to go for marriage counseling. With three youngsters there's too much at stake."

"I agree," Steve said. "Have you suggested counseling to your daughter?"

"Many times," Laura said, "but Vicki sees counseling as an admission of failure. She thinks that she and Tim should be able to work out their differences without outside help."

"Oh?" Steve's brows arched. "Then how come she moved in with you?"

"That's different," Laura said dryly. "I'm just her mother, and mothers don't count."

After their appetizers, Steve ordered soft-shelled crabs and pasta with a seafood sauce. Laura eyed the menu longingly, then settled on a chef's salad. No sense tempting fate, or all those extra pounds she'd finally managed to shed.

As they ate and talked, her tensions eased. Steve was a delightful companion, and she felt comfortable with him, almost as if their long separation had never occurred.

"Do you ever wonder what might have happened if I hadn't gone into the Army?" he asked, when the waiter had removed their plates and brought hot, fragrant coffee. "I was such a damn fool for not calling you, but I was so young, and it was such a kick being away from home . . . being on my own."

Laura felt herself drowning in his eyes. They were dark and hot with remembered passion, and Steve's gaze, so familiar and penetrating, made her own longings rush to the surface. She felt herself warming, opening. Get a grip, Laura, she told herself firmly. Take things slow and easy, one step at a time, and don't forget the pain this man once caused you.

"I won't pretend I wasn't hurt," she said honestly, "but like you I was awfully young, and as they say, time heals all wounds. I was just grateful I didn't get pregnant from that night we spent together." She was deliberately making light of it. She hadn't been merely hurt when Steve went away. For a while she had been devastated, but what was the point in bringing all that up now?

"God, do you realize I never even thought about that possibility until much later? What a callous ass I was!"

"Indeed," Laura agreed solemnly, then she couldn't help but laugh. "At the time I hated you," she admitted. "I thought about making a doll and sticking pins in it. Then I met Paul and forgot all about you." Laura wasn't very good at lying, and she could feel her face flush.

46

Luckily, Steve didn't seem to notice.

"I never forgot you," he said, "but after I got over sowing my wild oats I was too ashamed to get in touch with you. I was sure you'd kick me off your doorstep. Then I heard you were engaged and it was too late. And then there was Marcie. Is it too late now to say I'm sorry?"

Feelings were stirring inside Laura's breast, and all at once she was scared. She was on a roller coaster, and what if she couldn't get off? Everything was moving too fast . . . too soon.

"Apology accepted," she managed. "Now, how about changing the subject? All this talk of the past is making me feel old."

Steve looked like he wanted to protest until he looked into Laura's wide blue eyes and saw the lingering hurt, a hurt that he had caused.

"Sure thing," he said. "How about cheesecake for dessert?"

"I didn't know what to take out of the freezer for dinner," Vicki complained later, when Laura finally got home. Her voice was barely above a childish whine, "So I just made grilled cheese sandwiches for the kids. Are you hungry?"

"Not a bit," Laura said. "I ate far too much at lunch. I think I'll just have a cup of tea and a piece of fruit." She waited, then, "Did Tim call?"

Vicki shook her head, her eyes filling with tears of self-pity. "I wish Daddy was here," she muttered. "He'd tell me what to do. He'd tell me how to handle this."

"Honey, you know as well as I do that your father would never interfere in your marital problems. He always believed that was a sacred trust between husband and wife."

"Well, at least he'd be on my side," Vicki complained. "You always side with Tim."

"You know that's not true," Laura said, pouring hot water into her cup. "I just think that running away never solves anything. How can you and Tim ever work things out if you're not even speaking to one another?"

"If he doesn't call me soon I'm going to consult a lawyer," Vicki threatened. "Maybe I'll even file for divorce. He's not going to keep me dangling while he acts like a single man!"

"I'm sure that's not what he's doing, honey."

"See? You do stick up for him!"

"Vicki, I don't . . ."

"I don't want to talk about it anymore," Vicki said tightly. "I'll handle this in my own way." She glared at Laura and stomped off to bed . . . in Laura's room.

Laura sipped her tea thoughtfully. It might

be sneaky, but tomorrow morning she was going to pay a little visit to her son-in-law. This situation was getting out of hand.

At the end of her run the next day, instead of setting out for home, Laura changed her course and hailed a taxi. It was going to cost a bundle to get to Vicki and Tim's house, but it would be worth it if she could convince Tim to talk to Vicki.

Half an hour later she was knocking on her son-in-law's door.

"Good morning, Tim," she said, when the unshaven young man opened the door.

"Laura? Is Vicki with you? Are the kids okay? Has something happened?"

"Calm down, Tim. Everything is fine. I'm alone. May I come in?"

"Sure, oh sure. I guess . . . well, I wasn't expecting you to just drop in this way. I thought you might be mad at me."

Laura shook her head. "Vicki is miserable, Tim, and poor little Andrea is very confused. You know how the children adore you."

Laura's son-in-law paced the perimeter of his living room nervously. Laura couldn't help noticing the empty pizza box on the coffee table and the overflowing ashtrays. Newspapers were scattered on the floor, and one of Tim's shirts was lying on the back of the sofa. Vicki would be furious if she could see the mess. The house wasn't large or fancy, but Tim and Vicki had made it into a comfortable, attractive home. Now, the living room looked like a disaster area.

"I feel the same way about the kids and Vicki, but I'm getting fed up with Vicki's little games, Laura. For Pete's sake, when is she going to grow up? She'll soon be thirty years old. Andrea is seven years old. We'll be celebrating our ninth anniversary soon. Or maybe we won't," Tim muttered grimly.

"Can we have a cup of coffee?" Laura suggested gently.

"Coffee? Oh, yeah, sure. Come on out to the kitchen."

Once in the kitchen Tim seemed to forget why he was there, so Laura quietly filled the coffee maker with water, measured coffee grounds, and set out mugs, sugar and cream.

"What does Vicki want me to do anyway?" Tim asked, raking his fingers through his thick, sand-colored hair. "Do you think I should pass up this big promotion? Do you, Laura?" Without waiting for an answer, he went on. "I can't seem to make Vicki understand what this could mean to all of us. I'll be getting a sizable increase in salary, a company car, and some other really interesting perks. I thought that maybe once we got settled Vicki could hire someone to help her with the kids. She could even go back to school if she wanted to."

Laura poured them each a mug of steaming coffee and set a glass of orange juice and some buttered toast in front of Tim. He looked terrible, as if he hadn't been eating or sleeping for days.

"It sounds wonderful to me, Tim," she said honestly. Vicki had interrupted her college education to get married. Laura had always hoped she would go back one day and get her degree. "I really don't know what it is going to take to make Vicki see reason. Believe me, I'm on your side in this. Vicki is always accusing me of that anyway," she added, with a little laugh. "In this instance she's right. Much as I love my daughter, I'm not blind to her faults. She has always expected and demanded more than her fair share of attention, from me and her father, and also from you. I don't know why she's like that. She just is." Laura's voice softened. "Even so, warts and all, I believe you love Vicki a lot, and I know she feels the same way about you."

Tim set his coffee mug down carefully. "I love her more than anything in the world, Laura, but I don't think I should have to give up my chance for this promotion to prove it. Do you?"

"Of course not," Laura said.

Tim stared at Laura solemnly. "If I didn't love Vicki and the kids so much I'd be sorely tempted to throw in the towel and wash my hands of this whole deal. Vicki's got a lot of good qualities . . . I don't have to tell you. You're her mother. What should I do, Laura? How can we straighten out this mess?"

Laura thought for a moment, then she voiced a thought that she'd had in mind for a long time. "I think Vicki needs counseling to find out why the thought of moving away threatens her so much."

"I've suggested that on more than one occasion, but she always vetoes the idea. She said she's not crazy."

"Well, of course she isn't. Who said anything about her being crazy?"

"The thing is, she knew this would probably happen someday. We even talked about it, and she never gave a hint that she'd be unwilling to relocate. You know, she might even like Indianapolis, if she gave it a chance."

Laura finished washing the coffee mugs and set them to dry. "I know, Tim, but the thing is, thinking something may happen, and having the reality of it staring you in the face are two entirely different things. From a purely practical point of view, I don't see how you can afford to turn this promotion down." Laura put her hand on her son-in-law's arm. "I think Vicki is scared, Tim. She has always hated saying goodbye to familiar things, or to people she cares about. You remember how she was at Paul's funeral?"

Tim nodded miserably.

"I don't think you should let too much time go by before you try to talk to her," Laura said gently. "A separation isn't always a good answer to problems like these."

Tim nodded. "I miss her like crazy, and the kids too. Do you think I could drop by this afternoon? Will she see me?"

"I," Laura said firmly, lifting her chin, "will personally guarantee it!"

"You had no right to go see Tim, and you certainly should not have promised him I'd talk to him. Now that I know you pressured him into it . . ." Vicki was furious when Laura got home and told her about her visit with Tim.

"I did not pressure him into anything, Vicki, and the two of you simply have to end this cold war and talk things over. It's not just the two of you who are involved, you know. There are children sleeping upstairs who need their father."

Laura and Vicki were having a late lunch while the children napped. Laura had prepared a luscious fruit salad, but Vicki had hardly touched it.

"Well, I don't want to talk to him," Vicki stated flatly. "We'll only end up arguing again. That's all we ever do."

Laura looked her daughter square in the eye.

"You're exaggerating, honey," Laura said. "You and Tim have always gotten along far better than most young couples we know. Everyone has disagreements, and the reason you're arguing now is that both of you want something different. Instead of pulling in harness as married couples should, you're tugging in opposite directions. Just remember this, you have a good man in Tim, and there are three innocent children who need both their parents." Laura smiled. "There's a lot of truth in that old saying, 'Home is where the heart is,' you know."

"Would you have packed up and gone halfway around the world with Daddy?" Vicki challenged.

Laura considered a moment. Then she laughed. "I'd probably have done just about what you're doing. I'd have sulked a little, cried buckets of tears, and then, yes, I'd have packed up and gone with him."

Vicki looked away. She shrugged. "I guess I owe it to Tim to hear what he has to say. Will you look after the kids while we talk?"

Laura grinned. "What are grandmothers for?"

Three

Laura kept the children occupied in the back yard while Tim and Vicki talked. She was hoping against hope that her daughter and son-in-law would find a way to work out their differences.

She felt a tug on the leg of her slacks and looked down to see Andrea trying to get her attention. "What is it, sweetie?" she asked.

"Are Mommy and Daddy going to make up?" Andrea asked solemnly. "Are we going to go home to our own house soon?"

"I hope so, honey," Laura said honestly. "They're talking about that right now."

From Vicki's old sandbox where Kelly sat with her baby brother, came another question, this one not quite so timid.

"Maybe they'll get a divorce. Do you think so, Grandma?"

"Oh, Kelly honey, no! I'm sure that's not going to happen."

But in her heart, Laura wasn't sure at all. Vicki could be stubborn. And when Laura had last spoken to Tim, it had sounded as though he was just about at the end of his rope.

While Laura watched the children play, her thoughts wandered. She still couldn't get over the way Steve Walker had come back into her life. It was like something out of a movie.

High-school sweethearts reunited after thirty years. Of course, they weren't really reunited, not yet anyway. Laura flushed as she imagined herself making love to Steve. What would it be like? They weren't the same passionate, starry-eyed kids they'd been the night they climbed into the back seat of Steve's old car. They were mature adults, who had lived and loved and been parents. Their bodies were no longer quite as slim and supple. They both had laugh lines around their eyes and streaks of silver in their hair. The one time they had made love they had been fumbling and inexperienced, but now . . . if they went to bed together now, it would be very different.

Poignant memories came back to Laura as

she remembered the pleasures she had shared with her late husband. She and Paul had enjoyed a healthy, robust sex life right up to the night he had his stroke. It made her blush to admit it, but she was already beginning to long for the warmth and satisfaction of a physical relationship. How different things were now. At the time, what she and Steve had done in the back seat of his car had made her feel guilty and scared. For weeks she had been terrified of the consequences of her impulsive act.

But things were different now, Laura knew. People were more open about their physical needs, both women and men no longer felt that they had to be madly in love to enjoy a pleasant sexual relationship. The thing was, could Laura change her whole moral code? Could she take pleasure where she found it and not worry about promises or commitment? Could she move into the nineties and go with the flow, as her son Greg would say?

"Grandma, Bobby's diaper needs to be changed," Kelly piped, bringing Laura back to earth with a thud. "Yuk! He stinks!"

Leaving the two girls to play in the sandbox, Laura had no choice but to carry Bobby into the house to change him.

She grimaced and held the baby at arm's length. Kelly was right. Bobby did stink.

She quietly skirted the living room, not wanting to disturb Vicki and Tim, but she couldn't resist peeking in to see how things were progressing. One glance and her heart sank. Vicki was huddled in a corner of the sofa, her pretty face streaked with tears. Her eyes were red and puffy and it was plain she'd been crying for some time.

Oh no! Things weren't going well at all. Laura saw that her son-in-law's jaw was tight, and his dark eyes were sparking with angry frustration.

"You're acting like a spoiled brat," Tim accused harshly. "Your place is with me. How do you know you won't like Indianapolis?"

Vicki sniffed. "I can't leave my home," she said. "I won't know anyone out there. I'll be thousands of miles from my family and . . ."

"I thought the kids and I were your family," Tim said, his shoulders slumping dejectedly.

Laura moved towards the bedroom with Bobby in her arms. She felt guilty for eavesdropping, and she felt even worse when she realized that it was quite possible Vicki and Tim weren't going to be able to work out their differences. She wanted to force Vicki to act like an adult, and think about what she would be giving up if she refused to move with Tim.

Laura laid a vinyl pad on her bed and took a fresh disposable diaper from the box on her nightstand. Diapers on her nightstand. Only a few days earlier a lusty paperback romance had reposed in sensual splendor just waiting to bring secondhand excitement into Laura's life. Now, a large cardboard box sat there, proclaiming extrathick, no-leak diapers for toddler boys. Things certainly had changed.

"Here you go, pumpkin," she told Bobby, snapping the legs of his corduroy creepers. "All clean and dry. Doesn't that feel better?"

The baby boy gurgled happily and clapped his fat little hands.

Once again, Laura realized that Bobby was probably the one happy person in the entire household.

When she and the baby joined the girls in the yard, Tim was already there talking to them. Laura saw the sadness in Tim's eyes and her spirits fell.

"No good?" she asked gently, laying her hand on his shoulder.

Tim was kneeling next to the sandbox. He looked up and held out his arms to take Bobby from her. "You'd better go see to Vicki," he said. "She's pretty upset. I'd like to stay with the kids for a while, if that's all right."

"Sure," Laura said. "Take your time. The children have missed you."

"It's no use, Mother," Vicki sobbed, when Laura went in the house. "Tim absolutely refuses to give an inch, and I just cannot drag the children to the other side of the country like it's nothing. And besides, Tim doesn't pay any attention to me anymore. He treats me like an old shoe. I'm not his wife. I'm just his slave, the woman who washes his clothes, cooks his meals and takes care of his home and his children."

"I'm sure that's not . . ."

Vicki swiped at her eyes angrily. "Don't you dare stick up for Tim, Mother! You do it all the time, and it just makes me sick!"

"Now just a minute, young lady. This self-pity has gone on long enough. I do not stick up for Tim. I merely try to look at things objectively, and I still think that marital counseling would help both you and Tim, and it just might save the marriage you seem hell-bent on destroying!"

Laura was breathing hard. She'd never been so angry in her life. Laura felt like spanking her daughter.

"I think you need some time alone," she said quietly, heading for the door. "Maybe I do too."

"If you don't want me and the children here I'll make other arrangements," Vicki said, sniffing pitifully. "I certainly don't want to curtail any of your . . . activities, Mother."

"That," Laura said flatly, "does not deserve an answer. We'll talk later, when you calm down."

Tim was saying good-bye to the children when Laura went outside. Andrea was crying.

Laura's heart filled with pity for her son-in-law. Tim was a decent young man, and right now he wanted his promotion, and he also wanted his wife and family, and it looked like he couldn't have both. Closing her eyes against the pain she saw on Tim's face, Laura wished she could wave a magic wand and make all the problems disappear.

"I've got to go," Tim said, pushing himself to his feet and handing the baby to Laura. He turned to his daughters. "I love you," he muttered. "Don't forget that, okay?" He kissed Bobby's plump cheek and squeezed Laura's shoulder. "Thanks for trying," he said.

"Don't give up, Tim," Laura pleaded.

Tim shook his head. "I'm afraid Vicki already has," he said.

"Daddy said he's going away," Andrea informed Laura. "He said he might not be able to see us all the time. Why does he have to go, Grandma? Doesn't he love us anymore?"

"Oh, honey, of course he does," Laura answered, drawing Andrea into her arms. She looked at Kelly. Although she was usually the more stoic of the two girls, she looked unhappy too.

"Your Daddy will always love you no matter what happens, but you mustn't worry so much. Sometimes mommies and daddies get mad at each other. Sometimes they even live apart for a little while, but that doesn't mean they don't love their children."

"I don't want them to get di-divorced," Andrea whispered. "One of the girls in my class is divorced from her daddy, and she hardly ever sees him. She lives with her mom and her mom's boyfriend. I don't want Mommy to get a boyfriend."

Laura hugged the children close to her heart. She hated knowing the kids were hurting, and she hated not being able to do anything about it. That was the worst part of this whole mess. There was absolutely nothing she could do. She'd tried to intervene and it had been a disaster. Vicki was on the defensive now, and Tim was just about ready to throw in the towel. There was nothing Laura could do but stand by to pick up the pieces.

Once again she was left to feed the children and play with them until it was time to put them to bed. Vicki was closeted in Laura's room with a headache.

What about me? Laura thought, massaging her own throbbing temple. She had a headache too, and her back ached from carrying Bobby around. She wasn't used to having a twenty-five-pound baby straddling her hip. Nor was she used to the demands of three active children, or the tension that permeated the whole house.

She fixed a quick meal of scrambled eggs, toast and fresh fruit, then she settled Andrea and Kelly in front of the television to watch a children's show. Bobby sat on the floor with his blocks, happily babbling to himself. It wasn't a good idea to use the television as a babysitter. She'd heard Vicki say that over and over, but right now she didn't care. It wasn't going to warp the kids' minds, and she needed a breather.

How would it end, she wondered? Laura wasn't sure she could handle Vicki's moods and the confusion of three active children indefinitely, but what was the alternative? If she asked Vicki to leave, it was as if she was turning her back on her child in her time of need. But she didn't approve of what Vicki was doing. She was behaving like a spoiled child. She was hurting herself and her children.

Sighing, Laura snapped off the television and herded the kids upstairs to get ready for bed. She'd have to make Vicki understand that she wasn't going to take over the children every time she wanted to sulk. If they were going to share the house there would have to be some ground rules.

The next morning Laura made her speech over breakfast. Vicki's jaw dropped as the meaning of Laura's words sunk in.

"You're going to charge me to live here?" she asked incredulously. "Mother, how can you?"

"Feeding four additional people is expensive, Vicki, not to mention the electricity and water and . . ."

Vicki put down her fork and stared at her mother. "I cannot believe you are doing this," she said. "If Daddy were here he wouldn't . . ."

"If your father was still alive he would tell you the exact same thing, Vicki. You're a grown woman, not a helpless child. I can live comfortably on what your father left me, but I cannot afford to support you and your family."

Laura sipped her coffee. "Also, last night was the second time you went to bed and left the children to me. They're not my responsibility, Vicki, and I don't like being taken advantage of. You didn't even ask me if I minded taking care of the children. What if I'd had other plans?"

Vicki's dark eyes narrowed suspiciously. "Oh, I get it," she said stiffly. "The kids and I are interfering with your socializing, aren't we? Is that why you're acting so mean?"

"I'm sorry if you feel I'm being mean, but it's just a fact of life. I feel you should be responsible for yourself and your children."

"My own mother," Vicki muttered. "I can't believe this!"

Laura went out in the back yard. She looked around her neat, well-manicured lawn, the flower beds she'd planted with such pleasure. Then she stared up at the house she'd lived in for so many years. It was a wonderful house, and the walls were papered with warm, happy memories, but maybe it was time to think of letting it go. Maybe it was time for another family to enjoy the shelter she and Paul had lovingly created. The house was much too big for one person, and after only a few days, and the words they'd just exchanged, Laura knew

that she and her daughter could not live together on a permanent basis. She loved Vicki
and the kids. She loved Valerie and Greg as
well, but if she was strictly honest she had to
admit that she didn't want any of them living
with her. She wanted time for herself now, time
to explore who she was. There were so many
roads she could travel—but not with Vicki and
the children underfoot.

Was she being selfish, she wondered? For a
minute Laura thought she heard Paul's voice,
thought she heard him speak to her.

No father had ever loved his children more
than Paul, but he had believed that the kids
should be strong and independent. Laura
shrugged and straightened her shoulders. She
was doing the right thing. She had done her
job, and now it was time to start a new life.

She was surprised and pleased to get a telephone call from Steve that afternoon.

"I'll be in Miami tomorrow," he said. "Can
we get together?"

"Well, I don't know," Laura said teasingly. "What did you have in mind? Are you prepared to wine me and dine me in proper
style?"

"There's nothing I'd like better," Steve said.
There was silence for a moment. "I'll be look-

ing for an apartment this trip. Maybe you'll help me?"

"I'd love to," Laura said. It would be fun to help Steve find an apartment. Laura realized that it was really going to happen. Steve was actually moving to Miami. She was both excited and scared. There was a strong physical attraction between them. Steve was a healthy man in his prime. She was sure he wouldn't be content with a platonic relationship. She didn't think she would be either. She'd lain in bed on more than one occasion since Steve came back into her life imagining what it would be like to make love with Steve, to sleep beside him and wake beside him in the morning.

Frowning, Laura knew there was little chance of a romantic encounter while Vicki and the kid were around. But when Steve got his own place . . . she shivered with fear and anticipation. There was no doubt in her mind that it would happen. The only question was when.

"Another date?" Vicki asked the next day, as Laura pawed through her closet in search of a dress to wear to dinner that evening.

"Yes," Laura said. "Steve is back in Miami. He's going to be looking for an apartment and he's asked me to help him locate something. We're going out to dinner tonight to discuss it."

Vicki's face twisted. "You're not a realtor. Why doesn't he go to Home Finders or something?"

"I suppose because he wants me to help him. Actually, I'm looking forward to it." She hesitated, then decided there was no time like the present. "I'll probably be looking for something for myself one of these days, so this will be good practice. I'm putting the house on the market, Vicki, as soon as I get a painter in here and have some minor repairs done to the roof. I've thought about it a lot lately, and this afternoon I made some decisions."

"You're what? Mother, you can't be serious! This is the house you and Daddy bought together. It was the only home I knew until I married Tim. And what about Valerie and Greg? They aren't going to like this either."

"I'm sorry if that's so," Laura said. Then her tone softened. "This house has wonderful memories for all of us, honey," she said, "but now it's time for me to move on to something different. I know your father would approve."

"Then the kids and I have to leave?" Vicki asked, sounding young and scared. "You're kicking us out?"

Laura shook her head. "The house won't be sold overnight, honey. You'll have plenty of time to make other arrangements, and besides, you have a perfectly good home of your own."

Vicki frowned. "Not for long. Tim's transfer is scheduled for three months from now. He told me he was turning the house over to a realtor."

"You could have a new house in Indianapolis," Laura reminded her. "It might even be nicer than the one you're leaving behind. Don't you think it would be exciting to start all over in a new place, honey? You'd meet new people, see new places. Tim said he was thinking you might even want to go back to school."

"Why would I want to do that?" Vicki asked.

"Well, when you were younger you said you wanted to be a teacher. It's not too late, you know. I always thought you would make a wonderful teacher."

"Do you really think so?" Vicki asked, her eyes widening. "I guess there would be enough money for me to go back to school if Tim takes that promotion."

"Well, it's something to think about," Laura said casually, as she took a dark green jersey dress from the closet. It was the kind of dress that clung in all the right places, and the last time she'd worn it, it had been a little snug. She headed for the bathroom to try it on.

"I better go see what the kids are up to," Vicki said.

Laura congratulated herself. Vicki had definitely seemed interested in the idea of going back to school, and maybe it would be the best thing for her. Staying at home and being a housewife and mother wasn't fulfilling for her. Maybe that was why she demanded so much attention from Tim. Maybe if she had a compelling interest of her own, she'd be a little less demanding.

Slipping the jersey dress over her head, Laura sucked in her tummy. The dress had been one of her favorites, but she'd had no occasion to wear it lately.

When she had zipped it up, Laura stood and stared at her mirrored reflection. She turned to one side and then the other. Not bad for a fifty-one-year-old grandmother, she decided. "You're looking good, old girl," she said, sliding her hands down over her slender hips, then back up to her full breasts. Her bosom was not quite as high as it had once been, but she wasn't sagging by any means. With her hands under her breasts, Laura closed her eyes and imagined Steve touching her. She parted her lips and imagined his strong mouth crushing hers. She could almost feel his male hardness pressing against her belly, could almost feel his heated breath on her bare skin.

A low moan escaped her and her eyes flew open. Good grief! She was definitely ripe for the picking. Would Steve see how hungry she was? A part of her wanted to hold back, to wait and be sure. But what did she have to be sure of? This was the nineties. She didn't need a heavy commitment to enjoy a pleasurable relationship with a nice man.

"You've come a long way, baby!" Laura sang, as she let the jersey dress drop to the floor. She surveyed her underwear critically. Her cotton bra and panties were clean, plain and serviceable, and that was about all that could be said for them. It was time to do a little shopping, and think about love again.

Four

Laura peered into the mirror above her vanity table. She rarely wore green eye shadow, but somehow the occasion seemed to call for a little daring, and she wanted to emphasize the color of her dress.

She'd pinned her hair on hot rollers while she soaked in scented bath oil, and now as she finished making up her face, the soft, sensuous scent swirled around her. Vicki would definitely know that this was not "two friends getting together." Laura knew she had to face her daughter's sulky, disapproving face, if not tonight, then first thing in the morning.

But she'd deal with that when the time came, she decided, carefully lining her lips with a burgundy lip pencil. She wasn't going to allow Vicki's negative behavior to spoil her evening.

I deserve this, Laura thought, patting her soft, auburn waves into place. And I'm not doing anything wrong by going out with Steve.

At least she had the house to herself, and if she was lucky she could escape before Vicki got home. She wasn't anxious to have Vicki meet Steve. Vicki was too unsettled, too angry to be objective about her mother's friend. Then again, "friend" was really much too tame for what she and Steve had been to each other. Laura smiled. Despite how it had ended, those months with Steve had been special.

The door chimes sounded just as she finished spritzing a light cologne over her shoulders and in the hollow of her neck. For good measure she lifted her skirt and spritzed the back of her knees.

She straightened and smiled at her mirrored image. What you see is what you get, Steve, she thought. She hoped she measured up to his expectations.

He didn't move when she opened the door a few minutes later. He just stood there staring, as if he were mesmerized.

Finally he found his voice. "Laura, you look fantastic." He pulled his hand from behind his back and extended a bouquet of white daisies with yellow centers. He grinned. "The florist tried his best to sell me long-stemmed roses, but I insisted on daisies. I told him he didn't know my girl the way I do."

His girl. The words rolled off his lips so naturally. Laura felt the years waft away. She felt tears sting her eyelids as she gazed at the perky daisies. They were the only flowers Steve had ever given her, except for the rosebud corsage at the prom. She had declared her love of daisies over and over during their courtship. She blushed, thinking of the collection of porcelain and ceramic daisies resting on a shelf in her bedroom. Through the years, Paul had never guessed their significance.

"Thank you for remembering," Laura finally managed. "They're lovely."

Steve followed her into the kitchen when she went to find a vase. He looked around curiously, his dark brows arched. "Where is everyone? I thought you had a full house."

Laura frowned. "Actually I'd like to make a fast getaway before they get home."

Steve's dark eyes narrowed. "I take it your daughter doesn't approve? Is it me, or just the idea of your dating in general?"

"Mostly dating in general," Laura replied. "Vicki's pretty unsettled right now."

"Hey, I understand," Steve said, holding up his hand. "I'm sure it's hard for her to think of you with anyone but her father."

"That's part of it," Laura agreed, "but Vicki's own unhappiness is coloring all her emotions these days. What about your son? Does he know where you are and what you're doing?"

Steve grinned. He stood close behind Laura as she filled the vase with water and arranged the daisies. "I think men look at things like this differently," he said. "Steve realizes I have to get on with my life, and he understands that nothing or no one could ever take away from what his mother and I had together."

Laura swallowed. She felt all warm inside. She felt no jealousy towards Steve's late wife, or the memories he apparently cherished. And knowing that Steve had cared deeply for his wife only made her value him more.

"I'm glad you had a good life," she said softly. "I did too. We were both very lucky, weren't we?"

"Yes."

Laura felt Steve's breath on her neck, the light touch of his fingers against her cheek. Slowly, he turned her until they were face to face. "I won't ask for more than you're willing to give, Laura," he said, "and I won't try to rush you into anything you're not ready for. All I ask is that you give us a chance. We've been fortunate enough to have a second chance at happiness. I don't think we should pass it up."

Their lips were mere inches apart. Laura could see a light film of perspiration on Steve's forehead. She could let herself drown in the dark chocolate eyes, let her mouth melt into that incredible, all-encompassing smile. She felt herself sway, just as the front door slammed and the sound of children's laughter exploded around them.

"Uh-oh," Steve said, stepping backwards and shaking his head. "We waited too long. Now I have to face the firing squad."

Laura gave one last, lingering look at the daisies sitting on the kitchen counter, then she took Steve's hand and led him to the front room. "Maybe it won't be so bad," she said.

But it was worse than bad. It was a total disaster. Vicki was horrible. She glared at Steve mutinously, and she snapped and yelled at the children until Andrea ran upstairs in tears.

Laura looked at Kelly and Bobby's tear-stained cheeks and wavered. "Maybe I shouldn't go out tonight . . ," she said hesitantly. "The children . . ."

"Are your daughter's responsibility," Steve said firmly, taking Laura's elbow and edging her towards the front door. "They'll be going to bed soon," he whispered against Laura's ear, "and your daughter will be able to sulk all she wants."

"But . . ."

"Don't let her do this to you, Laura. This is your home. You have rights."

"I know, but she's so unhappy."

"Good night, Vicki," Steve said pleasantly, keeping a firm grip on Laura's elbow. "Perhaps we can get acquainted some other time, when you're feeling a little better. And don't wait up for your mother. She may be late."

Vicki stared after them, speechless, as Steve propelled Laura out the door.

"I'm not sure that was the right thing to do," Laura said. "Vicki has always been a very emotional girl and she . . ."

"Laura, there is no excuse for bad manners. I'm sorry to say it, but your daughter behaved like a spoiled brat tonight."

In her heart, Laura agreed with Steve, but she still didn't like hearing him say it. Vicki was her child, and nobody understood her the way Laura did. Laura knew how frightened she was. Steve didn't know, yet he felt qualified to judge Vicki. Something churned inside Laura and she edged close to the car door.

"My daughter is going through a difficult time, Steve, and she is a complicated person.

She feels deeply and she . . ."

Steve took his eyes off the road for a moment. "Let's not talk about children tonight, Laura. Let's just concentrate on each other. Can we do that? I have a feeling that you and I may see your situation with your daughter in different ways, and I don't want to end up fighting with you over a young woman I don't even know."

Laura didn't answer right away. It would be pointless for them to argue over Vicki, but was this a preview of things to come? Would Steve feel free to voice his opinion in regard to Laura's relationship with her brood? She wasn't sure she liked that idea, or if she was prepared to have someone in her life who would be openly critical of her children.

"What do you say, Laura? Can we forget everything but each other for the next few hours and just relax and enjoy ourselves?"

"All right," Laura said quietly. "We'll give it a try." It would be nice to put aside her worries about Vicki and the kids, Laura thought, and be a woman out on a date with an attractive man.

The restaurant Steve had chosen was new and the food was scrumptious. Laura made a valiant effort to think of nothing but Steve and the enjoyable surroundings.

"Paul and I used to eat out at least once a week after the kids grew up," she said. "He said the cook deserved a night off."

Steve nodded. He carefully speared a steamed shrimp and held it out to Laura. "Taste this cocktail sauce," he said. "It's great."

Laura opened her mouth and Steve levered the fork against her lips. She bit down on the tender, succulent shrimp and closed her eyes in ecstasy.

Steve squirmed uncomfortably in his seat. He'd never realized that a woman could be sensual eating a shrimp. Maybe most women weren't. Maybe it was just Laura. Remembering their high-school days, Steve realized that Laura had always had a special quality, even as an inexperienced teenager. His eyes never moved from her face as she chewed and finally swallowed the shrimp. She'd been cute as a young girl, but now, as a woman in the prime of her life, she was stunning. There was a warm, sensual maturity about her that made his belly twist into knots.

"Good?" he asked, surprised to hear his voice come out in a husky croak.

"Wonderful," Laura said. She smiled, and Steve had a feeling she knew exactly what he was thinking.

Later, the waiter brought them an after-dinner liqueur. Then a small band began setting up their equipment in the corner of the room.

"That's an awfully small dance floor," Laura commented, sipping her drink.

"The better to hold you close and tight," Steve said, his voice deep and promising. "I want to dance with you tonight, Laura, the way we did at the prom."

Laura smiled, then groaned. "I hope we can do a little better than that," she said. "You may not remember how you stepped all over my toes, but I do. My poor pink satin shoes had to be thrown in the trash."

"Then it's time I make amends," Steve said, undaunted. "Wait until you see how I've improved."

When the band began to play the first song, Laura's eyes widened. " 'Earth Angel,' " she said, sighing. "Oh, Steve, did you know this was a fifties band?"

He grinned, and reached across the table to take her hand. "I did a little research before I chose this place. It brings back memories, doesn't it?"

Laura didn't bother to answer. Wordlessly she rose to her feet and walked into Steve's arms. They made their way to the postage stamp dance floor. Other couples were already dancing, but to Laura it was as if she and Steve were alone on a private island.

His arms encircled her with an easy familiarity, as though the thirty-three years they'd been apart had never been. Laura closed her eyes and leaned into Steve. She was sixteen again, young and eager and excited by everything life had to offer. There were no grown children with marital problems, no crying grandchildren, no weighty decisions to make. There was just Steve and the magical music of their youth.

Steve kept an iron grip on his emotions. If Laura only knew, he thought. He wanted to crush her hard against the length of his hungry body. He wanted to pick her up and carry her off. As they swayed in time to the music, he found he couldn't remain uninvolved. His body was clamoring, his nerves were on alert. He wanted to hold Laura as he'd done so very long ago.

Momentarily closing his eyes, Steve could remember the wonder of knowing Laura for the first time, the splendor of realizing the full potential of his manhood with the sweetest girl in the world. He'd been frightened at first, scared of hurting her, afraid he wouldn't measure up. But then his youthful hormones and his feelings took over. He held Laura tight and it happened. He'd been stunned by the feelings and emotions that filled his young body. And then he left her.

Every time he thought of how their youthful romance had ended, he felt like a colossal heel, a creep of the worst kind. It was a miracle Laura hadn't slammed the door right in his face when he showed up on her doorstep. Yet, now she was here, in his arms, the perfumed warmth of her lovely body making him ache all over with longing. He hadn't made love to a woman since his wife's death. He hadn't wanted to. But now he was alive and alert and wanting. It was crazy. He was fifty-three years old, about to become a grandfather, and right now, dancing with the first woman he'd ever loved, he was as greedy as a hot-blooded young man of sixteen. He'd truly thought that kind of passion and longing was in the past, but he'd been wrong.

The song ended and Laura and Steve made their way back to their table. They sat down and looked at each other.

"We're not going to be able to keep our relationship casual, you know," Steve said. "There's too much between us, Laura. Too many memories and feelings."

She nodded. She couldn't speak. The feelings had rocked her mature stability to the core. She couldn't be sensible and safe with Steve.

When he held and touched her she was young and carefree, afraid of nothing.

They danced once more before leaving the restaurant. Then Steve knew he had to get out of the crowded room. He had to be alone with Laura, if only for a few minutes in a parked car. He was no longer a middle-aged widower. With Laura at his side he was a high-school football hero, and he wanted to kiss Laura so bad he ached.

"Let's get out of here," he said thickly.

Laura felt the same. She wished she had her home to herself, wished she could take Steve home with her and be alone with him.

In the car, in the soft, still darkness, they fell on each other like starving animals. Hands caressed and stroked, lips met and parted, then met again. Their tongues dueled sweetly, and Laura moaned when her full, ripe breasts were cradled in Steve's strong hands.

"Ah, this is what we need," Steve said. "We were made for each other, Laura. See? We fit perfectly." He drew away just a little, and his eyes dropped to that most private part of his body. He took her gaze with him, and Laura felt herself flush in the darkness. She ached to feel Steve against her, in her, but they couldn't make love in a parked car, could they? Oh, she wanted to; she would, except for the small, insistent voice of propriety. She was a mother and a grandmother, for heaven's sake!

"Steve, we can't," she cried, tearing herself away. "Not here. Not like this."

He groaned. "I know, and I'm old enough to know better than to start something I can't hope to finish. I don't want to take you to a hotel, Laura. Not you. If I had my own place . . ."

Laura managed a shaky laugh. There was a deep ache of longing in her belly, and her breasts throbbed where Steve had touched them. "Maybe you'd better see about that first thing tomorrow," she said.

Steve's eyes had adjusted to the darkness and he could see Laura's face plainly. At first she had been hesitant, not even sure if she was supposed to be dating, but now she was ready for their relationship to move to the next plateau. He grinned and touched his fingertip to her lower lip. "I'll make that my top priority," he promised.

When he dropped her off, the house was dark and silent, but Laura wasn't fooled. She was pretty sure Vicki was lying wide awake. They'd have to have a long talk tomorrow, she decided, but she wasn't up to a confrontation tonight. She was gloriously happy, and if anyone had told her she'd be feeling this way so soon after Paul's death she would never have believed it.

Surprisingly enough, she didn't feel guilty, or feel that she was betraying Paul's memory. She had given her husband all that she had to give, and she had stood by him until death parted them. Paul didn't need her anymore, and she was sure he would be the first person to tell her to get on with her life, to live each day to the fullest. She closed her eyes and she could almost imagine him smiling down on her, urging her on.

"I hate to let you go," Steve said, opening her door and helping her out, "but I guess I'd better get some sleep so I can hunt for an apartment tomorrow. Will you come along and help me find a place?"

"I'd love to," Laura said. "Pick me up around ten. That will give me a chance to talk to Vicki after breakfast."

Steve groaned. "Lots of luck."

They leaned towards each other and touched their lips together lightly. Laura could feel her breasts swelling and straining towards Steve's touch but she was careful to keep a safe distance between them.

"Easy does it," Steve murmured, when they parted. "Boy, I feel like a kid again."

"Me too," Laura said softly. "Me too."

She tiptoed into her house like an errant teenager, hoping against hope that Vicki was asleep, that she could get to her room and slip into bed undetected.

Luck was with her, or maybe it was Paul, smiling his approval. As she slipped between the sheets, Laura shivered. Steve was right. They'd been given a second chance. Even if their relationship never went beyond a brief love affair, it would still be meaningful. They were both alone and lonely. And they cared for one another. They always had, even though their lives had taken separate paths. Laura smiled into the midnight stillness, and wriggled into a comfortable spot in the narrow twin bed. Making love with Steve would be wonderful, of that she was sure. And it would most definitely not be casual or meaningless. And when it happened, it would be right.

"Really, Mother, you're acting like a . . . a hussy!" Vicki declared the next morning. "Mooning around over that man like some hot-blooded teenager!"

"Mm, I was one of those," Laura admitted, her lips curving in a smile as she remembered.

"See? That's what I mean! Ever since that Steve person showed up you've been acting like a . . . a . . ."

"Hussy," Laura said complacently. She sipped her coffee. Oh yes, it was just the way she liked it, hot and strong with a dash of cinnamon.

"It's not funny, Mother. It's embarrassing."

Laura had to laugh. When Vicki was annoyed, she called her "Mother," while any other time she was just "Mom." When the children were little, if Laura called them by their full names they knew she meant business.

"Well, I'm sorry if I'm embarrassing you, honey, but for the first time in my life I don't have to answer to anyone, and I like that freedom. I'm living my life and enjoying myself. I'm sorry if you don't approve." Laura was determined not to let Vicki rattle her. After all, even though Vicki was an adult, Laura was still her mother, and she deserved a little respect, didn't she?

Vicki spooned oatmeal into Bobby's open mouth and absently reminded Kelly to finish her orange juice. "It sounds almost as though you're glad Daddy's gone," she said spitefully.

Laura's coffee mug made a heck of a bang when it hit the table. Calling her a hussy was one thing, but insinuating that she was glad Paul was gone was different!

"Now you just wait one minute, young lady. You are overstepping your limits, and it's going to end right now. You are in my home, eating my food and sleeping in my bed, enjoying my hospitality. How dare you say something like that to me? I loved your father, and I will always cherish his memory, but he is dead, and I'm alive. I'm going on with my life whether you like it or not! If my behavior upsets you so much, perhaps you should make other living arrangements." There she had said it, and she wasn't sorry. Since she and the children moved in, Vicki had been a total bitch. She was unhappy with her own life, so she said ugly, hateful things to her mother, and she apparently expected Laura to sit back and take it.

"And another thing," Laura said stiffly. "Steve is coming by to pick me up shortly. I'm going to help him look for an apartment. I expect you to be civil to him when he arrives. I do not want a repeat performance of last night."

Vicki's anger melted and her face crumpled. "I'm sorry, Mom. I really am. I don't know what's gotten into me lately. My life is a mess, and Tim won't even try to work things out. He's adamant about taking that promotion."

"I don't blame him," Laura said. She quickly held up her hand when Vicki started to speak. "Hear me out," she said. "Tim is a hardworking, ambitious young man. He wants to provide well for his family. He loves you and the children very much. He deserves this promotion. How can you think of asking him to give it up? Do you realize how selfish that kind of thinking is?"

"You think I'm selfish?" Vicki said piteously, her eyes filled with tears. "Just because I don't want to go to the end of the earth and leave everything I care about behind?"

Laura touched Vicki's hand. "Honey, Tim and your children should be your top priority. Don't you remember your wedding vows, the part about forsaking all others?"

"But . . ."

"I think you need to put Tim's needs first for a while, Vicki. Give him this chance, and you might find out that Indianapolis isn't so bad. If you go back to school you could get your teaching degree, and when Bobby goes to preschool you can have a career of your own if you want."

Vicki looked thoughtful. She blinked and dabbed at her eyes. "You really think that's what I should do?"

Laura nodded. "If you love your husband and want to save your marriage."

"I do love Tim, but . . ."

Laura rose from the table and gave Bobby a kiss on his plump cheek. "I've got to get ready," she said. "Steve will be picking me up soon.

You think about things, honey. I'm sure you'll make the right decision."

Laura was just putting the finishing touches on her makeup when she heard Steve's car. He'd be at Vicki's mercy unless she hurried. She was so nervous she smeared her lipstick and had to wipe it off and start over. She tripped going down the steps and almost fell down the stairs. By the time she faced Steve in the living room, she was flushed and out of breath.

"I'm ready," she said.

Steve grinned. "So I see. Uh, did you want to button your blouse before we go?"

"What? Oh, my gosh!" Laura reddened and hastily buttoned her silk blouse, and tucked it into her slacks. "I was in such a hurry to get down here . . . I knew Vicki was . . ."

Steve laughed. "Relax. Everything is under control. Your daughter let me in, and she was very pleasant. I think she went to change the baby. He's a cute little devil, isn't he?"

"Yes, he is. Vicki was pleasant?"

"Scout's honor," Steve said. "She's really a very attractive young woman. A lot like her mother, I think."

"I don't know about that," Laura said, grimacing. "Look, maybe we'd better get out of here while she's still in a good mood."

Like kids sneaking off on an unknown adventure, they hurried out the door.

"I think I liked the last one the best," Steve said, several hours later, as they ate lunch at a small waterfront restaurant. "Even though it wasn't very big there was a feeling of spaciousness to it. I'm selling the furniture with my house. I figured it would be easier to buy new than transport everything. Besides, most of it wouldn't fit into a small apartment."

Laura looked thoughtful. "Do you know, I've just had a flash of insight. I really enjoyed looking at all those places this morning. I wonder if I should think about getting into real estate?"

"Are you looking for a job?" Steve asked.

Laura nodded. "I haven't actually been pounding the pavement, but I've been keeping an eye on the want ads. So far I haven't seen anything that really interests me, and since I don't have to work, I'd like to find a job I'll enjoy. Something with a bit of a challenge."

"I'm sure you'll be good at anything you want to do, Laura," Steve said seriously. "You'll have to take a course before you can become a licensed realtor, you know. How do you feel about going back to school?"

"I don't know." Laura's gray eyes grew pensive. She'd enjoyed school when she was young, but she wasn't sure how she'd fit into a classroom now. But a realtor's course was definitely an adult thing. She cocked her head to the side and grinned. "How do you think I'll look in a pleated skirt and penny loafers?" she asked.

"Do they still make those things? Penny loafers, I mean. Remember the white bucks we wore? Only they were never white. That wouldn't have been cool."

"Not to mention the fact that the word 'cool' wasn't really *in* back then. What words did we use anyway?"

"Would you believe I can't remember? I must be older than I thought."

Suddenly, the lighthearted banter stilled. Laura looked at Steve, and their eyes locked. She licked her lips and swallowed.

Steve thought it was an incredibly sensuous movement. He wished he could be the one to lick her lips. And then . . . "Let's get out of here," he said. "I'm going to put a deposit on that apartment!"

He dropped her off at four-thirty, but when Laura asked him if he wanted to come in, he shook his head. "Not tonight. Vicki might not be so happy to see me twice in one day. We'd better not push our luck."

Laura smiled, then she leaned over and impulsively kissed Steve's cheek. "I'm glad you're back in my life, Steve Walker," she said.

She ate supper with Vicki and the kids, and Laura noted that Vicki was definitely on her good behavior. They didn't discuss Tim, or the question of whether Vicki had decided to take Laura's advice. Instead, Laura devoted most of her attention to her grandchildren. Andrea looked a little peaked to her, and Laura said as much to Vicki when the little girl went to the bathroom.

Vicki nodded. "She takes everything so seriously, and she's missing Tim. The other two . . . well, Bobby's just a baby and Kelly's different. Nothing seems to bother her."

"She is an independent little thing," Laura agreed.

Vicki seemed a little anxious after she put the children to bed, and finally Laura asked what was wrong.

"I was wondering . . . would you mind taking care of the kids tomorrow so I can go and talk to Tim? I called him this afternoon and he agreed we should talk some more." Vicki frowned and bit her lip and her blue eyes filled with tears. "I've been acting like a bitch, haven't I, Mom? I really owe you an apology. You took me and the kids in at the expense of your own privacy. You tried to help and what did I do? I called you names and was rude to your . . . friend. I pushed the kids off on you and . . ."

Laura put her hand over Vicki's. "It's okay, honey. I know you've been unhappy and under a lot of strain, and you're doing the right thing to talk to Tim again. Will you promise me one thing?"

Vicki sniffed. "What?"

"No matter what, remember that Tim loves you and the children, and he's doing what he feels is best for everyone."

Vicki nodded, and managed a smile. "I think I finally figured that out, with your help, Mom. Boy, I'm almost glad Daddy isn't around to see me like this. He'd be disgusted with me, wouldn't he?"

Laura smiled. "Maybe just a teeny bit, but he'd still love you. That's the way parents are."

Laura quickly straightened up the house the next morning, and she was just folding some freshly laundered towels when the telephone rang. She was surprised and pleased to hear her son Greg's voice.

"Greg! How are you, dear? Are you calling from the hospital?"

"Hi, Mom," Greg answered. "I'm not at the hospital right now. I'm home. Something has happened."

A cold chill rippled down Laura's spine and she quickly sat down. "Greg, what's wrong? Are you sick? Has your asthma flared up?"

As a child Greg had suffered frequent attacks of asthma. On more than one occasion Laura and Paul had been forced to rush him to the hospital in the middle of the night. But as he'd grown older the attacks had lessened in frequency and severity. Greg's doctor had been unable to offer an explanation. All he could say was that they should count their blessings.

"Are you sick, dear?" Laura repeated, her heart hammering in alarm when Greg failed to answer right away. "Honey?"

"I'm okay, Mom. At least physically. Oh hell, I may as well spit it out and get it over with. One of my patients has charged me with malpractice. It isn't true, but the hospital suggested I take a little time off until things settle down. Mom, I feel rotten. Is it okay if I come home for a few days to sort things out?"

Laura hesitated, but only for a second. Another one of her chicks coming home to roost? And Vicki and Greg had never seen eye to eye. Greg thought Vicki was spoiled, and Vicki thought Greg was entirely too big for his britches. Laura closed her eyes and said a quick, silent prayer. Then she pressed the telephone receiver close to her lips. "Of course, dear," she said. "It'll be wonderful to see you."

Vicki came in then, Kelly and Bobby in tow. "I'm leaving now, Mom. Kelly's been begging for grilled cheese for lunch. Do you mind making them sandwiches?"

Laura shook her head. "No, of course not. Come here, sweetie," she said, taking Bobby from Vicki's arms. She gave her daughter a level look. "Greg is coming home for a while, Vicki," she said. "There's been some trouble at the hospital. A patient charged him with malpractice. He sounded pretty shaken, but I'm sure it's some kind of mistake."

Vicki's jaw dropped. "Greg's in trouble? How can that be? He's always come out on top."

"Not this time, I'm afraid. The hospital has suggested he take a few days off while they investigate the incident."

"Oh, God, that's terrible! Greg is . . . well, I'm sure he's a perfectly marvelous doctor. If he wasn't my brother I'd go to him myself."

Laura smiled. She hugged Bobby and kissed his rosy cheek. "Greg will enjoy knowing that," she said.

Vicki looked shocked. "Don't be silly, Mother," she said. "You can't tell him I said that! He'll think I've lost my senses!"

"But . . ."

"Don't worry, Mom. I'll be as sweet as molasses to Greg. I promise. I know I wasn't very nice when we were all growing up, but he was always so perfect, and every time he had one of those awful asthma attacks the whole family practically fell apart. I guess," Vicki admitted, smiling sheepishly, "I was jealous of all the attention he got. That's pretty stinky, isn't it? Being jealous of your own brother? Especially when he was sick?"

Laura grinned. "It's also very human, and I think it's very mature of you to come clean." She laughed and shifted the baby to her hip to walk Vicki to the door. "I think there's hope for you yet, kiddo."

After Vicki left, Laura played with the children, and around eleven-thirty she began fixing their lunch. Grilled cheese sandwiches and chicken noodle soup. As she worked, she considered the sleeping arrangements. Bobby was sleeping in Greg's old bed, with a guard rail on it. Vicki and the kids were in Laura's room, and Laura was sleeping in Vicki's old room. That left only Paul's den, or the sofa bed in the family room. She hated to put Greg on that. It wasn't comfortable, and he wouldn't have much privacy. Still, what alternative was there?

"Careful, sweetie," Laura said, as Kelly's cup of soup tilted precariously. She wiped the baby's face and cleaned off his high chair. Then she lifted Bobby and set him on the floor. The kids were adorable, if she did say so herself. Bobby looked like the famous Gerber baby. Kelly still had a little baby fat in her face, and her big blue eyes were as wide as shoe buttons. And Andrea . . . ah, Andrea was destined to be a beauty. Her eyelashes were so long and thick they looked like black fringe. She had skin as soft as silk and the sweetest smile Laura had ever seen.

But how could Laura have forgotten how much work children made, and how tiring motherhood was? After only a few hours with the kids she was worn out. How on earth had she ever managed to raise her own three?

You were a lot younger then, Laura, my girl, she reminded herself. You were younger, thinner, stronger, and you had Paul to back you up. As Laura finished cleaning up the kitchen she wondered if Vicki had even thought about how difficult it would be to raise the kids singlehandedly.

It took Laura a good forty-five minutes to get the kids settled down for a nap. Andrea was in school until three, so it was just Kelly and Bobby, but by the time she had the baby changed and in his bed, and had read Kelly a short story, she was totally exhausted. She wanted nothing more than to sit down and prop her feet in her easy chair and close her eyes for a few minutes.

After fixing herself a cup of herbal tea, Laura sank into her favorite recliner with a big sigh of relief. She leaned back and said a brief, silent prayer. Please let them make it up, Lord, she prayed fervently. Let Vicki and Tim mend the rift between them and let Vicki and the kids go home where they belong. Please, Lord. If you grant me this wish, I'll give double to the poor box, and I'll make sure I go to bingo every Wednesday night!

Five

Laura held her breath as she watched Vicki park her silver Chevy Lumina in the driveway. She couldn't see her daughter's face so she had no idea if Vicki was happy or sad. Then, she saw Vicki turn to look down the street, and wonder of wonders, Tim pulled in behind her in his little blue Ford Escort. Her jaw dropped as Tim hopped out of the car and grabbed Vicki by the hand. Then he tugged her into his arms and kissed her, and Vicki didn't offer one ounce of resistance.

"Hurrah! It worked! They've settled things! It's over! The cold war is over!"

The kids came running from the family room, and when they saw their mom and dad kissing in the driveway, the two girls started to giggle. Bobby, of course, didn't have the faintest idea of what was going on.

"All right, break it up, you two," Laura called teasingly. "You've been married too long to carry on like that in public."

"Ain't love grand?" Tim asked, pushing through the doorway to scoop Bobby up in his arms and grin at his girls. "We're going home, kids," he announced. "Mommy and I got all our problems worked out and we're all going home together."

Laura rolled her eyes heavenward. Thank you, Lord, she whispered silently.

"I knew you two would get your act together," she said, winking at Tim and giving Vicki a quick hug. "Is everything really all right?" she asked her daughter softly.

Vicki nodded. "I think so. We're going to work things out, Mom. Tim and I don't want to lose each other, and we don't want to split up our family. The kids need both of us."

Laura nodded. "What can I do to help?" she asked.

By seven-thirty that night Laura's house was empty and quiet. She twirled around her living room like a demented fool, singing and hugging herself. The toys were gone, and the pampers as well. Tonight she could sleep in her own bed again, and now she didn't have to worry about where to put Greg when he arrived. For a brief moment she thought about calling Steve and inviting him over for a drink, but she quickly decided against it. She'd had the care of the children for most of the day and she was exhausted. Much as she enjoyed Steve's company, she knew she'd enjoy the blessed luxury of being completely alone even more. And tomorrow her next houseguest would be arriving. Greg. Dear Greg. He was a good son, and a decent man. She'd been hoping he'd find a nice woman and settle down and start a family. He'd been so busy getting through medical school and then his internship, that he'd had little time for romance. She didn't want to see him drift into a lonely bachelor life. Men and women needed each other. She was convinced that married people were generally happier than singles. And it was a proven fact that married men usually lived longer than their single brothers.

Stretching out on the sofa and listening to the soft strains of one of her fifties love ballads, Laura wondered how any woman in her right mind would even think of accusing Greg of malpractice. Greg was a serious, dedicated physician, and he cared about all his patients. What could possibly have happened?

Laura shifted into a more comfortable position and idly traced the small cluster of spider veins just above her left knee. She was going to have to do something about that and soon. Her friend Gail had recently gone to a vascular surgeon and had injections to make the veins disappear. Laura decided she was going to look into the procedure. Maybe she couldn't stop the years from marching by, but at least she could do something besides lie down and let time tramp all over her.

The telephone rang, jarring her out of her comfortable, semisleepy state. She crossed her fingers, praying it wasn't Vicki calling to say she was coming back.

"Laura?"

It was Steve and he sounded excited and happy. "Hi," she said. "I didn't expect to hear from you tonight. Did you decide on an apartment?"

"Yep. The one I liked yesterday. I put a deposit on it and if all goes well, I'll be moving in about two weeks. In the meantime I'm going to need lots of help buying furniture and decorating the place. Can I count on you? I'm afraid I'm not much good with colors and fabrics and stuff like that."

Laura raised herself into a sitting position. All of a sudden she didn't feel so tired. "I'd love to help you pick out furniture, Steve," she said, "and there's not a woman alive who doesn't absolutely adore spending someone else's money."

Steve laughed. "Somehow that's just what I thought you'd say. I've never heard of a woman turning down an invitation to shop for furniture. When can we start?"

Laura suddenly remembered Greg and his imminent arrival. "Well, maybe not for a few days," she said slowly. "My son, Greg, is coming to stay with me for a little while."

"Wow! You really will have a full house, won't you?"

"Oh, that's right, you don't know, do you? Vicki and Tim patched things up. Tim came and packed them up and took them all home. Isn't that wonderful?"

"Hey, that is great. And now your son is coming?"

Laura could almost hear the disappointment in his voice. Like her, she knew he'd probably been hoping they could have some time together, and now she would have another houseguest.

"He's having some problems. I couldn't tell him not to come, Steve. I'm his mother. And I guess my sister-in-law, Blanche, was right. She said that children always need their mothers."

"Except that your kids aren't children anymore, Laura. Didn't you teach them to stand on their own two feet?"

"Wait a minute, Steve," Laura said quietly. "You don't even know my children. Don't you think it's unfair to assume that they're too dependent on me?"

"Sure, but it just seems like . . ."

All at once Laura was dead tired again, and she definitely wasn't up to arguing with Steve over her children. After all, he only had one child, and apparently things were going smoothly for young Steve, but what would he do if his son needed him? She couldn't imagine him turning his back, yet he seemed to think she should do just that.

"Steve, I'm really tired tonight. Could we talk about this some other time?" Or maybe not, she thought. Maybe the best thing they could do was steer clear of the subject.

"Okay. I'll call you tomorrow," Steve said. "Or should I wait until you call me?"

"Call me tomorrow if you like. Greg won't be arriving until midafternoon."

"All right. Good night, Laura. Sweet dreams."

She'd expected to have sweet dreams. Back in her own bed, with her house back to normal again, but sleep eluded Laura, and so did the peace she'd hoped for.

She couldn't help being a little angry with

Steve. What right did he have to criticize her children? He was entitled to his own opinion, of course, but did he have to be quite so vocal about it? During the years she and Paul were raising their family, they'd frequently disagreed on child-rearing methods. Paul tended to think Laura was too hard on the children, that she expected too much from them. Laura, on the other hand, had occasionally found herself feeling almost jealous of the rapport Paul had with his daughters and his son. It was always Daddy the girls went to when they had a problem, Daddy's shoulder they sobbed on when life treated them harshly. Oh, Laura knew they loved her too, but they were smart enough to know that they could get around Paul, while she usually remained firm.

Cut it out, Laura, she told herself, flopping on her side and punching her pillow into a comfortable shape. Paul's not here now, and the kids are grown up, and all in all, you didn't do such a bad job. Greg is a responsible, intelligent young man, a dedicated, caring doctor. Vicki is a wife and mother and a sweetheart— most of the time. And Valerie . . . in the darkness, Laura smiled. She'd always sworn she loved all her children equally, but in her heart she knew it wasn't strictly true. Valerie was her baby, her youngest, the last child she'd carried in her womb. And like Andrea, she was some-how softer than her sister. She loved babies and animals, and she was quick to cry at an injus-tice. At twenty-two, she was in her senior year of college. When she graduated next spring she would have her degree in business adminis-tration, and she was already interviewing for administrative positions in several top manufacturing firms. To look at Valerie, most people never suspected the savvy intelligence hidden behind the wide gray eyes and the mop of red-brown curls. She'd recently become en-gaged to a man she'd met at school, Robert Barnes, and although she wouldn't admit it, Laura suspected they were living together off campus.

When she stopped to think about it, it gave her a pang to know that her daughter, her baby, was "living in sin," as it was called in the fifties. Of course no one thought of it that way anymore, but Laura sometimes had a hard time adjusting to the new sexual freedom. She still believed in marriage, especially for her daughters.

Blushing, Laura admitted that she was defin-itely doing a "do as I say and not as I do" thing since Steve came into her life. She didn't like the idea of her daughter living with a man without benefit of matrimony, yet Laura was contemplating an affair! But her situation was different. She and Steve weren't about to make any babies, so that was a concern she didn't have. Also, she'd been married for most of her life, and she wasn't at all sure she wanted to do it again, especially now.

What for? Would the skies fall in if she allowed herself the pleasure of a romantic episode with a man she genuinely cared for? Would anyone really care?

Well, the kids might, especially Vicki. Laura was pretty sure Greg wouldn't care one way or the other, and Valerie would probably tell her to go for it.

On that happy note, Laura felt herself drifting off to sleep. If deciding whether or not to have an affair was the worst problem she had, she was pretty darned lucky! And that at the ripe old age of fifty-one!

True to his word Steve called her first thing in the morning. She was having her coffee out on the screened porch, and her portable phone was lying beside the morning paper.

"Good morning," Steve said. "I called for two reasons, but first of all I want to apologize. I was out of line last night criticizing your children. You may have noticed that I have a habit of opening my mouth and letting everything spill out. I am sorry if I offended you, Laura. That's the very last thing I want to do. It's just that . . . oh hell, I feel sort of protective towards you, and it feels like you're letting your children take advantage of you."

Laura smiled into the phone. Even though she didn't feel she needed protection, it was nice to know Steve cared so much. "Apology accepted," she said. "Now what's the second reason you called?"

"I just wanted to tell you again how much I enjoyed our evening together. I hope we can do it again."

Laura laughed. "Why I'm counting on it! Now that I've found a gentleman who wines and dines me in such splendid style I don't intend to let him get away."

"Good. That's what I was hoping you'd say. What time do you expect your son to arrive?"

"Midafternoon or thereabout," Laura answered. "I'm going to make a good old-fashioned. pot of chicken soup for dinner tonight. That always made Greg feel better when he was small."

Steve chuckled. "Once a mother always a mother, I guess. That's nice, Laura. I'm sure your son will appreciate being home with you."

"Well, I don't know what I can do about his situation," she said worriedly. "I probably won't even be able to offer intelligent advice." She hesitated, then blurted it out. After all, Steve was a friend and he wasn't about to spread her son's troubles all over South Florida. "I told you that Greg was a doctor, didn't I?"

"Yes. He's a gynecologist isn't he?"

Laura replied, "A very good one, if I do say so myself, but . . . well one of his patients has apparently charged him with malpractice, and he wants to come home for a few days to think things through. Of course, I'm sure it's some kind of mistake," she added hastily. "Anyone who knows Greg knows what a concerned, conscientious person he is."

For a long moment there was silence, and Laura was starting to be sorry she'd told Steve.

"I am sorry, Laura," he said finally, "and now I'm even more ashamed of the way I spoke out last night. I had no idea your boy was in trouble. Is there anything I can do?"

Laura stared down into her empty coffee cup. "No, but thanks for asking. I'm sure that once the hospital has time to investigate they'll get to the bottom of this mess, but at the moment I guess Greg needs someone to talk to."

"Sure, and he's lucky to have you to stand by him," Steve said. "Look, I'll call you in a couple of days. That will give you time alone with your son, but if you need me in the meantime . . ."

"I'll call," Laura promised, her lips curved in a smile. Even though she was enjoying being on her own, it was nice to know there was a strong male shoulder nearby, just in case.

After pouring herself a second cup of coffee and putting the folded newspaper in the house, Laura planned her day. Make chicken soup for dinner, and maybe some of her homemade cheese biscuits. All of her children loved those. If she had time she might even fix Greg a key lime pie. That had always been his favorite. And maybe she should run to the store and get more eggs for tomorrow's breakfast. Suddenly Laura realized what she was doing and froze, her coffee cup halfway to her lips. She was doing the Jewish mother thing, fixing her kid's hurts with goodies. She'd done it all the time they were growing up, and to her it had been part of the nurturing process, but now, with everyone so conscious of diet it seemed as though using food for comfort was sinful.

Well, maybe it was if you were fat and unhealthy, but she wasn't and neither was Greg, and maybe a good, homemade pie was just what they both needed!

As Laura cooked and cleaned and readied her home for her son's visit, she found herself wondering how Greg would take the news that she had decided to sell the family home. Would he feel betrayed the way Vicki apparently did? She doubted it. Greg usually took life in stride. She was pretty sure he would want her to do whatever was best for her. As she chopped celery and onions and grated carrots for the soup, Laura realized that she was actually starting to look forward to selling the house. It would be a big adjustment, moving from this large house into a small one-bedroom apartment, and it would mean disposing of some of the things she'd collected over the years. There would certainly be no place to display her collection of depression glass. She dumped the chopped vegetables into the chicken broth and stirred. Maybe she should give some of her handmade porcelain dolls to Valerie. Her youngest daughter had always loved the dolls her mother made, and perhaps when she married, Valerie would have a place big enough to display the dolls.

Sighing, Laura put the lid on the pot of soup and turned the burner to simmer. She had time to decide about her possessions. Houses usually didn't sell overnight.

By three-thirty that afternoon, Laura was ready. The house was clean, the pot simmered on the stove, sending the aroma of chicken soup wafting through the house. A pie was chilling in the refrigerator, and the bed in Greg's room was made up with freshly laundered sheets.

Laura sat in her living room and looked around. A nice house, she thought. But it was definitely time some young family had the chance to enjoy it. What did she need with four bedrooms, a large eat-in kitchen as well as a formal dining room, and living and family rooms. It was just too much house for a single woman, and that's what she was. Starting over. Second chance, as Steve liked to say.

She was at the window when Greg drove up in his almost-new Buick. Laura watched as her firstborn stepped out of the car. He was a little too thin for her taste, and his face looked pale and haggard. Well, no wonder. She'd be haggard too if someone was suing her for something she hadn't done.

She met him at the front door with open arms. "How are you, honey?"

Greg smiled crookedly. "I'm making it, Mom," he said, giving her a hard hug. "Boy, it's good to see you, and this place. It brings back a lot of great memories."

"Yes, this house has seen a lot. If the walls could talk, eh?"

Greg walked into the living room and put his

bag down. "Are we alone? Not taking care of Vicki's brood, are you?"

"Actually, Vicki just left last night," Laura said, watching Greg's reaction. "She and the children were with me for several days. Tim's being transferred to Indianapolis and Vicki didn't want to go."

Greg shrugged and dropped into Paul's old lounge chair. "I hate to say it, Mom," he said, "but that girl always wants her own way. What happened? Did old Tim come over and drag her home where she belongs?"

Laura laughed. "Not exactly. Vicki came to her senses on her own, with a little gentle nudging from me, of course."

"Well, all's well that ends well, I guess," Greg said.

Laura studied her son. He looked tired and worried, and his voice sounded old. "How about a glass of iced tea, hon? Are you hungry?"

"Tea sounds good, Mom, but I'm not hungry. To tell the truth I can't even remember the last time I sat down and had a full meal. This past week . . . well, it hasn't been the best time of my life."

Laura patted Greg's shoulder. "I'll get the tea and we'll talk," she said. When she returned with a tray holding two glasses of tea and a plate of cheese and crackers, Greg's feet were up and he was leaning back in the chair with his eyes closed. Laura's heart twisted with pity and concern. Parents always wished they could shield their children from the harsh realities of life, but in the end all they could really do was stand by and be ready to help.

"Here's your tea, Greg," she said, setting the glass on the table beside him, "and I fixed a little something to nibble on."

"Thanks, Mom, and thanks for letting me barge in on you this way, especially since you just got rid of Vicki. Boy, life is full of surprises, isn't it?"

"Yes indeed," Laura said, thinking of one particular incident that had put a whole new color on her life. She dragged her thoughts away from Steve. This wasn't the time. Her son needed her.

"What happened, hon?" she asked gently. "Can you tell me?"

Greg closed his eyes, then opened them and pushed his hands through his thick, dark hair. "It's the classic theme, Mom, only I never thought it would happen to me. One of my patients, a young woman twenty-four years old, has claimed that I touched her in an improper manner during a pelvic exam."

Laura felt all the color drain out of her face

as she sucked in her breath. "But how . . . don't you have a nurse in the room at all times? Isn't there a witness to prove that it isn't true?"

Greg rubbed his forehead. "I do have a nurse," he said, "but Janet had to leave the room for a couple of minutes to get some supplies. That's when the woman is claiming the impropriety took place, those few minutes we were alone. It boils down to my word against hers, Mom, and right now, there's been a lot of bad publicity about women being sexually harassed. People seem to want to believe that most men are out to get women. Oh hell, I don't know! Allison Montgomery is a troubled young woman. I knew that the first time she came to my office, but I never imagined anything like this. I never thought she'd do something so crazy! I can't figure out what she hopes to gain from it."

"How do you mean troubled?" Laura asked.

"Ah, she's young, and apparently her boyfriend just dumped her. She's taking it hard, and on top of that I had to tell her that she'd contracted a sexually transmitted disease from him. That really blew her mind. Right now, I think she probably hates all men. Maybe this is her way of getting revenge."

"Oh my God!" Laura was stunned. This was

even worse than she'd imagined. How could Greg possibly defend himself against something like this?

"What are you going to do? Is there some way to prove she's lying?"

Greg shook his head. "I think we may be able to show that she's emotionally unstable right now, but that's about all we can expect. As I said, it's her word against mine."

"But is the hospital behind you? Will they be fair? They don't believe those ridiculous charges, do they?"

"No, Mom, but they have to protect themselves, you know? The hospital has a reputation, and whenever there's an issue that generates a lot of public opinion . . ."

"Whatever happened to people being presumed innocent until proven guilty?" Laura asked indignantly. She'd never really questioned the justice system before, but then she'd never had to worry about one of her children being wrongly accused either.

Greg shrugged and tried to smile. "I don't know. Actually, right at this moment I don't know much of anything, except that it feels good to be home with you, in this house. The only other thing I could wish for is that Dad was still here so I could talk to him."

Laura swallowed around the lump in her

throat. "I know, son," she said, patting Greg's shoulder.

Later that afternoon, as she put the finishing touches on dinner and set the small table in the kitchen, she remembered the first weeks after Paul's death, when she had often found herself wanting to talk to him, wanting to ask his opinion on something. At those times the sense of loss was so acute it was an actual pain. But lately, those times had become less and less frequent as she learned to deal with life on her own. She was getting used to making her own decisions without help from anyone, and she was enjoying it. Smiling as she put warm cheese biscuits into a wicker breadbasket and covered them with a napkin, Laura realized that she'd literally gone right from her father's home to her husband's. There had been no period in between when she had had a chance to be independent. At home she'd been subject to her parent's rules and regulations, and after her marriage, she had to consider Paul's needs and wants. At fifty-one she was totally independent for the very first time.

"Here you are, hon," she said a few minutes later. "One of your old favorites, chicken soup and cheese biscuits." Laura felt a tug at her heartstrings as she noted her son's boyish grin.

Greg scooped two biscuits out of the basket

and slathered them with butter. "Good thing none of my colleagues can see me now," he said. "Cholesterol city!"

Greg was a lot like his father, Laura thought. He had the same infectious smile, the same thick, dark hair and dark, intelligent eyes. And he had his dad's values too. He really was a son to be proud of.

Seeing Greg's obvious enjoyment of the food she'd prepared increased Laura's own appetite and they both ate heartily. Finally, after a piece of key lime pie they took their coffee into the living room.

"I haven't even asked you how you're doing, Mom," Greg said. "I'm a self-centered jerk, aren't I?"

Laura smiled. "Not at all, and to set your mind at rest, I'm doing fine. I think I'm finally beginning to come to terms with everything."

Greg sipped his coffee, his dark eyes narrowing. "Meaning?"

"Well, for one thing, I've decided to put this house on the market. It's too big for one person and I'm getting tired of cleaning all the unused rooms. And I'm thinking of taking a course in real estate." And an old flame has come back into my life, Greg. What would you think about your old mom having a wild and passionate love affair? Laura flushed just thinking of the words she hadn't said aloud. She was pretty sure Greg could handle her selling the house and getting a job, but taking a lover? That was definitely another story! And anyway, that part of her life was her own business. It had nothing to do with her children, and it wouldn't affect her role of mother in any way.

Good Lord, she was rationalizing again. She seemed to do it a lot lately. She had the sudden realization that she wasn't as sure of her feelings as she'd like to think. When she was with Steve her thoughts automatically seemed to turn to an intimate relationship, but when she was alone she wondered if she really had the courage.

"You're going to sell this house? Hey, Mom, that's . . . well, it's great, if that's what you want. But where will you live?"

"I'm thinking of getting a small apartment. Something new and bright and easy to keep clean. If I'm going to be a working lady I don't want to spend all my time mopping floors and polishing furniture."

Greg grinned and shook his head. "You never cease to amaze me, Mom. Every time I think I have you figured out, you throw me a curve. Well, I think it's a good idea. You should have something small and easy to take care of." He shook his head again, and his grin intensified. "It's hard to imagine you as a career woman, but I guess stranger things have happened, haven't they?" A sudden thought struck him and his smile faded. "You're not having financial problems, are you? That's not why you want to go to work, is it? I was under the impression that Dad left you pretty well provided for."

Laura nodded. "He did, and I'm very grateful, and I'm glad that I was able to stay at home and be a full-time mother when you and your sisters were growing up, but I really think I'd like to get out of the house and do something different. It will also give me an opportunity to meet some new people."

Greg looked thoughtful. "What about all your pals here in the neighborhood? Lucy and Ann, and Betty Marshall?"

"I still see them, but not as much as I did before your father passed away. It's a funny thing, Greg, but all at once I'm an unattached woman, and somehow they see me as a threat. Oh, they still call me for lunch occasionally, but I haven't been invited to any of their houses for dinner in ages."

"If you ask me that's pretty lousy. What do they expect you to do, jump their husband's bones?"

"Greg!"

"Well, it's true, Mom. And what would you want with any of those old guys anyway? Don't those crazy broads realize you're a very proper grandma?"

"Are you forgetting that your dad was one of those 'old guys,' as you call them?"

"That was different." Greg's eyes narrowed. "Uh, you're not interested in finding . . . another husband, are you, Mom?"

Laura laughed at the worried look on Greg's handsome face. He'd said the word "husband" as though it consisted of four letters.

"No, I don't want another husband," Laura said, setting his mind at ease, "but who knows, I might want a boyfriend. Does that shock you, hon?"

Greg grinned. "You're forgetting that I'm a gynecologist, Mom. I know about menopause and how some women seem to bloom at midlife. Is that what you're doing, Mom? Are you about to burst into bloom before my eyes?"

"Stop teasing. You're looking at a rosebud that has definitely seen better days. You might say I've dropped quite a few of my petals." Laura paused, then spoke softly. "I just want to get on with my life, Greg," she said. "Can you understand that?"

"Sure. That's what I want to do too, but

right now I'm not sure how I'm going to accomplish that."

"It'll work out, honey," Laura said, hoping she sounded more positive than she felt. There was no doubt in her mind that her son was totally innocent, but she'd heard of too many cases where crazy women made false accusations and got away with it. Pray God, this wouldn't be one of them! She swallowed. "Why don't you just relax and try to unwind for a few days? I'll stuff you with good home cooking, and you can just be a slug."

Greg managed a smile. "Sounds good, Mom. I'll give it a try."

Six

Laura waited on her son hand and foot for the next couple of days. Greg looked so tired, so bewildered and beaten. She'd never seen him that way before and it was frightening. She talked on the phone to Steve twice, and she kept promising him that they'd get together soon to shop for furniture. He didn't sound too happy at being put off, but Laura just didn't feel right running off and leaving Greg alone to fend for himself.

She smiled to herself one morning as she fixed Greg's favorite breakfast of pancakes and sausages. Why was it that mothers frequently tended to spoil their sons and demand more of their daughters? Was it the age-old male-female thing? She loved all the kids, but somehow she felt that Greg needed mothering the most.

He came into the kitchen sniffing. "Umm, do I smell pancakes?"

Laura nodded. If it weren't for the problem that had brought Greg home she would have thoroughly enjoyed his visit. Part of it was that she knew it was only temporary, unlike the situation when Vicki and the kids moved in, and she'd been afraid Vicki would make it permanent. Greg was used to his privacy, and he was certainly well able to afford his own living quarters. He wouldn't be interested in coming home again.

"Are you feeling any better, Greg?" she asked, setting the plate in front of him. "Have you decided how you're going to handle things?"

"I'm going to fight it, I know that," Greg said quietly, slathering butter on the pancakes. "I just haven't figured out how."

"I wish I could help. I wish I could get my hands on that girl and shake some sense into her," Laura said angrily. "How can she do something like this?"

"I don't know, Mom," Greg said, with a crooked grin. "I studied psychology in medical school, but it wasn't my best subject. I'm not real good at figuring out what makes people tick."

"Well, it's all going to work out," Laura assured her son. "You'll see. That woman will

126

come to her senses. You'll see."

Steve called that evening, and this time Laura knew she couldn't put him off any longer. He'd be moving into his new place in a few days, and he didn't even have a bed.

"How about tomorrow?" she said, surprising both of them. "I'm sure my son can find a way to amuse himself for a few hours."

Sounding both surprised and pleased, Steve said he would pick her up at ten, and just before he hung up he warned her to wear comfortable shoes. "I like to browse," he admitted, sounding just a little sheepish. "You're not one of those quick shoppers, are you?"

Laura laughed. "No way," she said.

"I'm going out for a while tomorrow, Greg," Laura told her son before they turned off the television and called it a night. "An old high-school friend has asked me to help him shop for furniture for his new apartment. Steve just moved here from Arizona."

Greg's dark brows rose questioningly. "Steve, is it? An old beau, Mom? Do I detect a hint of a blush on that face of yours? Hey, you are coming to terms with things, aren't you, lady?"

"Go on, it's not like that," Laura protested, knowing even as she said it, that it was precisely like that. For all intents and purposes,

Steve was her boyfriend, but she felt compelled to deny it. "He . . . he's just a friend, hon. He lost his wife a couple of years ago, and his only son is married and . . . well, he has cousins here in Miami. I guess that's why he decided to move here."

Greg smirked. "Yeah, sure. Cousins. Right, Mom, and I'll bet they're helping him shop for furniture too, hmm?"

"Now you stop that, Greg Kinsey! You know I don't like to be teased."

"Ah, sorry. I'd forgotten. Well, you will keep your only son advised of any further . . . eh, developments, won't you, Mother?"

"Maybe, and maybe not," Laura teased. "Right now you are behaving like a real brat, Gregory James Kinsey. This is your mother you're talking to. Have a little respect!"

Greg immediately sobered. "Don't you ever worry about that, Mom," he said. "There's no one in this world I respect more. You're the greatest."

Laura had a hard time getting to sleep that night. How would Greg feel when he actually met Steve? Would he be able to feel the sparks between them? Would he be embarrassed by his mother's sexuality? She knew he'd deny it if she ever got up enough nerve to ask, but wasn't it normal for children to be uneasy about their parent's sexuality? Greg would feel honor-bound to deny it, because he was a doctor, and he was supposed to understand things a layman didn't.

In her darkened bedroom, Laura temporarily pushed her son out of her mind and thought about Steve. It was crazy, but she actually missed him. They hadn't spent all that much time together, but he was already beginning to insinuate himself into her life. She found herself wanting to discuss Greg's problem with him, even though she knew Steve could do little but sympathize. She hoped the two men would like each other, her son and her friend. Boyfriend. As her eyes finally began to grow heavy, Laura realized she liked thinking of Steve as her boyfriend. It brought back memories, and it made her feel young again, and strong and hopeful. And right now she needed those feelings very badly.

A few miles away, which could have been light years in view of the Miami traffic, Steve tossed and turned on the sofa bed in his cousin's living room. Rich had been good enough to put him up until his apartment was ready, so he couldn't very well complain about discomfort, but Steve knew that if he had to sleep on the lumpy, sagging sofa bed much longer he would be permanently disabled. His back already ached and he'd just lain down. By morning he would be stiff and sore over every inch of his body. Well, it wouldn't be much longer. A few more days and he'd be installed in his own place. He would be officially starting his new life, his second chance.

Unsuccessfully attempting to shift into a more comfortable position, Steve thought of his late wife, Marcie. His mouth curved in remembrance. Marcie had been a beautiful woman, not so much in looks, but in heart and spirit. Even after she was diagnosed with ovarian cancer she'd been beautiful, worrying more about him and Steve, Jr. than about herself. She'd made him promise her that he would go on with his life after she was gone. Steve remembered sitting by her bedside, holding her hand with tears streaming down his cheeks as he nodded, willing to promise her anything that would ease her mind and bring peace to her lovely gray-blue eyes.

"I'm doing it, Marcie," he whispered into the darkness. "I'm going on with my life. I'm doing what you told me to do, but I'll never forget you, or what we had together."

In his childhood bedroom, Greg Kinsey lay on his back, his hands behind his head, his eyes wide. He was in one hell of a mess, and all of his mother's well-meaning assurances didn't make him feel any better. He'd known that Allison was a troubled young woman. He'd actually felt her anger. He should have had enough sense to know that she was dangerous. Instead of letting down his guard he should have taken extra precautions. He should have been more aware. Well, hindsight wouldn't help him now, nor would self-pity. The only thing to do was to go back into the ring and come out fighting, like his mom was doing.

In the darkness, Greg felt his lips curve into a smile. She was some woman, his mom, a real inspiration. She'd held herself together after his dad's stroke, keeping the atmosphere in the house cheerful and relaxed for the man she'd built her life around. Well, maybe that wasn't strictly true, Greg thought. Maybe she hadn't built her whole life around her family. He'd always believed his mom was the perfect wife. Growing up he could rarely remember hearing his parents argue. But although his mom had always been there for her husband and her children, she'd managed to maintain a core of independence that was standing her in good stead now. Suddenly he remembered something she'd said earlier, about looking for a boyfriend. Had she been serious, or was it just her way of adding a little levity to the evening? Well, if she was serious, even if she had already found someone, he certainly wasn't about to censure her. She was a pretty neat lady, and she deserved whatever happiness she could find. Frowning, Greg wondered if his sisters would feel the same way, especially Vicki. She had always been close to their dad, and she was the one most likely to resent another man coming into their mother's life.

Greg flopped on his side and determinedly closed his eyes. Whatever happened, his mom would find a way to deal with it. She always did.

Laura flipped a picture-perfect omelet onto Greg's plate the next morning, and smiled at her son. "Feel a little better this morning?" she asked, almost sure that Greg's color had improved in the past few days. "Are things starting to come together?"

Greg eyed the omelet appreciatively and poured two glasses of orange juice. He hadn't realized how much he'd missed his mom's home cooking. "I don't know about that," he said honestly, "but at least I know I'm not going down without a fight. I'm going back to the hospital and I'm going to do everything I can to prove that Allison is an unstable, vindictive young woman, who is bent on getting back at men in general in any way she can. Maybe I'll call on you for advice."

"Any time," Laura said fervently. "Look, hon, I'll probably be out most of the day. How about we be really bad tonight and order in pizza for supper? How's that sound?"

"Perfect," Greg said. "I'll probably be out all day too. I'm going to head over to the library and do a little research."

"Good," Laura said. "Then I'll see you this afternoon. Would you mind if I invited Steve to share pizza with us?"

Greg shrugged and did his best to hide a grin. "Why not? Any friend of yours is a friend of mine, Mom."

Laura knew she blushed. She could feel the heat right up to the roots of her hair. Greg was a devil. If he suspected there was something going on between her and Steve, he'd never let up. Well, Laura had always believed in getting things out in the open. She shrugged as she went to her room to finish dressing. Let the chips fall where they may, she thought.

She was ready when Steve's Bronco pulled into the driveway. Peeking through the mini-blinds, Laura saw that it was an absolutely gorgeous Florida day. It was typical early spring weather. Warm and balmy, the sky clear and cloudless, the sun was a comforting mantle on her shoulders as she hurried down the walk and smiled good morning to Steve.

"My, you certainly are punctual, sir," she teased. "You must be anxious to spend your money."

Steve leaned over and opened the door on Laura's side. His smile left no doubt in Laura's mind that he was very glad to see her.

"It seems like years," he said seriously, as Laura slid into the passenger's seat. "I was beginning to forget what you looked like." She wore cream-colored slacks and a matching short-sleeved sweater. A gold charm in the shape of a sailboat hung on a slender gold chain around her neck, and gold button earrings decorated her earlobes. The soft, floral scent of her perfume wafted against Steve's nostrils as he admired the trim, well-proportioned length of leg beside him.

"You look marvelous," he said. Then his eyes slid down to her feet. He nodded approval. "Good. Sensible shoes. Thank God you're not one of those women who thinks she has to totter around on heels that were designed purely for torture purposes. I have a feeling we'll be doing a lot of walking today."

"I figured as much," Laura said agreeably, "So I thought I'd be more comfortable in pants than a skirt. You know, climbing in and out of the car."

Steve grinned, reading her thoughts. It was impossible for a woman to get in and out of a car without showing a little bit of leg, so Laura had apparently chosen to cover hers. "I hate to disappoint you," he said, his brows arched mischievously, "but you're still sexy as hell, even in pants. Were you really hoping to calm my raging hormones?"

Laura grinned back at him. "Did you say raging or aging?"

Steve pretended offense. "Now them are fighting words, lady! I may just have to prove you wrong."

"Maybe," Laura said, smoothing the gabardine material over her knees, "but not today, mister! We've got some serious shopping to do."

Their first stop was a huge warehouse-clearing store, where Laura had occasionally found some good buys. She didn't know how much money Steve planned to spend, or even what style of furniture he liked, but the warehouse usually had a pretty diversified selection.

"This place can be a little daunting," she explained as Steve helped her out of the Bronco. "They just stack the furniture every which way and that means you really have to use your imagination to visualize how it will look at home. Did you take any measurements of the apartment?"

Steve looked confused. "Measurements? For what? It already has blinds and drapes. Why would I need to measure?"

"Well, for wall space for one thing," Laura explained. "Will you want a king-sized bed or something smaller? And how about the living room? What kind of sofa do you have in mind? Something modern like a sectional, or do you just want comfort?"

"I definitely want comfort," Steve said, taking Laura's arm as they entered the warehouse, "but I want it to look as nice as possible too. Can we manage that?"

Laura let herself enjoy the feel of Steve's hand on her elbow for a moment, then looked up at him and smiled. He had a nice face. It had evolved from the handsomeness of youth to the dignity of middle age quite nicely, she decided. "We'll give it our best shot," she promised.

It took all morning for Steve to settle on a bedroom set he liked, and one that he also thought would fit into the apartment's bedroom. Actually, there were two bedrooms, but he planned to use the smaller one as a combination office and guest room. "I don't think the kids will be visiting too often," he said, "especially after the baby comes, but I do need an extra bed. And Steve, Jr. may want to stay over when he comes through Miami on his route."

"Then you might want to think about some kind of sofa bed," Laura said. "That will save space, and give you room for a small desk and a comfortable chair."

"What would I do without you?" Steve said, draping his arm over her shoulders casually. "I'm not much good at this kind of thing. Picking out furniture and decorating was always Marcie's department."

Laura felt a pang. For a moment Steve looked lost and lonely, then he smiled and the sun came out again. Like her, he was having good days and bad days, happy moments and times when things came down on him with the force of a dynamite blast, like now, when he remembered all the things his wife had done.

"Hey, you're in good company," she said, taking his hand and squeezing it.

The salesman assured Steve that the bedroom set would be delivered in three days' time. Steve took one last, lingering look at the plainly styled walnut dresser, chest and headboard he'd picked out, then, like a naughty little kid, he plopped down on the mattress and bounced.

Both Laura and the salesman laughed.

"I don't like rock-hard mattresses," Steve said sheepishly. "Actually . . ." He hesitated, and color rose in his cheeks.

"What is it, sir?" the young salesman prompted. "Do you want to try some more mattresses?"

"Well, I was wondering . . . do you carry water mattresses?"

"Water mattresses?" Laura squeaked. A vision popped in front of her, of her and Steve together on a sensuously undulating water mattress. Good grief, she was going crazy! She was standing in the middle of a furniture warehouse with Steve and a salesman young enough to be her son, and she was having erotic daydreams! What next?

"Why, yes we do," the grinning salesman said quickly. "May I show them to you, sir?"

"You may indeed," Steve said, taking Laura's hand and swinging it between them as though he was sixteen instead of heading towards sixty. He leaned over and whispered in Laura's ear. "I always wanted to make love to a beautiful woman on a waterbed, but Marcie thought they were decadent. She was convinced that only drugged-out hippies slept on waterbeds."

"Oh." Laura was completely stunned. She was rendered speechless by this new and unexpected development.

The cheeky young man showed them several different types of water mattresses, and Laura was quite sure that he was thoroughly enjoying himself. Once he even winked at her.

Some of the mattresses had baffles so there was less movement, and some were controlled so each person in the bed could have a different degree of softness or firmness.

"Personally, I say to hell with the baffles," Steve said. "What good is a waterbed without movement? Isn't that the whole idea?"

Laura blushed, and the salesman's grin widened.

"My sentiments exactly, sir," he said. "Why don't you go with your instincts and try the plain mattress? We offer a thirty-day guarantee of satisfaction on all water mattresses. If after sleeping on it for thirty days you decide you don't like it, we'll exchange it for another type. How's that sound? Fair enough?"

"Perfect," Steve said. "You've got yourself a deal."

"My goodness," Laura said, as they walked out to the Bronco. "I had no idea you were so . . . so . . ."

"Decadent?" Steve asked, putting his arm around her waist and squeezing gently. He looked down at her and smiled. "The way I see it, Laura, I'm only going to live once, and I may as well squeeze all the enjoyment from life I can. Make sense?"

Laura thought for a moment, her head tilted to one side. Actually, it made perfect sense to her. Steve was right. Life was short, and you only got one go-around. But what did other people think when they saw middle-aged couples doing things that were usually reserved for the young?

She stopped walking right in the middle of the parking lot as a sudden thought struck her. Why in the world should it matter what others thought? Who cared anyway?

"Go for it, Steve," she said. And then she stood on tiptoe and kissed his cheek, not caring if the whole world saw her.

"I'm having fun," Steve said later as they sat in a small Cuban restaurant having lunch.

Laura nibbled a piece of fried plantain and nodded. "This is the nicest day I've had in a long time. Helping you pick out furniture, this delicious lunch. I think *boliche* is one of my favorite Cuban dishes. This beef just falls apart."

"I like *piccadillo*," Steve said, "and the roast pork. Unhealthy as hell with all that fat, but worth every cholesterol-laden bite."

Laura nodded agreement. "It's great to throw caution to the wind, isn't it?"

"Umm, I certainly did that today, didn't I?

I'm still having a hard time believing I actually bought a waterbed. Wait until my cousins find out. They'll want to have me committed."

Laura smiled. "You'll probably think I'm making this up, but I always wanted to see what it was like to sleep on a waterbed, only Paul wouldn't even think of giving up his posturepedic mattress."

"Well, well, my lady has an adventuress streak after all," Steve said. His eyes were dark and warm, and they pinned her to her seat. "Maybe we can work something out."

Laura squirmed uncomfortably. She was plagued with longings these days, sometimes vague and sometimes quite explicit, and she didn't know whether to feel guilty, or be glad she was alive to have feelings at all!

"Am I moving too fast?" Steve asked, his smile fading as he noted Laura's discomfort. "I promised I wouldn't rush you and I meant it, but sometimes I get the feeling that you feel at least some of what I'm feeling, Laura."

She started to shake her head, then changed her mind and nodded. "I do," she admitted, feeling somewhat shy, "but I guess I don't know how to handle my feelings. This is all so new to me. I've never done anything like this. Besides you, Paul was the only other man I ever dated, the only man I ever . . ."

Steve covered her hand with his, and his eyes, those dark and wonderful eyes, were misty with tenderness. "I know," he said softly, "and that's what makes what I'm feeling now so special. It feels right, Laura, as if this is the way our lives were destined to work out."

For just a second Laura closed her eyes. Memories. There were so many memories. And the last memory, of the way Steve left her, was still sharp and painful after all the years between. Would she ever be able to exorcise the ghosts?

"One step at a time, Steve," she said, her voice just a little unsteady. "Right now, we need to polish off this delicious flan and get back to business. We still have a kitchen set and living room furniture to buy, unless you plan on eating off the floor and watching television while perched on an old crate."

Steve groaned. "No way, lady. These old bones wouldn't stand for that. Come on, back to work."

By five-thirty Steve had finally managed to find an armchair he felt comfortable in, as well as a contemporary sofa and loveseat. These, together with an oak coffee table and two end tables, a table lamp and one floor lamp, promised to make his living room habitable for the time being. He decided he would buy pictures and other accessories in a more leisurely manner. With the living room taken care of they quickly selected a small, round dinette table and four matching chairs. "In case I decide to throw a formal dinner party," Steve joked.

"Okay," Laura said tiredly, as she climbed back into the Bronco. "I guess that's it. At least you've got the basics. The only other things you need are cooking utensils and dishes, some basic cleaning supplies and equipment and linens. We'll do that another day, okay? Right now I'm starved, and I promised Greg we'd have pizza tonight."

Steve looked disappointed. "Oh. You have to go home?"

"Not have to, want to," Laura said. "Comfortable shoes or no, my feet are dead. All I want to do is kick back and relax in my own comfortable living room. You like pizza, don't you?"

"Why? Am I invited?"

Steve looked like a kid who's won the prize at a country fair. Laura patted his cheek and laughed. "If you'll carry, I'll buy," she said, "and one of the pizzas has to have mushrooms."

"Damn! And I wanted anchovies," Steve said, slapping his forehead.

"Yuk! No anchovies. Greg and I are both allergic to them."

Steve shrugged. "I bow to the greater numbers," he said. "Mushrooms it is."

They stopped at a pizza parlor not far from Laura's house, and they shared a cold beer while waiting for the pizzas.

"Nothing like a nice cold beer," Steve said. Laura agreed.

It was a typical pizza joint, and music from the juke box blared over and around them. A hefty young waitress went by, balancing a tray with a steaming pizza and several soft drinks. Laura's stomach growled and she hoped the pizza maker would hurry.

"How would you feel about remarrying?" Steve asked, out of the blue. "I mean someday . . . if the right man came along?"

Laura looked at Steve, completely stunned by his question. His eyes were earnest and questioning, and his jaw looked a little tight, as if he was trying hard to hide his true feelings.

She shook her head. "I can't answer that, Steve," she said, "at least not right now. I'm not sure how I feel about remarrying."

"Oh. Well, I suppose that's normal, for you anyway. As far as I'm concerned, I don't think much of the single life."

Laura nodded. "Being single has its drawbacks," she agreed, "but it also has some plus factors. There's no one to answer to, no one but yourself to consider, your own wants and needs. There's privacy and space . . . and a certain freedom." She quickly shook her head when Steve started to reply. "Don't get me wrong. I loved being married. I enjoyed being a wife and a mother, and I wouldn't trade the past for anything, but just now . . . well, I'm perfectly satisfied with things as they are."

"Oh," Steve said again. "Well . . ."

"Order number 123," the young counter boy called. "Two pizzas to go, one with mushrooms, one with sausage and extra cheese."

"That's us," Laura said, jumping up. She'd been saved by the bell.

Greg was home when they got there. He fixed a level, cautious gaze on Steve as Laura introduced the two men, but he didn't hesitate to shake hands with Steve.

"Did you get all your shopping done?" Greg asked politely, after offering Steve a beer.

"Thanks, but your mother and I already shared one. I'll just have iced tea with my pizza." Steve sat down on the sofa across from Greg. "We got the main pieces," he explained. "A bed, a comfortable chair, a table and chairs for eating." He smiled. "The necessities of life."

Steve returned the smile. "I know what you

mean. You should see my apartment in Atlanta. I have all the necessities, but none of the niceties, at least that's what my last girlfriend told me."

"Well, your mom was a tremendous help," Steve said, finding it hard to tear his eyes from Laura's well-shaped posterior as she bustled around the kitchen, getting plates and filling glasses with ice. "I'd probably still be back in the furniture store if she hadn't agreed to help me out."

"Not true," Laura yelled. "Steve knew exactly what he wanted, and he wasn't afraid to say so," she added, advancing into the room with the goodies on a large tray.

"Here, let me help you," Steve said, jumping up to help her lower the huge tray to the table.

Their hands touched, and Laura felt herself flush, wondering if Greg would notice how she jerked her hand back. Although Greg claimed he understood that women didn't automatically start knitting and swear off men after menopause, she was sure it would be different when the woman was his own mother.

"Hurry up, Mom. I'm starving," Greg said, "And don't forget, the piece with the most cheese is mine!"

It was a fun meal. They stuffed themselves with pizza and washed it down with lemon-spiced iced tea. Steve spoke of his years as plant supervisor for a computer software firm, and Greg confided that he loved messing with computers in his spare time.

"Not that he has much," Laura complained. "I thought once Greg finished his school and became a real doctor, it would be easier for him, but if anything he seems to put in more hours. If he's not caring for patients he's doing research or something. You have to take time to smell the flowers, son."

Greg's expression sobered. "I may have plenty of spare time in the future," he said. "Maybe more than I want or need."

"Your mother told me about your problems, Greg," Steve said. "I'm sorry."

"Thanks. So am I, and what makes me so mad is that I think I could have prevented the whole thing."

"You mean by making your nurse stay in the room?" Laura asked.

"Yes, that, and I probably should have tried to get Allison to see a psychiatrist. I knew she was troubled."

"Well, hindsight isn't going to help now," Laura said, "but I know everything's going to be all right, Greg."

"You're right," Greg said, smiling. "Remember what Dad always said, that if you told the truth you couldn't go wrong?"

"And he was right," Laura said.

By the time she had disposed of the pizza boxes and was loading the tea glasses into the dishwasher, Laura couldn't stop yawning. Steve picked up the paper napkins and smiled.

"Well, I guess I should take the hint and say good night," he said. "You're about to fall asleep standing up."

Laura turned to face him and shrugged apologetically. "I'm sorry. It must have been all that walking we did. I feel like I could sleep for a week."

"Then I will say good night," Steve said, moving forward and gripping Laura's shoulders. "But first let me thank you for a wonderful day. It was the best day I've had in a long, long time. I'm beginning to think I really can start over."

He was standing very close, his lips mere inches from hers. Laura wondered if he would kiss her. If she wanted him to.

As though he read her thoughts, Steve dipped his head and whispered against her ear. "No, I'm not going to kiss you, even though there's nothing I'd like better. Your son is in the other room, and I'm saving all my energy for a time when we're all alone."

Laura shivered with a combination of anticipation and fear.

"I had a nice time too," she managed. "There's nothing more fun than picking out furniture, unless it's eating pizza with extra cheese."

"Good," Steve said, nodding. "A cheap date, every guy's dream. Instead of a five-course dinner, I'll order a pizza with extra cheese. Maybe I'll even throw in some mushrooms."

"Whoa, boy, I love pizza, but I also like the five-course deal too. I'm a woman of varied tastes."

"Good," Steve repeated. "I'll enjoy discovering just what they are!"

She walked him to the door, conscious of her son watching from the comfortable old lounge chair.

"Good night," she said, careful to keep a sedate distance between herself and Steve.

"Good night," he answered. "Sleep tight."

Laura shut the door and turned around. "Well," she said. "I'm glad you two got to meet each other."

"So am I," Greg said. "He's more than just a friend, isn't he?"

"I don't know," Laura said honestly. "Steve and I go back a long way. He was my first real boyfriend, so I suppose I'm a little sentimental about him."

"Well, he seems okay," Greg said, "and I say, do whatever makes you happy, Mom. You've spent practically your whole life taking care of your children and your husband. Maybe it's time for you to do something just because you want to."

"Maybe," Laura said, sitting down on the sofa across from her son.

"I guess you get pretty lonely here in this house all by yourself," Greg said.

"Actually, I'm not, or at least I haven't been yet. Oh, those first few weeks after your dad's death were terrible. The house felt like a mausoleum, but now . . . well, I've got Buttons," Laura said, pointing to the fluffy fur ball curled into a corner of the sofa. Now that Vicki and the kids were gone, he'd come out of hiding. "And I also have my 'lady friends,' as your dad used to call the girls," Laura said. "And when I take my real estate course and start working I'll be too busy to be lonely."

"Mom, you are really something," Greg said, grinning. "I sure am proud of you."

"Well, thank you, son, and I am equally proud of you."

Greg leaned back in the chair and looked thoughtful. "I think I better go home tomorrow," he said. "I'm going to stand up and fight instead of running around with my tail between my legs. If my mom can overcome widowhood and make a new life, then I guess I can work my way through this little roadblock."

"Atta boy, Greg," Laura cheered.

The next morning Laura spent several hours dusting and rearranging her collection of porcelain dolls. She loved them all, from the clown with rhinestone teardrops on his cheeks to the baby doll with a cloth body and the face of an angel. It hurt to think of parting with any of them, but Laura knew she really should give some of them to Valerie and Vicki. After all, when she sold the house and moved into a small apartment she simply wouldn't have room for them. Not to mention the fact that after she took her real estate course and began working, she simply wouldn't have time for all that dusting.

After packing the satin-garbed clown in a box and stuffing tissue all around it, Laura put it aside and went to the small desk in her bedroom. Squaring her shoulders, she sat down and picked up the telephone. An hour later, her fate was sealed. She'd gotten all the information on the real estate course and had promised to send the woman a check for the course fee. If all went well, and she passed the course she would soon be a licensed realtor. She was scared and excited at the same time. Scared that she might fail, but excited that she'd had the courage to take the chance. Nothing ventured, nothing gained, right? Smiling to herself, Laura thought it odd that so many of Paul's old sayings were coming back to her lately. He'd had a million of them. It was almost as though he were standing by, ready to prod her when she faltered. Well, maybe that's the way it was with couples who had shared more than three decades. Maybe even death couldn't separate mates of that long standing.

Laura went in the bathroom and splashed water on her face and combed her unruly auburn hair before going downstairs. She'd make Greg some lunch and then see if he needed any help packing.

But like most men, Greg had his own method of packing for a trip. He just stuffed everything in, not caring how wrinkled it got, and then, if necessary, he'd sit on the lid.

Laura smiled as her son loaded his bags into the trunk of his car. She'd miss him, but it was right for him to go home and stand up for himself. They each had their own lives to live.

"I'll stop and see Vicki and Tim and the kids tomorrow before I head out," Greg said. "I've spoken to them on the phone a couple of times, but frankly I wasn't ready to see them until now."

"I'm sure Vicki will understand," Laura said. She'd spoken to her daughter several times since Vicki went back home, and so far everything seemed fine. Vicki sounded content with the decision she'd made, and she and Tim were preparing for the move to Indianapolis. Laura smiled. Too bad she hadn't taken the real estate course earlier, she could have listed their house.

"How's Val doing?" Greg asked as he and Laura ate tuna salad sandwiches on the patio. "Has she been home lately?"

Laura shook her head. She hadn't seen her youngest daughter for several months, but they kept in touch by telephone and letter. "You know how senior year is, Greg," Laura said. "Valerie has all she can do to keep her grades up, and she's also interviewing. And besides, there's that young man she's engaged to. I imagine he takes up a lot of her time."

Greg helped himself to a serving of fruit salad and nodded. "I wish I could meet him. With Dad gone . . . well, I feel like I should be looking out for my baby sister, you know?"

"A nice thought, but I doubt if it will work, Greg. Valerie's always been an independent girl. I'm sure she believes she's perfectly capable of looking after herself."

"Umm, I hope so," Greg said. "I was thinking the other day how ironic it is that she and

I are so close, while Vicki and I seem to set off sparks every time we get together. Why do you suppose that is?"

"Just different personalities," Laura said vaguely. There was probably more to it than that, but at the moment she wasn't interested in delving into the mysteries of sibling rivalry. She was thinking of herself. What if she couldn't pass the real estate course? What if her hopes were dashed before she even began? What if she made a complete fool of herself and failed miserably?

"Mom? Is something wrong?" Greg was frowning, and now he leaned over and took her hand. "You look scared."

Laura made an attempt to smile and failed. "I am, son," she admitted. "I'm scared silly."

Seven

Laura waved good-bye to her son as he backed out of the driveway. She said a silent prayer that Greg's misguided patient would come to her senses and tell the truth.

When Greg's car had disappeared from her sight, Laura went to her bedroom to get dressed. She had to register for her realtor's course. She laughed out loud as she pulled slacks and a tailored pink shirt from her closet. In two weeks she would be a student again, after being out of school for over thirty years. What would it be like? Would she be able to keep up with the other students? What if she couldn't?

"You can, Laura," she said firmly. "You can do it. You may not have a college degree, but you're nobody's dummy, and you can learn anything you want to learn."

A pep talk always made her feel better, Laura

thought. Perhaps her days as a high-school cheerleader hadn't been a total waste after all.

The telephone rang just as she finished buttoning her blouse. Laura said hello, aware that her voice held a trace of irritation.

"It's me, Blanche," she heard. "Goodness, Laura, can't you pick up the telephone once in a while and let us know you're still alive? Jim and I worry about you. How are you, dear? How are you getting along?"

Laura briefly closed her eyes. She definitely did not need a dose of Blanche today of all days, but short of being downright rude, there was nothing she could do except listen to her ramble on.

"Well, I just told Jim that if you didn't answer the phone I was going to march right on over and see what was going on. A single woman living alone . . . well, you have to be careful nowadays."

"I haven't exactly been alone, Blanche," Laura said. "Vicki and the children were with me for a few days, and then Greg came for a short visit. I've been pretty busy entertaining." Not strictly true, but maybe it would satisfy Blanche, at least for the moment.

"Isn't that nice? Why, how sweet of the children to visit you and keep you from being lonely. You must just rattle around in that big house all alone."

"Yes, I do," Laura said, and suddenly she made a decision. No use beating around the bush, or hiding her head under a blanket, as Paul would have said. It was best to just spread all her cards on the table. She couldn't help chuckling. Paul certainly had collected a bunch of old sayings. Amazing how they just popped into her mind at exactly the right moments.

"I'm selling the house, Blanche. It's much too big for one person. Some other family can enjoy it. I'm going to find myself a small apartment."

"You're selling Paul's home?" Blanche asked. "And all your precious memories?"

"The memories don't go with the house, Blanche. They belong to me forever, but yes, I am selling the house, and it was my home too, not just Paul's."

"Well, of course. I didn't mean . . . oh, dear, this is such a surprise . . . such a jolt. I never thought . . ."

"Life goes on, Blanche. I know Paul would want me to do what's best for me, and I think this is it. I'm taking a course in real estate and once I start working I won't have time to look after such a big house. An apartment will be easier for me."

"You're going out to work? Oh, Laura, are you in financial distress? Why didn't you say something? You know Jim and I will help in any way we can."

"That's sweet of you, Blanche, but there's no need. Paul left me very well provided for. I'm going to work because I want to. I think I'll enjoy being a realtor and meeting new people. I'm not ready to sit in a rocker and knit the hours away."

"Well, for heaven's sake, no one expects you to do that, but I just can't imagine why you would want to go out to work when you don't have to. I mean you have those sweet grandchildren of yours to spend time with, and you could join my ladies' garden club. You know we meet every Tuesday and . . ."

"Blanche, I'm sorry, but I have to go. I'm registering for my real estate course this morning, and if I don't hurry I'll be late. I'll give you a call."

She hung up on Blanche's sputtering and shook her head. The ladies' garden club indeed! She knew for a fact that Blanche got together with her cronies simply to exchange gossip and eat sweets and drink tea. There was very little gardening done.

As she drove through the Miami traffic, Laura thought of Blanche and her three "lady friends," as Paul had always called Laura's three pals. They were all basically decent women, but like Blanche they were stuck in a time warp. All products of the fifties, they cooked and cleaned and waited on their balding, paunchy husbands. They babysat with their grandchildren and went to the grocery store one day a week with carefully itemized lists and a calculator in their purses. They were resigned to having sex once every two weeks or so, and Lucy had once declared that she didn't care if she ever "did it" again. It was a big bore, she claimed, and highly overrated. Betty Evans was clearly unhappy in her marriage, but would never even dream of leaving her verbally abusive husband, Jake. Divorce was a sin in her eyes, an admission of failure. And besides, what would she do if she left Jake? What man would want an overweight, nearsighted fiftyish grandmother? And how could she possibly live all alone after almost thirty-five years of marriage?

Laura sighed and pulled into the parking lot next to the realtor's office. She wasn't like those women, and couldn't imagine how she'd ever thought she was. Even when Paul was alive she'd occasionally thought of what she would do if she was left alone. That was just reality, being prepared for whatever curves life threw you.

Now that she was alone, it made her feel good to think she could manage her own affairs in a reasonably intelligent manner. Paul, she knew, would have been proud of her.

With that thought firmly entrenched in her head, Laura slid out from behind the wheel of her tan Buick and smoothed the creases in her slacks. I can do it, she reminded herself.

* * *

"Well, we're glad to have you aboard, Laura," the trim woman with her thick, curly gray hair said, shaking Laura's hand with a surprisingly firm grip. "Personally, I feel that we women make better real estate salespeople than the men. Of course, maybe we'd better not let Mr. Brigs know we think like that. He is convinced that men rule the world, and women are just pretty ornaments."

Laura laughed. She already liked Isabelle French and the other people she'd been introduced to. There would be thirty people in the class, she'd been told, and it wasn't the easiest course to pass. Still, Isabelle seemed convinced Laura could do it, if she really wanted to.

"I believe in the power of positive thinking," she explained, shuffling some papers around on her desk. "Do you know what I earned in commissions last year?"

Laura shook her head. She really didn't know much about the real estate business and she'd chosen it merely because she liked meeting people and visiting homes and apartments. It had sounded like a fun way to make some extra money and meet new people. Only now, with Isabelle gazing at her intently, a pencil shoved through the fluff of gray at her temples, Laura suddenly realized that it wasn't a game, or even a pleasant pastime. It was serious business. Isabelle apparently made her living this way.

She smiled and shook her head again. "I'm afraid I couldn't begin to guess," she said.

"Well, I'll tell you because I'm damned proud of myself," Isabelle said. "I grossed $47,000 dollars last year, and I expect to top it this year, even though sales have been a little sluggish lately. Not bad for an uneducated granny, eh? I barely finished high school before I married and started having babies. Most women didn't work in those days. You just stayed home and made hamburger casseroles and did the laundry and rocked the babies."

Laura nodded. That was pretty much what she'd done, even though she was a few years younger than Isabelle.

"Well, I did all that, and did it pretty well, if I do say so myself. Then, just when the kids were going off on their own and my hubby and I thought we could take things a little easy, Bill up and had a heart attack. Just like that," Isabelle said, a trace of remembered pain clouding her eyes for a moment. "One day I was a wife, and the next I was a widow. We didn't have much insurance, about enough to bury Bill and keep me for a few months. I knew I had to do something, but what?"

Laura said to herself, "So you saw the ad for the real estate course in the paper, and the rest is

161

history, right? Why don't you cut this nice lady a break, Isabelle, and make the story short and sweet?"

Laura found herself looking into a pair of unusual gray-green eyes. They belonged to a rugged, outdoorsy-looking face, and a sturdy, slightly overweight body that was tucked into a crisp white shirt and black trousers.

"George Ryan," the man said, putting out his hand to Laura. "You one of the new students?"

Laura nodded. "Yes."

"Well, don't let Isabelle the Great here intimidate you, honey. She's really a pretty neat old gal, but sometimes her tongue does run away with her. The best way we've found to shut her up is to pop a cinnamon biscuit between those flapping gums."

"George, one of these days your big mouth is going to get you in a bunch of trouble. I can just imagine what Laura thinks of us after that spiel of yours. She's probably convinced we're both certifiably insane."

"She's probably right," George said, with an evil smirk and a wink in Laura's direction. "Anyway, welcome aboard, Laura. We're glad to have you."

"Crazy man," Isabelle said, wrinkling her nose. "I don't know why I put up with him."

Laura laughed, and the last of her doubts fell away. "I think I'm going to like it here," she said.

"So, how did it go today?" Steve asked that evening. Laura had gathered her courage and invited him to dinner. She wanted to tell him all about her new experiences, about Isabelle and George and yes, even Blanche, but most of all she was hoping to end the evening in his arms. She needed warmth and touching. It wasn't sex so much, but just the sweetness of another human being touching her. A hand on hers, a shared smile, a warm, breathing body. Isabelle's little story had touched her, had reminded her how fragile human life really was.

"It was incredible, Steve," she said later. "I feel like a new woman. Everything seems so fresh and exciting. I'm not even scared about going back to school anymore."

"Well, I hope you don't change too much," Steve said. "I kind of like the old Laura. Uh . . . I didn't mean old as in elderly. I mean . . ."

Laura laughed and passed the potatoes to Steve. She'd spent the afternoon cooking all the foods she thought a man like Steve would enjoy. Tender pot roast, roasted potatoes, fresh corn on the cob, and strawberries with cream for dessert.

"I hope you like plain home-cooked food, Steve. I've never been much of a gourmet. I can fix a mean stew, and roast the tenderest chicken this side of heaven, but I don't know a quiche from a goose egg."

"No problem," Steve said. "Marcie liked to experiment in the kitchen. She was always trying out some new recipe. Some of them were good, but there were also quite a few disasters. I think I'm past the stage of wanting surprises with my dinner. Plain food is fine with me."

"Good, because I plan to concentrate on my studies in the upcoming weeks and someday maybe I'll top Isabelle's $47,000. I don't plan to have much time to fuss with fancy foods."

"If we get a craving for something fancy we can always eat out," Steve said. "I can't have my working woman slaving in a kitchen every night, now can I?"

"How's your new job coming?" Laura asked, buttering a second biscuit. She usually avoided biscuits because they tended to go with butter, but tonight, calories be damned!

"We open Monday," Steve said. "We've been getting everything set up these past few weeks. Hard work, but kind of exciting. A new venture is always invigorating. And of course there's always that little kernel of fear. What if it doesn't fly? What if we fall flat on our faces and my cousin loses his life savings?"

Laura sipped her wine and nodded. "That is scary. And I suppose that if it didn't do well, you would feel responsible?"

"Sure. Who else? I'll be managing the place.

It's my finger that will be on the pulse, so to speak, but I'm going to make sure it does succeed. I'm not going to let Rich down."

They finished eating in a comfortable silence. Laura realized that during the months after Paul's death she'd gradually gotten used to eating alone, and sometimes she even enjoyed it. At lunch she sometimes propped a book on the table as she ate, not exactly something you would do with another person sitting across from you. But having a congenial dinner partner was nice too, and she decided to wring every possible drop of pleasure from this evening.

"So," Steve said. "Greg get off all right?"

"Yes, and I have a feeling this unfortunate situation is going to work out just fine. My son is strong, and he's a decent young man."

Steve drained his wine glass and pushed back his empty plate. He groaned and rubbed his belly.

"Laura, that was a wonderful dinner, but I'm afraid that if I eat like this too often I'd end up as wide as I am tall. Did your husband have a problem controlling his weight?"

Rinsing and stacking the dishes in the dishwasher, Laura kept her head bent over her task. There was nothing wrong with Steve's question, and she should have been pleased that he was so complimentary about her culinary skills, but somehow having Steve mention Paul, even in

165

such a casual way, had ruined the mood of the evening. It was not that she felt guilty, she assured herself. After all, she wasn't doing anything wrong. She was single and perfectly free to date if she wanted to.

Then why do you feel like an adulteress, Laura Kinsey, she questioned herself? Why does the mere mention of Paul make you feel disloyal? Vicki had brainwashed her, Laura decided, with her talk of letting another man take Paul's place.

"Laura? Are you okay?" Steve asked. "Did you hear what I said?"

"Yes. I heard you," she said, pushing the uncomfortable thoughts to the back of her mind. She straightened and forced herself to smile. "Paul never had a weight problem," she said. "He was one of those people who can eat everything, without gaining an ounce."

Steve stood up, grinning. "The kind of guy you love to hate, huh?"

Laura shook her head, and now she knew the mood was totally destroyed, at least for this evening. "Everyone loved Paul," she said, "especially his family."

"Does it bother you for me to speak of your husband?" Steve asked later, when they were comfortably settled in the living room with coffee. "You're awfully quiet."

Laura shifted her position and added a few inches of space to the distance separating her and Steve. "I don't mind your speaking of Paul," she said slowly. "It's just that sometimes my memories of him are very sharp and clear, and it seems as though he's still here."

"Oh." Steve set his coffee cup down and Laura knew he understood exactly what she was trying to tell him. "Ghosts, huh?"

"I guess," Laura said, hopping up from the sofa when it looked as though Steve was about to reach out to her. Part of her still longed for his touch, old and yet new again. Passion from the past, and hope for the future, but right now it was as if Paul was sitting between them, and their children were grouped around him. It was as if her family had formed a solid buttress to prevent her from knowing another man. She wondered briefly if she was going crazy, if having her first love come back into her life this way had tampered with her sanity.

"Let it go, Laura," Steve said, his voice firm and gentle at the same time. "You and I have no deadline to meet, and I don't want pressure to be a part of our relationship, so just relax and don't worry about anything. Let's talk about your future career in real estate."

Laura felt the tension rush from her body. She was filled with tender appreciation for Steve's sensitivity. No matter how he'd acted as a young man, he had definitely matured into a decent, caring man.

"I'm going to be a great realtor," she said, standing tall and confident. She laughed. "Positive thinking. That's what my new friend Isabelle French swears by."

Her smile made him ache with longing, to hold her against his chest, to feel her head resting against his shoulder, to breathe in her warm, womanly scent. But he'd promised himself he'd never pressure Laura, and he meant to keep his word. She'd been a lovely young girl, and now she was a beautiful and gracious lady. He was determined not to do anything to mar the fragile trust forming between them. He'd betrayed Laura's trust once. He wasn't looking to do it again.

"You're going to be a sensation," he said. "You'll take Miami by storm!"

When Laura walked Steve to the door to say good night, she was filled with tender, almost maternal feelings. On impulse she stood on tiptoe and kissed his cheek.

"Thanks for being so understanding," she said.

Steve lightly touched his fingertips to Laura's cheek, leaving an imprint of heat that traveled all the way to her toes.

"We're rebuilding a friendship, aren't we? It's a friend's job to understand."

Laura smiled. "You've certainly grown up, Steve Walker," she said. "Like me, you've come a long, long way!"

There was no restless tossing and turning for Laura that night. After washing her face and brushing her teeth, she climbed into bed and turned off the light. Her body gently relaxed into the mattress and she yawned, feeling her eyelids flutter heavily against her cheeks. It was almost as if Paul was in the room with her, but there was nothing threatening about his presence. He was merely standing by to guide and protect her as he had in life. And when the time was right, he would let her go. Laura suddenly knew this. Paul would step back and away when she was ready to go forward, and not a moment sooner.

Eight

Laura started class on Monday morning. At first she felt awkward and unsure of herself. What made her think that after years of being a housewife she could suddenly become a successful realtor?

But why not, Laura? — she asked herself, pulling a pad and pencil from her leather tote bag. Why can't you do just about anything you set your mind to? As she waited for the class to start Laura found herself remembering the first days and weeks after Paul's death. It had been expected, but it was still a wrenching shock, and then, after the initial emotional anesthesia had worn off, pure panic had set in. What to do about the stocks and bonds Paul had accumulated? How to handle the IRA account, and the CD's he'd scattered in several banks around the city? What about the Social Security death benefit? How should she go about having the house changed over into her name alone? What about the car? Those were all things Paul had taken care of, things he had told her not to worry about.

She sat on the side of their bed one day, with the contents of the safety deposit box in her lap, and cried until there were no tears left. Then she'd pulled herself up and made an appointment with an accountant, William Henshaw. After several meetings with that knowledgeable gentleman, and a few visits to the banks, Laura had become comfortable handling her finances. Oh, there were still questions, things she didn't fully understand, but at least she had learned how to get the necessary answers. She no longer felt like an aimlessly drifting rowboat. She was a smooth-sailing vessel now, with a carefully charted course. No unexpected squall would catch her unprepared.

"Laura, hi," Isabelle French called cheerfully, stopping beside Laura's seat. "Are you all set?"

"I'm as ready as I'll ever be," Laura answered, inwardly smiling at the colorful absurdity of Isabelle's outfit. On some women it would have looked ridiculous, even tacky, but on Isabelle it was just right. A purple print blouse, a red and blue striped skirt, a sequined headband. "I had a brief panic attack earlier," Laura added, "but I think I'll make it."

"I know you will," Isabelle said. "I can spot strong women at fifty paces." She grinned. "I just sold a handsome piece of property, and believe me, there's nothing like a good sale to perk up one's ego. And that first sale is in a class of its own. Do you know I copied and framed the agreement of sale? It hangs in my bedroom at home."

Laura smiled as some of the other students began to file in. A couple of women her age, a man in his twenties, three older men, and a pretty girl who looked all of eighteen.

"Are minors allowed?" she asked Isabelle.

Isabelle rolled her eyes as she sharpened a pencil. "Kids like that make me crazy," she said. "I've got nothing against youth, but most girls that age can think of nothing but the next date, and the latest shade of nail polish."

Laura laughed. "Not all of them. My daughter is graduating from college in the spring, and she is very level-headed."

Shrugging, Isabelle gathered up a stack of papers. "We'll see, she said, her tone slightly ominous.

By the time her first class ended Laura knew she was going to have to concentrate if she hoped to pass the course. It wasn't just a matter of showing someone a pretty house and having them sign on the dotted line. There were things like escrow to learn about, mortgage percentage points, creative financing, prevailing interest rates, as well as the fine art of dealing with customers and keeping them happy.

"Whew," she confided to Isabelle, "There's more to this than I realized. I hope I haven't gotten in over my head.

Isabelle laughed and patted Laura's shoulder. "It's more than looking pretty and smiling a lot," she agreed, "but I love it, and I'm betting you will too. How about going for a drink before you head home? There's no one waiting for you, is there?"

"Only my little dog, Buttons," Laura said. "And he's pretty patient."

Steve was at the auto rental agency a full hour before they were scheduled to open the doors for the first time. Any new venture was exciting, and this was no exception. He'd been in on the planning stages, and the job perfectly suited his managerial skills. He'd been the supervisor of a computer software manufacturing firm for many years. The position had earned him a comfortable salary and confidence in his expertise in management. Originally Rich had invited Steve to join him as a full partner, but Steve had reservations about co-owning a business with a relative. Working for Rich was one thing. If things didn't work out, they could part amicably, but if they jointly owned a business . . . well, it was a risk he hadn't wanted to take. He had, however, invested a sizable portion of his savings in the venture, and if things worked out the way they all hoped, he would eventually reap a handsome return on his money.

"Well, this is the big day," Rich said, striding into Steve's spacious office. "Are we ready?"

"No problem," Steve joked. "The question is, is Miami ready for us? This is a new concept, renting dream cars. I sure hope your market studies were accurate."

"No sweat," Rich said, grinning. "We're in the business of selling dreams, and that's never going to go out of style."

He'd vouch for that, Steve thought, as he wandered around the lot outside a few minutes later. A gleaming red '55 T-bird sat in royal splendor next to a '57 Chevy convertible. Across from that was a '62 Mustang. Toys for rich little boys, Steve decided, knowing that only the well-heeled would patronize their rental agency.

He wanted the venture to be a success for a lot of reasons. And one of those reasons was Laura. When his cousin Rich had written and told him about her husband dying, he'd felt bad. He was still grieving for Marcie, and he hated thinking of someone else having the kind of pain he had endured. After spending the bulk of your life with a person, when you suddenly found yourself alone there was a gaping hole in your world. He'd gone through it, and when he heard about Laura's husband, he knew she was going through it too.

It was like a light bulb going on in a dark attic

when young Steve told him that Laura was eager to see him. He wouldn't have blamed her if she'd sent him a hate note for having the audacity to look her up after more than thirty years. But when he saw her again, he understood why she hadn't done that. Laura was just as soft and sweet and kindhearted as she'd been as a girl of eighteen. She didn't have a mean spot anywhere in her lovely body. When he hugged her it was like coming home. His feelings for her took nothing away from the relationship he'd had with Marcie. If anything it enhanced his memories.

Running his finger over the highly polished chrome hood ornament on one of the cars, Steve felt his lips curve in a smile. Laura had always been soft and too tenderhearted for her own good. His smile melted into a frown. Her kids apparently took advantage of that softness. He remembered how angry he'd been at the way Laura's daughter talked to her, at the way she tried to shove the responsibility of her children off on Laura.

Her son had seemed like a decent young man, but Steve felt strongly that Greg should have handled his career crisis on his own, without involving his mother. There was another daughter that Steve hadn't met yet. He wondered what she was like. Would she be as self-centered as her older sibling? Was Laura strong enough to stand up to her children?

"Steve? Hey, it's that time. Dreams for Rent is officially open. We're on our way, coz. Fame and fortune awaits us!"

"I'll settle for financial solvency," Steve said dryly. He tucked his thoughts of Laura into a corner of his heart and put a welcoming smile on his face. It was time to go to work.

"So, I'm not interested in getting married again," Isabelle said, shrugging. "I mean, what for? I don't need a daddy for any little babies. I can support myself very nicely, thank you, and who needs to pick up some man's dirty underwear and smelly socks?" The bar Isabelle had suggested was the typical watering hole. Dim and slightly smoky, even in the afternoon, the strains of a love ballad competing with the clink of glasses, the laughter and chatter of the patrons.

Laura laughed. "There's a bit more to marriage than that, Isabelle, and you know it."

The gray-haired woman across from her shrugged again and twirled the wine glass in her hand. "Maybe, but I just don't think there's anything a man has that I can't do without."

"Well, I don't know about that either," Laura said, grinning mischievously. She liked Isabelle. Her new friend reminded her of a colorful, exotic gypsy. Laura was fascinated. Isabelle was a strong, gutsy lady, a woman who wasn't about to take a back seat to anyone, male or female. "Would you believe my high-school sweetheart recently showed up on my doorstep?"

Isabelle's dark eyes widened. "No kidding? Out of the blue, with no warning? How come? Did he tell you he's carried a torch all these years? Gee, we must be talking about nearly thirty years, huh?"

"Almost thirty-three," Laura said. "Steve was happily married, and so was I, but now we're both alone and he seems to think we've been given a second chance."

Isabelle narrowed her eyes. "And what do you think?"

Fiddling with a couple of peanuts, Laura avoided meeting Isabelle's eyes. Those eyes were penetrating, all-seeing, and Laura wasn't ready to reveal her innermost thoughts and feelings. It was nice to have another woman to talk to, and confide in, up to a point, but her feelings for Steve were too new and fragile to be pulled out and examined under a microscope.

"I don't know yet," Laura answered truthfully. "I enjoy his company, and there's a strong physical attraction between us, but I'm not sure how involved I want to get."

"I know what you mean," Isabelle said. She glanced at the plain wristwatch on her arm. "I've got to run," she said. "I have a cat at home who likes to be fed on schedule." She smiled at Laura.

"Maybe we can do this again sometime. I almost feel like I'm back in school again, sitting and chatting with a girlfriend."

"I *am* back in school again," Laura said, nodding towards the books stacked on the table, "and I enjoyed the girl talk too."

"Great. Then we definitely will do this again." Isabelle picked up her purse and grinned. "Good luck with your homework," she teased.

Laura let herself into the house half an hour later and waited for Buttons to leap on her. But instead of the little dog's joyous barking, there was silence. A prickle of alarm inching up her spine, Laura moved through the house, calling the little dog.

When she found him she nearly went into cardiac arrest. "Oh no! Buttons . . . what's wrong?"

The little dog lay on his side. He was still breathing, but barely. He didn't seem to know Laura was there. Suddenly all Laura's strength and competence flew right out the window. She couldn't handle this alone. She wanted, needed someone to help her, someone to hold her if the worst happened.

Her hands shook as she dialed Steve's cousin's number. By the time a man answered, Laura was sobbing. She managed to make the man understand that she needed Steve, and then as Buttons began to convulse, the receiver slipped out of her hand.

Somehow she broke the connection, and dialed her veterinarian with trembling hands.

"Bring him in, Laura," Dr. Elsie Weylich said promptly. "I'll meet you at the clinic."

Laura found a large towel and carefully wrapped Buttons in it. Thank God, he'd stopped convulsing, but at any minute she expected to see him also stop breathing.

"Hang in there, little buddy," she begged, as tears streamed down her cheeks. She wanted Steve, but she couldn't wait. She grabbed her purse, cradled Buttons in her free arm and started for the door.

"Laura, what in the world is going on?" Steve was white-faced and shaken as he raced up the walk. He immediately spotted the bundle in her arms. "The dog!" There was relief in his voice, but it quickly turned to concern when he saw Laura's tear-stained face. "What happened to him?"

"I have to get him to the vet. Will you drive me?"

"Come on," Steve said, propelling her out the door. "Let's go!"

She sat in the back in case there were any problems, while Steve negotiated the evening traffic.

"What happened?" he asked again. "Was he hit by a car?"

Laura's voice was harsh with fear. "No. I don't know what happened. He was fine when I went to class today, but when I came home I knew some-

179

thing was wrong. He didn't greet me at the door, and then I saw him . . . barely breathing . . . I don't know what happened!"

Steve let her out at the front door of the animal clinic and went to park the car. Laura looked at Buttons's glazed eyes and fresh tears streaked her cheeks.

She gave Buttons to Elsie and nearly collapsed on a chair next to the examining table. "I don't know what happened," she babbled. "I found him this way when I got home . . . and then he started convulsing and . . ."

"It's poison," Dr. Weylich said, gently feeling the little dog's swollen, rigid abdomen. "He's not good, Laura, but I'll do my best. I'll give him an antidote and then we'll just have to wait and see what happens. Was he running around loose last night or this morning?"

"He was in the yard, but it's fenced," Laura said. Then she remembered. "Oh no! Oh, Elsie, I think I know what happened!"

Three hours later, after drinking a gallon of strong, hot coffee, and pacing a path in Dr. Weylich's carpeted waiting room, Laura got the word. Buttons was going to make it. He'd be weak and wobbly for a few days, but he was going to be okay.

"It would be best if you leave him here overnight, Laura, so I can monitor his heart rate and respiration. But barring any unforeseen complications I think he's going to make it."

Laura almost wanted to kiss the vet. Buttons was her little pal. She'd cried buckets of tears into his soft white fur after Paul's death, and he'd kept her feet toasty in the wide king-sized bed. He was a warm, breathing presence in her life, something she could love and nurture as much as she wanted.

"Don't use that particular brand of roach poisoning again, Laura," Dr. Weylich cautioned. "Or if you do, make sure you dispose of the empty containers in a place Buttons can't get at."

"I've learned my lesson," Laura said, giving her little friend one last gentle pat. "I'll call tomorrow before I come by to pick him up, and thank you from the bottom of my heart."

The vet smiled. "It was definitely my pleasure."

Throughout the ordeal, Steve had stayed close, his shoulder ready if Laura needed it. He'd been gentle, encouraging and everything a man could be to a woman he cared about. Laura turned to him as they got in his Bronco.

"How can I thank you?" she asked. "I was just beginning to believe that I'm a strong, independent lady, and then this happened, and I fell apart. I crumbled like a stale cookie."

Steve smiled. He made no effort to start the car. Instead he draped his arm over Laura's shoulders and hugged her. "Hey, you were entitled. Buttons is a cute little guy. If he were mine I'd probably have panicked too. I'm just glad everything turned out okay."

Laura felt closer to Steve than she had in all the weeks they'd been seeing each other. How could any woman not adore a man who was so gentle and loving, so kind and caring? Her eyes met Steve's and she felt as if she were drowning, drifting deep down into a warm, azure sea. What was it Isabelle had said earlier about not needing anything a man had to give? Well, maybe that was true for her, but Laura knew she needed the care and concern Steve gave so generously. She needed it like a flower needs water and sun, like a baby needs its mother's protection and affection. Perhaps she didn't need Steve to take care of her financially, and she didn't need him to shield her from the realities of life, but she needed to know that another human being cared about what happened to her. That someone hurt when she wept, and smiled when she laughed.

"You're a nice man, Charlie Brown," she said, reaching up to pat his cheek. "I think I like you."

Steve bit back a groan. "Like" was much too tame a word for what he felt for Laura. He ached for her, her touch, her scent, her soft, gentle voice. He wanted her in his life. What he felt took him back to the glorious days of his youth, that brief time when he possessed Laura's heart and her lovely body. And then, with the stupidity and cruelty of youth, he'd thrown it all away. Now, through an odd trick of fate, they'd found their way back to each other. But you couldn't go back. That was something Steve was starting to learn. Life moved forward or stood still. There was no reverse gear.

He reached out and smoothed the hair off Laura's forehead. She was relaxed now, knowing that Buttons was out of danger. Her eyelids drooped wearily and she felt soft and pliant. Steve held himself in check and leaned down to gently slide his lips across her mouth. He wanted to crush her against him, wanted to feel her ripe, full breasts flatten against his chest. He wanted to make her breath come in short, hot gasps, wanted to feel her writhe against him in a fury of need, but it was the wrong time. She was too vulnerable right now, too weak from the emotional turmoil she so recently experienced. When they made love he wanted to be the only thing on Laura's mind.

"Come on," he said, taking his arm away and sliding behind the wheel. "We'd better get you home. You look like you're about to collapse. You've had a long day."

"Umm," Laura murmured sleepily, leaning her head back against the seat. "That was a nice kiss, Steve. It was . . . just right."

"I'm glad," Steve said, smiling, "because I aim to please."

"Oh, you do," Laura mumbled tiredly. "You do."

Steve insisted on going in the house with Laura, just to make sure everything was all right.

"This is nice," Laura said, "having someone take care of me. Mind you, I don't really need a caretaker, but once in a while it's nice."

Chuckling, Steve looked around, making sure the house was secure. It was much too big a place for a woman alone, but he wasn't about to say that to Laura. If and when Laura decided to give up her home, it would have to be her own decision.

"I'm moving into my apartment in a couple of days," he said. "Boy, am I going to be glad to get off my cousin's sofa bed!"

"And into that jelly-belly waterbed," Laura joked. "I just hope that thing doesn't spring a leak!"

Steve finished his security check and stood by the front door. He wished he could stay and just hold Laura, but she was dead tired. Her eyes were glazed with weariness and her shoulders slumped.

"Okay, I'm going to get out of here and let you get some sleep. I'll give you a call tomorrow night and see how Buttons is doing."

"I've got a better idea," Laura said. "I owe you for all the moral support tonight. How about coming for dinner tomorrow?"

"Hey, all right!" Steve said. "I have to tell you that my cousin Rich is definitely not a gourmet chef. Shall I bring white or red wine?"

Laura cocked her head and thought a moment.

"Red," she said finally. "A nice, robust red."

After a quick kiss on the cheek, and a final check to make sure the front door was securely locked, Steve almost skipped down the walk to his Bronco. He tried to whistle, but he wasn't any better at it then he had been as a kid. Oh well, he didn't need to whistle to feel good. He had a date with a beautiful woman and he felt eighteen again!

Laura got ready for bed quickly. She was completely exhausted, mentally and physically. She felt as though she could sleep for a week. She turned on her side, and closed her eyes as a soft smile curved her lips. She might not want to get married again, but it was awfully nice to have a man in her life.

Nine

The telephone rang just as Laura was putting the finishing touches on the strawberry shortcake the next afternoon. Buttons was home, content to rest in his basket and be pampered. Laura licked whipped cream off her index finger and picked up the receiver, slightly irritated at the interruption.

"Hello?"

"Mom? It's Valerie. How are you?"

"Honey! It's so good to hear from you. I'm fine. How about you?"

"I'm okay," Valerie said. "Mom, there's . . . look, could I come home for a few days? I'll bring my class work with me so I don't get behind, but I really need to talk to you about something."

"Well, of course, hon. Is Robert coming with you?"

There was a moment's heavy silence, then Valerie's voice. "No, Mom. Robert can't come. Are

186

you sure you don't mind? Greg called me a few days ago. He told me about Vicki and the kids staying with you, and then him dumping himself on you. I don't want to be a pain."

"Don't be silly. This is still your home, even if you are about to become a college grad and a big business tycoon. Come ahead, honey. When shall I expect you?"

"I'll leave in the morning," Valerie said. "I should be home late tomorrow night."

"Okay, sweetheart. I'm looking forward to seeing you. Drive carefully."

Laura's brows knitted thoughtfully as she hung up the phone. Of course she'd be glad to see Valerie. It had been a while since her youngest daughter had been home, but there had been something in Valerie's voice that troubled her. "She better not be thinking of dropping out," Laura said, stirring the beef burgundy with a vengeance. She couldn't imagine Val wanting to do that, but lately life seemed to be full of surprises, and not all of them were pleasant.

By six-thirty everything was ready. Laura had set the small round table off the kitchen. It was much cozier than the big table in the dining room. She had dressed with care in a jade jumpsuit, and she was liberally spritzed with her favorite cologne. Doing a quick check in the hall mirror, Laura was satisfied that she looked her best. Her makeup had been artfully applied to conceal a line here, a wrinkle there, and her hair framed her face with soft, shining auburn curls.

She was a little nervous, but not so much as if she were about to entertain a complete stranger. There was a certain familiarity with Steve, a comfortable camaraderie that made her feel warm and safe.

Straightening the leg of her jumpsuit, Laura wandered back to the kitchen to check on the noodles she was preparing. She could only hope the genuine affection she had for Steve would help her get through this night, for there was something she needed to discuss with him. She'd worried about it from the beginning, and then last night, after the scare with Buttons, her feelings had become clear to her. She had her fingers crossed that Steve would understand.

Promptly at 6:45 the doorbell rang. When Laura opened the door Steve smiled at her, and held up a bottle of wine. "Is this robust enough?"

Laura read the label and nodded her approval. Then she stepped back so Steve could come in. "Hungry?" she asked. "Dinner is just about ready."

Steve's eyes traveled appreciatively over Laura's well-proportioned body. The jade color she wore accentuated her reddish brown hair, and was a striking contrast to her gray eyes. He grinned like a boy. She smelled good too. He was hungry all right, but not just for food! The light, floral scent of Laura mingled with the tantalizing aroma of rich beef and wine, and the soft background music only added to the warm, appealing setting.

"This is wonderful," he said. "Did you really go to all this trouble just for me?"

Laura thought for a moment, then laughed. "Only partly," she teased. "This is a celebration dinner. Look at Buttons. He's getting stronger with every passing minute."

"Hey, little fella," Steve said, bending over to pat Buttons's head. "You were a pretty lucky little guy."

Laura shuddered as she turned the burners low under the main dish. "If I'd stayed out a few minutes longer . . ."

"Hey, you didn't, and Buttons is going to be fine. No recriminations, okay? Hindsight doesn't do anyone any good."

"You're right," Laura said, taking Steve's hand and leading him into the living room. There was a tray of cheese and crackers and raw vegetables on the coffee table, and beside it, an ice bucket with a bottle of chilled wine. Laura poured them each a glass and sat down next to Steve.

"I'm glad you're here," she said. "It's no fun to celebrate alone."

"Well, let's drink to Buttons's good health, shall we?"

Laura lifted her glass, held it to her lips and then forgot to sip as Steve's penetrating gaze pinned her to the sofa. She was a kid again, a bumbling, awkward teenager.

Then, just as the tension became unbearable, Steve winked, releasing her. He took a swallow of his wine and promptly proposed another toast. "This is to us, Laura. May we always be there for one another, in good times and bad."

"I . . . I'll drink to that," Laura managed. But the wine lay in her throat like liquid lead. She was frozen, unable to swallow. Was this really what she wanted? Did she want Steve always to be there? Was she prepared to be there for him? Or was that too heavy a commitment to make at this time of her life? Did she really want to give up her newfound freedom?

"Steve, there's something I . . ."

"Later," Steve said, putting his hand over hers and silencing her with his eyes. He laughed and his eyes sparkled with pleasure. "Right now I need to be fed, woman! I can't remember when I last enjoyed a good, home-cooked meal!"

Laura pushed her ambivalent thoughts away and decided to relax and enjoy. "Well, I've always been a softie where starving men are concerned," she said. "Let the feast begin!"

It was a happy, thoroughly pleasant meal. Laura was so relieved about Buttons that her spirits were high, and Steve seemed almost euphoric to be sitting in her kitchen eating a home-cooked meal.

"I know the prices and flavors of all the frozen dinners by heart," he confessed. "While I was still living in Arizona, young Steve and his wife invited me for dinner once in a while, but I didn't want to take advantage, you know? I mean, they're young and they're busy with their own lives. I really felt like a fifth wheel. So most of the time I ate alone."

Laura shook her head disapprovingly. "I can't understand why so many men hate to cook."

"I don't hate it," Steve said. "I just don't know how. Recipes confuse me. For instance, what's the difference between whipping, beating or mixing? Isn't it all the same?"

"There are subtle differences, but it can make a whopping change in the finished product."

Steve shrugged and grinned. "I'll stick with frozen," he said, "and maybe once in a while a certain kindhearted lady I know will take pity on me. I'll tell you, Laura, this stew is a gourmet's dream."

"Stew! Why I'll have you know that you are eating beef burgundy, not stew!"

Steve shook his head, his grin widening. "It's all the same, isn't it, just this has a fancy name?"

Laura stood up and put her hands on her hips.

"No dessert for you, Steve Walker," she threatened, "unless you take that back!"

Steve laughed. "Sorry," he said, tongue in cheek. "My mistake. What do I know anyway?"

"Well at least you admit your ignorance," Laura said, waggling her finger in his face. "I do not," she emphasized, "make beef stew. I prepare beef burgundy!"

"I stand corrected," Steve said, "now whatever it is, may I have a second helping, please?"

By the time the strawberry shortcake had been reduced to a few crumbs on their plates, Steve was groaning. "I'll never be the same again," he complained. "I feel like a fish, all stuffed and ready to be mounted on someone's wall."

"Well, you don't look like a fish," Laura assured him. "Why don't you take your coffee into the living room while I tidy up here?"

"No way," Steve said, picking up his empty plate and carrying it to the sink. "After all you did to fix such a fantastic meal, the least I can do is help load the dishwasher."

"Okay, I accept your help. Do you think we could go for a short walk around the block when we're finished? I ate more than I should have."

"A walk is fine," Steve said, "But don't even think of asking me to jog. My body will definitely not cooperate on that level, not now."

"What a wimp!" Laura teased, rinsing the

dishes as Steve passed them to her. She'd forgotten, how nice it was to have someone work beside her in the kitchen, how pleasant it was to hear the sound of another human voice as you went about your daily chores.

She remembered her earlier determination to speak to Steve, and now she found herself wavering. If she was going to be honest, she had to admit that she didn't want to lose this. She didn't want to be without Steve's warm, delightful companionship, but she still felt she wasn't ready for an intimate relationship, not yet anyway. Her heart knew it, but her body said otherwise, and from the looks of things, Steve's body was sending out storm signals too. So, how to handle this? Would Steve understand if she told him she simply wasn't ready for that kind of intimacy? Would he think her foolish for wanting to get better acquainted before taking that crucial step? Because despite all the modern-day messages regarding women's new sexual freedom, Laura was still a product of the fifties. She wanted to go forward and keep up with the times, and maybe she would someday, but she couldn't be in a hurry. She had to do things at her own pace, take it one slow, steady step at a time. Could she make Steve understand all this? The physical attraction between them was strong, and it was rearing its head more and more frequently.

At first Laura believed she could switch gears, from a proper, staid, middle-aged matron to a modern, thoroughly hip woman of the nineties. And maybe she still could, but it wasn't going to happen overnight.

"Okay, let's take that walk," Steve said, neatly folding the dish towel and laying it on the counter. "I peeked out the window and there's a beautiful Miami moon out there just waiting to bathe us in its golden glow."

Seeing Laura's raised eyebrows, he chuckled. "All right, so I'm corny, and it didn't rhyme. Would it hurt you to pretend that I'm handsome, intelligent, charming, not to mention witty, wealthy and . . ."

"Stop!" Laura cried. "What happened to plain old, ordinary Steve? Did my 'stew' alter your personality?"

"Come on," Steve said, dragging Laura behind him as he headed for the door. "I can't handle all this abuse!"

They walked in companionable silence for a few minutes. Laura allowed her tensions to drift away, and just enjoyed the moment. Sometimes it was still hard for her to believe that Steve had come back into her life. How many times had she dreamed of that before she met and fell in love with Paul? And even after her marriage. Despite the fact that she was happily married, she'd never really forgotten her first love. She'd occasionally daydreamed about him, wondered if he was married, if he had children, if his wife was pretty. And always, inevitably, she asked herself why he hadn't come back to her.

Well, he was back now, and he seemed to think that they'd been granted a second chance, that they could pick up where they left off and go blithely forward.

"What are you thinking, Laura?" he asked, giving her hand a little squeeze. "You look awfully solemn."

"I was just thinking," she said slowly, "about us. About all those years in between. You went your way, I went mine, and now . . ."

Steve's steps slowed, almost as though he sensed what was coming. He wasn't stupid and he had sensed the restraint in Laura. He'd felt her lean forward, then pull back. Her ambivalence had touched him, and now he looked at her with some trepidation. Had she decided there was no chance for a relationship between them? In just a short time she'd already become an integral part of his life. His thoughts were of her last thing at night, and first thing in the morning.

"What is it, Laura? What do you want to say to me?"

"I've done a lot of thinking," she said. "It was like an old, old dream finally coming true when you showed up on my doorstep. I didn't know that all those old feelings would come rushing back. I never expected to feel what I'm feeling now. When Paul passed away I really thought all that was over."

Steve let his breath out slowly, and his heart, suspended between beats, resumed a regular rhythm again. "You mean you're not . . ."

"Wait," Laura cautioned. "Let me get this out, okay? I'm not very good at this kind of thing. What I'm trying to say is, I care for you, Steve, and maybe in time it will develop into something more . . . more serious, but for now . . . I can't jump into a physically intimate relationship with you. Not yet."

She paused and a slow flush colored her cheeks. "I can't deny that I'm attracted to you, and you're starting to haunt my dreams at night, but I just can't handle that kind of closeness yet. Am I making any sense?"

Steve nodded and gave Laura's hand another squeeze.

"You may think I'm making this up, but I'm not. Strange as it may seem, I've been having the same kind of thoughts. You were a pretty young girl, Laura, and you've matured into a beautiful woman. When I'm near you I want you so bad I ache. My belly twists up in knots, my palms get sweaty, and I feel like I'm eighteen again, but somehow the time just isn't right yet. I think it will be one of these days, but not just yet."

Laura nodded wordlessly. At the moment there was nothing else that needed to be said. Steve understood. He even felt the same way. It was more than she'd dared to hope for.

She spent the day getting ready for Valerie's visit. Fortunately her real estate classes only met three times a week, so she would have plenty of time to enjoy her daughter's company.

"Val's coming home, Buttons," she told the little white dog.

He'd perked up considerably in the last twenty-four hours, and Laura estimated he'd be completely back to normal by the next day.

Funny, she thought, how much a pet came to mean to you, especially when there was no special person in your life. Like her daughter, Laura had always loved animals, especially dogs and cats, but when Paul was alive Buttons was just a pet, a much loved pet, but a pet. After Paul's death, the little pooch became her friend and confidant, her sounding board. Laura smiled. Buttons never disagreed with her, and he never offered unsolicited advice. Best of all, he never raised his eyebrows if she ate an extra piece of chocolate.

"Well, Val will fuss over you and pamper you to extremes, little buddy," Laura told Buttons, "so get ready!"

She'd made Val's favorite, seafood chowder, figuring that it could easily be reheated if Val arrived very late. There was also a chocolate mousse pie chilling in the refrigerator, and a packet of her daughter's favorite bubble bath beside the tub in the second bathroom.

As she waited for her daughter to arrive that evening, Laura leafed through her photo albums. The past leaped out at her. She saw herself young and bloated with her second pregnancy, holding Greg by the hand. Then there were pictures of her with all three of the kids, Greg and Vicki shoving each other, a sweet-faced Valerie propped on Laura's lap.

There were far more photos of her and the children than there were of Paul, Laura realized. But then she supposed that was the way it went in most families, especially in the sixties and seventies. The daddies went off to work, and the mommies stayed home and did the homemaker thing. Now, everything was different. Very few young women stayed home with their children. Laura shook her head. She was ambivalent at times about being over fifty. There were good and not so good points about being mature, but she was glad she'd raised her family. She wouldn't trade the memories of those busy, chaotic years for a million dollars.

Valerie drove in at 10:30, just as Laura was starting to get concerned. It was a long drive, and Laura, like any anxious mother, couldn't rest until her chick was safe and sound under her roof.

Mother and daughter hugged, then Laura held her youngest at arm's length. "Let me look at you, honey," she said. "It's been a long time since you were home."

She had a hint of pallor that Laura instantly picked up on. Why? Val had always spent as much time as possible outdoors, soaking up sunshine. Of course the weather wasn't the same at Texas U. as it was in Miami, but still . . . "Honey, have you been sick?"

"Not exactly," Valerie said. "I'm really tired from the drive, Mom. Could I have something to eat before we talk?"

Laura reheated the chowder while Val went into the bathroom to splash cold water on her face. Something was very wrong. The vibes were strong. Maybe it had something to do with Valerie's engagement. She hadn't thought to check if Val was still wearing her diamond. Well, if that was all, Laura would be greatly relieved. All kinds of weird thoughts had been dancing circles in her head since Val's phone call.

Valerie sat down at the kitchen table and looked

at the steaming bowl of chowder in front of her. She smiled wanly. "My favorite." She sniffed, then turned a vivid shade of green. She jumped up and fled to the bathroom.

Laura sat, feeling as if she'd suddenly turned to stone. Now she knew what was wrong.

When Valerie returned a few minutes later, Laura was still frozen in her chair. Her eyes brimming with tears she looked up at her pale, shaken daughter. Laura put out her hand. "You're pregnant, aren't you?"

Ten

"It's not as if I can't support a child, Mom," Valerie said quietly, after Laura cleared away the chowder and made tea and toast. "Once I graduate and start working I'll be making more than enough money to support myself and my child, but it's just not how I thought it would be. You know how much I love kids. I always pictured myself happily married, like you and Daddy. I want to be a good mother like you, and I want my kids to have a father as great as mine was." Valerie looked down at the table. When she raised her head, her gray eyes were swimming with tears.

"How could I have been so mistaken about Robert? Why didn't I see what a self-centered creep he is? Do you know what he said when I told him I was pregnant? He shook his head and said it was really a shame, that I should have been more careful. Then he wanted to know when I was going to have my 'little problem' taken care of. He spoke of our baby as a 'little problem,' Mom. It's nothing but a nuisance to him."

"Didn't you ever discuss having children?" Laura asked. She was shocked and stunned, not so much by her daughter's unexpected pregnancy, but by the circumstances surrounding it. How could an intelligent young woman like Valerie agree to marry a man and know so little about him?

Valerie halfheartedly nibbled her dry toast. She took a sip of tea and nodded. "Sure we did, Mom, and he said that when we were both out of school and settled we'd talk about starting our family. But when I told him about this baby, he said that it just wasn't a convenient time. After he graduates he has student loans to pay back, and right now neither of us has good medical insurance. He . . . his advice to me was to 'get rid of *it*' and be more careful from now on." Valerie ducked her head again. "I threw a lamp at him, Mom." She looked up and managed a weak smile. "I'm sorry to say I missed. Anyway, I packed my stuff up that same night and moved into the dorm with a girlfriend. I think I can stay with her until graduation. I'll be about six months along by then."

It wasn't so much what her daughter was saying that made Laura feel so sick and sad. It was the things she wasn't saying. She joked about throwing a lamp at her ex, but Laura knew that Val was devastated. Valerie had strong values and high morals, and even though she was about to become an unwed mother, she never had been promiscuous. She had genuinely loved Robert and had planned to have a life with him, and now all those dreams had turned to dust.

"Come here, honey," Laura said, standing up and opening her arms. "Give me a hug."

That night Valerie slept in Laura's king-sized bed beside her, with Buttons cuddled against her chest. During the night Laura woke, reached over and touched Val's slightly rounded tummy. Her grandchild was sleeping in there, a child who would be every bit as loved and precious as Vicki's three. How could any man turn his back on his own child? How could Robert have cared so little about Valerie that he would let her walk out of his life for the sake of convenience?

Well, Val would be all right. She was a strong, determined young woman. And soon she would be a wonderful mother. But this wasn't the way Laura had hoped to become a grandma again. She'd dreamed of seeing Valerie walk down the aisle as a beautiful, radiant bride. Then, afterwards, when the time was right, the babies would come. This way, Valerie would have all the problems and pains of being a single parent. She would have to raise her child single-handed. There would be no one there to help her when her child was sick or cranky, and no one to rejoice at the first word, the first steps.

Laura's heart ached for her child, but there was nothing she could do but offer her loving support. Valerie had already made her decision, and for her, it was the only decision she could have made. She couldn't have an abortion. She valued life too highly, and adoption, although a viable alternative for many women, was clearly not for Val. She wanted her child, and, financially at least, caring for it would not be a problem.

Laura sighed and flopped on her side, hoping her restless tossing wouldn't wake Valerie. She was going to become a grandma again, ready or not, and her baby was about to become a mother. It wasn't a tragedy. In many ways it was an occasion for rejoicing, but it was just that it should have been different.

"So, why did you really come home, honey?" Laura asked the next morning over breakfast. It looked like it was going to be Val's lucky day. She'd wolfed down the scrambled eggs and sausage hungrily, and so far it was staying down. Thank the Lord for small favors, Laura thought as she waited for Val to answer her question.

"Well, I knew I had to tell you soon, and . . . I guess I wanted to make sure you weren't going to be mad at me, Mom. I need somebody on my side now, you know?"

Laura smiled gently. "What good would it do either of us for me to get mad? I can't pretend I'm happy about the situation, but I do understand how you feel, and I'll help you in any way I can."

"Thanks, Mom," Valerie said softly. "That's what I was hoping you would say. Claire, that's my roommate, said that her parents would disown her if she ever turned up pregnant and unmarried."

Laura sipped her orange juice, then shook her head. "That happened a lot in the years when I was growing up. In those days an unwed mother was a disgrace. Parents hid their pregnant daughters or sent them away to have the babies and give them up for adoption. And, of course most young women were not as well prepared to support their babies as you will be. That does make a big difference. Still, although society has changed its opinion on the subject, I think you need to be prepared for the fact that not everyone is going to smile and pat you on the back. There is still some prejudice against fatherless babies, hon."

Valerie nodded. "I know. Would you believe that Claire's boyfriend told me I'll have a hard time finding a husband if I go through with the pregnancy?"

"Let's not worry about that right now," Laura said. "The main thing is for you to stay well, finish school and have a healthy baby. You can worry about a husband later."

Val stood up and shook her head. "A husband is the last thing on my mind right now," she said flatly. "I'd be afraid of running into another Robert."

How badly would this experience scar her daughter, Laura wondered later as she tidied the kitchen and tried to decide on something for supper? Val had always been a sweet, trusting little girl, and she'd grown into a loving, trusting young woman. But what would happen now, as her pregnancy advanced and the reality of Robert's cruel desertion sunk in? Would she be able to handle it without becoming bitter? Laura sighed, hating the thought of anything or anyone changing her daughter's softness into ice. She'd always thought that of all her children, Valerie was the one with the most love to give, but would she be afraid to give it in the future?

"Mom, I'm going to lie down for a little while. I'm starting to feel a little queasy again."

"Go ahead, honey. We'll have something light for lunch."

An hour later the telephone rang. "Hi. It's me."

Steve's voice made Laura's eyes water. She wished he was with her, holding her, and comforting her. Ever since she'd heard Val's news she felt on the verge of tears.

"How's the new business going?" Laura asked, turning away from the phone to sniff. "Are you renting all those old relics?"

"I beg your pardon, *madame!*" Steve said, sounding shocked. "Those old relics you speak of so disrespectfully are classic automobiles, treasures from the past."

Laura heard Steve laugh, then lower his voice. "I'll bet you would auction off your best girdle to get a ride in the '55 T-bird I've got here."

"I don't wear girdles," Laura said tartly, "and if I remember correctly, you promised me a ride in the car of my choice. Nothing was said about my having to auction off my underwear."

"I'm glad about the girdle," Steve said, his voice low and husky. "I never did like all that stiff elastic stuff."

"Me either," Laura said, laughing. Then she remembered. "Steve, my daughter's here. Valerie, my youngest. She . . . has a little problem and she wanted to spend some time with me."

"When did she arrive?" Steve asked, his tone somber. "She's not sick, is she?"

"Not exactly."

"Well, what is it? What's the problem? Is it something I can help with?"

"I don't think so," Laura said. "Valerie is pregnant."

"Oh. I see. Well . . . are you happy? That's good news, isn't it?"

"I don't know. I'm a little ambivalent. Valerie is not married, and now she tells me she isn't planning to be married, at least not in the foreseeable future. Steve, you and I both know it's not easy being a parent, and Valerie will have to do it all alone. It breaks my heart."

"I thought she was engaged? Didn't you tell me your youngest daughter was planning to be married after her graduation?"

"Yes. She was, but he doesn't want a baby right now. He told her it was inconvenient. He wanted her to have an abortion, and Valerie won't do that."

"Good for her," Steve said. "What kind of creep was she hooked up with anyway? I wish I could get my hands on him. I'd show him what was inconvenient!"

Laura couldn't help laughing. The image of Steve, a calm, collected middle-aged man, beating up on a young man who could be his son was slightly ridiculous, but it was sweet of him to care, and she told him so. "I want you to meet Val while she's here. I know she'll like you."

"Damn, Laura, I wish there was something I could do! You must be worried sick about all this."

"It could be worse. At least Valerie will be able to support her child after she graduates. It's not like she's a sixteen-year-old drop-out or something."

"Yeah, I guess. Look, I've got to run. Rich looks like he's having a problem with a customer. May I stop by tonight, or would you rather be alone with your daughter?"

"Please do come by. I think Val and I can both use a little cheering up. Why don't you come for dinner? I'll fix something easy and we'll all relax."

"Sounds great," Steve said.

When Valerie woke from her midmorning nap she looked more like herself. Some of her natural color had returned and she looked well rested. "I guess I missed my old bed, Mom," she said, smiling. "Why is it that you always want to go home when you have a problem? Was it terribly immature of me to come running home to you?"

"Just the natural, normal thing, hon," Laura said, putting a chef's salad on the table. She'd baked rolls to go with it, and there was fresh fruit for desert. "Try and eat something," she told her daughter. "The baby needs nourishment."

"The baby. I still can't get used to hearing that. My baby. It's a funny feeling knowing there's a tiny, helpless little baby inside me. It's wonderful and yet scary at the same time."

Laura helped herself to salad and nodded. "I know. When I discovered I was pregnant with Greg I couldn't quite believe it. It wasn't until I started outgrowing all my clothes that I really began to believe there was a real, live baby in my belly."

"And was Daddy happy?" Val asked wistfully.

"He was ecstatic," Laura said, her lips curving softly as she remembered. Paul had been an exemplary father from the very beginning. Even before their first child was born he had started planning. That was what she wished Valerie could have, but they'd just have to make it on their own. One thing Laura knew for sure. She wasn't going to desert Val in her time of need.

"You'll have enough love for your baby to make up for the lack of a daddy, hon," she said gently. "It will be hard on you, but I know you can do it. Do you want to come home after graduation and stay with me until the baby comes?"

It would mean postponing the sale of the

house, and she'd have to rethink some of her personal plans, but what else could she do? This was her daughter, and the baby would be her grandchild.

Tears filled Valerie's eyes. "Oh Mom, that's what I was hoping you would say, but I . . . was almost afraid to ask. Lately your letters have sounded different, like you're getting on with your life, and doing your own thing. I don't want to interfere with that. I don't want to be in your way."

"I am getting on with my life, honey, but I can postpone things for a few months. You're going to need some help."

"Nice to meet you, Valerie," Steve said that evening, with a warm smile. He stood in the middle of the living room, looking from mother to daughter and shaking his head. "You look just like your mother did when we were dating. It's uncanny." He turned to Laura and grinned. "It's like you cloned her."

Both women laughed. Laura had prepared Valerie for Steve's arrival by telling her he was an old school friend, but she hadn't said anything about dating.

"Oh, so you and Mom were sweethearts?" Valerie asked, a devilish grin curving her lips.

"You didn't tell me that, Mom."

"Mothers don't have to tell their children everything," Laura said, lifting her chin.

"Well, anyway, I am glad to meet you, Valerie. I've met your older sister and your brother, and I've been looking forward to meeting you."

"Normally I wouldn't be home now," Valerie said, "but Mom told me you know about my . . . pregnancy."

Steve sat down on the sofa and nodded. "Yes. Congratulations. You must be excited. I'm going to be a grandfather soon, you know. My daughter-in-law is going to have a baby in a few months."

"That's nice," Val said.

Laura watched her daughter, saw the smile melt into wistfulness again. Was Val thinking that her baby would be cheated out of a grandpa? With her own father dead, and Robert refusing to participate, all this baby would have was a mama and a grandma. Well, so be it, Laura thought angrily.

She left Steve and Valerie to get better acquainted and went out to the kitchen to check on dinner. As she'd told Steve, she'd made it simple. Her family favorite meatloaf recipe, baked potatoes, and a green bean casserole, with homemade apple pie for dessert. As she spooned sour cream and chives into a small dish, Laura found herself listening to the muted sounds coming from the living room. So far so good, she thought. Val hadn't seemed shocked to learn that her mother had a man friend, and Steve was being very kind and considerate of Valerie's feelings.

Oh, if only he knew how much that young woman needed a strong male figure in her life right now! She knew Valerie was missing her daddy very much. If Paul had been here he would have held his daughter in his strong arms and promised her that everything would be all right. He would have been a buffer against the storm, a pillar of strength for Valerie to lean on.

Laura sighed as she lifted the meatloaf from the oven. The tangy aroma of tomato and spices drifted out to her. Paul wasn't here, and Valerie was on her own. Well, not quite. She had a brother and a sister who would both be supportive when they heard the news. Laura was convinced of that. Vicki might be slightly self-centered, but she had a strong sense of family loyalty and she loved Valerie, and Greg had always been protective of his little sister. And she'll have me, her mother, Laura thought.

Dinner went even better than Laura could have hoped. Steve managed to keep Valerie laughing throughout the meal with comical tales of his recent experiences as manager of Dreams for Rent.

"There was one man," he said, between bites of meatloaf and extravagant praise for the green bean casserole, "who must have weighed three hundred and fifty pounds. He came in wanting to rent our '55 T-bird. Let me tell you, it took some diplomacy to convince him that he'd enjoy driving the '59 Caddy convertible much more." Steve grinned. "At least we knew we'd be able to get him out of that one."

Valerie laughed until tears came to her eyes. "Mom, where did you find this guy? He's better than HBO!"

"You always were a ham, even back in high school," Laura said teasingly, offering Steve a second helping of meatloaf. "I guess there are just some things we never outgrow."

Without conscious thought, her eyes met Steve's. The teasing glint faded, and was replaced by vivid, technicolor memories. Steve, pulling her hair when he sat behind her in study hall. Chasing her around the empty football field after a Saturday afternoon game. Sending her silly notes in English class that made her giggle uncontrollably. How could she remember all those little things after all these years? And why did the memories make her feel all soft and squiggly inside? Those feelings were for kids, for young people like Val and Greg, certainly not for fifty-two-year-old grandmas!

She could tell by the expression on Steve's face that the memories were assaulting him too. A kaleidoscope of emotions crossed his face as they stared at one another. Then suddenly the spell was broken.

"Break it up, you two," Valerie teased, her eyes sparkling with mischief. "You're making me feel like a spare tire here." She giggled like the youngster she still was. "Boy, is this what I have to look forward to when I'm old?"

"Old! Wash your mouth, young lady!" Steve said. "Your mother and I are just entering the Prime of Life! And the way I feel right now, I'll never be old!"

Laura laughed. "Good for you, but just wait until that little grandbaby of yours starts climbing all over you, and you try toting a twenty-five pound toddler around for a couple of hours. You'll discover aches and pains you never knew you had!"

"I'm depending on you to give me lots of practical advice," Steve said. "After all, you're a pro."

Valerie looked at her mother and smiled. "She's a good grandma. My baby is going to be very lucky."

Steve smiled at the two women. One he already loved, and the other he knew he could easily learn to love. "I'll drink to that," he said.

"So, what's the deal here, Mom?" Valerie asked, as she and Laura finished putting the clean dishes away. Steve had gone home after declaring that his belt had to be let out a notch, and that he'd have to take up jogging if he continued to eat this way. The two women were alone, and the moment Laura had been dreading had arrived.

"How do you mean?" she answered cautiously. "I told you Steve was an old school friend."

"Come on, Mom, this is me you're talking to, your daughter who just finished Psychology I, and with a B +, I might add. Friends don't look at each other the way you two did tonight. Is there a romance brewing?"

Laura dried her hands on a paper towel and untied her apron. "I'm really not sure, honey," she said. "Does it bother you to think I could care about a man other than your daddy?"

"Mom, Daddy wouldn't want you to be lonely. He would want you to go on with your life and be happy. Personally, I think Steve is pretty neat." She grinned, then added, "For an old guy!"

Laura laughed. She opened her arms and Valerie moved into the circle of her mother's love.

"I really do love you, Mom," Valerie said, "and you'll never know how much I appreciate you standing by me this way. I was so afraid you were going to be disappointed and angry with me."

Her daughter's voice was muffled, and Laura knew Valerie was fighting back tears. It had been an emotional time for both of them, the news of Valerie's pregnancy, the introduction of Steve in their lives. But love and respect was the thread that held everything together. If nothing else, Laura had to respect her daughter's strength and courage, and her determination to stand up for what she believed in, just as she now knew Valerie would respect her mother's right to start a new life.

"We're a pretty good group, if I do say so myself," Laura murmured, her cheek against her daughter's silky hair. "We done good, honey."

Eleven

Isabelle laughed as Laura entered the room the next morning, loaded down with books and notepads.

"So, you decided to hang in there, eh? Good for you. Do you have any idea how many people drop out after only one class?"

Laura deposited her things on the nearest available desk and looked at her friend incredulously. "Are you serious? After one class?"

Isabelle nodded vigorously, her iron gray curls bobbing. "Cross my heart. I guess they come in thinking it's going to be easy and when they realize that they're actually going to have to work a little, they change their minds. Anyway, I'm glad you're not a dropout."

"Me too," Laura said. "I don't think much of quitters."

George Ryan wandered in then. He stopped

beside the two women and winked at Laura. "So, Isabelle didn't manage to scare you away. How you doing, Laura?"

Laura sat down and made herself comfortable. "So far so good," she said, "although I didn't get as much chance to absorb everything these past few days as I would have liked. When I went home the other night I found my little dog nearly dead of poisoning. I spent hours at the animal clinic until I found out he was going to be okay."

"How awful," Isabelle said. "How did it happen?"

"It was all my fault," Laura admitted. She still felt guilty when she thought of it. "I put out some roach traps and I dumped the empty containers in a wastebasket. Apparently Buttons got in the wastebasket, and there must have been just enough of the powder on the packages to make him very, very sick. Believe me, I learned a hard lesson."

"Is your dog okay now?" George asked. "I don't know what I'd do if I ever lost my dalmatian. My boy gave him to me last Christmas, and he's about the best friend I've got."

"Buttons is completely back to normal," Laura said. "It was a close call, but he's fine. And I know what you mean about your dog being your best friend," she told George. "I don't know how I would have gotten through those first weeks after my husband passed away, if not for Buttons."

Isabelle nodded her agreement. "Pets are worth their weight in gold. Sometimes I like my cat better than my kids!"

By the time her second class was over, Laura was convinced that she'd made the right decision to take the realtor's course. Just chatting with Isabelle and George lifted her spirits and added a little spice to her life. Isabelle had a wonderful dry sense of humor, and George was a perpetual jokester. They both made her laugh, and she suddenly realized that she was looking at the world around her with a whole new perspective. She knew she would never be as flamboyant as Isabelle, but she was already looking forward to buying a briefcase, wearing handsome suits and low-heeled pumps, and best of all, her first sale.

Sticking a pencil behind her ear, and opening her notebook, Laura realized that she was indeed starting a whole new life. The things she was anticipating now were things she would never have dreamed of when she was raising her children and being a wife.

"Mrs. Kinsey?"

Laura looked up, startled, to see the class youngster standing beside her. At close range the young woman looked more like eight than eighteen. Her face was so small and vulnerable, and she was obviously painfully shy.

"Call me Laura," she said pleasantly. "What can I do for you?"

"I was wondering . . . well, I guess I should start by telling you my name. It's Sheila. Sheila Brooks."

"Hi, Sheila," Laura said. Although she looked nothing like Valerie, there was something sweet and shy and gentle about the young woman, and Laura felt very protective.

"Hi. Well, anyway, what I was wondering was . . . do you think I could see your notes from the first class? I guess I'm sort of confused."

Laura hesitated. She didn't mind helping a fellow student, but would she be helping or hindering? Then she looked at Sheila's anxious face and smiled. "Sure, this time anyway. But try to take your own notes for this class, okay? I think you'll get more out of it that way."

A few minutes later the class got rolling and Laura quickly became absorbed. There was a lot to learn and she was determined not be left behind.

"Well, what do you think now?" Isabelle asked, when the session was over. She stood next to Laura, and this time she was dressed in a wildly patterned jersey jumpsuit and bright purple heels. There was a velvet band holding her gray curls in place, and dangly silver earrings touching her shoulders.

"You like?" she asked, grinning as she noted Laura's interested gaze lingering on the sparkling tubes of silver.

"They're wonderful," Laura said. And they were. For Isabelle. Laura knew she'd never dare wear anything so bold and flamboyant, but it was definitely Isabelle.

"Here are your notes, Laura. Thank you."

Sheila walked up, holding out a sheaf of papers. "Your notes were much clearer than mine," she said. "I think I understand everything better now."

"Well, good," Laura said, taking the papers and stuffing them in her notebook. She smiled at the young woman. "Have you met Isabelle?"

Sheila nodded. "Yes. Hello, Ms. French. I like your outfit," she said, then ducked her head shyly.

Isabelle looked at Laura and rolled her eyes heavenward. "Thanks," she said. "Well, I've got to run. "See you all next time."

"She isn't very friendly," Sheila said, when Isabelle was gone. "At least not to me. I don't think she likes me."

Laura had a crazy urge to hug Sheila as close as she would have held one of her daughters. "I'm sure that's not true. Isabelle is a very nice person. She's just a little brusque."

"Well, I want her to like me," Sheila said shyly, "and I want to do well with this course."

Laura looked at the girl standing in front of

her. Sheila could be a very pretty girl, but she was so shy and timid she wasn't making the most of herself. As a very little girl, Valerie had been painfully shy, and Laura had helped her gain confidence by praise and constant reassurances. Now, although she still retained her sweet gentleness, Valerie was a strong, confidant young woman.

"What are you doing for dinner tonight?" Laura asked impulsively. "How would you like to come home with me and meet my daughter, Valerie? She's home from college, and she's not much older than you. I'll bet she'd enjoy having someone her own age to talk to."

Sheila blushed and smiled. "Oh, gosh . . . you mean it? Gee, I'd love that, Ms. . . . uh, Laura. Can you wait while I call and let my family know I won't be home until later?"

As Laura gathered her things and waited for Sheila to make her call, she found herself remembering. At Sheila's age she'd been shy too, but her mother had never even tried to help her overcome it. Instead she had laughed and made fun of Laura's attempts to fade into the woodwork. It was a wonder she'd ever gotten a date with Steve, and later fallen in love and married Paul. A smile softened Laura's features. She'd been lucky in love, despite how her first romance with Steve had ended. Both men had been caring enough to bring her at least partly out of her shell. And marriage and motherhood had completed the transformation. After all, how could the mother of three rambunctious children sit in a corner? There were PTA meetings, Girl Scout cookie drives, conferences with the teachers. Before she even knew how it had happened, Laura was brave and confidant, facing the world with strength and determination.

As she waited for Sheila, Laura's head was already spinning with ideas of how to help the young woman gain self-confidence. She was sure Val would have some ideas too.

Sheila followed Laura home in her own little car.

"My daughter will be going back to school soon," Laura explained as they went in the house. "She's just visiting for a few days."

Buttons came running to greet them, and then Laura heard Val's voice. "I'm in the living room, Mom."

"Oh, we have company?" Val smiled welcomingly as they went in. "Hi," she said, holding out her hand to Sheila. "I'm Val."

"Sheila Brooks," Sheila managed. "Your mother was kind enough to invite me home to dinner. I hope you don't mind."

"Not at all," Valerie said. "Here, sit down. Are you in Mom's real estate class?"

Satisfied that Val could keep a conversation going, Laura headed for the kitchen to see what she could prepare for dinner.

She was staring morosely into the refrigerator when the telephone rang.

"Laura? It's Steve. How was your second day in class?"

"Good. There's a lot to learn, but I'm really enjoying it." She thought for a minute, then shrugged her shoulders. "Want to come eat with us? I brought one of my young classmates home with me, and I'm just going to throw together something simple."

"I've got a better idea," Steve said. "How about if I pick up an assortment of Chinese dishes. Does Valerie like oriental food?"

"She sure does, and I do too. Are you sure you want to do this?"

"I'll be there in about an hour," Steve promised. "Now why don't you just sit down and prop up your feet?"

"A knight in white armor has decided to rescue us, girls," she informed Val and Sheila. "Steve is bringing Chinese food for our dinner."

"Great," Val said. "I could eat a good egg roll. Do you like Chinese food, Sheila?"

"I love it," the young woman said. She smiled up at Laura. "Your daughter is beautiful, Laura, just like you. I was afraid to approach you today, but you have such a nice face. You don't look like you're ready to bite off my head like Ms. French."

Valerie laughed. "I don't know how long I'm going to be beautiful. Pretty soon I'll be as big and fat as a cow."

Laura sat down across from the girls. "Valerie is having a baby," she told Sheila. "She's making me a grandma again."

"A baby? Oh, how wonderful! And you're still in school?"

"Just until May. Then I'm coming home to stay with Mom until the little stranger arrives. Once I get that all taken care of I'll have to get a job and look for a place of my own."

"Oh. Then you're . . . not married?" Sheila asked.

"No. I'm going to be a single mother."

"Aren't you scared?"

Valerie shrugged, then smiled at Laura. "I would be, except for that lady over there. I was so shy when I was little that I hid behind her skirts when strangers came anywhere near me."

"I have to confess that's why I brought you home, Sheila," Laura broke in. "I started remembering the way Valerie was and I thought maybe between the two of us we could help you open up a little. No one knows better than my daughter and I how much it hurts to be shy."

Tears filled Sheila's eyes and she shook her head. "I've never had anyone be this nice to me

226

before. I feel like I'm dreaming."

They all laughed then, and Val dragged Sheila up to her bedroom to experiment with makeup. Laura smiled and did as Steve had suggested. She leaned back, closed her eyes and propped up her feet. Amazing how tired she was even though she'd been sitting down all day. But it was a nice tiredness, she decided. She felt as though something had been accomplished. She gained a little more knowledge of the real estate business, and she had a good feeling about helping Sheila. All in all, life was pretty good, Laura thought, and hopefully it was only going to get better.

"Okay, ladies," Steve said, setting the cardboard containers on the table. "I bought a little of everything. We have won ton soup, egg rolls, spicy chicken wings, shrimp fried rice, pork egg foo yong, chicken chow mein . . ."

"What, no fortune cookies?" Laura said, forcing a pout. "What's a Chinese meal without fortune cookies?"

"Never fear," Steve said, pulling one last bag from behind him. "Fortune cookies!"

Laura was touched by the gentle way Steve treated Sheila. Even without being told he seemed to sense that the young woman needed tender handling. He kept both her and Val laughing with

227

new tales of his experiences in the auto rental business. And to the young woman he paid subtle compliments that brought a pleased flush to her cheeks.

As Laura carried the garbage out to the kitchen she heard Sheila whispering to Val. "Is that your mother's boyfriend?"

She couldn't hear Val's answer, but her cheeks pinked in response. Indeed! She felt a little self-conscious knowing that the young women were discussing her private affairs. A giggle caught in her throat. Affair. Now that was definitely a loaded word!

When the kitchen was cleaned up they all sat around and watched a video Steve had picked up. It was a comedy and they all laughed until their sides were sore. Several times during the evening, Laura glanced at Sheila and saw that she looked relaxed and unafraid. She was glad she'd followed her instincts and invited the girl home.

But later that night, Laura's happiness turned to fear and despair, as she called an ambulance to rush her daughter to the hospital.

They left her waiting in a tiled room with stiff, cold chairs and out-of-date magazines. Valerie had been fine when she went to bed shortly after midnight, but a couple of hours later, Laura had been awakened from a sound sleep by her daughter's cries for help. It happened suddenly. One minute Laura was sleeping soundly, the next she was stumbling around in the dark, nearly paralyzed with fear.

"Oh, Val," she said, when she saw her daughter doubled over with pain on the side of her bed. "Honey, what's wrong?"

"It came . . . all at once, Mom . . . these terrible, sharp pains. I'm scared!"

"Don't worry, sweetheart, it's going to be okay," Laura soothed, dialing 911 with shaking hands. Lord, she didn't want Valerie to lose her baby! In just a few days she'd begun to think of the baby as a real little person. Both she and Val already loved the tiny scrap of life.

The ambulance came quickly, and the attendants gently bundled Val up and lifted her onto the stretcher. Valerie was crying quietly now, her cheeks streaked with tears, her beautiful eyes wide with fear and dread. "Come with me, Mom," she pleaded. "Please?"

Nodding, Laura grabbed a light jacket from the sofa and followed the stretcher. Nothing in the world could have made her leave her daughter's side.

Then the tense, fearful waiting began. Laura paced quietly, desperately. She didn't think Valerie would be able to stand it if she lost the baby. She'd already lost the man she'd thought she loved in the cruelest possible way. If she lost the baby too, Laura wasn't sure how Valerie would cope.

As she waited for word, Laura remembered. Val had been the child who brought home stray kittens and wounded birds. She'd babysat for the neighbors from the time she was twelve years old. Laura knew she would be an excellent mother. She would be warm and loving and gentle. It wasn't fair for her to lose her baby!

At last, when Laura was beginning to think she couldn't stand it another minute, a white-coated doctor came hurrying towards her.

"She's holding her own," he said, "and I think she can keep the baby, but she's going to have to take it easy for the rest of her pregnancy. It was touch and go there for a while."

"Do you have any idea what caused it?"

The doctor shook his head. "I couldn't find anything specific, but as I said, I think she's going to come out of this all right."

"May I see her?"

"For a few minutes, but then I want her to rest. She had a bad scare, and she's pretty shaken up. I gave her a mild sedative."

Laura tiptoed into the semidarkened room, her heart not quite daring to rejoice. Valerie lay with her eyes closed, the pallor of her skin stark against her red-brown curls. Laura swallowed, wishing she could hug her daughter close and keep her safe from all harm. How hard it was for a parent to stand by and not be able to help a child. How terrifying to know that there was nothing you could do to change things.

"I'm here, honey," she said softly.

Maybe Val was just too young and this was nature's way of preventing . . . no. Laura shook her head. Val was young, but not that young, and she would grow up quickly now, with her own child depending on her.

"Honey, can you hear me?"

"I . . . still have my baby, Mom," Val whispered, her eyelids fluttering softly. It was as if she wanted to wake up, but couldn't.

"You're going to be all right, sweetheart," Laura said, "both you and the baby."

"I know," Val murmured sleepily. "I love you, Mom."

"Good Lord, Laura, why didn't you call me? Don't you know I'd come out at any hour of the day or night for you? Are you sure Valerie is okay? Is it definite that she's not going to lose the baby?"

Steve sounded frantic, almost as though Valerie were his daughter too. It was sweet of him to be so concerned, but in truth Laura had thought of calling him, and had quickly rejected the idea. She had called him when Buttons got sick, but that was different. This was much more serious. Valerie was her daughter, and her responsibility. As much as Steve was beginning to mean to her, he wasn't her children's father, and he never would be. If Paul had been alive he would have been by her side all night. Together they would have watched over their daughter and unborn grandchild. But Steve was outside all that, and it wouldn't have been right to involve him. He was already becoming too much a part of her life.

She tried to explain her feelings to him, and failed miserably.

"What you're saying is that I'm an outsider, right? You don't want me to care about your family, is that it? Well, I'm sorry, Laura, but I do care. I care about you, and I can't help it if my affection spills over on your offspring. Is that such a terrible thing?"

"No, of course not, but . . . I felt it was an imposition to involve you in a family crisis."

"Thanks," Steve barked, sounding bitter. "I thought you and I were slowly growing closer, that you were learning to trust me. I guess I was wrong."

Laura wearily shifted the phone to her other hand. She was dead tired, and still worried about Val and the baby, and the last thing she wanted or needed was an angry confrontation with Steve.

"Look, I'm sorry if I hurt your feelings," she said. "But in this past year since Paul's death I've learned to be independent, to handle things on my own, and I like it that way." She closed her eyes and her voice softened. "You're not my husband, Steve, and you're not Valerie's father. I didn't think it was appropriate for you to be at the hospital last night. And for that matter, I didn't even call Valerie's sister. There wasn't anything Vicki could have done, and I didn't see any need to disturb her in the middle of the night."

"Well, good for you. I'm glad you feel you don't need other people in your life, Laura. It must be nice to be so strong and secure."

Laura's eyes flew open and her jaw dropped. She was stunned by Steve's anger. In her wildest dreams she had never expected him to act like this. It was as though he was threatened by her independence. As if he were right beside her, she suddenly heard Paul's voice, telling her that the best course was always honesty.

She took a deep breath and spoke quietly into the telephone receiver. "I'm sorry if I hurt your feelings, Steve. That wasn't my intention, but yes, I am strong and secure, and it wasn't easy getting to this point. I won't surrender that to anyone. I have to go now. We'll talk later, if you like."

Steve held on to the telephone for several minutes after he heard the click that told him Laura had hung up. Had he come on too strong? Was he pushing Laura when he'd promised he wouldn't?

But he couldn't help feeling the way he did. He cared for Laura . . . oh hell, he more than cared. He was in love with the woman! He was hoping that their relationship would grow into something strong and permanent. He wanted her to be his wife, his partner for the rest of his life. He didn't like being single, and he had no desire to play the field and act like a playboy. Every woman he saw failed to measure up to Laura. He was smitten with her beauty, her kind heart and gentle nature. As far as he was concerned the only fault she had, if she had one at all, was her stubbornness and determination to be so damned independent. Why couldn't she see that he wanted her to lean on him . . . that he wanted to be there for her, in good times and bad? Why couldn't she feel even half what he was feeling?

Twelve

She picked Valerie up at the hospital that afternoon, and the two women went home together, quiet and subdued by what had happened, and by the threat of what could still happen.

"I've always been so healthy," Val said, shaking her head. "When I found out I was pregnant I thought I'd sail through these months with hardly an ache or pain, and now the doctor is saying I have to take things easy. It's going to be like walking on eggs the next few months, Mom."

Laura nodded, taking her eyes off the road briefly to regard her daughter's pale complexion and worried eyes.

"Look, darling," she said. "I know you're disappointed about not being able to finish this last semester, but if you want to have a healthy,

235

beautiful baby, you don't have much choice."

"I know," Valerie said. "It's just that I thought I had everything all figured out. I was going to finish school, get my degree and then I'd be able to take care of myself and my baby. Now I have to rethink everything."

"Well, for now let's just do what the doctor suggested and see how things go in the next few days. He did say you might be able to go back to school, if that was all you did."

Laura pulled into her driveway and brought the car to a stop. To be perfectly truthful, she was more upset than she wanted Valerie to know. Prenatal care was expensive enough under the best of circumstances, but if there were complications it could be devastating. Laura's medical insurance would cover Valerie until she graduated, but Laura wasn't sure if pre- and postnatal care would be covered. And if Val couldn't finish this last semester, it would delay everyone's plans. Val would have to wait until after the baby's birth to complete her studies and get her degree, and it would take her much longer to get settled in a job so she could take care of herself and her child. Laura didn't mind helping out, but she wasn't sure how much help she could reasonably afford to give Val. It was a scary situation, and as she helped her daughter out of the car and into the house, she voiced the question that had been on her mind all day.

"Val, do you think there's any chance that Robert will help. I mean, when he learns you're having problems . . ."

Valerie shook her head. "He's in school on a scholarship and student loans, Mom. He's barely scraping by as it is. He didn't want me and the baby when he thought everything was fine. Do you really think he'd want to get involved under these circumstances?"

"I suppose not," Laura said slowly. "I guess I was just grasping at straws."

She helped Valerie get settled on the sofa, turned on the television set and went out to the kitchen to make some tea. Tea was the answer to just about everything, Laura thought. It made you feel better when you were sad, helped you think when you were confused, and it seemed to give strength when you felt weak.

It was a scary situation, and not one she would ever have expected her daughter Val to be in. Laura buttered hot toast and placed some of Val's favorite cookies on a plate. But accidents happen, she supposed, and when they did you had to deal with them. She sighed. She hated having Val in this kind of predicament, and although Laura felt guilty admitting it, she was just a little angry that she had been drawn into it.

Everything had been going so well, her plans to sell the house, her real estate course, even her budding relationship with Steve, and now everything was turned upside down. Well, there was no help for it, and nothing she could decently do except stand by her child and help as much as possible.

Valerie smiled wanly as she finished her second cup of tea. "Nothing tastes as good and tea and toast when you're not feeling up to par. Thanks, Mom," she said, looking like a frightened little girl. "I know you didn't bargain for all this when I showed up on your doorstep."

The doctor had given Valerie a prescription for mild sedatives, and she had taken one just before she started to eat. Now, as Laura watched, her daughter's eyelids began to droop.

"How about a little nap now?" she asked. "The doctor said you should rest as much as possible in the next few days."

"Okay," Valerie said obediently. "I do feel kind of sleepy."

"Good. Then close your eyes and dream about the beautiful, perfect little baby you're going to have in a few months. I have a few chores to take care of."

Laura made it to the kitchen before she

238

broke down. Then she quietly sobbed into a dish towel. She hadn't cried in months, and she was ashamed of herself for caving in now. She thought fleetingly of Steve, and wondered what he would think if he could see her now, the strong, independent woman, dampening a dishtowel and ruining her makeup. Well, she'd handled things pretty well so far, and she'd cope with this too. But it would have been comforting to have a pair of strong arms holding her, even if she didn't really need it.

"What is going on at your place, Laura?" Blanche demanded the next morning.

Laura had taken the call on her bedroom extension, and now she was glad. If she'd been in the kitchen with Val, Blanche's grating voice would surely have carried around the room.

"How do you mean?" Laura asked cautiously. She'd hoped to keep the news of Valerie's pregnancy to herself for a while, at least where Paul's sister was concerned. Blanche was very opinionated, and she had very outdated views of unwed mothers.

"Well, I met Helen Parker in the grocery store yesterday, and she told me that her friend, Betty, who works in the emergency room, said that you were in with Valerie. I didn't even know my sweet little niece was home, and then to find out that she's sick?

What's wrong with her, Laura? And why haven't I been kept informed? My own dear brother's children . . ."

"I would have called you, Blanche," Laura said carefully, trying hard to hold her temper. "But everything happened so suddenly, and right now my main concern is Valerie's health."

"Well, of course, mine too. What is wrong with her, Laura? It's not serious, is it?"

Laura took a deep breath and plunged in. "Valerie is pregnant, and the other night she almost lost her child. She's doing all right now, but we're still not sure how things are going to turn out." Twisting the phone cord nervously, Laura said a small, silent prayer that for once in her life, Blanche would think before she spoke.

"Pregnant? But . . . how can that be? She didn't run off and elope, did she? And she wouldn't . . . oh dear, are you telling me . . ."

"She's not married, Blanche, and she has no plans to get married any time in the near future. I'm going to help her as much as I can."

"Oh dear! I can't believe this! I always thought so highly of your daughters, Laura, and Paul was so proud of his girls. Oh, I'm almost glad he isn't here to see this terrible shame come down on his family! It would have been a blessing if Valerie had lost the child!"

"Why, you bitch!" Laura's face was fire red and she had difficulty getting her breath. She couldn't ever remember being this angry before in her entire life. "Valerie is still the same sweet, loving girl she was before this happened, Blanche, and if Paul were here he'd be furious at what you just said. We want this baby, both Val and I, and she's going to make out fine, and if you weren't so damned narrow-minded, you'd be asking what you could do to help, instead of making nasty comments!"

"Well! I must say I've always suspected you didn't care much for me, Laura, but I've tried to be a good sister-in-law, and I can't imagine . . ."

"That's the whole problem, Blanche. You can't imagine what it is to be young . . . to be human . . . to have needs. You can't begin to imagine how frightened and unhappy my daughter is right now, and to say it would be best if she lost her child! How can you be so cruel?"

"But I only meant . . ."

"I'm sorry. I can't talk to you anymore right now. I have to check on Val."

Laura was shaking. This was the second altercation she'd had in the past few days. First Steve, now Blanche. What next? By the time she went downstairs, Laura was more determined than ever to keep a handle on things. Her daughter and her grandchild's health depended on it, not to mention her own emotional stability. She'd held herself together through much worse than this. Paul's stroke, those anxious days and nights while they all wondered if he would even live, and then the pain of knowing that he would live, but that his lifestyle would be permanently altered, that he'd never again be the same man.

It had been a terrible, trying time, and there were many days when Laura had been certain she wasn't going to make it, but she had, and when it was all over, when Paul's suffering ended and he was finally laid to rest, she'd felt justifiably proud of how she'd handled things.

"And I can do it again," she vowed, fixing a tray of fruit juices, crackers and cheese, and cookies. Valerie will have her baby, and I will go on with my life. It was just a little setback, a test of her fortitude.

"What happened to Steve?" Val asked that afternoon, when she woke from her nap. "I miss him. He makes me laugh."

Secretly, Laura agreed. She missed Steve too, and a good laugh would have been more than welcome, but she couldn't call him. She didn't know what to say, how to make him understand.

242

"I'm afraid Steve is a little angry with me, hon," she told Val. "He thinks I should have called him the night you were in the emergency room. I think he feels that by not calling him, I'm shutting him out of my life. I didn't mean to do that, but I just thought it was inappropriate."

Valerie laughed. "Oh Mother! Who cares about whether or not something is appropriate? Who do you have to impress anyway?" She grinned, and her eyes sparkled mischievously. "After all, it's not as though dear Aunt Blanche is looking over your shoulder, you know."

Laura groaned. "If only you knew!"

"Oh? So she did find out. Boy, that woman has the nose of a bloodhound, doesn't she?" Valerie tried to look properly repentant and failed. "I suppose she is terribly disappointed in me, isn't she?"

Laura couldn't help smiling. She helped herself to a cracker and a slice of cheese. "You might say that."

Val laughed. "I'm not surprised. Look, Mom, I hope this doesn't upset you, but I really don't like Aunt Blanche. As a matter of fact, I never did, and I don't think Daddy liked her either, even if she was his sister."

Laura rolled her eyes heavenward. "I don't think she'll be calling me for a while. I'm sure

I'm on her list."

Valerie sobered. "Who cares? Who needs people like that anyway?"

"Not us," Laura said firmly.

She was breading chicken for dinner when the doorbell rang.

"Stay where you are, hon," she called to Valerie who was lying on the sofa watching television. "I'll see who it is."

Laura's questioning look turned into a huge smile when she saw Sheila. "How nice of you to come by," she said. "And how pretty you look. Are you here to see Valerie?"

Sheila nodded. "Isabelle told me what happened. Is she okay? She didn't lose her baby, did she?"

"No, she's fine. In fact, she's in the living room watching television, but I'm sure she would much rather talk to you."

Sheila smiled. "I have a little something for her . . . actually it's for the baby. Is it okay to give it to her?"

"I think she'd love to get a little present right about now, Sheila. That was very thoughtful of you."

"Well, she was really sweet about teaching me some stuff about makeup and hairstyles, and she said we could do it again, so I thought

I'd like to do something for her."

"Well, go on in. I know she'll be delighted to see you."

Sheila ended up staying for dinner, and afterwards, as Laura finished cleaning up the kitchen, she found herself strangely restless. And she kept thinking of Steve. She couldn't stop remembering the hurt in his voice, the way he sounded just before she hung up on him, and all the nice, kind things he'd done for her, for all of them for that matter. He'd been pleasant and supportive of Greg, and he'd put up with Vicki's tantrums, and Val . . . well, Laura was sure he had a soft spot for her youngest daughter, even as she did.

Before she could change her mind, she whipped off her apron, peeked in the mirror in the hall, and quickly finger-combed her hair.

"Girls, do you think you'll be okay for an hour or so? I have an errand to run." She wouldn't even dream of leaving if she thought Val was in any danger, but she'd done well since she came home from the hospital, and there was no reason to think there would be any more problems.

"An errand?" Val asked cheekily, her eyes wide and innocent, her lips twitching. "By the name of . . ."

"Hush, you fresh child," Laura said. "I just

need some fresh air. I haven't been out of this house in two days."

"Then go on and get," Val said, waving her off with her hand. "Leave me and Sheila alone so we can do some serious girl talk!"

"Okay, but I won't be too long. And if you need anything, just . . ."

"We won't need anything, now go. We'll see you later."

After a hasty trip to the bedroom to pick up her purse and car keys, Laura stepped outside and shut the door behind her. It was true. She hadn't been outside for more than forty-eight hours, and she wouldn't leave now if Valerie was alone. But she had Sheila with her. There was no real reason Laura couldn't take a little break.

Steve was in his new apartment now. She'd thought about that all day. She wondered who had helped him move in. If his cousins had helped him set up his waterbed, if he was even now lying on it and thinking about her. Fat chance, Laura, she told herself. After the way you cut him out, you'll be lucky if he doesn't slam the door in your face. Well, maybe he would, but she was betting he wouldn't. She didn't think that was Steve's style.

But even though she told herself that Steve would probably give her a chance to state her case, she was as nervous as a cat on a telephone pole when she finally located his apartment building and parked her car. What if he decided she simply wasn't worth the trouble? After all, Steve was an extremely attractive man. There must be scores of women who would be delighted to get to know him. Women who were not encumbered by the problems of their grown offspring. Women who would be only too happy to help Steve cure his loneliness. And he was lonely. Laura had known that from the very beginning. Unlike her, he didn't seem too fond of his own company. He didn't like being without a wife. He wasn't interested in the swinging singles scene.

She knocked on the door, her insides twisting with apprehension. If he was still angry . . .

But he was anything but angry when he opened the door and saw her. "Laura? Is it really you? You're the last person I expected to pop in! Come in, please. How's Valerie?"

Laura stepped inside the apartment. There were boxes stacked against the walls, mute testimony that Steve was still getting settled.

"Val's doing well," she said, "but I didn't come here to talk about her, or any of my children. I feel terrible about what happened the other day. I was just so tired and distraught, and when I heard the anger in your voice my back went up."

Steve took her light jacket and led her into the living room. The sofa and love seat they'd picked out together were nicely arranged, along with the tables and the lamps.

"It looks good so far," Laura said. "Do you think you're going to like it?"

Steve nodded. He indicated that Laura should take a seat on the sofa, and then he sat down across from her on the love seat.

"I'm sorry for coming on so strong, Laura. It's just that I was concerned about Valerie, about both of you . . . and the baby, and it was like you were telling me I had no right to care."

"I know, but I really didn't mean it that way," Laura said. "I'm afraid that I'm just so anxious to be independent that I saw your concern as a threat. Stupid, isn't it?"

Steve drank in the pleasure of being able to look at Laura's soft, lovely face. For the past two days he'd wondered if he'd ever see her again. He wished he'd bitten his tongue before saying those hurtful words, and yet, he'd meant them then, and they were no less true now. Laura had shut him out. She had made him feel like an interloper.

Hell, he knew he couldn't step in and be a dad to her kids. It was too late for that.

Laura's brood was all grown up, and they'd had a wonderful, loving father. They didn't need a substitute. But even if he couldn't be their dad, couldn't he be their friend?

And what about what he wanted to be to Laura? With her it had to be more than friendship, more than a casual relationship. It was going to have to be all or nothing with Laura, because he was already realizing that mere friendship would never be enough. And it wasn't just that he physically desired her, although there was certainly a strong attraction between them. She felt it too. She'd already admitted it. But she'd also said she wasn't ready to act on those feelings, and he understood that. He was willing to wait, as long as he knew that Laura, his precious treasure, would be waiting at the end of the rainbow.

"What are you thinking?" she asked, as she watched the changing expressions on his face.

"Oh, lots of things. I'm thinking of how I'd like to be friends with your children, and of how I don't want to be friends with you."

"You don't want to be friends?" Laura's spirits took a nosedive.

"No," Steve said, and now he rose from the sofa and stood in front of her. He held out his hands and Laura gave him hers. He pulled her to her feet and looked at her intently. "Not just friends. I'll be your friend, but I also want to be your lover, and maybe even your husband, when you're ready. I don't want us to drift apart again, Laura."

"Steve, I don't know how I feel about that. I'm not sure I . . ."

"Shh," Steve said, touching his index finger to her lower lip. "I don't want an answer now. I just don't want you to write me off."

"I won't. I don't think I could," Laura said. Her breasts were flattened against Steve's chest, and she desperately wished he would stop talking and kiss her. When he started to speak again, she shook her head, then took the initiative and silenced him with her mouth.

Her lips sighed against his as he wrapped his arms around her tightly. All the old sweet hungers broke loose inside Laura. She pressed tighter against Steve's masculine warmth and let her fingers caress the back of his neck. It was easy for a moment to believe that she was eighteen again, easy to remember the way she'd felt when she first surrendered herself to this man.

Steve was in heaven. His mouth tasted Laura's warmth, his lips drank in her sweetness. His hands, pressed hard against her back, held her passionately. Erotic thoughts spun in his brain as he imagined himself carrying her off to his gently undulating waterbed. He imagined himself sinking down into the velvety softness with her, moving sensuously against her, holding her close and tight, and finally, the ecstacy of blending his body with hers.

"Oh, Laura," he moaned. "What you do to me!"

His words broke the spell, and she reluctantly moved away. As much as her body clamored, she wasn't ready to take that final step. But she was moving closer. She knew it, and so did Steve. It was no longer if, it was merely when.

They sat down again, carefully seated across from one another. "I'll have to get back soon," Laura said. "I don't want to leave Valerie for too long."

"She's not alone, is she?" Steve asked, sounding worried. "If she is, maybe . . ."

"Sheila is with her," Laura explained. "That's why I thought it was safe to skip out for a little while. I was getting a little claustrophobic."

"Well, I'm glad you came here," Steve said. "Can I give you a cup of coffee, or a drink? Wine?"

"A glass of wine would be lovely," Laura said, "But I got what I came for. I can go home now and relax, knowing you're not mad at me."

"When will I see you again? Could I bring

dinner for you and Valerie some night this week? It doesn't have to be Chinese. I'll even cook, if you have a barbecue grill."

Laughing, Laura crossed her legs, and settled into a more comfortable position. "Did you ever know a Floridian who didn't?"

"All right, how about steaks and fresh corn tomorrow night? My specialties."

"Why not?" Laura said, shrugging. "If you're cooking, Val and I will be happy to eat. I have a class tomorrow." Her brow knotted with worry. "I'm not sure I should leave Val."

"Is she going to be able to go back to school?" Steve asked, handing Laura a glass of white wine. "It would be a shame if she had to drop out now, with such a short time to go."

Laura sipped the wine, then turned her face up to Steve.

She was worried about her daughter. It was in her lovely gray eyes and in the lines of strain around her mouth. He wished he could lift some of the burden from her shoulders, but he was afraid to make any suggestions. They'd already established that Laura's family business was her own affair. That she didn't want or need any interference.

"We don't know yet," Laura said, in answer to his question. "The doctor wants to see her in a couple of days, and in the meantime she has to stay in bed." Laura finished her wine and stood up. "I'd better go," she said. "I think I'll ask my next-door neighbor to keep an eye on Val while I'm at class tomorrow. And I can call home on my break. I'd really hate to give up my real estate course at this stage."

Steve nodded. Once a parent, always a parent, he thought, and how could it be otherwise? He did believe that children should be taught to be independent, but in a case like this, where a baby's life was at stake, how could a parent not respond with all the love and care necessary? If it were young Steve's wife, he knew he would be just as worried as Laura was. But he worried about Laura. She looked tired and strained. She had apparently just started to put her life back together when all her children and their problems descended on her. It really wasn't fair.

"Tomorrow?" he asked, as he walked Laura to the front door. He held her hand and he was loath to let go. Without her, her warm smile and intelligent eyes, he knew the apartment would be dark and dreary. With her, the sun came out and the air was perfumed with the promise of pleasure.

"Tomorrow," Laura said, giving his hand a squeeze before she released it. "I'll look forward to it."

And that was all. It had to be enough for the moment. Steve smiled into the darkness. Tomorrow was another day, a new beginning, and if he knew anything at all about Laura Cramer Kinsey, she would handle this latest crisis and forge ahead with her own new and exciting plans.

Thirteen

"So, it's been a hectic few days," Laura explained to Isabelle when she got to her class the next morning. She'd arranged for her next-door neighbor, Phyllis, to look in on Val, and she had promised her daughter she'd call at each break.

Val had seemed content to have her go. Laura had left her propped up on the living room sofa, with a small table beside her with a pitcher of ice water, a new novel and a couple of pieces of fruit.

"I'm sorry, Laura," Isabelle said. "Kids sure can turn you gray, can't they? Well, I hope everything works out all right for your daughter, and for you. Life is never dull, is it?"

Laura thought about Isabelle's words as she got out her notes from the last class and sharpened her pencils.

Life certainly wasn't dull, and it was a far cry

from what she'd expected when she was struggling through the maze of grief immediately following Paul's death. Then, it had seemed as though her life was all but over. Oh, she knew her children still cared about her, and there were the grandchildren to love, but her life as a woman, as the nurturer of her little family, was gone. Laura smiled ruefully. Not quite, she thought. It seemed she still had a little nurturing to do, and she was too busy to give up and sit in a rocking chair. There simply wasn't time!

She hardly recognized Sheila when the young woman approached her. "Sheila? Is it really you?"

Touching her softly waved, newly hi-lighted brown hair, Sheila smiled, still shy, but a step closer to confidence. "Do you like it? It's my new look . . . at least part of it. Valerie told me how to do it. She's going to help me with my makeup too."

"You look lovely." Laura said, "Like an up-and-coming realtor. I wouldn't be surprised if you became quite a sensation around here."

Sheila giggled and ducked her head. "I don't know about that, but I already feel different, you know? And it's not just my hair. I think a lot of it is just knowing that people like you and Valerie care about me. That you really want to help me."

"Well, you remind me a lot of Val when she

was your age, and myself too, and I just thought maybe my daughter and I could give you a few tips."

Sheila hesitated, then reached out to hug Laura. "Thank you," she said, "for being so nice. I'll never forget this."

So she'd made a new friend, Laura thought, albeit one young enough to be her daughter. But what did that matter? Where was it written that friends had to be the same? Wasn't variety the spice of life? Another of Paul's beloved old sayings, Laura thought, with a silent groan. They popped into her head at the oddest times. She looked up as the instructor entered the room. At least she hadn't said it out loud!

She called home on her first break, and Val assured her she was feeling fine.

"In fact, I'm sure I'm well enough to go back to school, but . . ." Val paused, and when she continued speaking her tone was worried. "I guess if I do go back to school I'll have to give up my part-time job, and I don't know . . ."

"I've already been thinking about that," Laura said. "We'll work something out. I don't want you to worry, hon. It's not good for you or the baby."

"Okay. I'll be good. Hey, have you seen Sheila today? Did she fix her hair the way I told her?"

"She did and she looks wonderful. You girls must have had fun while I was out last night."

Valerie giggled. "Not as much as you probably had. How does Steve's apartment look?"

"I . . . how on earth did you know that's . . ."

The giggle got louder. "Come on, Mom, I don't need a crystal ball to see what's going on right under my nose. My mother's got herself a beau, and a very nice one at that. It's okay, you know. I like Steve. I think he'll be good for you."

"Well, I'm glad I have your approval, although I'm not sure exactly what it is you're approving of. Steve and I are just . . ."

"I know. You're just friends. Tell it to the birds in the back yard, Mom. I wasn't born yesterday, you know! Anyway, I'm looking forward to that steak he's going to cook for us tonight. How about you?"

"I'm looking forward to the day you give birth to that baby you're carrying so I can take you over my knee and give you the thrashing you deserve for being so fresh. Have you no respect for your elders?"

"Sure, but where are they?" Val asked teasingly, "All I see around the house these days is a sexy lady and a handsome hunk giving each other the eye."

"Valerie Kinsey, you are an impossible brat, and if you weren't already confined to bed, I'd ground you!"

Val laughed. "Too late, Mom. My little baby son or daughter already did that!"

"Everything okay on the homefront?" It was George Ryan, and he looked genuinely concerned as he walked up to Laura at the soft drink machine. "Isabelle told me about your daughter. I hope everything is all right."

"Thanks," Laura said, putting two quarters in the machine and selecting a diet soda. "I think Val is going to be okay, and the baby as well, but it gave me quite a scare."

George nodded. "I know the feeling. It's funny, but after my divorce, when I realized that the kids were all grown up, I thought my job as a daddy was done, but I soon discovered differently. It seems like there's always one crisis or another, and 'dear old Dad' is the only one who can help."

"Don't even think of putting the make on her, old man," Isabelle warned, coming up behind them. "You'll have to watch this guy, Laura. He thinks all widows are fair game."

"Don't listen to her. She's got the hots for me! She tries to scare away all other interested women!"

Isabelle guffawed loudly. "Now I have heard everything," she said. "George Ryan, you are something else. I just haven't figured out what!"

"Actually, I think you're cute, George," Laura said, joining in with a broad smile. This was what she needed, what she would have missed if she'd stayed at home, tending her flowers and

living on memories. This playful exchange between new friends. Suddenly, Laura thought of
her sister-in-law, Blanche. Maybe this was what
Blanche needed, something to get her out of the
house and away from thoughts of the past and
dreary predictions of the future. She was almost
sorry she'd spoken the way she had to Blanche,
but she really had deserved a tongue-lashing for
what she said about Val and the baby. Probably,
Blanche was hurting, just as Laura was for the
bitter exchange. Soon, when everything got
straightened out at home, Laura would pay
Blanche a little visit. After all, she was Paul's sister and the children's aunt. It wouldn't hurt to
try.

When the class was over, Laura said good-bye
to everyone and hurried to her car. She was anxious to get home now and see how Val was doing, not to mention the fact that Steve was
coming over and she wanted time to shower and
change before he arrived.

As she drove, Laura hummed to herself, a
peppy show tune she'd always loved. She hadn't
scurried around this way for years, she realized.
During the last months of Paul's life she'd done
everything she could to keep things as quiet and
peaceful as possible. She'd carefully constructed
a gentle cocoon around her husband to keep him
safe and content. There were no loud noises in
the house, no angry words or sudden moves.

She'd isolated and insulated their life so Paul could drift gently into the next world.

Now, everything was happening at once. She had to hurry to school and home again. She had Val to look after and worry about, and Vicki's move and Greg's malpractice suit to think of. And then, Steve. At the hub of it all was Steve. Patiently waiting for her to get it all together, to settle her grown-up kids and make room for him in her life. But how long would he be patient, Laura wondered? Would he get tired of hanging on the sidelines and demand to be allowed inside? And what if she simply couldn't do that? She wasn't at all sure she could, despite the way his kisses made her feel, and despite all the memories.

Before she went into the house, Laura took a moment to look around. Her small lawn and her flower beds were not quite as neat and well trimmed as they'd once been. She'd have to get her neighbor's son over to mow the lawn and do some yard work. In the past she'd done it all herself, but now there was simply no time, and when Val moved in to wait for the baby's birth, there'd be even less time. There would be lots to do to prepare for the baby's birth. Laura's lips softened into a smile as she bent and plucked a dead blossom from one of her plants. A baby was a miracle, no matter what, and despite how much she had always loved puttering in her yard, she would enjoy spending time with her daughter even more. And besides, she rationalized, young Tim could use the money he earned doing yard work. He was saving to buy his first car.

"Hi. I'm home," Laura yelled as she opened the front door.

"And I'm right where you left me, Mom. I've been as good as gold all day, and Buttons will swear to it."

Laura found her daughter contentedly watching a soap opera with Buttons cozily ensconced at her side.

"So, you've transferred your allegiance, have you?" she asked the little white dog. "What about me? Am I the forgotten mistress?"

Buttons opened his shoebutton eyes a sliver, peered up at Laura, then settled back into a sleepy ball of fluff.

"Traitor!" Laura said. Then she looked sternly at her daughter. "Is this the thanks I get for taking care of you? You alienate my dog's affections? Don't you realize he always greets me at the door?"

Val smiled sweetly. "He knows I'm pregnant," she said, "and he's protecting the baby. See how he's cuddled up to my stomach?"

"Oh, honey!" Laura went to her knees beside the sofa, and held her daughter tight in her arms. "The baby's not going to need protection.

You'll see. He's going to be strong and bright and beautiful. Everything a baby should be!"

"I want to believe that, Mom, but I've been so scared," Val confessed, her tears dampening Laura's blouse. "I even thought maybe I was being punished for . . . moving in with Robert and letting myself get pregnant."

"That's not the way it works, sweetie. You had a little scare, but I know that's all it was. Lots of women have strange things happen during their pregnancies, and most of them go on to have perfect, healthy babies."

Val looked at Laura with tear filled eyes. "But what about the ones who don't, Mom?"

Laura sat with Valerie for half an hour, assuring her that the worst was over, and her baby was going to be fine. Then, when she was convinced that Val was content, she rushed upstairs to shower and change her clothes. Valerie was due to see the doctor tomorrow, and he'd said he might have to run some tests to see what was going on. Then, if everything checked out, he might allow Val to go back to school. At that, she would have to promise to do her schoolwork and nothing more. No part-time job, no strenuous extracurricular activities.

Thank God, her insurance was going to cover Val's prenatal care and the baby's delivery. She'd called her insurance agent and discovered that they were covered. At least that was one thing they wouldn't have to worry about. As she stood under the stinging shower spray, Laura found herself wondering if Vicki would mind contributing some of the children's outgrown baby clothes. It wasn't as though she'd be using them again, because during her estrangement from Tim, Vicki had confided that after Bobby's birth, she'd had her tubes tied. She'd given Tim a son, as well as two beautiful daughters, and she had declared herself officially out of the baby business.

It was just as well in this society, Laura thought, stepping out of the shower and wrapping herself in a thick, apple green terry towel. Raising children was expensive, not to mention emotionally draining at times. Three was plenty. She didn't blame Vicki for feeling her family was complete.

And she still didn't know about Valerie. Several times they'd started to call her and tell her the news, but something always held them back. Not that she thought Vicki would be nasty about it. She and Val had always been close, and Laura was sure Vicki would be more than willing to lend whatever support she could. Maybe it was just that it was one more family thing Vicki wouldn't be a part of. She'd be settled in Indianapolis by the time the baby came, and Laura doubted she'd be able to fly home so soon after relocating.

Things were pretty stable in Vicki's household these days, and Laura hated to stir anything up. She wasn't sure she could cope if Vicki decided not to go with Tim at the last minute and came trooping home, with all three tots in tow.

"Think nice thoughts, Laura," she told herself. "Steve is cooking you a steak on the grill, there's wine chilling in the refrigerator, and Val and the baby are hanging in there. What more could you ask for?"

By the time she got back downstairs Steve had arrived. He was sitting across from Val chatting.

"Hello," he said, his dark eyes roving approvingly. "Nice outfit."

"Oh, this is old and comfortable, but I'm glad you like it."

She'd picked the soft green lounging outfit because the color went well with her hair, and like any normal female, she wanted to look nice for her man.

But was Steve her man? Would he ever be, or was their relationship going to die a slow death while family problems steadily separated them?

"Valerie has been looking forward to your cooking, Steve," she said, to cover her sudden confusion. "What can I do to help?"

Steve stood up and laughed. "Get out some plates and silverware, and how about some iced tea? It feels like summer today."

"I wish I could help," Val said wistfully. "I'm

awfully tired of lying on this sofa."

"Well, tomorrow you go back to the doctor and I'm betting he gives you a clean bill of health, but until then I want you to stay right where you are. I'll set up a card table in here so we can all eat, together."

"Fair enough," Val said. "Thanks, Mom. You're being very good to me. I do appreciate it."

An hour later they settled down to eat. One bite convinced Laura that the steaks were done to perfection. There was corn on the cob to go with it, and baked potatoes with sour cream and chives. And Laura had caught a glimpse of Steve stashing her favorite praline ice cream in the freezer.

"This could be habit-forming," she said, laughing as Val chewed a piece of steak and rolled her eyes in ecstasy. "You may find yourself cooking for us seven days a week."

Steve grinned and shrugged. "No problem. My barbecued chicken is pretty good, and I can make omelets too. As long as you don't mind alternating between those three things . . ."

The two women exchanged amused glances, and once again Steve was struck by the resemblance. Valerie was simply a younger, slightly thinner version of her mother. She had the same gray eyes, the same shiny auburn hair, the same warm smile.

"You two really could pass for sisters," he said.

"Not in a couple of months," Val cried. "I'll be out to here by then, and Mom will still be slim and trim. Boy, I hope I look as good as you when I'm old," she said, smiling at Laura.

Laura twisted her face, then looked at Steve and shrugged.

But there was a mischievous glint in her eye, and Steve had a pretty good idea what she was thinking. He smothered a chuckle of his own. If Valerie only knew!

Chronologically, he and Laura were classed as middle-aged, or, if you were inclined to be gentle, "in the prime of life," but any way you sliced it, most people thought they were old, especially youngsters like Valerie and Sheila. He'd bet a week's worth of auto rentals that neither young woman could imagine him or Laura being consumed by a fiery passion, and yet that was exactly what did happen whenever he and Laura were alone. Steve could count on one hand the times he and Laura had been completely alone. Last night had been one of them, and he had been more than a little surprised and pleased when she showed up at his door.

She caught Steve feeding Buttons scraps of meat under the table, and she finally had to warn him that if he did it one more time she'd make him do the dishes.

But by the time Laura was ready to clean up

the kitchen, Valerie had fallen asleep, with Buttons once again curled protectively against her stomach. She motioned for Steve to follow her out to the kitchen, and she started a pot of coffee.

"I'm glad she's sleeping," she said. "She needs all the rest she can get. I'm anxious to see what the doctor says tomorrow."

"Laura, I don't want to pry, and I promised myself I'd mind my own business, but I can't help worrying. Are you going to be able to manage financially? Because I can help if you'll let me. I know how draining medical expenses can be, and since the baby's father isn't going to contribute . . ."

"You're sweet and I thank you, Steve, but everything is under control, really. My medical insurance covers Valerie until she graduates, and it does have a clause for prenatal care."

"That's a relief," Steve said. He sat on a stool at the kitchen counter while Laura measured coffee into the pot. Her kitchen was nice, he decided. It had a warm, cozy feeling.

"Did your husband design this kitchen?" he asked.

"No. I did. I must have made a hundred sketches until I came up with what I wanted, but I've always felt that the kitchen is the heart of a home. I spend a lot of time in my kitchen." She laughed. "At least I used to. Now that I'm a student again I'm looking for quick and easy ways to fix a meal."

"Nothing wrong with that. I'm sure you've got plenty of hours behind the stove." He accepted the coffee Laura poured him, and stirred milk into the cup. "Marcie loved to cook. It seemed as though she was always trying out some new, exotic recipe. Like I said before, some of them were great, but we also had some disasters. That's how I learned to cook. Every once in a while I used to force her to take a night off. I'd grill steaks or barbecue chicken." He laughed. "Marcie didn't think much of my culinary talents."

"Well, I thought the steak was fantastic, and the potato was superb."

"And you say it with a straight face," Steve said, shaking his head in amazement. Suddenly he sobered. "What do you really think, Laura? Is your daughter going to be okay? She's not going to lose her baby, is she?"

All the pleasure of the evening went away as Laura thought about what the next day would bring. "I haven't let myself think that she will," she admitted. "I think it would almost kill her, Steve. She's putting up a brave front, but Robert's betrayal has hurt her deeply, and if she loses the baby too, I'm not sure she'll be able to handle it."

"Then we'll keep believing that she won't,"

Steve said firmly.

Somehow, and she never knew exactly how it happened, Laura found herself in Steve's arms, her head against his chest, his arms holding her safe and tight.

"Go ahead, let go," he urged her gently. "You deserve a good cry. It's all right."

He knew she wanted to cry, sensed that she needed the release, but she was holding herself under rigid control. She was keeping all her fears and uncertainties inside, and if she wasn't careful one of these days she would explode.

"I'm all right," she mumbled, struggling to regain her equilibrium.

But she wasn't, and they both knew it. She was hanging on by a thin thread. One snap and she'd be gone. She'd fall down into a deep, dark well of despair. He wanted so badly to help her, but she wouldn't allow it.

"Laura, please let me help you."

She shook her head, and then, unexpectedly she lifted her face to him, offering her lips. "Just hold me and kiss me," she whispered. "I don't want to talk."

Steve hesitated only a moment before his lips descended to hers, before he let his arms tighten around her possessively. She felt small and fragile, as though she truly were in need of his protection, but he knew if he said that she would shy away like a frightened bird. So he pushed his instincts deep down inside and just let himself feel the glory of holding Laura in his arms. His Laura. She had always been his, even through the long years they'd been separated. He'd never forgotten her. He never would, and somehow he'd make her understand that she could love and let herself be loved without sacrificing all of her independence.

Laura wallowed in the honeyed touch of Steve's lips. He was strong, yet gentle, his touch firm, yet nonthreatening. He represented love, warmth and a wonderful, sweet feeling of security.

When they separated there was a terrible feeling of loss, a disappointment so strong Laura wanted to weep. She was starting to trust this man again, learning to lean on him for comfort and protection. It scared her. For the first time in her life she was independent. She was accountable to no one. She was frightened that it would all change if she allowed herself to need Steve. And then, with the suddenness of a wild windstorm, she realized that was now her greatest challenge, to figure out how to love Steve without surrendering her freedom. Because she did want to love him. Oh, how she wanted to love him!

Fourteen

The doctor's visit went well. Valerie and Laura spent most of the morning at the hospital while the doctor ran various tests to try and determine the status of Val's pregnancy. While there were no ironclad guarantees, the final verdict was that Val could safely finish her last semester as long as she was careful not to overdo.

Both women were euphoric as they left the hospital.

"Thank heavens!" Laura said. "Aside from the fact that you'll be able to get your degree on time, I wasn't looking forward to having you on bed rest for the next few months. I'm sure we would both be climbing the walls long before the baby arrived."

Val laughed.

Laura thought that her daughter's color was good, and that she looked vastly relieved. She put her arms around Val's shoulders and squeezed. "Everything is going to work out all right, honey," she said, "and someday you'll look back on this and laugh."

"Is that one of Daddy's pearls of wisdom?" Val asked, wrinkling her nose and rolling her eyes.

"He had a few, didn't he?" Laura smiled. It was good to start remembering the happy times, to be able to think of Paul with fondness instead of that awful, raw pain.

"Mom?" Val looked a little embarrassed, and somehow Laura sensed what was coming.

"What, hon? What is it?"

"I was just wondering. I know you really like Steve, and I think that's great. I like him too. But . . . well, the way you feel about him . . . it doesn't take away from what you had with Daddy, does it?"

Laura felt the tears sting her eyelids. "Oh honey, of course not! I do care for Steve, but I had a wonderful, happy life with your father, and I wouldn't trade those years for anything. No matter what happens from now on, I will always honor and cherish my memories of your daddy."

"Oh Mom! Thank you! I needed to hear that! In my heart I knew that's what you would say, but I still needed to hear you say the words. Now I can go back to school and just concentrate on graduating with decent grades."

Laura smiled as she slid behind the wheel of the car. "Before we go home, there's one stop I think we should make. We have to tell Vicki what's going on. She's going to be hurt that we kept things from her this long, but you can't go back to school without talking to her."

Val nodded. "I know, but after all the trouble she and Tim just went through, I was afraid of adding fuel to the fire, you know? Vicki has always wanted to be right smack in the middle of everything, and now she'll be long gone before my baby is born."

"Yes, I know," Laura said, nodding, "and that's going to hurt her. She does seem to need to stay close to her family."

Telling Vicki was actually easier than Laura had anticipated. At first she was angry and hurt that she hadn't been told about what was going on right from the start.

"I feel like I'm not even a member of this family," she complained. "All kinds of things happen, and no one even lets me know!"

Val was sitting on the floor playing with Bobby. She looked radiant, and Laura was reminded of what a good little mother she would be.

"Honey, after what you just went through, Val and I didn't want to upset you. Look at this,"

Laura said, spreading her arms wide to encompass the room that was filled with boxes, some filled and securely taped shut, others only partially filled. "Now that Val's going back to school, I'd like to come over and help you pack."

"Sure," Vicki said absently. "That would be great. But let's not talk about that now." She turned to her younger sister, and her face was anxious. "Are you really okay, Val? You're not just saying that to keep me from worrying? Because I'm not going to fall apart, you know." She glanced at her mother and grinned. "I'm getting counseling, Mom, just like you suggested, and I'm learning a few things about myself. I'm going to be okay."

For the second time that day Laura's eyes filled with tears. "Oh, honey, I'm so proud of you. It takes courage to admit that you need a little help. Now I know you're going to make it, and your marriage too."

Vicki smiled, but she wasn't ready to let her sister off the hook. "Well, I think what that creep did to you was lousy, and I hope he gets his, but what about you, Sis? How are you going to handle this? Babies are great, but it's not easy, even when you have someone to help you."

Val nodded. She stood up and went to her sister. "I know. Mom and I have already discussed all that. I wish my baby could have a great daddy like your kids have, but I guess it just

275

wasn't meant to be that way, so I'll just work extra hard to be the best mom around."

"I won't be here to be your Lamaze coach," Vicki said regretfully, "so I suppose Mom will have to do it. What I will do is sort through all the infant clothes that have been languishing in the attic. I'll wash them all and give them to Mom before I leave. How's that?"

Laura was stunned. Was this really her emotional, never-want-to-let-go daughter? Vicki was calmly accepting the fact that she couldn't be a part of her sister's big moment.

"Well!" she said. "I don't know who is counseling you, hon, but he or she is doing one hell of a job!"

Vicki hugged her little sister and turned to her mom. "I'm growing up, Mom," she said, arching her eyebrows and grinning. "It happens to the best of us!"

"Boy, that was really a surprise!" Val exclaimed when they were back in the car. "I thought we were in for a major scene. Didn't you?"

"Absolutely," Laura said. "Whatever your sister is doing, I hope she continues. Tim must be thrilled."

Val nodded. "Good old Tim. Are you sure he doesn't have a brother tucked away somewhere?"

Laura laughed and started the car. "Don't I wish! No, I'm afraid there's only one Tim. I'm just glad Vicki woke up and realized what she had. For a while there I was afraid the marriage was going down the tube."

"Well, at least one of your children is happily settled. Now if Greg could just get that stupid malpractice thing straightened out."

With that thought both women fell silent. Valerie looked out the window and Laura kept both eyes on the road.

She was beginning to realize that life never kept a straight course for long. Every time you thought things were just about the way you wanted them, something would happen to shake you up. And maybe that was good.

Maybe, Laura thought ruefully, but right now a little peace would be very welcome.

She dropped Val off at home and promised to be back in time for a late-afternoon cup of tea. "There's something I need to take care of."

As she drove the short distance to her sister-in-law's house, Laura found herself thinking back over the years, remembering all the times Blanche had irritated her, all the times Laura made excuses to avoid spending time with her. Back then, she'd thought she was justified. Blanche was a depressing person to be around. In her mind, things were always a hundred times worse then they really were. And when there was no trouble on the horizon, Blanche could usually manage to invent some. But was she really a nasty person, or just terribly lonely and unhappy? Both of her children were so far away, her son all the way out on the West Coast, and her only daughter working overseas with the Peace Corps. It wasn't that Laura didn't respect what Patty was doing, but she knew Blanche must miss seeing and spending time with her daughter. And Jim, Jr. hardly ever came home. Laura suspected it was because his mother depressed him too, but how terrible if Blanche had pushed her children away and wasn't even aware of it.

As Laura parked her car in front of the modest frame home where Blanche had spent her whole married life, she was determined to give it her best shot. She'd hold her temper and try to remember that maybe Blanche's apparent cruelty stemmed from her unhappiness. And she'd try to remember that she was Paul's only sister.

"What do you want?" Blanche asked coldly, when she opened the door and saw Laura. "You hung up on me the other day. Why are you here now?"

Blanche's face was puffy, and it was plain that she'd been crying. Laura's irritation melted.

"Blanche, I'm sorry about what happened the other day. That's why I'm here. I was hoping we could talk."

"What about? I guess now that Paul's gone you figure you don't have to be nice to me anymore." Blanche was determined to keep her defenses up, but she stepped back so Laura could enter the house.

Laura moved into the living room and sat down. "You hurt me very much by what you said the other day, Blanche. I'd like to think you didn't really mean it. Yes, Valerie is going to be an unwed mother, and it's not what I would have chosen for her, but what you and I both have to remember is that things aren't like they were when you and I were girls. In those days it was a terrible disgrace for an unmarried woman to have a child, but now no one seems to care. Many young women are making a conscious decision to be single mothers."

"Well, it's not right," Blanche mumbled, not meeting Laura's eyes.

"Maybe not, but if we're going to live in this world we have to move with the times, Blanche. Valerie will graduate from college in a few months. She's already had offers for several good positions. She'll be able to support herself and her child. There was just no other option for her than to keep her baby. She doesn't believe in abortion, and she couldn't handle giving the child up for adoption. Actually, I'm proud of her for standing up for what she thinks is right."

"But what about the baby's father? Oh dear, it's not one of those situations where . . ."

Laura's temper, so tightly reined in, started to rise. She swallowed, counted to ten and held up her hand. "Don't say it, Blanche, and don't even think it. Valerie was engaged to the father of her baby. They were planning to be married after graduation, but he doesn't want a baby now. He told Val it would be too inconvenient."

"What? Why, how terrible for poor Valerie! Oh, that poor, poor child!"

"She doesn't think of herself that way. She's just grateful she didn't lose the baby, and all she wants now is to complete her studies and get her degree. After graduation she'll be coming home to stay until the baby is born. I was hoping, well, I thought maybe you would want to be a part of the big event. After all, it will be Paul's grandchild."

Now the tears flowed freely down Blanche's face. "Oh dear . . . oh, what a silly fool I am! How could I have said those terrible things to you? Of course I didn't really think it was better for Valerie to lose the baby, but I just couldn't think how she was going to manage. I should have known. With a mother like you . . ."

Laura managed a smile. "I didn't believe you when you said that children always need their mothers, but lately I've found out it's true. What do you say, Blanche? Can Val and I count on your help and support? You know how helpless I am at sewing, and I was wondering about that old bassinet I have in the attic . . ."

"Oh my goodness, I'll fix it up so beautifully

280

Val will think it's a designer original! But what color should it be, pink or blue? Oh, I'll have to get Jim to clean and oil my sewing machine. I haven't done any sewing in ages!"

"Blanche, if you'll fix that bassinet, Valerie will be thrilled, and what about a soft, pretty yellow? That would be good for either a boy or a girl."

"Yellow? Well, of course. That's perfect. Oh, this is so exciting, a new little life . . . maybe Valerie will want me to babysit once in a while."

Blanche's excitement finally ebbed, and a look of longing came over her face. "I used to dream about the day Patty would have a baby," she said, "but I don't think that's ever going to happen. She's just so involved in her work. Of course I'm proud of her, but it would have been nice to be a grandma."

"Well, maybe Jim, Jr. will get married one of these days. He's still young enough."

"He might," Blanche said, "But that wouldn't do me much good. All the way out there in California . . . when would I ever see the child?"

Laura stood up and patted Blanche's arm. "It's difficult when your children grow up and move away. Blanche, what would you think about taking a class at the local college? Or maybe just starting a new hobby? What about your sewing? You just said you haven't sewn in ages, and you do such beautiful work. I'll bet you could have a little home business, if you wanted."

Blanche smiled through her tears. "I don't know. I can't imagine anyone actually paying me for my sewing." She hesitated. "Can you?"

"Yes, I can. Why don't you give it some thought? If you feel like talking about it, give me a call. I don't know much about sewing, but I'll give you my honest opinion."

"Well, maybe I will," Blanche said. "But in the meantime, you get that bassinet down from the attic so I can start working on it, you hear?"

"Right away," Laura said. Then, on impulse, she hugged Blanche.

Her sister-in-law looked startled, then pleased. Her plain face flushed. "Well, my goodness, what was that for?"

"It was to celebrate a new beginning," Laura said, "for you and me."

Valerie listened, wide-eyed, her mouth hanging open in amazement as Laura related her visit to Blanche.

"I could kick myself for not realizing it before," Laura said. "She's lonely, Val, and bored. So she dwells on the past and minds everyone else's business. She's so unhappy with herself that it spills over in bitterness to others. You should have seen her face when I mentioned my old bassinet. I'll bet it will be a work of art." Laura smiled. "And more importantly, a labor of love."

"Mom, you continue to amaze me. Aunt Blanche smiling? I guess I'll have to see it to believe it."

Laura laughed. "Don't knock it. She's looking forward to babysitting for you."

After a simple dinner, Laura helped Val pack. There wasn't much to do because Valerie had only brought enough clothing for a few days. She'd never intended a prolonged stay.

"Now remember what the doctor said," Laura reminded Val, as she handed her a check for spending money for the upcoming month. "Avoid stress whenever possible." Her eyes narrowed. "I think you should stay away from Robert, honey. Arguing with him wouldn't be good for you or the baby."

"Don't worry, Mom. If I never lay eyes on that man again, it will be too soon. Any man who could say the things he did, and think of his own child as an inconvenience . . . well, I don't want any part of him."

"Good for you, hon. And remember, if you need me, I'm only a phone call away."

"I know," Valerie said, putting her arms around Laura and giving her a hug. "You've always been here for me, Mom. I knew you wouldn't let me down this time."

They spent a quiet evening, talking about the baby and Valerie's plans for the future. Her daughter laughed at Laura's dreams of becoming a top-selling realtor someday.

"I have no doubt you'll do it, Mom, if you really want to, but I've got one question. Where does Steve fit in?"

Laura sobered. After weeks of thinking of her children and their problems, and pushing her relationship with Steve to the back of her mind, she suddenly realized she was rapidly running out of excuses. Once Val was gone, Steve would expect a larger share of her time. Was she prepared to give it to him?

"I wish you hadn't asked that, honey, because I'm still trying to figure things out. You already know that I care for Steve. In a way a part of me always has. I never really forgot him. And there is a . . . strong physical attraction between us."

Valerie laughed at Laura's flushed cheeks and averted eyes.

"Mom, I think this is even worse than when you tried to tell me about the birds and the bees, but don't worry, I get the picture. You want to jump his bones, right?"

"Brat," Laura snapped. "Why do I even try to talk to you?"

"Because you love me, and you know I love you, and I just want to see you be happy. You deserve someone nice in your life. Not to mention that you have great legs for an old broad, and it would be a shame to see them go to waste!"

Laura closed her eyes and counted to forty. Ten or twenty definitely wouldn't do it.

"You are a shameless little hussy, and I should wash out your mouth. Okay, you're right. I do want to . . . uh . . . Steve is a nice looking man. Any woman would . . ."

"Say it, Mom," Valerie taunted. "You lust after his body. I can see it in your eyes. It burns hot and bright and . . ."

"Oh my God! I knew those hours in front of the boob tube watching soap operas would turn your brain to mush!"

"And I read steamy romance novels in my spare time," Val said cheekily. "Anyway, for what it's worth, you have my blessing. If you decide to marry the guy, great. If not, that's fine too. This is the nineties, Mom. You've got to get with it."

Laura nodded. What could she say? Marriage to Steve was a possibility. He'd already said that was what he wanted. The problem was, Laura wasn't sure what she wanted. If she were younger, there would have been no question, but now it was like a whole new life was opening up for her. There were different paths she could take. Being a wife carried certain responsibilities and duties, and Laura simply didn't know if she was prepared to swap her freedom for that. It was nice to be able to eat when she pleased, go to bed when it suited her, and have the whole Sunday paper to herself. Little things, but did she really want to give them all up?

When the two women finally went to bed, Laura's future was still undecided. Maybe she would marry Steve, and maybe she wouldn't. Maybe he would be content with a loving relationship without benefit of matrimony, and maybe he wouldn't. Maybe they would part the way they had thirty-odd years earlier. Laura sighed and snuggled under her light blanket. It would all work out in time, one way or the other.

She stood at the window the next morning and waved as Valerie backed out of the drive and headed back to school. If all went well, she'd be back in three months, and then they'd settle in to wait for the baby's arrival. It was amazing, but even though she already had three lovely grandchildren, Laura was starting to get excited about the latest little bundle.

There was something about babies that softened even the meanest of temperaments. Blanche was a perfect example. She'd turned from a hissing, spitting feline into a purring kitten right before Laura's eyes. This might even be the trigger that turned Blanche's life around.

Since she had no class that day, Laura decided to take care of some chores around the house and cook a really nice dinner. And she'd invite Steve to come over. She felt like celebrating!

But when she called the auto rental agency, she learned he wasn't there. "Is this Laura?" a strange voice asked.

"Yes, it is. Is something wrong? Steve isn't sick, is he?"

"No, he's fine. It's his boy. Had some kind of accident, and he's in the hospital in Arizona. I think it's pretty serious."

"Oh. I didn't know. When did this happen?" Laura had the oddest feeling, like she was all empty inside. Why hadn't Steve called her?

"Sometime yesterday morning, I think," the voice answered. "Is there any message you want me to give him when he calls? I'm expecting to hear from him any time now."

"I . . . no, that's all right. I'll see him when he gets back."

"That might not be for a while. If young Steve is really bad, I imagine he'll stay a while."

"Of course. Well, you can tell him I called then, and tell him I'll say a prayer for his son."

"I'll do that. Bye now."

Laura slowly replaced the receiver, feeling dazed. She ached for Steve, because she understood the fear and helplessness he would experience when he realized there was nothing he could do but stand by and wait. But worst of all, was the fact that he hadn't even bothered to let her know what was happening in his life. Why? Was he punishing her for not calling him when Val was sick? But that was a different situation, wasn't it? Or was it? If she didn't want to involve Steve in her personal affairs, why should he feel any differently?

You reap what you sow, Laura, my girl, she told herself, dredging up yet another of Paul's beloved little sayings. But it wasn't funny.

Fifteen

"What's the matter, Laura?" George Ryan asked the next morning when she went to her class. "You look a little down."

She forced a smile. She liked George and Isabelle, but she really didn't want to discuss the situation with Steve with either of them. "I'm all right," she said. "It's just a little letdown, I guess. It's amazing how quiet the house is all of a sudden. I have to get used to it all over again. Even my little dog misses Val."

George handed Laura a steaming cup of coffee. "Have some java," he said. "That always perks me up."

"Thanks," Laura smiled. She'd drink the coffee, but she doubted it would make her feel any better. She couldn't stop thinking of Steve, couldn't stop worrying about how he was feeling, what he was thinking. At times like this people needed friends, they needed to know that others cared. And she didn't even know what hospital young Steve was at. She didn't even know how to contact Steve. But she could find out if she really wanted to, she knew. All she had to do was call Steve's cousin and ask.

And that was part of the problem. She wasn't sure she wanted to know. She wasn't sure she wanted to take that step and involve herself in Steve's private life.

Yet, if she didn't, would he think she didn't care? Of course he would, just as he'd been hurt and disappointed when she failed to tell him of Valerie's illness.

Steve wanted intimacy. He seemed to want to share his life with her.

It was a problem, Laura knew, and not one that could be easily resolved. She was going to have to think the matter over very carefully. This was her life she was tampering with, and Steve's life as well. They had both been married, and had raised children. They'd been happy, and they'd known the pain of loss. Now, at midlife, they didn't need any more loss. They needed sunshine and laughter. At least a small measure of contentment as a reward for a life well lived. That wasn't too much to ask, was it?

But maybe they each had different measures for contentment. Maybe what would bring Laura happiness, would not work for Steve.

"Hey, Laura, are you with us?"

Isabelle's voice brought Laura back to earth with a thump. First things first, she told herself. Right now she needed to pay attention unless she wanted to fall behind in her work.

She saw Sheila briefly after class was over.

"Yes, Val went back to school," she said in answer to the young woman's questions. "She only has about three months left and then she'll come back to wait for the baby's birth. I have her address at school if you'd like to write to her. I know she'd enjoy hearing from you." Laura smiled. "I think she's secretly wondering who will get the highest grade, you or me. I don't know how much faith she has in her old mom."

"Well, you're not old at all, and I wouldn't be surprised if you leave me by the side of the road," Sheila said. "Really, all I care about is getting my license. I think I'm going to like selling houses. Did you know I'm taking a class at the college on assertiveness?"

Laura's jaw dropped. "Really? When did you decide on that?"

"After my new hairdo," Sheila said proudly. "I feel so much better about myself I decided it was time to try and learn to stand up and be

291

counted. I can't be shy if I'm going to be a successful realtor, can I?"

"Wonders will never cease," Laura muttered as Sheila happily waltzed away. She wondered for a moment if she'd created a monster, but then she decided that all the changes in Sheila were for the better.

Reluctant to go home to her empty house, Laura accepted Isabelle's invitation to go shopping for some new clothes. After all, it was spring, Isabelle reminded Laura, and there was nothing better than a little shopping spree to perk up a woman's spirits.

They went to a nearby mall and had a wonderful time wandering in and out of the various stores, but in the end they bought only a couple of things. Laura found she simply could not resist a lovely jade silk blouse, and Isabelle fell in love with a bright red sequined shell, that she said would be perfect for a party she was giving.

When they began to get tired, Laura suggested they grab a bite to eat at one of the mall restaurants. She was embarrassed to admit it, but she was addicted to junk food. She loved nothing better than a fat, juicy burger smothered in fried onions and melted cheese, and slathered with catsup.

"Laura, you can't eat like this all the time," Isabelle complained, eyeing Laura's plate with longing. "If you did you'd weigh three hundred pounds."

Laura laughed just before she took the first scrumptious bite. She chewed for a moment, swallowed and grinned sheepishly. "I only do this on rare occasions. I decided today was a day to treat myself."

"You miss your kid that much?" Isabelle asked, moving pieces of her fruit salad around without enthusiasm.

Laura flipped her friend a few sinfully greasy fries, and smiled as Isabelle ate them with obvious enjoyment.

"The house does seem awfully quiet after having Val around, but it's not just that." Earlier she hadn't wanted to talk about it, but now she felt differently. "Steve's son had an accident in Arizona. He went back to be with him, and he never even called and told me."

"Oh. I see how that could rock your cradle. Do you have any idea why he didn't let you know?"

Laura nodded. "That's just it. I know exactly why and I have very ambivalent thoughts. You see, I did the same thing to him the night Val nearly miscarried. I bundled her off to the emergency room and never called him. Actually, I didn't call anyone, not even Valerie's sister. I guess I just thought I could handle it on my own."

"Sure. I can understand that, but I guess Steve felt left out, huh?"

"Exactly," Laura said, nodding. "He said I was shutting him out of my life. Oh, we patched things up a few days later, or at least I thought we did, but now I'm not so sure."

"Would you really want Steve to include you in his family situation?" Isabelle asked. "I mean, once you start doing that kind of stuff, can wedding bells be far behind?"

"I don't know," Laura said, shaking her head helplessly. "That's the crux of the whole problem. I simply don't know. I don't know what I want from him. I don't know how I want to live the rest of my life. Am I crazy?"

"No. I think it's more that you're finding yourself after years of being lost. You know what I mean, Laura. When our children were small, we started to think of ourselves as Susie's mama, and Harry's wife. In a sense we lost our identities. Maybe that's not so terrible, but now it's as though we're finally able to see ourselves as women again, as individuals. We can find out what we like and don't like. I think a lot of men are threatened by that attitude."

"Steve is, I think," Laura said. "It's as if he feels that my wanting to be independent means I don't care about him."

"Well, it's not an easy situation," Isabelle said, beginning to gather up her things, "but what the heck, what's life without a challenge, right?"

"Right," Laura said, and she stood up too. Buttons would be waiting. There was no Val to cuddle up to now, and he would be hungry for human companionship. She smiled to herself. The house wasn't really empty. She had Buttons, and her memories, and her hopes for the future.

But when the phone rang at ten-thirty that evening, she jumped to answer it, hoping it was Steve. Her elation melted into disappointment, then leveled out as she recognized her son's voice.

"Greg! How are you? I was thinking of you earlier. How's everything going for you?" She was loath to mention the word malpractice, because it was so unfair. It suggested carelessness, at the very least, and she knew her son would never be careless in his concern for a patient.

"That's what I called to tell you, Mom," Greg said, sounding pleased. "Allison hasn't retracted her story yet, but she has agreed to see a therapist. I'm hoping she'll realize what she's doing and tell the truth. That's really my only hope. If it goes to court, it's her word against mine, and if I happen to get a judge who's heavy on the sexual harassment thing, I could be in big trouble."

"I'm sure it isn't going to come to that, son,"

Laura said. "It just can't. It wouldn't be fair."

"Well, my fingers are crossed," Greg replied. "Anyway, how is Val doing? Did she go back to school?"

"Yes. She left yesterday and she was feeling fine."

"What a bummer," Greg said. "That jerk leaving her in the lurch the way he did. I'd like to have a go at him. Val is probably better off without him, but I hate to think of my little sis going through such a tough situation. I spoke to her doctor, you know. He thinks she's going to be okay."

"That's what we're all praying for, Greg, and we're also hoping things work out for you as well."

"I know, and it helps just talking to you, Mom. Did I ever tell you you'd make a great cheerleader?"

"Only because I've got a winning team," Laura said, feeling the familiar pride. "How can we lose?"

After hanging up with Greg, Laura decided it was time for bed. She was tired, and she had promised Blanche they could go shopping tomorrow for material for the bassinet skirt she was making for Val's baby. Laura hadn't gotten the bassinet down from the attic yet, but Blanche said they could take measurements from a bassinet in the store. They were all basically the same. And she seemed anxious to get started.

Laura brushed her teeth, thinking of everything that had happened since the day Steve showed up on her doorstep. It was mind-boggling. Vicki's marital problems, Greg's malpractice threat, then Val and her pregnancy and the miscarriage scare. And now, Steve's son.

She thought of the young man she'd met so briefly. She could only hope his injuries were not severe. There was a baby on the way, and he was Steve's only child.

Laura hadn't prayed much since her husband's death, but now she knelt on the side of the bed and said a little prayer, for Steve's full recovery, and for her own children. They all had problems and obstacles to overcome, and she only wanted them all to be strong enough to cope with whatever life gave them. She couldn't hope for any of them to have a life free from pain and grief. Bad times came to everyone, but after the rain, there was always sunshine. That was what they all had to remember.

She picked Blanche up at ten o'clock the next morning. Laura was amazed at the visible change in her sister-in-law. She could barely see the lines of discontent that had always marred

Blanche's expression. She was actually smiling when she got in the car.

"You'll have to tell me what kind of diet you follow, Laura," she said. "I really must lose some weight. And while we're out today, do you think you could help me pick out some new cosmetics, and maybe a new outfit?" Blanche blushed and giggled like a teenager. "Would you believe my Jim asked me out on a date? Why, we haven't gone out on the town in ages, and out of the blue he decides we should go to dinner and go dancing afterwards. Can you imagine me dancing at my age?"

"Why not? I think it's wonderful, and I'd love to help you pick out a snazzy new outfit."

Laura was surprised at how much she genuinely enjoyed Blanche's company. They found the perfect fabric for the bassinet skirt, a soft yellow organdy. Then they bought yards of snowy lace and tons of yellow ribbon, and they laughed like young girls as they cooed over soft baby blankets and tiny booties.

Then, after a nice salad for lunch, they went shopping for Blanche. Laura helped her sister-in-law pick out a lovely dress in a delicate shade of blue that seemed to soften the lines in Blanche's face. They bought foundation cream and loose powder, a soft peach blusher cream, some eyeshadows in different colors so Blanche could experiment, and finally, a tiny bottle of cologne that the saleslady said was unconditionally guaranteed to turn any man's head.

"My goodness, I feel like a bride!" Blanche said, blushing prettily. "Am I being silly?" The worry lines in her forehead started to come back as she gestured towards her purchases. "After all, I'm not a girl anymore. I thought I was past all this foolishness."

"Oh, Blanche, don't you know it's never too late to be happy and enjoy yourself."

Laura smiled and touched her sister-in-law's arm. "Tell the truth, Blanche. Aren't you a lot happier today than you were last week at this time?"

Blanche looked surprised for a minute, then she smiled. "Why yes," she said. "I believe I am!"

Laura laughed, and Blanche followed suit, and after more than thirty years of knowing one another, the two women felt the stirrings of friendship. But Laura was determined not to look back. There was no point in regretting those wasted years. This day and this moment were all that mattered. She smiled. Paul would be pleased.

As soon as she got home that afternoon Laura checked her mailbox, and then her answering machine, hoping for a message from Steve. The machine was blank, mute testimony that Steve was going it alone. Her heart ached for him because she knew exactly how he must be feeling. She was well acquainted with the despair and frustration he was feeling, and with all her heart she wished she could help. But even if she were standing beside him there would be little she could do, except act as a sounding board.

She thought about calling Steve's cousin to ask for more information. Steve wouldn't consider that interference, would he? No, of course he wouldn't. In her heart Laura knew that if things had been different, if she hadn't been as adamant about guarding her independence, Steve would gladly have included her in this part of his life. But he probably thought she wouldn't want to get involved, that she wouldn't want to be dragged into caring about his son.

Sighing, Laura wandered out to her kitchen and made herself a cup of instant decaf. The thing was, she did care. She cared about Steve and his son, and she even cared about young Steve's wife, even though she'd never met the girl. How could you not care about a fellow human being in trouble? And caring and helping Steve through this difficult time didn't have to spell a lifetime commitment, did it?

Before she could change her mind, Laura picked up the telephone and called Steve's cousin. Right or wrong, she knew she would go crazy if she didn't find out what was going on.

"Then it looks like everything is going to be all right?" she asked a few minutes later. "Young Steve is going to be okay?"

"As far as we know," Rich said. "Apparently it looked a lot worse than it was. Of course, Stevie is going to be laid up for quite a while, and his wife is pregnant, you know. There's some rough times ahead for those kids, but we're all grateful that there isn't going to be any permanent damage."

"Thank goodness for that," Laura said. "Do you have any idea how much longer Steve will stay out there?"

"Not yet," Rich said. "Say, do you want the number at Stevie's place? I'm sure Steve would like to hear from you."

"Yes, please," Laura said. "I'd like to call and just let him know I'm thinking about him and young Steve."

Laura jotted the telephone number down and thanked Steve's cousin. Then she slowly replaced the receiver, feeling weak with relief.

She hesitated only briefly, then dialed the number Steve's cousin had given her. After only three rings she heard Steve's voice.

"Steve? It's Laura. How are you? How's your son?"

"Laura?"

He sounded surprised to hear from her, and she wished she'd called sooner.

301

"I wasn't expecting to hear from you," he said.

"Well, I was worried," she admitted, "about you and your son. Is he really going to be all right?"

"Yes, in time. He's got a long road ahead of him, but thank God, he's going to recover."

Laura was at a loss as to how to continue the conversation. Steve sounded polite, distant and cool, as if he were talking to a stranger.

"Steve, I . . ."

"Thank you for calling, Laura," he said, and then his voice softened. "I didn't want to bother you with my problems. You've had enough of your own."

"I care, Steve. Is there anything I can do?"

"Thanks, but I can't think of anything. It does help to know you care."

"Then give young Steve my best wishes for a speedy recovery, will you? Do you . . . have any idea when you'll be home?"

She thought she heard a sigh, but she couldn't be sure. The connection was a little fuzzy. "I'm not sure yet, but I'll be in touch when I get back. And thanks again for calling."

She hung up the phone, feeling oddly unsettled. Steve had said all the right things, all the proper, polite things, but there had been no warmth in his voice. He could have been on the other side of the world.

Well, isn't that what you wanted, Laura, she asked herself? Didn't you want to keep a respectable distance between yourself and Steve? Didn't you want to keep the relationship from becoming too close and intimate?

Laura stood up and carried her empty coffee cup into the kitchen. Sometimes she had a hard time figuring out just what it was she did want. She smiled to herself. Just like a teenager, she thought, wanting one thing one minute, something else the next. Being happy as a bud in bloom one second, and ready to weep buckets the next. Hormones, Laura thought, happy to have something to blame her confusion and ambivalence on. It was all due to hormones. She thought it terribly unfair that women had all these crazy ups and downs, while men escaped the dread midlife thing unscathed. Or did they? She'd have to ask Steve the next time she saw him. As she locked up the house and got ready for bed, Laura fervently hoped it would be soon.

Sixteen

Leaving his daughter-in-law, Joyce, at his son's beside, Steve stepped out in the hall to take a little break. Just the day before young Steve had been declared stable and out of any immediate danger, but it was still hard to see him all bruised and bandaged and hooked up to all the various machines. But the doctors were reasonably sure there would be no permanent damage. Steve's badly fractured leg would heal in time, and with the proper therapy he might not even have a limp. His internal injuries were less severe than originally thought, and the concussion he'd suffered was mild. Steve leaned against the wall and closed his eyes. He couldn't even imagine what would have happened if . . . no, he wasn't even going to think about it. Steve would recover, and that was all that mattered.

He stuck his head around the door, saw Joyce holding Steve's one unbandaged hand and talking softly. He smiled. The kids didn't need him right now. He decided to go down to the cafeteria for a cup of coffee.

A few minutes later, as he sat at a small round table, an untouched cup in front of him, he let himself remember the quick surge of joy he'd experienced the night before when he answered the telephone and heard Laura's voice.

But when he hung up he warned himself not to make too much of it. Laura was just naturally a kind, caring person. She would have felt the same about any one of her friends who was going through a family crisis. The fact that she had called didn't mean she'd had a change of heart, that she was suddenly ready to forgo her hardwon independence and surrender herself to him.

Steve's lips curled. Now that was definitely a macho thought, if ever he'd had one. Surrender, indeed! Why should Laura have to surrender anything? Why should he expect it? She was a warm, lovely woman, and she'd spent the better part of her life caring for a husband and children. Who could blame her if she wanted a little something for herself before it was too late?

And she never said she didn't like him, Steve reminded himself. She'd admitted that she cared, and that she felt physical desire, just as he did. But she just wasn't ready to give all of herself to a man, not yet.

The more Steve thought about it, the more he realized that to have any kind of relationship with Laura, there would have to be compromise on both sides. He was the kind of man who needed the reassurance of a woman's love. Laura, he was beginning to learn, wanted and needed love just as much as he did, but she was afraid of losing herself in the process.

There had to be a way they could come together and have the love and security all human beings craved, without giving up the essence of who they were.

Smiling ruefully, Steve stood up. All you have to do is find the magic number, Steve, old boy, he told himself.

Several days later, Steve stood at his son's bedside, heartily relieved to see some of the color coming back into his son's face.

"So, are you sure you don't want me to hang around a little longer?" he asked his son and daughter-in-law. "Rich isn't going to fire me if I stay a little longer, you know."

Young Steve tried to shake his head, but it was practically impossible. He was still heavily bandaged and any kind of movement was a major undertaking.

"Dad, we appreciate everything you've done, coming here like you did, looking after Joyce for me, but I'm going to be okay. It's just going to take a little time, and you've got your own life to get back to. So, go on and get out of here and go chase that pretty lady of yours. You'll be coming back in a few months anyway, when the baby comes."

Joyce laughed. "Steve is right, Dad. We'll be fine. He's on the mend now, and my folks are here. They'll keep an eye on us. It's been great having you here, but now it's time for you to go home."

Steve grinned. "Well, I guess I can take a hint. You two kids want to be alone, huh?"

Again, Joyce laughed. She stood up and patted her round belly. "Right," she said. "I'm as round as a beach ball, and your son is swathed in bandages like a mummy. Not much chance of a hot romance here, Dad."

Young Steve managed a weak smile. "Just a temporary condition, my dear," he told his pregnant wife. "You won't be able to keep me down for long. I'm a chip off the old block. Just take a look at Dad, still going strong at the ripe old age of . . ."

"Don't push your luck just because you're lying in a hospital bed, son. I'm as young as I

307

feel, and right now I'm feeling pretty darned good!"

Raising his unbandaged hand, Stevie made a V for victory sign. "See what we've got to look forward to, Joyce?"

Steve threw his suitcase in the trunk of his car that same afternoon. He'd thought about waiting until morning, and decided against it. He was anxious to get back to Miami, anxious to see Laura and tell her what he'd discovered. And maybe now, with her children all settled, at least for the moment, she'd be willing to give some of her warm affection to him. The thought propelled him behind the wheel and out onto the highway, and it kept him company all the way home.

Laura was humming right along with her real estate classes. She was more than a little surprised at how much she enjoyed studying again. And it seemed to come fairly easily to her. She'd been afraid she would be rusty, that her brain might have atrophied from all the years as a homemaker, but instead she found that her academic skills only needed a little polishing.

"Hi, Laura," Sheila said one morning, as Laura settled herself in class. "What do you hear from Valerie these days?"

"She's doing fine. She's not even having morning sickness. I'm happy about that. It would have been hard for her to keep up if she was sick every morning."

"I just can't wait until she comes home," Sheila said. "I feel like she's my sister."

Laura laughed. "She thinks a lot of you too. By the way, I like your outfit. Is it new?"

Sheila flushed prettily. "You don't think it's too loud?"

Laura rolled her eyes. "Have you ever noticed some of the outfits Isabelle wears? What you have on is actually tame compared to some of her things. But the look is perfect for her, as this is for you. How's the assertiveness class coming?"

"Great. I never realized it would feel so good to speak up and say what was on my mind. It's still kind of scary, but I'm learning more every day."

"Good for you," Laura said. "So am I."

After class, Laura stopped off at Blanche's house. Her sister-in-law had called the night before to say she was almost finished with the bassinet skirt she was making. She wanted Laura to see it, and there were some things she wanted to discuss with her.

As she knocked on the door, Laura smiled to herself. The change in Blanche was almost unbelievable, and it was reflected in Jim's behavior as well. Both her sister and brother-in-law seemed happier these days, and Laura was glad for both of them.

"Here I am," she said, as Blanche opened the door. "Where is that gorgeous bassinet skirt you wanted to show me?"

"Oh, Laura, it's perfect, if I do say so myself! Valerie is going to love it!"

"I'm sure," Laura said, following Blanche into her sewing room.

Years before, when Blanche's children were small, she had been an avid seamstress. She'd made nearly all her daughter's clothes, and even some of her own. And she'd even made a wedding gown for a close friend. But through the years she'd lost her enthusiasm for the craft and had all but given it up.

Now, as she stepped into the room Blanche had always used as a sewing room, Laura looked around in amazement.

"Blanche! My goodness! What is all this?"

"I thought about what you said, about setting up a little business. I made some inquiries and I put a little ad in the paper, and you can't imagine the response I got. I have all kinds of work lined up for alterations, and one woman wants me to make a prom dress for her daughter. And then, since the bassinet skirt turned out so well, I was thinking I might want to sew some baby things. What do you think?"

Laura shook her head, almost unable to believe what she was seeing and hearing. The room that had so recently been cluttered with odds and ends, was now a sparkling clean sewing room. Someone, probably Jim, had built cabinets on three sides of the room. Blanche's sewing machine, newly oiled and cleaned, sat in the middle of a long counter. On the walls were shelves for materials and patterns and sewing notions. There was a dressmaker's dummy in one corner, and a professional pressing machine in the other. The eager, expectant smile on Blanche's face was all the illumination the room needed.

"Blanche, this is incredible! When did you do all this?"

"Jim and I worked on it all last week," Blanche said proudly. "We just finished up this morning. Didn't Jim do a lovely job with the cabinets?"

"That's right, he still has his woodworking shop in the garage, doesn't he?"

Blanche nodded happily. "Yes, but he hasn't done anything for years. Do you know, Laura, I suddenly realized that Jim and I were stagnating here in this house. All we did was sit and worry about everyone else's business." She lowered her voice. "It isn't good for Jim not to have something constructive to do, so I asked him to help me fix up my sewing room, and I believe he truly enjoyed it. Do you know what he's doing now?"

Laura shook her head. She was still stunned. It really was a miracle.

"He's out in his shop making a wooden rocking horse for Valerie's baby. Isn't that something?"

"It certainly is. Blanche, I'm thrilled for both of you, but where's the bassinet skirt? I'm dying to see it."

Blanche beamed. "That's the next part of my surprise. The best part, I think. Follow me, Laura."

She followed Blanche to the next room. It had once been Patty's bedroom, but it had been empty for years.

Blanche stooped outside, hesitated a minute, then flung open the door. "Behold!" she cried proudly.

Laura's jaw dropped. She blinked, but it wasn't a mirage. Blanche had transformed the empty room into a dream nursery. A room fit for a tiny prince or princess.

"What in the world . . . ?"

"It's going to be my showroom, Laura. That's Valerie's bassinet, but I'm going to do another one, and then, when I start advertising my custom-made nursery decorations, I'll have samples to show. Don't you think that's a good idea?"

Laura was speechless for a moment. Then

her face split into a huge smile. "It's perfect, Blanche. Absolutely perfect, and you were right, the bassinet is gorgeous. Valerie is going to be thrilled."

She shook her head and touched the beautifully quilted bumpers Blanche had made. "I knew you were an excellent seamstress, but I had no idea you could do something like this."

"Well, I don't expect to become an instant millionaire," Blanche said, "but Jim and I both feel that a little extra income would make our lives a lot nicer, and we'll be doing something we both enjoy. I really think it will work, Laura. Don't you?"

"I don't see how it can fail. When people see your things they'll be beating a path to your door."

Blanche laughed, and Laura was surprised at how pleasant it sounded. She wanted to hug her sister-in-law, and she did just that.

"Oh my," Blanche said, her cheeks pink with pleasure. "I think you and I are finally going to be friends. Imagine! After all these years!"

Laura could not stop smiling all the way home. Wonders never ceased, as Paul would have said. And Blanche had just discovered that old dogs could learn new tricks!

Then, as she pulled into her driveway, her

heart felt like it skipped a beat. Steve's Bronco was parked right in front of her!

She nearly tripped getting out of the car, and she couldn't believe how happy she was that he was back.

"Steve?"

"Here I am," he said, getting up from where he'd been sitting on the steps. "I thought you were never coming home." He stood close now. "It's good to see you, Laura. I feel like I've been away for months."

They stood facing each other, close but not touching, and for a moment there was a curious awkwardness, then Laura smiled, and Steve followed suit, and then they were where they belonged, in each other's arms.

This was a day full of surprises, Laura thought dizzily, amazed at how good it felt to be close to this man again. She'd missed him, but she hadn't realized how much until now. But as she took in the warm, masculine scent of him, as she inhaled his familiar spicy aftershave, and felt the hard strength of him, her heart began to sing. She'd missed this, and she didn't want to give it up. Her life was full now, with her new friends, her realtor's course, and her children. But there was still room for Steve in her life and in her heart.

"Let's go inside before we make a spectacle of ourselves," she said. "I'm so glad to see you!"

And it seemed she had so much to tell him, about Sheila's new hairdo and blossoming self-confidence, about Blanche's fresh new attitude and business plans, but mostly she wanted to tell him how much she'd missed him, how empty her days and nights had been without having him near.

"Is this what they mean when they say absence makes the heart grow fonder?" Laura asked. She stood just inside the doorway, in the circle of Steve's arms, and she was feeling very fond. She looked up at him, gazing at a face that had become increasingly familiar and dear in the past weeks and months. A face that had never totally faded from her memory for more than thirty years. "Steve, I . . ."

"Don't talk," he murmured huskily, "just hold me as I'm holding you. I missed you so much. I'm having a hard time believing this is real." His lips, gentle as butterfly wings, fluttered across her eyelids, as she closed her eyes and leaned into him.

It was heaven, or as near to it as she was likely to get while still warm and breathing, Laura decided. She'd been backing away from this man for weeks because she was confused and uncertain about the way she wanted to live the rest of her life. But young Steve's accident had shaken her. And she had to tell Steve how she felt.

"Don't," she said, gently disentangling herself. "Wait. I have to tell you something."

Steve briefly closed his eyes, then he opened them and held Laura mesmerized with a penetrating gaze. "What is it, Laura? What do you have to tell me?"

"About Steve's accident . . . it made me stop and think. In the beginning, when you didn't even know how serious it was . . . I realized again how fragile life is, how precious every moment is. I've been dancing around on tiptoe, afraid of letting you get too close, afraid of letting myself really care, but then I found out that it's too late. I already do care, and I'm ready for us to be close."

There was silence when she finished. Steve stared as if he were trying to decide if she was serious. He seemed afraid to believe it.

"It's true," Laura said, smiling gently. "I still love you, Steven Walker. I guess a part of me always has." She stiffened her shoulders and looked him right in the eye. "And I'm tired of pussyfooting around!"

For a moment Steve looked startled, then he burst out laughing, and he gathered Laura into his arms. "So am I, kiddo!"

It was an evening of discovery and renewals. Laura had worried that Steve might be disappointed when he made love to her. What had pleased an eighteen-year-old boy might not necessarily do the same for a fifty-three-year-old man. And she wasn't the same girl she'd been then, all those years ago. Her body was different, and her life experiences had taught her things she hadn't known then. She was sure she was a better lover now than she had been at seventeen, but there were other factors. Her body wasn't the same. Her breasts were not so firm, and childbearing had left its mark on her. But all the fears and doubts were swept away in a tidal wave of warm sensations when Steve slowly lowered her to the sofa. Then he was beside her, warm and strong and impatient, and suddenly, as his lips and fingers worked their magic, Laura found that she was eager and impatient too.

"I don't care if this is right or wrong," she whispered against his neck. "I just know it has to be."

"Yes. It has to be," Steve echoed. Then he began to love her, as he had once before, so very, very long ago.

It was like going back and yet it wasn't. It was old, yet new at the same time. They touched and sought each other, feeling the form and outlines of bodies no longer young, but not yet old.

"You're just as beautiful now as you were then, my Laura," Steve murmured, his lips against the soft warmth of her breasts. "Then

317

you were a girl, and now you're a woman . . . my woman, always."

A shiver of delight rippled over Laura at the dear, loving words. She was filled with sweet, aching desire, and the awkwardness she had feared was no more. This was Steve, her Steve. He had been the first man in her life, and now he would be the last.

"You are my darling," she whispered, her hands stroking and fondling, driving him to a fever pitch of sensual excitement. She gloried in her woman's powers. To know that she could do this to him excited her beyond all reason. Her flesh tingled where he touched her, and she raised herself to help him as he removed her clothing with exquisite care. When she was naked before him, she felt a moment of shyness, Then, as his dark eyes devoured her, she laughed with joy. In those eyes she was beautiful, no matter the ravages of time.

Hands on her breasts, Steve felt the fullness of her, as she helped him shed his slacks and shorts. He was still lean, still firm and strong, and Laura flushed as he caught her lingering gaze.

"Do I suit?" he asked, his voice rich with joy and laughter.

"Oh yes," she replied hastily, as his mouth descended to her nipples. "Oh yes, you suit just fine."

They were young with desire, and old with experience, as they met and merged, hearts as well as bodies. The beauty of it all took Laura's breath as she rose higher and faster to the peak of the mountain. She shivered on the peak, then held Steve tight as together they began a slow, languorous descent.

They held each other as if they were afraid to part, as if what they had just experienced would disappear in a puff of smoke, and it would all have been a mirage. Then finally, when her less-than-youthful limbs began to cramp, Laura was forced to move.

"I'm sorry," she said, "but I've got to get up. I'm getting a charley horse."

Steve moved so quickly he nearly fell on the floor, and Laura exploded with laughter at the stunned look on his face.

"A sofa like this was not meant for this kind of activity," she said, holding her discarded blouse against her as she struggled to sit up. Now she felt shy again, and it didn't help when Steve openly ogled her.

"I love a naked woman," he said, giving her a lecherous wink, "they're so helpless . . . so at my mercy."

"Oh yeah! You want to bet? Do I look helpless to you?"

"No. You look adorable. You also look satisfied, satiated, fulfilled . . . and well and thoroughly loved." Steve laughed, and then he sobered. "Are you as happy and content as I am at this moment?"

Laura looked at Steve. "Yes," she answered softly.

Seventeen

It was time for Vicki and Tim and the children to leave. Steve went with Laura when she went to see them off.

He was flattered that she'd invited him, but he wondered how Vicki would feel seeing them together at such a time.

He was pleasantly surprised to see that Laura's daughter had undergone an attitude adjustment since their last meeting. She was polite and pleasant, a perfect lady.

The house had been sold, and the new owners would be moving in within days. Laura caught Vicki looking at the empty house longingly, but then she bravely squared her shoulders and turned away.

Steve helped Tim carry the last of their possessions out to the huge moving van that would meet them at their new home in Indianapolis.

"We're renting a place until we decide what and where we want to buy," Vicki said, sounding very confident about the whole thing. "I know it will be hectic for a while, until the children adjust, especially Andrea in her new school."

Laura gave her eldest grandchild an extra hug before they all climbed in the car, and then she turned to Vicki. Despite her vow not to cry, she felt tears sting her eyelids.

Vicki smiled, and her own eyes watered. "Don't, Mom," she said. "Please don't. This is hard enough."

"I know, and I'm sorry. It's just that it didn't seem real until now. I'll miss all of you."

Vicki looked at Steve. "Maybe you'll drive her out to visit us when we get settled," she said.

Steve grinned. "I'd be delighted, Vicki. I wish you and your family the very best of luck in your new life. I know you're all going to be happy."

Then there was a last round of hugs and kisses all around, the slam of car doors, and the almost frantic waving until the car was out of sight. And only then did Laura release the tears she'd been holding back.

"I didn't know I'd feel this way," she sobbed, soaking the collar of Steve's shirt. "I thought I was resigned to them moving away. I know it's best for them . . . the opportunity was too good for Tim to pass up, but I just didn't realize it would hurt so much to watch them drive away.

Will you take me out there when they get settled? Would you do that for me?"

Steve put his fingers under her chin and lifted her face so he could look into her eyes. "I would do just about anything for you, Laura. Haven't you figured that out yet?"

And she knew it was true. Steve had done everything in his power to make her feel loved and cared for. He'd given her his love and his trust, he was ready to be there when she needed him, and all he asked was the same love and loyalty from her.

"Let's go home," Laura said. "I need you to hold me."

But Steve drove to his apartment instead of taking Laura to her house. "I have a bottle of bubbly, a loaf of bread, some sharp cheese, and the sweetest grapes this side of heaven," he said, by way of cajoling her into staying at his place. "It's all guaranteed to raise your spirits and cure the blues, and besides, I think it's time you got a chance to try out my waterbed."

Laura couldn't help blushing. Wine and bread and cheese, and Steve's waterbed? How could she stay depressed with all that to look forward to?

"I'm putty in your hands, sir," she said, looking up at him and batting her eyes flirtatiously. "Do with me what you will."

And he did. They sat on huge pillows on the floor and ate bread and cheese by candlelight.

They drank champagne until Laura was wonderfully lightheaded, and then Steve fed her some lusciously sweet grapes. Finally, when they'd kissed and teased each other into a frenzy, Steve guided her to his bedroom and his huge, gently undulating waterbed.

This time Laura undressed herself while Steve watched unashamedly. Then she turned to him and began slowly unbuttoning his shirt. The delicious torture lasted only minutes, and then Steve finished the job himself. Then they were on the bed, laughing as they rolled together, and then apart, until passion and deep, aching need took over, and the laughter stilled.

Each time Steve loved her was more beautiful than the last, Laura thought, just before she drifted off to sleep in his arms.

But she wouldn't stay the night. Hours later, despite Steve's sleepy protests, she insisted on getting dressed and going home. She used Buttons as an excuse, but they both knew it wasn't true. Staying over meant giving up a tiny piece of her independence and she couldn't do it, at least not yet.

That was what Steve hung on to, the thought that with time Laura would feel safe and secure with his love, and be willing to surrender herself into his care.

Anyway, what choice did he have, he asked himself as he drove back home in the dark of night? He had to hang in there with Laura, or else give her up, and he wasn't prepared to do that. They had something rare and beautiful, and they'd been lucky enough to find each other again after three decades apart. Wasn't a relationship that promised so much, worth a little patience?

"So, how's your love life these days, coz?" Rich asked Steve the next day. "Has that pretty lady of yours finally succumbed to your charms?"

"How could she resist?" Steve asked jokingly. "Let me put it this way, Rich. My love life is doing as well as our business venture here."

Rich whistled and grinned. "Wow! That good, huh?"

Steve just grinned. "We are doing pretty good here," he agreed. "I have to admit that I was a little concerned. I knew we had a good concept, but you never know how something like this is going to go over."

Steve's cousin nodded. He was younger than Steve, and he still had two kids in college, and a third in high school. His expenses were high, and starting the business had been a calculated risk. Now, thank goodness, it looked as though everyone was going to be able to relax soon.

Steve worked the rest of the day in high spirits. He'd shared a wonderful evening with Laura, even though he hadn't been able to get her to spend the night. He thought about waking up with Laura beside him, of seeing her lovely face first thing in the morning. That was one of the things he missed. He didn't like waking up alone. For so many years Marcie had been at his side, soft and warm. Her smile had been the first thing he saw upon waking. She had spoiled him for the single life, no doubt about it.

Laura juggled her key in the lock and opened the door with a weary sigh a few days later. She was beginning to think she'd opened Pandora's box when she suggested that Blanche do some sewing at home. The woman was tireless these days, and she wanted Laura's company whenever she went out shopping. This morning she'd called all in a flutter. She needed fabric and some trim for a new crib bumper she was designing. Laura groaned as she slipped off her shoes and rubbed her aching feet.

Anyway, Blanche knew Laura's class schedule now, and she'd badgered Laura into going shopping with her for fabrics. It had seemed innocent enough, but when Laura drove by to pick Blanche up, the fun started.

Blanche came hustling down the sidewalk at a pace faster than Laura had seen her use in years.

Laura's jaw dropped as she got a good look at Blanche's outfit.

"Why, Blanche, you look . . . different," she finished lamely.

Blanche wedged her ample frame into the front seat beside Laura and smiled. "Isn't this a lovely color?" she asked, indicating the vivid purple chemise she was wearing.

Actually, the dress wasn't half bad, Laura thought. It was just the color. It did funny things to Blanche's skin tones. But her sister-in-law was smiling from ear to ear and that was a definite plus, so Laura held her peace and smiled and nodded.

"Well, I thought we could go to that wonderful fabric place I found several years ago," Blanche rattled on, as Laura drove, following orders like a uniformed chauffeur.

"They have wonderful prices on their fabrics, and just about every imaginable trim. I just can't believe I wasted all those years sitting on my duff eating sweets and watching those silly soap operas! Why, do you know that I got three more alteration customers in just this past week?"

"That's wonderful, Blanche. You must . . ."

"But Jim said that I may need even more room for my supplies, so maybe we'll put some shelving in the garage. Although, with Jim's woodworking tools . . ."

"Well, if Jim . . ."

"Oh, I don't know!" Blanche interrupted again. "But we'll figure it out. Oh, Laura, everything is so exciting these days! It's fun to get up in the morning again."

"I'm glad. I . . ."

"Now, hurry up. Let's get to the store. I have a list a mile long!"

Laura subsided then, and just concentrated on her driving. It was a Monday and the traffic was fairly heavy. It was wonderful to see Blanche so happy and animated, but Laura had to wonder if she'd ever be able to get a word in edgewise again.

When they got to where the fabric store was supposed to be, Blanche looked around in bewilderment. "Why, there's a restaurant on that corner, and I distinctly remember . . ."

"When was the last time you shopped here, Blanche?" Laura asked.

"Well, I'm not exactly sure. It was several years ago, but how could they have moved? It was one of my favorite stores!"

"Not anymore," Laura said, resisting the urge to scream. It was getting warm, and the air conditioner in her car wasn't working very well, and she was starting to get a headache.

"Well, never mind. There's another store that's almost as nice. Of course it's on the other side of town, but . . ."

"And when did you last shop there?" Laura asked.

"It's been a while," Blanche said. "I'm not really

sure, but they couldn't go out of business too . . . could they?"

"I'll find a telephone booth and we'll look it up," Laura said. "I'm not going on another wild-goose chase, Blanche. And what's wrong with the store where you usually buy your fabrics?"

Blanche waved her hand dismissively. "Oh, they have a very limited selection. I probably wouldn't be able to find half the things on my list." Suddenly she looked alarmed. "You don't mind driving a little out of our way, do you, Laura? I certainly don't want to impose, but since you don't have a class today I figured you didn't have anything really important to do. You don't, do you?"

"Not a thing, dear," Laura said. "I'm at your disposal."

Much to Blanche's dismay, the second store had also ceased to exist, but they found a new store just recently opened and Blanche hopped out of the car almost before Laura had brought it to a complete stop. She gestured for Blanche to go in without her, and took a moment to catch her breath, and then, as she realized just what she'd done by encouraging Blanche to take up her sewing again, Laura began to laugh. It was a full fifteen minutes before she could get herself together enough to join Blanche in her quest for unique fabrics and fabulous trims.

So, it was after five before Laura dropped Blanche off. At home she felt like a wilted carnation as she rubbed her aching feet and massaged the small of her back. Yet, as tired as she was she couldn't help smiling as a vision of Blanche, in her vivid purple dress, swirled around in her head. A lavender tornado, Laura thought, remembering how Blanche had whipped through the stores, picking fabric here, yards of trim there, and boxes of pins and spare needles, and thread to match all the fabrics.

The telephone rang, interrupting her thoughts, and she hobbled over to answer it.

"You sound tired," Steve said. "Did you and Blanche have fun?"

Laura groaned. "Don't even ask. I'm sure there's no flesh left on the soles of my feet, but I can't really complain. Blanche is happy for the first time in years."

"Well, that's good. I thought maybe we could go out for dinner, but you sound like you're about to fall asleep."

Laura experienced a spurt of disappointment, but Steve was right. She wouldn't be fit company for anyone. All she wanted was a cup of tea and some toast, a warm bath and her bed.

"I really am exhausted," she said apologetically. "Do you mind if we do it another time? I'd be lousy company."

Steve chuckled. "I can't believe that, but sure, we'll take a rain check."

"Thanks," Laura said, grateful for his understanding. She felt bad about breaking their date, but it couldn't be helped. There was no way she was going to get shoes on again right now.

Steve hung up the phone, and tried to decide between a hamburger from a fast-food restaurant, or a frozen TV dinner. He'd looked forward to having dinner with Laura tonight, but she'd sounded as though she were about to fall asleep standing up. He smiled to himself. Women and shopping! And apparently Laura's sister-in-law was hot to trot. Oh well, he and Laura would have other evenings together, and the last thing he wanted to do now was crowd her. He was trying to show her that she could have a warm, loving relationship without sacrificing herself.

He finally settled on a frozen turkey dinner from his freezer. He grimaced as he popped it in the oven. At least it was one of the ones with dessert.

Laura settled herself in her easy chair and raised the foot rest. Ahh, wonderful. The relief was instantaneous. She took a sip of her tea, decided it was just right, then leaned back and closed her eyes. Was there anything better than a quiet night at home after a strenuous day of shopping? She couldn't imagine anything more wonderful than what she was doing right now. The house was blessedly still. She could even hear Buttons snoring. She felt warm and rosy from her bubblebath, and she was cozily wrapped in an old flannel nightgown and robe. Her hair was uncurled, her face free of makeup, and it didn't matter because there was no one to see her. These were the moments she was loath to give up, even for the love of a good man like Steve.

She sighed. For now, she wasn't going to worry about it, but she knew that one of these days she would have to make some decisions, because Steve wasn't going to wait around forever.

Laura woke the next morning, with the soles of her feet still sore, but otherwise she was fine. As she got ready for her class, she decided that from now on she would monitor Blanche's shopping trips a little more carefully.

She debated calling Steve before she left the house, but decided against it. She'd call him at work on her break.

But when she got to class she found all the students in an uproar. Sheila took her aside and told her what had happened.

Isabelle had suffered a heart attack and was in the hospital in serious condition.

"Oh no! When did it happen? Is there anyone

with her? Any family?"

Sheila shook her head. "Not that we know of. You know her husband is dead, and she has three children, but they all live a long distance from here. George said she insisted they not be notified unless her condition becomes critical. But I don't think she should be alone at a time like this, do you?"

"I certainly do not," Laura said firmly. "Are they going to have class today?"

Sheila nodded. "George said we have to go ahead with our schedule."

"Well, will you please take notes for me? I'm going to the hospital to see how Isabelle is doing, and maybe I can convince her to let me contact her children. There comes a time when a person can be too independent."

Laura drove the short distance to the hospital feeling shocked and stunned. Isabelle was the last person she would have expected to have a heart attack. George, with his paunch and his incessant cigar smoking, seemed a much more likely candidate, but instead it was Isabelle.

She hadn't known the woman long, but she had become very fond of her. Isabelle was honest and down-to-earth, the kind of person you instinctively knew you could trust. And she had a great attitude about life. When she wanted something, she went out and fought for it. Laura admired her spirit, her ready sense of humor, and her aspirations. She could only hope that the heart attack was a mild one.

But the news was not good. When Laura got to the hospital and went up to the CCU, they didn't want to admit her.

"Only family is allowed in CCU, ma'am," one of the nurses explained politely. "If you're not related to the patient . . ."

"Look, she doesn't have any family around here. She's all alone, and I'm her friend. Can't you make an exception?"

The nurse looked uncomfortable, and she started to shake her head.

"Please," Laura said earnestly. "Would you want to be all alone at a time like this? I won't stay long, and I won't say or do anything to upset her, but I just want her to know that someone cares."

"Well, all right. I do know that the lady has no family in the area. But five minutes only." The nurse lowered her voice and put her hand on Laura's arm. "Her condition is still very serious. She could go either way at any time. She probably won't be able to talk to you."

Laura's stomach did a flip-flop as she followed the nurse to Isabelle's bedside. The whole atmosphere of hospitals brought back painful memories of the awful time after Paul's stroke.

"Here she is," the nurse said softly. "You have a visitor, Isabelle."

"Is she . . ." Laura hesitated.

"I'm sure she knows you're here," the nurse said quietly, "but she is very weak, and she may not be able to respond to you. Just let her know that you're here, let her feel your concern. That will be a big help."

Laura approached the head of the bed cautiously, stunned by Isabelle's pallor, by the tubes in her nose, and the wires attached to her chest. She'd seen this kind of thing before, of course, but it was still hard to believe that it was Isabelle lying there. The last time she'd seen her, Isabelle had been trying on a red sequined top and planning a party. Now it looked as though her partying days were over.

"Isabelle, it's me, Laura. I came as soon as I heard. Is there anything I can do for you, anyone you'd like me to notify?"

Just the slightest shake of her head, but it indicated that she'd heard and understood.

"What about your children? Wouldn't you like to see them?"

Again the shake of her head, and now her eyes were agitated.

"Okay, never mind," Laura said quickly. "Whatever you say is what we'll do. You just rest and get well. Before you know it you'll be back on your feet, scaring the daylights out of all the realtor students."

Once more Isabelle managed a weak shake of her head, and this time there was a sheen of tears in her eyes. As Laura watched, tears slowly slid down Isabelle's cheeks.

"No, that's not so," Laura said, hearing the words Isabelle was unable to say. "You're going to be fine. You'll get well and laugh about this little interruption."

She felt herself choke up. "You've got to hang on, dear," she said, knowing she sounded desperate and afraid, and hating herself for not being in better control.

"Time's up," the nurse said, coming up behind Laura. "She needs to rest as much as possible."

Laura bent down and gently kissed Isabelle's cheek. "I'll be back," she promised. "You be good and do what they tell you so you can get out of here quickly."

Without waiting for the negative shake of Isabelle's head, she hurried out into the hall, where the tears finally came.

"I'm sorry," she sobbed, when the nurse came to see if there was anything she could do. "It's just that she seems so alone, and she's so very sick. I guess I didn't realize . . ."

"We've notified her children," the nurse said, nodding, "even though she indicated she didn't want us to bother them. Her condition is quite grave, and we thought the family should know."

"I'm glad," Laura said. "She should have her family around her now, but she's a very independent lady."

The nurse nodded. "I know, but this is not the time for her to try and prove how strong she is. She has every right to lean on her loved ones now."

Laura was allowed to see Isabelle once more before she left, but her friend was sleeping, and she was careful not to wake her.

Everyone was waiting for a report when Laura returned to class.

"How is she? Any improvement? Is she going to make it?"

Laura could only shake her head. She didn't protest when George Ryan put his arm around her. "Buck up, girl," he said. "Isabelle's a strong lady. She'll pull through."

"You didn't see her," Laura said. "She's so weak. She couldn't even talk to me."

"That's now," George said. "A few hours from now she could be dramatically improved."

But she wasn't. Two hours later the hospital called. Isabelle was gone, and she had died before her children had a chance to say good-bye.

Eighteen

Laura had not expected to be so depressed over Isabelle's death. Of course she mourned her friend, but she hadn't known Isabelle very long, or even that well. Her grief and despair seemed out of proportion, and she said as much to Steve.

"I don't understand why I feel this way. All of the students feel bad, and George Ryan has worked with her for years. He really took it hard. They had a special relationship, a genuine friendship. But I didn't know her that well, and yet I feel such a terrible sense of loss."

Steve nodded, and gently coaxed Laura's head down on his shoulder. They were at his apartment. Laura had gone there directly after class, feeling a deep need to be with him, to have him hold her and chase the demons away.

Was it just that she had once again been reminded of the fragility of human life? Had she seen herself in Isabelle's pale face and shadowed eyes? Had she visualized herself dying all alone, with no one to hold her hand or touch her cheek?

"This is silly," she said, finally pushing herself into an upright position. "I'm acting like a baby. What is that poem? There is a season, a time to live and a time to die. It was just Isabelle's time."

"Sure, but that won't stop you from missing her," Steve said reasonably. "Don't be so hard on yourself, Laura. There's nothing wrong with having deep feelings."

"It's just that she was so alone," Laura said softly, unable to meet Steve's eyes. "Her children must feel terrible."

Steve nodded. "It seems as though she cheated them as well as herself by refusing to have them notified. But," he added softly, "I'm sure she believed she was doing the right thing. I suppose everyone wants to spare their loved ones pain and worry."

They stopped talking about Isabelle then. What more was there to say? She had lived the way she wanted to live, and she had died the same way. It had been her choice, and now it was over, too late for regrets.

"Come on," Steve said a few minutes later. "Let's go get the fattest, juiciest cheeseburger we can find. I'll even spring for a milkshake and fries."

"Oh, I don't know if . . ."

"Say yes, Laura," Steve said. "Say yes to life. We're here together. We're alive. Say yes."

"Yes," Laura said, smiling through her tears.

So they gorged on hamburgers and french fries and drank thick, creamy chocolate milkshakes. Laura even splurged and ate one of the little apple pies the fast-food restaurant was famous for.

And when they were finished eating she felt better. Life wasn't always fair, she decided, and sometimes bad things happened to good people, but all you could do was pick yourself up and go on.

"Do you think we could go to my place and take Buttons for a long walk?" she asked Steve. "I feel like moving, and it's a beautiful evening."

Steve grinned, and gave her a quick hug. "I can't think of anything I'd rather do," he said.

So they walked and talked, and let the soft Miami evening soothe away the pain. Spring was in the air, and it had been an unusually cool winter. Laura was looking forward to sunshine and warmth, to swimming in her pool and sunbathing beside it. And if she wanted, she could have Steve beside her.

"Where are we headed, Steve?" she asked softly, as they strolled along, Buttons trotting happily beside them. "I'm still not sure."

"I know where I want to go," Steve said. "I want us to be together for the rest of our lives. I want to be able to count on you in bad times as well as good. I want to know that you'll be here for me, as I'll be here for you. And I can wait for a while, Laura, but not forever. I'm not as brave as your friend, Isabelle. When the end comes, I don't want to be alone."

So, it was as she'd thought. Steve was being as patient and understanding as possible, but he wouldn't wait forever.

As Paul had always said, Laura knew that honesty was the best policy, the only policy she would be comfortable with. She slowed her steps and touched Steve's arm.

"All I can promise you now is that I'll always be honest with you. I'll try never to mislead you, and I'll try not to hurt you, but beyond that I can't go right now. I love being with you, and it's wonderful to know that you're here for me, but I just can't make any commitments. Not now."

Steve took her hand, raised it to his lips and tenderly kissed each fingertip. "I promised I wouldn't pressure you, and I said I could wait, and I will, but ultimately we'll both have to make some decisions, Laura, and what we decide will affect the rest of our lives."

"Yes, I know," Laura said softly, "and that's why I have to be sure."

Steve could have stayed over, but he didn't. They had never been together in Laura's bed, the bed she had shared with her husband. It seemed wrong, as though it would have defiled her marriage and her memories. And Steve knew that he would not have made love to Laura in the bed he had shared with Marcie. That bed, which he had sold when he moved to Miami, was a part of his past. And he sensed that Laura had a lot to think about, that she needed this time alone. He had helped her through the first terrible hours, when the shock of Isabelle's death was fresh and hurting, and now she needed some space.

As he always did, he checked to make sure the house was securely locked for the night, then he took her in his arms and kissed her tenderly. "Try to get some sleep," he said, "and we'll talk again tomorrow."

Laura nodded. She was drained, emotionally spent from all that had happened in the past few hours. She'd lost a friend and gained a little wisdom, or had she? She was still unwilling to totally commit to Steve, and what if she woke up one day and found herself alone and lonely and full of regrets? She shook her head, trying to chase the worrisome thoughts away. It was late and she was too tired to think. Standing on tiptoe she kissed Steve's cheek. "Thank you," she said simply.

And so they lay in separate beds, Steve feeling the gentle motion of his waterbed every time he shifted positions. Sleep was elusive, jumping away from him every time he got close. He thought of Laura . . . hell, he'd thought of little else since the day he walked back into her life. And it was perfect, or at least it could have been, if only she wasn't so scared of commitment.

Staring into the darkness, Steve thought about it, trying to see things from Laura's perspective. And he had to chuckle. Usually it was men who were unwilling to commit, men who were afraid of the responsibilities of marriage. He was sure it wasn't responsibility Laura was afraid of. Look how she handled the situations with her grown children. She didn't shy away from trouble then, and she gave unstintingly of her time, her love and her concern. No, it was more a fear of losing her newfound freedom as a single person. And even though Steve knew himself to be a man who pulled well in harness, he knew that there were freedoms that would disappear in a marital relationship. But it seemed a small price to pay for love and companionship, and someone to share your life with. Sighing, Steve turned on his side and punched his pillow into a comfortable shape. It was late. He was tired of thinking.

After Steve left her, Laura took a long bubble bath. Somehow, soaking in a tub of warm, scented water always seemed to soothe her. It softened the rough edges of pain and helped her sleep when she was troubled.

Why had Isabelle taken such a hard line when she was so sick? Had her relationship with her children been less than what it should have been? Or was it just her need to be independent and stand alone, even at a time when family and friends would have meant the most? She'd never know now, but it forced Laura to think hard about her own life. If Steve insisted on marriage, was she willing to let him walk away, go out of her life again?

The water in the tub grew cold, and Laura finally got out, shivering as she wrapped a thick towel around her nakedness. She pulled a comfortable old nightgown over her head, quickly brushed her teeth and creamed her face, and then she crawled into bed and cuddled Buttons next to her. She couldn't think anymore. She was too tired.

George Ryan called at eight-thirty the next morning. Isabelle's children were in town, and they were making funeral arrangements. George wondered if Laura would want to come over to the office after lunch and meet them.

"I'll understand if you decline," he said. "I'm not looking forward to it myself, but Isabelle's son and daughter seem to want to talk to all the people she knew."

"Of course," Laura said. And she didn't even have to stop and think about it. It was the least she could do for Isabelle's memory. "I'll be there a little after one," she said. "I'm glad you called me."

And when she met Isabelle's son and daughter she was doubly glad George had called her. Naturally, they were upset by their mother's death, and the suddenness of it had shocked them, but they were philosophical about everything, and they were happy to meet and talk with their mother's friends and coworkers.

"Mom was pretty unique," Sam French said to Laura, as his sister spoke quietly with George. "She always was a bit of a loner, and I'm sure that's why she didn't want anyone to call me or Angel." The man's face clouded for a moment. "I would have liked to have been here, but I have to believe it was Mom's choice."

"Yes," Laura said. "I enjoyed knowing her. She definitely was unique."

After a few minutes with Isabelle's daughter, Angel, Laura felt a calmness settle over her. Apparently Isabelle's children didn't feel cheated as she had expected they would. They accepted their mother's independence, and they were at peace with her decision. It made Laura realize that people looked at things differently.

Isabelle was buried two days later. Laura attended the service with George and some of the other students from the realtor's course. Steve had offered to go with her, but she had insisted it wasn't necessary.

"You're sweet," she said, "but you didn't know her, and it's probably better if just friends and family attend."

Steve had nodded. "I understand." And he did. He didn't feel threatened because Laura didn't need him, and he had just wanted her to know that he was there for her.

Actually, he was glad not to go, because funerals bothered him. They were too final, the losses were too devastating, and he'd never dealt well with loss. He still felt his wife's loss keenly, even though the initial pain of her passing had softened. A huge chunk of his life that had been cut away. He was functioning, but he was incomplete. He didn't expect Laura to replace Marcie. That could never happen, but he needed to fill the void left by her passing. He needed a companion to walk the paths of life beside him.

Laura cooked dinner for Steve the day after Isabelle's funeral. She woke that morning feeling that she was writing a new page, starting a new stage of her life. Her friend's death had made her examine her deepest feelings closely. There were still areas of confusion, still some doubts lingering at the edge of her consciousness. The one thing she was sure of was that she didn't want Steve to go out of her life again. He had matured into a strong, self-confident man, a man with compassion and consideration, and a rare gentleness that touched her. When they lay together in the darkness, filled with the bliss of belonging, it was easy to dismiss her fears, but in the light of day they always resurfaced.

Laura bustled around her kitchen contentedly. There was still some soul-searching to do, but somehow she felt confident that things would work out for the best.

* * *

"Daisies," she said happily, when she opened the door to him that evening.

Steve stood there, carrying a huge bouquet of them, and grinning boyishly. "They were easier to get this time," he said.

"I've always loved daisies," Laura said. "I guess they represent all the magic of the past . . . of our youth."

Steve wrapped his arms around her and swung her around in a circle. "The present is what I'm interested in," he said, pretending to growl, "and what is that wonderful smell?"

"Pot roast," Laura said, laughing, and pushing reluctantly away from his embrace. If she let herself get too close, dinner might end up being considerably delayed, and she was hungry. Hungry for good plain food, and hungry for a man to sit across from her and enjoy it with her. Eating alone was no fun, except for an occasional quick, casual lunch. But at night, at the end of a day, it was lovely to have someone you cared about sitting across from you.

"Would you like a beer?" she asked. "You can go sit in the living room and watch the news while I finish up in here, or you can perch right over there," she paused and pointed at a kitchen stool, "and talk to me."

"I'll perch and talk," Steve said, flipping the

tab on his beer. He tilted his head back and took a long swallow. "Umm, that just hits the spot. It got warm today, didn't it?"

"And it's about time," Laura said. "I've lost all my tan. If it stays like this for a few more days, I'm going to start getting the pool ready."

"I'll be glad to help," Steve said. "That was one of my favorite jobs at the house in Arizona. Marcie always said she couldn't have survived without that pool."

Laura shook her head. "Not in that heat, but just wait until we get in the soup here. You may find it hard to adjust to the humidity after the dry air in Arizona."

Steve crossed one long leg over the other. "I'll manage," he said. Laura looked different tonight. Maybe it was the way she'd fixed her hair, or the silky shirt she was wearing. Her cheeks were flushed and her eyes were very bright. Her movements seemed a little jerky, and yet she didn't seem nervous. It was more that she was slightly anxious about something. He wondered if she had come to a decision about them and their relationship, or was it still too soon?

"What do you hear from your kids?" he asked. "Is Vicki getting settled in the new place?"

Laura smiled as she stirred flour into the

gravy to thicken it. "She called last night, and said that Andrea loves her new school. Tim is finding his way with his new coworkers, and she is still unpacking. It takes time to settle a whole household, but at least she didn't sound like she was sitting around sobbing in her teacup."

"Good," Steve said. "I think that little family is going to make out just fine. They may have some rough spots, but basically I think your girl has a good head on her shoulders, like her mom, of course."

It was one of the best dinners Steve had tasted in a long time. The meat was tender and delicious, the vegetables cooked to perfection, and the rolls were light and flaky.

"Laura, I thought you said you weren't a gourmet cook? This is great."

She laughed. "Pot roast hardly qualifies as exotic fare. I think it's the first thing you learn how to prepare in Home Ec. But I'm glad you enjoyed it. I was worried about having a lot of leftovers, but I don't think that's going to happen. Maybe I'll just mix a little of the meat and vegetables in with Buttons's dog food and give him a special treat."

"Well, I'd love another helping, but my stomach can't take it," Steve said, pushing himself away from the table. "If I eat like this too often I'll have to start jogging again."

"Good. We can go together. I try to jog at least five days out of every seven. It keeps my metabolism going."

Steve was quiet as Laura poured coffee and served them each a piece of homemade cheesecake. Then, when she sat down across from him, he spoke.

"What's wrong, Laura? You seem a little anxious. Is there something you want to tell me? Have you made a decision?"

She lowered her eyes and shook her head. "No. And that's what I wanted to tell you. I don't know when I will, or even if I can. I promised you I'd be honest, and that's what I want to do. I want you to understand that I'm not stringing you along, and I'll understand if you don't want to hang around waiting for me to make up my mind. I won't be happy if you decide to skip out, but I will understand."

"Hey, wait a minute. What's all this about skipping out? Didn't I tell you I'd wait, at least a while longer while you sort things out?"

"Yes, but . . . how long is a while?"

"I don't know," Steve said honestly, "anymore than you know when you'll reach a decision. I'll be as honest with you as you're being with me. That's all I can say."

Laura groaned and dropped her head into her hands. "This should be so simple. I love you. There, I said it, and I haven't been struck by lightning, and you . . . you love me too, don't you? Isn't that what this is all about? Loving?"

Steve was stunned. They'd made sweet, beautiful love to one another, but they'd never said the words. Not that he hadn't wanted to, but he'd been afraid, scared of pushing Laura. Now she had said them first and he felt like a kid again. He wanted to run out into the streets shouting, letting the whole world know. "Laura loves me!" he cried, beaming.

"Oh, you nut! It's a good thing my neighbors are away on vacation."

"Oh no," Steve said, "I've got it. The jackpot at the end of the rainbow. Laura loves me!"

She was blushing, but she wasn't displeased. How could she be when Steve was so overjoyed? But there was more that she had to say. Things she could only hope he would understand. Words he might not be so happy to hear.

"I do love you," she repeated softly, her eyes glowing, "but love isn't always the answer to everything, Steve."

"It can be," he argued. "It should be."

"No." Laura shook her head adamantly. "I love you and I enjoy being with you, having dinner with you, making love with you, knowing that I can call you if I need a strong shoulder. All of those are things that you can and do give me, and in return I can do the same for you. But I'm not at all sure I want us to live together as man and wife, Steve. I'm Laura. I don't want to become just Steve's wife."

Steve looked stricken for a moment. He swallowed, tried to speak and failed. Then, "I . . . see," he said. "You think that by becoming my wife you have to lose your identity?"

"I don't know," Laura said. "That's what I'm trying to figure out."

They talked a while longer, and the cheesecake sat, uneaten, while the conversation went in circles. He did, she didn't. He was, she wasn't, and finally, when Steve could stand the ambivalence no more, he gently lowered her to the sofa and made passionate love to her, as if he could brand her with his love, as if their mating could make her believe in the love they shared, as if it could banish all her doubts and make her want him as much as he wanted her. But it didn't, and he'd known all along that it wouldn't.

He filled her with warmth and light and contentment, and she wanted all of that to go on and on, but she couldn't sign the papers and take the steps that would legally bind her to this man.

Nineteen

Laura passed her realtor board exams with flying colors. She went out with George and Sheila and some of the others to celebrate, and then, when she went home, the first person she called was Steve.

"That's great," he said warmly. "Do you feel like celebrating?"

"Yes, I certainly do. You have no idea how nervous I was about that exam. I was sure I was going to disgrace myself forever." She took a deep breath. "May I come to your place? I don't feel like being with crowds of people. I'd rather it was just you and me."

There was a short silence, then Steve's husky response. "Hurry over," he said. "I'll chill the champagne."

But before she could even get in the shower, the telephone rang, and it was her son, Greg.

355

"How did you make out, Mom?" he asked. "Did you manage to squeak by?"

"Brat," Laura muttered. "I'll have you know I passed with plenty of room to spare. How are you, honey? Any news?"

"That's one of the reasons I called. Allison admitted that she was lying. Her psychiatrist got her to tell the truth. All charges against me have been dropped."

Laura started to cry. The tears slid down her cheeks, even as she laughed out loud. "Oh Greg . . . oh, honey, that's wonderful! I'm so happy for you!"

"Yeah, me too, Mom, and you can bet I'll make sure nothing like this ever happens again. I'll glue my nurse to the door, if I have to, but I'll never let myself be that vulnerable again."

"This really makes my day now," Laura said. "The only thing that would make it better was if you were here to celebrate with us."

Greg laughed. "Us, as in you and Steve?"

"Well, yes. He's cooking dinner for me and chilling a bottle of champagne and . . ."

"And you wish I was there with you?" Greg asked. "Mom, you're slipping. I'm sure you and Steve can manage very nicely without me."

"All right, we'll do our best. Congratulations, son."

"Thanks. The same to you, and now I'm going to go pick up my date and do my own celebrating."

"Date?" Laura's ears perked up. "Someone special, dear?"

"Wouldn't you like to know?" Greg teased. "Sorry, Mom, no info today, but maybe one of these days I'll bring her home to meet you. How's that?"

Laura grinned. "You just answered one of my questions, son. Have a nice evening."

She hung up feeling as if she wanted to dance and sing and twirl wildly around the room all at once. After weeks of nerve-racking worry, Greg's ordeal was finally over. That made two of her children who seemed to be moving in the right directions. Now if Val was able to finish her studies and have a healthy baby, everything would be just about perfect.

And as soon as Val and the baby were settled, Laura would put her house on the market. From what she'd learned in her realtor's course, she should be able to get a decent price for the place, and then she'd start looking for a small apartment. Of course, she could move in with Steve if she wanted. He'd hinted on more than one occasion that he'd like nothing better, but why couldn't he understand that she was looking forward to fixing and decorating her own little place? She'd never done that before.

This house, lovely as it was, had been decorated with Paul's tastes in mind as well as her own. This apartment would be all hers. It would be the first time in her life she'd be free to indulge her wildest ideas, her fondest fantasies. Laura laughed happily. Everything was wonderful!

As promised, the champagne was chilled to perfection when Laura arrived at Steve's place. She hugged him, then looked around with interest. It seemed like every time she came over, something new had been added. Steve seemed to be enjoying his apartment immensely.

"I like that print," she said, indicating a picture of a ship in full sail bobbing atop white-capped waves.

"Thanks. Would you believe I found it at a garage sale? Marcie never cared much for that kind of thing. She didn't like flea markets either, but sometimes I enjoy browsing through other people's throwaways."

"I love flea markets," Laura said. "When I get my apartment, I'll be haunting them all."

"Well, I'll be happy to offer expert advice," Steve said, handing Laura a tall, fluted champagne glass. "Let's drink to your success," he said. "This is quite an accomplishment." They lightly clicked their glasses together.

Steve insisted that Laura relax while he put the finishing touches on dinner, but she was equally insistent on joining him in the kitchen while he worked.

Steve laughed as he squeezed by Laura to get to the refrigerator. "This kitchen was definitely not designed for family-style cooking. The bare necessities are here, but that's about all."

"It's what we realtors call functional," Laura said soberly. "All the necessary elements to prepare and serve food, but none of the frills." She smiled and shook her head. "You're right, a true gourmet chief would not be happy here."

"Yet it's perfect for me," Steve said. "What would I do with all those fancy gadgets they keep coming out with?"

"I think I'll look for something with a kitchen just a little larger than this one," Laura said, looking around thoughtfully. "Because I do like to fool around in the kitchen when I have time."

"Umm, you like to fool around?" Steve came up behind her and pulled her against him. She felt the masculine hardness of him even as his large, warm hands cupped her breasts from behind.

"So, this is how you prepare a meal, eh?" Laura felt warm and happy, and she loved the feel of Steve's hands on her body. It made her remember that above all else, she was a woman. When they stood close like this she could forget the years, forget that she was a parent, that she'd already buried one husband. Steve helped her feel young and free again, vibrant and hopeful, as if all the good things life had to offer were still ahead of her.

"I better get back to business," Steve murmured, reluctantly releasing Laura and moving back to the stove. "Unless you're not hungry right now?" he asked hopefully, waggling his eyebrows lecherously.

"I'm starved," Laura said, laughing at the disappointed look on Steve's face. "Dinner first, dessert later," she promised, batting her eyes flirtatiously. "And I promise you it will be worth the wait."

When they sat down at the small, round table, Laura nodded appreciatively. Steve had given his wife's china to his son and daughter-in-law, and had bought himself a simple set of stoneware in soft grays and blues. The tablecloth picked up the blue of the dishes and the napkins were gray. In the center of the table was a bud vase with a single white rose. There were two pewter candle holders with tall white tapered candles. The effect was casual, but lovely.

"Rich's wife helped me pick out the tablecloth and stuff," Steve said sheepishly, as he watched Laura's reaction. "I don't know much about things like that."

"Well, it's lovely. I'm impressed," Laura said, lifting her spoon to taste the onion soup Steve had prepared. She sipped, then nodded. "Wonderful," she said. "You know this is blowing my whole image of bachelors. I always pictured a single man eating out of cans, with the kitchen littered with pizza boxes and frozen-food trays."

Steve grinned. "Well, I've never gotten into eating from cans, but you can find an occasional pizza box, and I do eat frozen dinners once in a while. But this is a very special occasion."

When they finished eating, Steve did allow Laura to help him load the dishwasher, then they took coffee and brandies into the living room.

"This is actually a double celebration for me," Laura said, settling herself comfortably in a corner of Steve's sofa. "Greg called just before I left the house. The woman who accused him of malpractice finally told the truth. He is clear of all charges. Isn't that wonderful?"

"Hey, that's great! Tell Greg I said congratulations, will you?"

Laura nodded happily. "And he had a date too. He wouldn't tell me anything about her but he said he might bring her home to meet me one of these days. That sounds encouraging, doesn't it?"

Steve moved a little closer to Laura and laughed. "Now that definitely smacks of a meddling mother. You know, it's not as if you don't already have grandchildren. Why do you care whether or not he gets married?"

"Well, I suppose he doesn't have to get married, but I just want him to have someone, you know? He works so hard, and he's a good man. A woman would be lucky to have him."

Steve chuckled. "You couldn't be just a wee bit prejudiced, could you?"

Laura's eyes widened innocently. "Me? Prejudiced?"

It was nice being together like this, Laura thought, nice to feel comfortable with a man, and yet know that when the time was right, sparks would definitely fly. She felt a tingle just thinking about it, the times she and Steve spent in each other's arms. As a lover, Steve had to be right up there with the best of them, and he made her feel things she'd never expected to feel again. It still amazed her to realize that she could be so passionate, could desire a man so much that she actually ached.

As though he read the emotions on her face, Steve moved closer. He put his coffee cup down and opened his arms, and without hesitation Laura moved into the welcoming circle.

They made love right there on the sofa, slowly and languorously, as though they had all the time in the world, and for a few minutes it seemed that way. There was no reason to hurry, no reason for haste to make them miss one second of pleasure.

They tasted and touched, like lovers young and new, and then, as the passion built up, their movements became perfect for them. The years of experience came into play, and they both drew upon all the ways they had learned to please and pleasure a lover. And it was wonderful. New and bright and glorious. It was endless, bringing a youthful glow to their bodies, a warmth to their souls. Laura felt warm, salty tears on her cheeks. Tears of joy and fulfillment.

"I don't ever want this to end," Steve said, as Laura straightened her clothing. He thought she was the most beautiful woman in the world, especially now, all flushed and rosy from his loving. And he knew it meant as much to her as it did to him. It had to. She was not the kind of woman to indulge in casual sex. When Laura gave herself as she had given herself to him, it meant something.

"Everything ends eventually, Steve," Laura said softly. Everything felt soft. Her voice, her body, even the secret places of her heart. Soft with loving. "I'm beginning to believe that we must take every moment and squeeze every ounce of enjoyment from it, because you never know."

"Thinking of Isabelle?" Steve asked. He loved watching Laura fix her hair and smooth her clothing. He loved the slightly rumpled look of her.

"Yes, and Paul too. Until his stroke Paul was a healthy, vital man. It never even occurred to me that he would suffer a debilitating stroke. And Isabelle . . . she was such a vibrant woman, so alive and funky. And then poof. It's all over, and sometimes you don't even get a chance to say good-bye."

Steve nodded. He had his memories too, some bittersweet, some still too painful to examine. But at least he'd had a chance to say good-bye. He'd had a chance to begin to prepare himself.

"Were you able to say good-bye to Paul?" he

asked gently, taking her hand in his. It had grown cool now, and some of her pleasure was fading as she remembered.

"Yes. Paul knew his time was short, and we had lots of long talks. He told me that I had always been the . . . sunshine of his life."

"Just as you are now, for me," Steve said huskily. "We've been doubly blessed, Laura. We've each had the love and devotion of a wonderful mate, and now we've found each other."

"I know. I guess I didn't really think much about it until Paul died and I was left alone, but there is a lot of loneliness and unhappiness all around us. We are very lucky."

And there was. She knew it, and evenings like this made her realize that she didn't want to be all alone. She wanted Steve to stay in her life.

She took a deep breath, closed her eyes briefly and decided it was time to change the subject. She wasn't ready to delve any deeper just now. "How is Steve, Jr.?" she asked, "And how is Joyce feeling these days?"

Steve straightened, swallowed his disappointment and released Laura's hand. "He's coming along," he said. "In fact, I called them yesterday, and his cast will be coming off in a couple of weeks. Joyce said she's as round as a beachball, and she hasn't seen her toes in months.

She swears the baby is practicing for the varsity football team."

"And what are you hoping for, Grandpa? A little boy or a girl?"

Steve grinned. "Will you think less of me if I say I've got my fingers crossed for a girl? I know most men say they want boys, but I've always had the urge to spoil a dainty little girl."

"Girls are sweet," Laura said, "and they make the most darling little clothes for them these days. I'm hoping Val has a girl too. And in her case I just think a girl will be easier."

"That creep didn't come to his senses?" Steve asked. Val wasn't his daughter, but he felt very fatherly towards her anyway. It made his blood boil to think of her being hurt that way by some selfish, self-centered boy.

"I talked to her a few days ago," Laura said, shaking her head, "and she said she'd heard rumors that Robert is transferring to another university. I suppose he's worried that Val will make some kind of claim on him."

"She probably should," Steve said, sipping his brandy. "Even if he doesn't want to get married and be a father to his child, he should at least pay support."

Laura shook her head. "Val doesn't want that. She feels that once she gets her degree she'll be able to take care of the baby by herself, and since Robert feels the way he does, she doesn't want him to have any claim on the child." Shrugging, Laura continued. "I have to admit I agree with her. The child will be better off with one loving, caring parent than a father who resents its very existence."

"I can't imagine a man feeling that way," Steve said. "And there are so many people who would love to have a child."

"Well, Valerie's baby is going to have plenty of love," Laura said. "There'll be no shortage of hugs and kisses for my grandchild."

Steve smiled, and then he pulled Laura back into his arms for a kiss. Just a kiss, nothing more. For the moment he was satisfied just to hold her, to breathe in her scent, to feel the rise and fall of her chest against his. For the moment it was enough.

Laura decided it was time for a payback. She called Blanche and refused to take no for an answer when Blanche hesitated about accompanying her on a shopping trip.

"There is nothing that can't wait one more day, Blanche," she said firmly, "and you owe me. After that last trip for fabrics . . . well, I may need an objective opinion today, so get dressed. I'll pick you up in forty-five minutes."

To her credit, Blanche was ready and waiting, and this time she was wearing a bright, forest green tent dress. Laura thought her sister-in-law looked like a huge, swollen flower bud, and she vowed that if they had time she would give Blanche some pointers on dressing to disguise extra poundage.

"Hurry up," she said, as Blanche climbed in the car. "I have an appointment for a haircut and style at eleven." She tried to look innocent. "Oh, and I made an appointment for you too. I thought maybe it was time you had a change."

"Me?" Blanche squeaked. "Oh my, I don't know. I've worn my hair this same way for . . . why, I can't remember how long it's been . . . and Jim likes it this way."

"Only because he's never seen you any other way. What would you think of a rinse, Blanche? Just something to cover the gray?"

"A dye job? For me?"

"No, just a rinse," Laura said. "Rinses aren't permanent. After a few shampoos they wash out, so if you really don't like it, you're not stuck."

"Well, I don't know. Do you think I really need it?"

"That's up to you," Laura said. "I'm having the works, a cut and styling, and a rinse. I haven't decided whether to deepen the auburn or lighten it. What do you think?"

"Well, my goodness, I just don't know," Blanche said. Then her eyes narrowed and she stared at Laura intently. "For heaven's sake, Laura . . . do you have a beau?"

Laura laughed. She'd dreaded this moment for a long time, but now she was beginning to think it might not be so bad.

"Actually I do. He was my first real love back in high school. He lost his wife to cancer a few years ago, and he recently moved here from Arizona. At first I thought we would just be friends, but now . . . well, it's developed into something more."

"You . . . are you planning to marry him . . . this old boyfriend?" Blanche looked horrified, and Laura hastened to reassure her.

"Marriage is not on the agenda, at least no. right now, but would it be so terrible if I did remarry someday, Blanche? Don't you think that would be a sort of testimony to the happiness Paul and I shared?"

Blanche cocked her head to one side and pursed her lips. Then she began to nod. "Why yes, I suppose it would. I never thought of it that way, but I believe you're right." Her eyes narrowed, Blanche leveled a stern look on her sister-in-law. "So, this man, he's the reason for all this primping?"

"Only partly," Laura said truthfully. "Now that I have my realtor's license I want a new look, something modern and chic. I'm going to buy some business clothes and shoes, and I may even treat myself to a briefcase."

"Oh, Laura, I'm proud of you! I think what you're doing is just wonderful. Paul would be proud of you too. Oh, dear, was that the wrong thing to say? I'm trying not to dwell on the past these days, but I can't just forget my dear brother, can I?"

"Of course not," Laura said. "But going on with our lives doesn't tarnish Paul's memory, dear."

Blanche digested that for a minute, and then she smiled and nodded. "You're absolutely right, Laura," she said staunchly. "I always knew you were a clever lady."

It turned out to be one of the nicest days Laura had enjoyed in a long time. She and Blanche left the beauty salon looking like new women. The stylist had given Laura a very short, layered cut that took full advantage of her naturally wavy tresses. Then he suggested a rinse to lighten her hair and give it highlights.

When Laura saw herself in the mirror, her eyes seemed larger and she looked years younger, and the stylist assured her that it would be an easy style to manage.

For Blanche the new look was even more traumatic. She'd worn her hair in the same flat way for as long as Laura could remember, and her hair was streaked with gray and it had lost all its shine.

She had a different stylist than Laura, but he turned out to be equally talented. When Blanche stood up, Laura could not believe it was the same woman.

"Oh, Blanche, you look wonderful! How do you like it? Are you pleased?"

"Oh my," Blanche said, turning this way and that in front of the mirror.

The stylist had shaped Blanche's thick, straight hair into a smooth, sleek cap that framed her features beautifully, and he had rinsed it with a gold-brown rinse that gave Blanche's skin a soft glow.

"Jim will love it," Laura said. "It's perfect for you."

"You don't think it's too youthful?" Blanche asked anxiously. "Goodness, it's been ages since I've done more than run a comb through my hair, and now look at me!"

"All right then, we're off to the dress shops

now," Laura said, slipping the stylists a nice tip. Cheap at twice the price, she thought, to see Blanche so happy and animated.

She bought three basic dresses, one suit in a delightful shade of peach, two skirts—one navy, one black—and three blouses. Then she stocked up on pantyhose and bought three comfortable pairs of midheeled pumps to mix and match with all her outfits.

Blanche trotted along offering advice and comments, some helpful, others not, and finally Laura was satisfied with her working woman's wardrobe. Now for Blanche.

"How about a couple of new dresses, Blanche? Now that you're earning all that extra money you can afford to treat yourself."

"Oh, I don't know. Jim and I don't go out that much and I have plenty of dresses."

"Yes, but I'll just bet Jim would enjoy seeing you dress up once in a while. Look at this navy shift. Doesn't it look cool and comfortable for the warmer months? And how about this light blue over here? Jim likes blue, doesn't he?"

And so it went, and before they left the store Blanche had purchased four new outfits, all of which were styles that would camouflage, rather than call attention to her excess weight.

Just before Laura dropped Blanche off, her

sister-in-law made a rather startling statement.

"You're all right, Laura," she said. "I used to think you didn't like me, but I guess I was wrong, wasn't I?"

Laura felt Paul's presence very strongly at that moment, and she simply could not lie. "I like you now, Blanche," she said honestly.

Blanche gave her a funny look, but then they were pulling up in front of her house, and she began to flutter as she got her packages from the back seat. "Oh, I do hope Jim likes the new me," she said worriedly. "Do you think he will?"

"Absolutely," Laura said, "and just wait until you try on one of your new dresses. I wouldn't be surprised if you two end up going on a second honeymoon one of these days."

"Get out of here," Blanche said, flushing. "My goodness, I'm much too old for that sort of thing . . ." Suddenly, Blanche's eyes narrowed. "I'm only two years older than you and you're . . . oh, my goodness! I just can't imagine . . ."

"You're never too old, Blanche," Laura said, smiling. "And don't knock it until you've tried it!"

With those words, she put the car in gear, and drove off, leaving Blanche standing on the pavement, staring after her in amazement.

Laura laughed so hard she finally had to pull off the road to wipe her eyes. Then, when she had herself under control, she took out her compact, powdered her nose and touched up her lipstick. And she headed for Steve's apartment. She could hardly wait to see how he liked her new look.

Twenty

"You look gorgeous," Steve said, "but that's nothing new. How about letting me take you out to eat? You can show off your new look."

"Why not?" Laura said. "Steve, just wait until you see Blanche . . . oh, that's right, you've never seen her at all, so you wouldn't know. Well, let me tell you, that lady is a walking miracle!"

Steve laughed. "That good?"

"Better," Laura said, nodding. "She was such a grouch before. No one liked her. My kids couldn't stand to be around her. And now she's looking forward to when Val has her baby. She even offered to babysit. Her hair looks wonderful, and with the new clothes I talked her into buying . . ."

"Whoa, slow down," Steve said, grinning.

"You're making me a little nervous. Who is next on your make-over list? Me?"

"Oh no. You're perfect just the way you are," Laura said, her eyes sparkling with mischief, "although maybe . . ."

"Let's go," Steve said, taking her arm and guiding her out of the apartment. "We'd better hurry if we want to get to the restaurant before it gets crowded."

"Chicken," Laura taunted, bending her arms and flapping them like wings.

Without a word, Steve turned and grasped her in a bear hug that literally took her breath away.

"So, I'm a chicken, am I?"

Steve's eyes were dark with passion.

The teasing smile slid off Laura's face as she met his gaze.

Then they were in each other's arms and the earth was spinning as it had years before, when everything was young and new.

"My goodness," Laura said a few minutes later, when Steve finally, reluctantly released her. "I'll never call you a chicken again."

Grinning crookedly, Steve took her arm and walked her outside and down to his car.

They ate at a small dockside restaurant. It was casual and inexpensive, but the food was fresh and plentiful.

"I've always liked this place," Laura said. "I

love just sitting here and watching the boats go by, looking out over the water."

"I love the clam chowder," Steve joked. "And the steamed shrimp. I think fresh seafood was one of the things I missed most when I lived in Arizona."

"But your wife loved it there."

"Yes." Steve laid his fork down and looked out over the water. "Marcie's family was there, and like your Vicki, she wasn't anxious to leave them. And I liked it too. The desert has its own unique beauty. I'm sure young Steve will raise his family there."

"And you really don't mind being so far away from your only child?"

Steve looked thoughtful, and then he grinned. "Look how easy it is for me not to be an interfering father."

"But you'll miss a lot, not being able to watch your grandchild grow up."

Steve nodded, and now his dark eyes were sober. "I know, and I do feel bad about that, but the way I look at it is that I have my life to live, and Steve has his. Just because we're not right next door to each other doesn't mean we can't have a good relationship. Didn't you feel the same way when you encouraged Vicki to go with Tim to Indianapolis?"

"Touché," Laura said. She tasted her seafood pasta with relish. "But now that they're gone

I'm beginning to realize how much I'll miss watching the children change and grow. I'm not going to get out to Indianapolis that often."

"That's the way of things now," Steve said. "Families are scattered all over the country, and there isn't much we can do about it. From what you told me Tim couldn't afford to turn down that promotion."

Laura shook her head, and sipped her ice-cold beer. It tasted wonderful. "Financially, they're better off, and that's what I keep telling myself whenever I start missing them, but it would have been nice if Tim's opportunity had kept them a little closer to home."

Steve reached across the table and covered her hand with his. "I guess both of us are cutting the apron strings, aren't we? How come no one told us how much it would hurt?"

They went for a ride after they finished dinner. It was a beautiful moonlit night. The sky was clear and filled with stars. They held hands the way they had more than thirty years earlier, and Laura felt perfectly content.

"Did you ever think of how our lives would have turned out if we'd stayed together? What our children would have been like?" Steve asked. In the soft evening darkness his voice was deep and slightly husky.

Laura felt a momentary pang. Then she breathed deeply, taking in the sweet scent of oleander. She sucked the familiar fragrance into her lungs and laughed. When Steve first came back into her life she'd thought about that, and at first there had been a lingering touch of pain. But now, since they'd gotten reacquainted, she was completely satisfied with the path her life had taken.

"Having a case of the 'what-ifs'?" she asked. "What's the point, Steve? We're together now. Isn't that all that matters?"

"I suppose, but every now and then I can't help wondering, and then I get mad at myself all over again for being such a callous jerk."

"Let it go, Steve," Laura said softly. She stopped walking and regarded him solemnly. Then she reached up and touched his cheek. "You're a good man," she said. "You were a good husband and father, and now you're an excellent lover." She smirked. "Wha da ya want, egg in yer beer?"

Steve smiled, then he caught Laura's hand before she could pull it away. He brought her hand to his lips and gently, reverently, kissed each fingertip in turn.

Laura felt like an ice-cream cone on a summer day. "Steve, I . . ."

"Let's go home, Laura love," Steve said huskily. "I want to be alone with you."

"You should get a dog," Laura said later, when they entered Steve's silent, empty apartment. "Don't you hate coming into an empty place?"

"I'm afraid a dog won't do it for me, Laura," Steve said softly. "I want to come home to you."

Laura tried to turn it into a joke. She hadn't wanted the conversation to take this kind of turn. "What makes you think I'd get here before you?" she asked, hands on her slender hips.

Steve studied her, loving the bright, animated look on her face, the trim contours of her body. No longer youthful, but still appealing and intriguing. He shook his head. She was quite a woman, his Laura. But was she his? Would she ever be his?

There would be no answers tonight. He could see it in her eyes, and he didn't want to spoil the wonderful mood of the evening.

"Come here, woman," he said, pretending to growl. "I want to manhandle you!"

Laura laughed throatily. "I can hardly wait!"

By the time she drove home Laura was pleasantly tired, and totally content. Steve insisted on following her in his car to make sure she got home safely. It made her feel warm and cared for, and yet it worried her. What did Steve think she would do if he weren't around?

* * *

Turning from side to side, Laura checked the hemline on her skirt. She loved getting dressed every morning and going to the office, loved telephoning potential buyers, and most of all, she loved showing homes.

It was a whole new world, and her only regret was that she hadn't taken the course and gotten her license sooner. But Paul hadn't wanted her to work, and she had been content cooking and baking and puttering in her garden, and after Vicki's children were born, being a grandma. Now, suddenly it was as if she had found her niche. Even George complimented her. He said she had a way about her that the customers liked. He told her she could be very successful if she wanted to be.

"Successful! Me! Just imagine," she thought, lifting her soft auburn curls and lightly spritzing them with hair spray. When she was ready, she picked up her briefcase and went out to her car.

"Yes, Mrs. Thomas," Laura said later that same afternoon. She was in her office talking to a woman she'd shown several houses to. "Well, there is one more home I can show you that fits in your price range. How about tomorrow morning at ten?"

"Whew! That Mrs. Thomas is one picky lady," Laura said, when she finally hung up. "I have one more house on the list to show her tomorrow, but if she doesn't like that one I'm done."

George snuffed his cigar out in the ashtray on his desk. "Any day now you're gonna make that first sale, and when you do, we'll celebrate, eh?" His homely faced sobered. "Too bad old Isabelle isn't here to join us."

Laura nodded. "She was something, wasn't she?"

They both looked up when the front door slammed. "Now who in the . . ."

"Sheila!" Laura exclaimed. "You look like you just won the lottery, or is it just a new boyfriend?"

"Even better," Sheila said. She was glowing, and her eyes were shining. "I made my first sale! I sold a house!"

"Oh, honey, that's wonderful!" Laura jumped up and hugged the girl, and she wouldn't have been any happier if she'd been the one to make the sale. "What were you just saying about a celebration, George?" she asked the paunchy realtor.

"All right, all right," George said, laughing. "Powder your noses, and let's go, ladies. Every first sale deserves a celebration."

"So, I guess my assertiveness training paid off," Sheila said later, as she sipped a pink lady. "A year ago I would never have believed I could do this."

"Positive thinking," Laura said, lifting her wine glass. "Here's to your first sale, and many more to come. Congratulations, Sheila. We're all proud of you."

George lifted his glass and Sheila beamed proudly. "Wait until Valerie finds out," she said. "She'll be surprised."

Laura grinned. "Maybe not as much as you think. She told me she thought you had a lot of potential."

"She's so sweet," Sheila said. "I got a letter from her the other day. She said she can't wait to get finished with school so she can come home and wait for her baby. She's going to be a great mom, isn't she?"

"I think so," Laura said, "but I still wish things could have been different for her."

"Hey, girls, am I missing something here? Valerie is your daughter, isn't she, Laura? Is there some kind of problem?"

"I guess it depends on how you look at it," Laura said, sipping her wine. "Val isn't married. She was engaged to the baby's father, but he doesn't want a child right now. He said it would be inconvenient. He wanted my daughter to have an abortion."

"Why that . . ."

Laura held up her hand. "Don't, George. I've already decided that he isn't worth it, and Valerie feels the same way. She's going to have the baby and she's going to be a wonderful mother, and she'll get along just fine without Robert."

"That kind of thing makes my blood boil," George ranted. "What's the matter with the young men today? Don't they have the guts to take on any responsibilities? And what is this going to mean to you, Laura? Is it going to put a burden on you?"

Laura smiled. "No. I'm going to be fine. Val will have her degree and once the baby is born she'll be able to get a good job. She'll be able to support herself and the baby easily. Of course, I'll help her get on her feet in any way I can, but basically I think she'll be all right."

"Well, it's still a rotten shame," George growled. "Leaving a young woman in the lurch that way! Whoever he is, he ought to be ashamed!"

As they all drove back to the office, Laura found herself sneaking peeks at Sheila's glowing face. Laura wondered if she was going to look like that when she made her first sale. She hoped so, because a woman her age could use all the glow she could get. She smiled to herself. Success certainly was lovely.

"You should have seen her face," Laura told Steve when he phoned that evening. She was lying on the sofa with a briefcase full of listings, and a glass of iced tea. She'd had a long, relaxing bubble bath, and she felt wonderfully content. Steve, on the other hand, seemed to be all out of sorts.

"That's nice," he said shortly. "Sheila seemed like a nice kid."

"Well, actually she's not a kid. She . . . Steve, what's wrong? You sound angry or upset or something. What's bothering you? Is there anything I can do?"

"No, there's nothing anyone can do," Steve said. "I'm going to have to go back to Arizona for a while. Young Steve's leg isn't healing the way it should, and he's going to have more surgery."

"But I thought they were getting ready to take the cast off?"

"Yeah. They did. Nobody seems to know why, but something went wrong. It looks like the leg will have to be rebroken and reset, and that means more pain and convalescence for Steve, and the baby is due in just a few weeks."

"Oh, Steve, I'm sorry! I had no idea. How are they making out financially?"

Steve sounded helpless and scared. "That's the least of their worries right now, Laura. Steve will get a settlement from the accident, and he's collecting disability payments. Joyce's parents are helping out as much as possible, and so am I, but what I'm worried about now is Steve's frame of mind. Joyce said he's awfully depressed."

"I can imagine," Laura said. She felt as helpless as Steve sounded. It was terrible. And it was unfair. And there was nothing either of them could do about it. At what should have been one of the happiest times of his life, young Steve was facing more surgery and an extended recovery time. That had to put a shadow on the impending birth of his child.

They talked for a long time, but there was really very little Laura could say to make Steve feel better. It was just a bad time they would all have to get through.

"It will all work out, Steve," she said. "In a few months, when all this is behind you, you'll . . ."

"Don't tell me I'm going to look back on this and laugh, Laura," Steve said sharply. "There's nothing funny about this situation."

"Of course not, but you can't let it get you down, Steve. Your son will need you to keep a positive attitude."

"That's easier said than done," Steve replied. "Look, I'd better hang up and let you get some sleep. I know you have to work tomorrow."

"Yes, I do, but . . ."

"Goodnight, Laura," Steve said flatly. "I'll be in touch with you when I get back from Arizona."

"Sure," Laura said softly, "Sure." But she was talking to the dial tone.

"So, I'm doing really good, Mom. I've only gained fifteen pounds so far, and the doctor said that was great. I spoke to him about transferring my records and he said he would, so it would be really great if you could call Dr. Reynolds and tell him what's going on. You don't think he'll mind delivering the baby under these circumstances, do you?"

"I don't see why he would," Laura said. She was in the backyard by the pool with her portable telephone. Her tan had disappeared during the cooler winter months and she felt like a real paleskin.

"Wait until you see the bassinet Blanche made for the baby. It's gorgeous. You'll love it, and so will the baby."

Val laughed. "Can you believe it? I'm having a real, live baby? I'm really starting to get excited, Mom, and I've been feeling great ever since I came back to school. Isn't that good?"

"It's wonderful, hon," Laura said. She idly smoothed suntan oil on her legs as she and Valerie chatted. In three weeks she would be attending her daughter's graduation from college, and then Val would come home to wait for the baby. Everything seemed to be working out perfectly, in sharp contrast to what was happening with Steve's son and daughter-in-law. If the complications with young Steve's leg weren't bad enough, Joyce had gone into premature labor and had been delivered by caesarean section. The baby, a little girl, weighed less than five pounds and was suffering from jaundice. Laura sighed. Poor Steve. It was just one problem on top of another.

She hadn't seen him in two weeks. He'd gone to Arizona for Steve's surgery and then stayed on when the baby came along. He'd called a couple of times, but he sounded distracted and far away.

"So, how is Steve's new granddaughter?" Valerie asked. "The baby's going to be all right, isn't she?"

"I'm sure she will be, honey," Laura said, hoping she sounded confidant. The last thing Val needed now was to hear bad news, especially when it concerned a newborn baby.

"I saw Robert yesterday, Mom," Val said quietly. "He looked right through me, then turned and walked the other way. And you know what? I didn't even care!"

But she did. It was in her voice, in the pain she couldn't quite hide.

Laura hung up the phone and shook her head. It was hard, but it would work out. It had to.

* * *

She was really ready for some good news when Vicki called a few days later.

"How is everything, honey? Does Andrea still like her new school?

"Everything is great, Mom, except that we all miss you. I've been checking out the university here, and when everything is a little more settled, hopefully by this fall, I may go back to school."

"Oh, that is wonderful! Are you going after your teaching certificate? I can't help thinking you would make a fantastic teacher."

"Thanks, Mom. I am interested in teaching, but Tim and the kids will always be my top priority. Anyway, we'll see how it goes. How are things on the home front? Val wrote to me. She said she's feeling good. She didn't mention that jerk she was engaged to. I guess there's no chance of them getting together?"

"I doubt it. Val said he's been avoiding her. I think she'll probably be better off without him. Who needs a guy like that anyway?"

"Not our Val," Vicki said. "Well, I just wanted to check in with you. Greg wrote me about his good news. I'll bet you were relieved, weren't you?"

"To say the least," Laura said.

"What about you, Mom? Val mentioned

something about you taking on Aunt Blanche as a project of some sort. What did she mean?"

Laura laughed. "You'll have to see it to believe it, honey. Tell you what, I'll take some pictures the next time I see Blanche and send them out to you. You know what they say, one picture is worth a thousand words."

"That good, huh? Well, okay. I guess I better hang up. Write me a nice, long, newsy letter, okay? I love getting letters."

Laura caught the sound of homesickness in Vicki's voice. She had never been prouder of her daughter than she was at that moment.

"Give the children a hug and a kiss from grandma," she said, "and honey, you're doing great. I'm proud of you."

"Thanks, Mom. I love you. Bye."

Laura stared at the telephone thoughtfully. All of her children were doing well, but for Steve one disaster after another seemed to be piling up. She knew he was probably worried sick about the baby, and it was the little girl he'd wanted.

He'd told her once that he didn't handle loss very well, but who did? And hopefully there wouldn't be any losses.

She made her first sale on a Tuesday, to a doctor and his young wife. It was their first home, and they were ecstatic, especially the wife, who was pregnant with their first child.

All the young woman could talk about was the nursery, and how she couldn't wait to start decorating it, but she was unsure of how she wanted to do it.

"My sister-in-law makes beautiful nursery decorator items," Laura said. "Her name is Blanche, and I know she would be happy to show you her samples. That might give you some ideas."

So she made her sale. It was a lovely ten-room tudor-style house, with a large, screened lanai and an in-ground swimming pool. She would earn a handsome commission, but best of all was the boost to her self-confidence. Now she knew she could do it, and there would be no stopping her!

But there was also no one to celebrate with. George was out of town, and Sheila had gone away to visit her ailing grandmother. And Steve was still in Arizona.

Laura ended up taking a long, scented bubble bath, and pouring herself a glass of champagne. She also poured a tiny bit in Buttons's water dish, but the little dog sniffed it and turned away.

"Okay," she said, lifting her glass to her lips. "Be that way. See if I care! I made the sale and that's all that matters!"

But drinking champagne alone wasn't much fun, so she called Blanche. Laura's sister-in-law was very excited, especially when she learned that she might acquire a new customer.

"Honestly, Laura," she said rapidly, her words almost ramming head first into one another, "I just don't know how I ever managed to sit around this house doing nothing all those years, and now I'm just busy all the time. But I'm excited about your first sale . . . have you told all the children? Won't they be surprised . . . no, of course they won't . . . I'm sure they knew all along that you would be successful in whatever you decided to do."

"Well, one sale doesn't exactly make me an overnight success, Blanche, but it's gratifying. At least I proved I can do it, and now I have to start thinking of the next one," Laura said, when she could finally get a word in edgewise.

"And that will be even easier," Blanche said firmly. "You know, you really must think positively, Laura. Someone told me that once. I just forget who, but anyway, I believe it's true. Did I tell you that Jim is taking a course in advanced woodworking? No, well, sometimes I forget what I've told you. There's just so much on my mind these days . . . but that's good, isn't it? Use it or lose it, wasn't that one of the things Paul always said?"

Laura started to giggle. Was it the champagne, or Blanche? She wasn't sure, and she really didn't care. She felt pleasantly mellow and relaxed, and she didn't feel quite so lonely anymore.

"Blanche, I really enjoy talking to you these days. Now I suppose I better hang up. I'm getting a little sleepy."

"It's the excitement," Blanche said. "That always makes me sleepy."

But it wasn't excitement with Laura. Her sleepiness was the direct result of her third glass of champagne. Usually she only sipped one, but tonight for some reason it had gone down very easily. So she poured a second glass, and finally, a third. And now when she stood up she was a trifle wobbly, and she couldn't seem to stop giggling. It reminded her of when she was in high school, and had gotten together with a few girlfriends. One of them would say something silly, and they'd all start giggling, and first thing they knew, they couldn't stop.

So, giggling and wobbling, Laura made her way into her bedroom and practically fell on the bed. And a few minutes later, when Buttons joined her, she was fast asleep.

The faithful little dog licked Laura's face, sighed, then curled up in a ball beside his mistress and fell asleep.

Twenty-one

Steve got back a week before Valerie was due to graduate. He came to Laura's house the first evening, and she was shocked by his appearance. He looked so tired, so dejected. Laura went to him and put her arms around him. She just held him, not speaking.

Later, after he'd managed to eat a bowl of soup and drink two cups of tea laced with honey and brandy, he looked a little better. But he sighed heavily as he settled himself on the sofa and looked around. "I was beginning to think I'd never see this place again, never see you again, Laura. It's been hell."

"I know. I've thought about you every day, wondered about how you were coping, how young Steve was handling this . . . and the baby on top of everything else."

"Well, thank God, she's doing fine. They

named her Sandra Lee. If she continues to gain weight, Joyce should be able to take her home next week. It's going to be rough on the kids. A new baby and Steve needing a certain amount of care. And they're so proud, so determined to handle everything on their own. I finally got them to agree to let me pay a woman to come in and clean their house once a week, so Joyce won't get burned out. Poor kid. She was at the hospital night and day, even after they released her. And she was torn between spending time with Steve, trying to cheer him up, and being with her baby."

"What about Steve's leg? What's the story on that?"

Laura sipped her brandy and resisted the urge to smooth a few stray hairs off Steve's forehead. She sensed that he needed to talk. So she settled back to listen.

Steve shook his head. "I guess we'll never know the true facts on that. All I know is what the doctors were willing to say. It seems that the break was a bad one, and it just did not heal the way they anticipated it would. When they took the cast off they realized things weren't right. If they left the leg the way it was, Steve would have a bad limp, and probably a lot of trouble in the future. So, even though Steve was devastated by the idea of being laid up for another eight to ten weeks, we talked him into having it taken care of now. When I left he was starting to come out of his depression, but for a while he really had us worried."

"I'm so sorry all this has happened, and I wish there was something I could do to help."

Steve stretched his legs straight out in front of him, raised his arms and stretched. "You do help just by being you, by being here and listening to me. Do you have any idea how much I've missed you, how badly I wanted to come back to you?"

"About half as much as I missed you?" Laura teased softly. "I made my first sale a few days ago, and there was no one to celebrate with. It took a lot of the pleasure out of it because I couldn't share my joy with you."

Steve's eyes lit up. "Your first sale! Well, congratulations! That's wonderful, honey. Of course I never doubted you could do it, but this is just great. I'm sorry I wasn't here when it happened, but it's never too late to celebrate. Maybe we'll plan something special for next week. How does that sound?"

"It sounds wonderful, but you get yourself settled first, and then we'll worry about celebrating. Anyway, I did have a celebration of sorts. I took a long, leisurely bubblebath, and then I drank champagne all by myself. I tried to get Buttons to join me, but he pooped out." Laura rolled her eyes and laughed. "Boy, did I have a whopper of a hangover the next morning!"

Steve chuckled. "And they say dumb animals! Buttons knew what he was doing."

For the first time since they'd been together, Steve stayed the night at Laura's house. At first he seemed hesitant, but she hastily reassured him. "You won't be sleeping in Paul's bed," she said softly. "While you were in Arizona I bought a new bed. I never cared for that extrafirm mattress anyway, and it was time."

"We never really talked about it, so how did you know what I was feeling?"

Laura moved over to sit next to Steve. She took his hand and lifted it to her cheek. "I felt it too, as though there would be ghosts in that bed, even though I know Paul would heartily approve. That was my marriage bed, and it belongs to a different time of my life. You and I are starting over, aren't we?"

Steve found himself speechless. That Laura would do such a thing filled him with joy. It was much like what he had done when he was finally able to clean out Marcie's closets and give away all her clothes and personal items. It was a final good-bye, realizing that part of your life was over, and that you had to move forward. He had taken that step before he moved to Miami and first knocked on Laura's door, but he had felt her holding back, even after they had become intimate.

"We don't have to . . . what I mean is . . . we can just sleep. It's just nice to be together." Laura blushed furiously, and she wondered if she should take Sheila's assertiveness-training class. But Steve was smiling, and he looked less weary than he had when he first arrived.

"You're right, it is nice just to be together." His eyebrows rose and he attempted a lecherous leer, "but we do have to, Laura. We definitely do have to!"

And it was a glorious experience for both of them. It was soft and gentle and filled with caring. It was slow and easy, and the sweet pleasure seemed to go on forever. And when it was over they fell asleep in each other's arms, warm and content.

"I knew it would be wonderful to wake up with you beside me," Steve said the next morning, only moments after his eyes opened. "Even with your hair all rumpled with sleep, you're beautiful."

"What are you hoping to gain with that flattery, sir?" Laura asked, propping herself on one elbow to look down at Steve. She thought he looked young and vulnerable. The lines of weariness that had crisscrossed his face the previous evening were all but gone, and his smile, the smile she had never been able to forget, was back. Impulsively she leaned forward and kissed him.

"Well, what was that for? Does that mean my flattery worked?"

"Don't push it," Laura warned. She sat up, holding the sheet to her chest. She was wearing one of the lacy nightgowns she'd bought on her last shopping trip with Blanche.

"I like that color," Steve said, letting his warm fingers smooth over the peach-colored satin that covered Laura's back. "And I love that soft, silky feel. You women definitely know how to work on a man's senses."

"Oh? Is that what I'm doing? Just because I like pretty lingerie."

"Hey, I'm not knocking it," Steve said quickly, and now his warm hand cupped her left breast. "Umm, I do love that softness," he murmured. "Do you suppose . . . ?"

"No. Absolutely not," Laura cried. "I have to go to the office. I have several appointments scheduled today."

"Ah, the price of success. All right, you win.

I better get going too. Poor Rich has been carrying on alone ever since all this happened. He'll probably be sorry he ever got involved with me."

"I'm sure he understands," Laura said, slipping into a robe. "I'll make some coffee, and then I'll shower. There's cereal in the cabinet and milk in the refrigerator. I'm afraid I don't have time to fix breakfast."

"Hey, no problem. If you have eggs I can whip us up an omelet."

"Not for me, thanks. I've had my quota of eggs for the week, and I really don't have time to sit down and eat. I'll just grab some fruit."

"Oh, sure. Well, maybe I will have a bowl of cereal. I won't be holding you up, will I?"

Laura stopped on her way to the bathroom. "This is the way it would be, you know. If we . . . lived together. Mornings would be hectic, and there wouldn't be much time to linger over big, sinfully rich breakfasts. We'd see each other at our worst, even have to suffer through morning breath."

Steve grinned. So, Laura had been thinking about what it would be like for them to live together. Well, marriage was what he wanted, the whole shebang, but maybe living together could be the first step. Maybe that way Laura could ease into the idea of being a twosome. "Laura, have you . . ."

But now she got that closed look on her face, and she hastily backed through the doorway. "Not now, Steve," she said, shaking her head. "I'll be late for work."

So he sipped his coffee alone while she showered, and when he heard her coming towards the kitchen he deliberately wiped the self-satisfied smile off his face. Slow and easy, Steve, old fellow, he reminded himself. In some ways Laura was like a bird, all flighty, ready to fly away at the slightest movement. She was life-wise and commitment-wary, and Steve knew he was going to have to use all his powers of persuasion to convince her that she simply could not live without him. Well, he'd always enjoyed a challenge, so why not?

"All right then," Laura said, tucking a stray hair into place and picking up her briefcase. "You'll lock up when you leave?"

"I will, and don't worry about Buttons. I'll walk him just before I leave."

"Thanks. That will be great."

"Oh, what about tonight? Will I see you?" Steve felt like a kid, asking for the second date. His belly was jumping as he waited for Laura's answer.

Halfway to the door, she turned and shook her head. "I'm sorry, but one of my appointments isn't until six-thirty this evening, and I have no idea how long I'll be. By the time I get through I'll probably be ready for a bath and bed."

Steve swallowed. It was just like being eighteen again. His disappointment was sharp, and what made it worse was that Laura didn't seem to care. How could she turn her feelings on and off this way? Last night she'd held him as if she never wanted to let him go, and now he felt like a casual acquaintance who had stopped by to have coffee.

"Well, I've got a lot of catching up to do anyway, so it's just as well," he said.

Laura nodded, her mind already racing ahead to the office and her first appointment. It was to show an expensive condo, and if she made the sale it would mean a hefty commission. But the buyer had purchased properties from Echo Realty before, and he was known to be difficult. It promised to be a real contest.

Steve finished his coffee thoughtfully. Laura certainly seemed to be enjoying her new career, and he was glad. But was it going to be an all-or-nothing deal? Would she make room in her busy new life for him, or would her personal affairs be pushed to the side? Only time would tell. He had a feeling he was going to need all the patience he could gather.

* * *

"What do you think, Mr. Elliot?" Laura asked that evening, after showing the condo to her prospective buyer for the second time that day. "Is the apartment adequate for your needs?"

"Possibly," James Elliot said, "but I'm not sure I'm really happy with the location. I would like to be a little closer to the mainstream, if you know what I mean."

"Of course, but then you won't have this nice, peaceful atmosphere."

"I suppose you're right. We can't have everything, can we?"

No, Laura thought, as her headache increased in intensity, but what she had right now was one picky customer. She was trying to be patient, but her smile was beginning to feel forced, and her feet hurt. She tried not to breathe too deeply because the pungent scent of Mr. Elliot's cologne was clogging her sinuses.

Normally women were the ones accused of using too much fragrance, but James Elliot must pour his scent on with a pitcher!

"Mr. Elliot, perhaps you'd like to see the apartment again tomorrow, in the daylight. It is getting rather late, and maybe after a good night's sleep you'll have a fresh perspective."

"Umm, yes, I believe you're right. It is basically what I'm looking for, but I just want to be sure. You understand, don't you?"

"Of course," Laura answered, gathering up her briefcase and her purse before Mr. Elliot could change his mind.

By the time Laura dragged herself into the house her headache had accelerated to a nine plus on a scale of one to ten. Her feet ached, and she was absolutely certain she would never get the smell of Mr. Elliot's cologne out of her nostrils.

She hadn't had any dinner, but she felt too tired to eat. All she wanted was a bath and her bed, just as she'd told Steve that morning. But the telephone started to ring as she slipped off her shoes, and she quickly hobbled across the room to answer it.

"Laura?"

It was Steve, and even though she knew it was crazy, the sound of his voice irritated her. Why was he calling now? She'd told him she was working late, and that when she did get home, she'd be dead tired. So why was he calling? Didn't he understand plain English?"

"Yes, Steve," she said. "I just got in the door."

"Oh, great. I was afraid you might not be home yet. Look, I know you don't feel like cooking, and you probably don't want to go out

404

either, so why don't I pick up some Chinese take-out and we can . . ."

"Steve, I'm not hungry. I'm going to take a bath and go to bed. I've got a headache, and my feet hurt, and right now I don't feel like making conversation with anyone."

"Oh, well, if you're really that tired . . ."

"Yes, I'm that tired, and I told you this morning that I probably would be."

"Laura, for Pete's sake . . . what's the matter with you?"

Closing her eyes, Laura felt her teeth grind as she fought for control. She was so tired, and she just wanted to be left alone.

"The only thing the matter with me is that I'm dead tired and I need to go to bed, and if I stay on this telephone much longer you and I are going to have one hell of a fight."

Silence for a moment, then, "I'll make it easy for you. Good night, Laura. I hope you feel better in the morning."

Click.

Laura held the receiver in her hand for a moment listening to the hum of the dial tone. I'm a bitch, she thought. I'm a pure bitch, and Steve is insensitive, and right now I don't even care!

She took a shower instead of a bath, because she was afraid if she climbed into a warm bathtub, she'd fall asleep, slide down under the water and drown.

And when she dragged her aching body into bed, she snuggled down, closed her eyes and fell asleep almost instantly, unaware that a few miles away, Steve was furiously pacing back and forth, and he was sure he'd never be able to fall asleep.

"Look, Steve, I don't want to argue, and I said I was sorry. Let's just forget it, all right?"

"No. I don't think we can, Laura. It's not the fact that you were tired and cranky. It's that I was a bother to you. Do you have any idea how that makes me feel?"

"But that's not what I meant. It was just . . ."

Steve grimaced, and Laura's eyes widened in surprise. "What's wrong? Are you in pain?"

"Just a pulled muscle," Steve explained, rubbing his arm. "Rich got an urge to arm wrestle and I forgot my advancing age."

Laura grinned. "I have some liniment, grandpa. I'll go get it."

She came back with a tube of something that smelled like mint and felt like ice when she massaged it into his aching muscles.

Steve groaned with pleasurable relief. "Oh,

Laura, that feels wonderful. Don't stop."

She laughed, and for a moment the tension between then was forgotten. "Careful how loud you say that," she warned. "My neighbors will think we're being lewd and lascivious."

"Want to?" Steve wheedled. "My arm isn't that sore."

But he looked at Laura's suddenly sober expression, and he knew that there'd be no lovemaking, not until they got things settled between them, if they could.

"I almost forgot," Steve said.

"Me too."

"I don't want to argue with you, Laura, but I don't think we can just let this pass. It isn't just a case of a woman with PMS. It goes a lot deeper than that, and we both know it." He pulled his arm away from her, and waved the tube of liniment away. "I'm not a yoyo. I can't bounce back and forth at will. Now you want me, now you don't. 'Steve, I missed you so much.' 'Steve, I want to be left alone.' I don't know where I stand with you, Laura. I thought I could be patient and wait quietly while you figured things out, but now I don't think I can do that. I need to know whether or not I'm important in your life. Am I expendable?"

"No, of course not! I . . ." Laura's voice trailed off helplessly. The minty smell of the liniment tickled her nostrils, and made her eyes water. Or were those natural tears?

"Valerie is graduating in four days. I have to go. Maybe when I come back we can talk and figure everything out. I'm not trying to put you on hold, Steve. It's just that right now I don't know what to say."

He nodded, and then he stood up and picked up his jacket. "Tell Valerie congratulations," he said, "and drive carefully."

The door closed behind him, and the tears, not from the liniment at all, trickled down Laura's cheeks. "Good-bye, Steve," she whispered softly.

The air crackled with excitement, with the vigor and hopefulness of youth. Laura craned her neck, trying to see the graduates as they filed down the aisle between the double rows of seats. She wished Vicki and Greg could have been with her, but neither of them had been able to get away. Vicki because she was still trying to get her little family settled, and Greg because he was up to his ears in patients. Which was good, of course, and Valerie understood. She'd said that as long as her mom was there, everything would be okay.

Laura felt a touch of sadness as she thought

of her late husband. Paul was the one who should have been here. He had encouraged all his children to do and be the best they could be, and he would have been proud of Valerie as she came down the aisle, her swollen belly pushing out the front of her gown. And she wasn't the only pregnant student. Laura saw at least three others. But maybe they were married, and maybe they weren't facing what Val was facing.

She raised her hand in a wave, and winked as Val swayed past. And her daughter, her baby, the last to leave her womb and the family nest, smiled broadly and formed a V with her fingers.

Her tears flowed freely as Val received her diploma and turned to smile in her mother's direction. Laura turned to the woman next to her. "That's my daughter."

The woman nodded and smiled, and pointed to a young man in the second row. "My son," she said proudly. "Graduating with honors."

Then the graduation ceremony was over, and Laura suddenly realized that not once had she even thought of the young man who had made her daughter pregnant, nor had she heard his name announced when the diplomas were given out. Had he really transferred to another university to avoid Valerie?

"Congratulations, darling," Laura said a few minutes later, when she finally managed to find Valerie. "Come on, let's get away from this crush of people," she said. "I'm afraid that baby you're carrying is going to get smooshed."

Valerie was radiant. "I did it, Mom. I really did it! I'll be able to take care of my baby now, and I won't have to depend on anyone. Did I tell you I've had a couple more job offers?"

"No, but I'm not surprised," Laura said, maneuvering Valerie away from the laughing, excited crowds of students and their families. "Look, honey, can we go somewhere and get a cup of coffee and something to eat? I was too excited to eat any lunch. How about you?"

Valerie laughed. "Same here, and now that you mention it, we, my baby and I, are starved. How about pizza, with mushrooms and pepperoni? I crave pizza all the time now."

"Then pizza it is," Laura said. "You're the star of the show today."

They sat in a booth in the pizza parlor, munching pizza and drinking ice-cold root beers.

"Umm, I love root beer," Valerie said, closing her eyes in ecstacy. "Don't you?"

"Absolutely," Laura said. "Now, tell me. How

are you feeling? You look wonderful."

Valerie grinned. "Yeah, for a basketball. I feel great, Mom, except for when the baby decides to do somersaults and upsy-daisies. Then I sometimes find it hard to get in a comfortable position."

"I remember that well, and you deserve what you get, my girl. Of all three of my children, you were the most active in the womb. It was as if you were in a big hurry to get out and see what the world was like."

"Mom, I love this baby so much already. I can't even imagine what I'm going to feel when it finally arrives. And I can't help wondering how Robert can be so callous. Did I tell you he left school? I guess he couldn't stand seeing me walking around with my belly growing bigger every day."

"Put him behind you, honey. He's not worth a moment of your time. You don't need a self-centered young man like that, and neither does the baby."

Laura stayed overnight, camping out with Valerie and her roommate, Gail. The three of them sat around eating pretzels and drinking cheap red wine, except for Val, who had milk. The girls were high on life, filled with triumph for their achievements. They told silly jokes and talked about men, about what a rat Robert

411

was, and about the guy Gail was currently drooling over, and finally Val turned the conversation to Steve.

"My mom's got a sweetie," she said teasingly. "Haven't you, Mom? How is old Steve anyway? And how's his new granddaughter?"

"The baby is fine as far as I know," Laura said, "and Steve sent his love and congratulations. Sheila did too. She wanted to come up with me, but she had a settlement today. You're going to be surprised when you see her again. She's really blossoming."

"I'll bet," Val said. "But what about Steve, Mom? How's your love life these days?"

Laura couldn't help it. She blushed, and both girls giggled.

"Boy, if I teased my mom this way, she'd probably ground me for life," Gail said. "Don't let her get to you, Mrs. Kinsey. She's just a big tease."

"How well I know," Laura said, rolling her eyes. She looked at Val sternly. "For your information, young lady, my love life is not up for discussion. Steve is fine, and so am I. That's it."

"Ohh, trouble in paradise, Mummy?" Valerie probed. "Did you lovebirds have a tiff? Well, don't worry. My psychology prof said that fights clear the air. Of course he didn't call

412

them fights. He referred to them as altercations. Did you and Steve have an altercation, Mom?"

"I think so," Laura said, taking a big sip of her wine, "and believe me, it was a honey!"

Early the next morning Laura headed back home. Her head felt a little funny from all the wine she'd drunk, but she was anxious to get home. A neighbor was looking after Buttons, and she had several appointments to show houses the following day. And in three days Val would be home to wait for the birth of her baby.

As she drove home Laura was filled with ambivalent feelings. Was Valerie's psychology prof right? Did fights clear the air? And had she and Steve just had a fight, or was it more than that?

She felt bad when she thought of how she'd spoken to Steve, but she couldn't guarantee it wouldn't happen again. She was only human, and when she was backed into a corner she came out hissing and clawing. But Steve didn't realize he'd cornered her. He didn't understand how she felt. And she didn't know how to explain it to him . . . not without breaking his heart, and maybe her own in the bargain.

Twenty-two

Steve paced around the auto rental lot. The business was doing even better than he had hoped it would, and he should have been jumping for joy. He would have been, except for all the problems his son had suffered through, and his tiff with Laura.

And it was much more than a tiff. As he'd told Laura the last time he saw her, it went much deeper than that. It had to do with her inability to commit. She'd already admitted that she loved him, and even if she hadn't said the words, her actions had proved it. A woman like Laura wouldn't go to bed with a man unless she had strong feelings for him. And Laura had done a lot more than go to bed with him. She'd loved him in just about every way a woman could love a man, with her hands, her lips, her body, and finally, her heart.

"Hey, buddy, why so solemn? You haven't had more bad news from Steve, have you?"

Rich came to stand beside Steve, and now he clapped a hand on his cousin's shoulder. "Hang in there, pal," he said. "Better days are coming."

"Yeah, so I heard. Steve's doing okay, and they brought the baby home, so everything's all right in that department."

"Then what's bugging you, coz? Woman trouble?"

Steve grimaced and kicked a stone with his foot, the way he had as a boy. "You might say that. Laura's giving me fits."

Rich grinned and slapped Steve on the back. "I know what you mean. Women are good at that, aren't they? Casey makes me crazy sometimes too."

Steve shook his head and ran his hand over the smooth exterior of the hood on a '64 Mustang convertible. The metal was warm from the sun. "Not like that, Rich," he said. "I love Laura, and I want to marry her. Hell, you know how I am. I'm not the swinging bachelor type. I'm more for home and hearth, you know? And I always thought that's what women wanted, a guy who was willing to make things all legal and tidy. But not Laura. She's dragging her feet. She said she's not sure she wants to marry again, that she likes being free and unencumbered. She's really getting into this real estate business now and I feel like I'm perched somewhere on the sidelines."

Rich shoved his hands in the pockets of his pants and shrugged. "Now that is a switch. Usually it's the man who feels that way, and the little woman who's begging for a ring."

"Not this time, and not with my lady . . . oh hell, she's not my lady yet, and sometimes I think she never will be. Sometimes I can almost feel her slipping away from me."

"Well, I sure don't know what to tell you, coz. Have you tried a little loving persuasion?"

Steve shrugged and ignored the pointed question. He wasn't a kiss and tell guy, and he never had been. What had happened between him and Laura was private . . . almost sacred. At least that's how he thought of it. He wasn't sure anymore about what Laura thought.

"So Elliot finally bought something," Laura said. She shook her head and frowned. The man who had been indirectly responsible for her fight with Steve had turned around and bought a property from another realtor. Of course he had every right to do that, but it just

416

annoyed her to think of all the time she had spent with him, all for nothing.

"Those are the breaks of the game, Laura," George said philosophically. "It happens that way sometimes."

"Well, if he comes here again, I'm going to be otherwise occupied," Laura said, slapping a folder down on her desk with more than usual force.

"Hey, what's up, pretty lady? Problems?"

Laura started to shake her head, and then stopped. Every now and then George liked to pretend that he was flirting with her, but they both knew there would never be anything but friendship between them, and maybe it would help to look at this from a man's point of view.

"Answer a question for me, will you, George?" She perched on the corner of his desk, carefully covering her knees with her skirt. "If you had a girlfriend, and you wanted to get married and she didn't . . . what would you think?"

George grinned. "I'd thank my lucky stars that I had the good sense to pick such an intelligent woman. Look, honey, I was married twice. The first time it ended in divorce, and the second, my wife died. You know what they say about three strikes and you're out? Well,

I'm not about to try for that third strike. I date, when I find a lady who likes bald, somewhat paunchy men, and at the end of the evening I take my date home. It's better that way."

Laura slid off the desk and began to pace. "That's sort of the way I feel. I had a good marriage with Paul, and I wouldn't trade my memories for all the silver on the *Atocha*, but I'm just not sure I want to do it again. I've tried to explain my feelings to Steve, but he ends up getting defensive. He thinks the fact that I'm not dying to rush down the aisle means I don't care enough."

"Do you?" George asked seriously.

"Yes, I do," Laura said, "and that's what makes this so hard." Her face softened. "I love Steve, but I'm just not sure that marriage is necessary at this stage of my life."

"Then, if you're not sure, don't do it," George advised.

One of the other realtors came in then and George was called away. Laura sat down at her own desk and opened the file folder she'd put there earlier. It was a deal she was currently working on, a sale where the home's present owner was offering to hold part of the mortgage for the buyers. Laura had spent several days working out terms that were satisfactory to both parties, and now she was finally ready to present the agreement of sale for signing. Her eyes skimmed the figures one last time, and then she closed the folder, feeling the satisfaction of a job well done. Some areas of real estate transactions were still confusing to her, but she was learning more every day, and best of all, she was enjoying everything she did, with the possible exception of dealing with difficult customers like James Elliot.

But she couldn't win them all, and basically she was pleased with the decisions she had made since Paul died. Starting over was never easy, but she had done it, and once Val had her baby and Laura was able to sell her home and settle into a small, cozy apartment, the transformation would be complete, except for Steve.

Terrible as it sounded, and as much as she loved him, he was a thorn in her side. She didn't want to be without him, but she didn't know how to keep him without giving up what she most cherished, her freedom.

The telephone rang. Laura shrugged and picked it up. "Echo Realty," she said. "Laura Kinsey speaking. How can I help you?"

* * *

"Valerie will be home tomorrow evening, so I thought we should have a talk while we still have some privacy," Laura said. She'd pleated and repleated a paper napkin until it fell apart in her hands. And now she looked up at Steve pleadingly. "If I could just make you understand," she began.

"I think I'm beginning to understand," Steve said soberly. "You have feelings for me, but they're not strong enough to make you want to give up your newfound freedom and independence."

Laura jumped up from the sofa, and the shredded napkin fell to the floor, the bits and pieces scattering in every direction. Buttons darted over and tried to catch them. "You make it sound so . . . cold, and it's not like that at all, Steve. Don't you know that?"

"Look, Laura, I'm not sure what I know anymore. When I first saw you again, after all the years we were separated, it was like a miracle, like someone more powerful than us was giving us a second chance. I was awed by the feelings I had for you. From that first moment I knew I wanted to spend the rest of my life with you. There was never any doubt in my mind. I've never been much of a loner. I want you in my

420

life, and I'm willing to take the bad with the good. Hell, I know we're both probably a little set in our ways, but we could work around that, couldn't we?"

Laura bit her lip, and then she tasted the warm salt of her blood. A part of her wanted to fall into Steve's arms, to make crazy wild love with him and let the future take care of itself. But when the lovemaking was over and they dropped back to earth, what then? If Steve couldn't accept her need for space of her own, after years of giving her all to her family, how could they make a marriage work?

She went to him, knowing she shouldn't, but unable to stay away. She sat beside him on the sofa and gave him her hands.

"Steven Walker, I love you. No matter what happens, I hope you will never doubt that. I think a tiny part of me has always loved you." She stood up and tugged him with her. "Come with me. There's something I want you to see."

She led him to her bedroom, hoping that what she was about to show him would help him understand.

"Here," she said softly, lifting her hand to touch the side of his face with a feathery caress. "This is what I wanted you to see."

She turned on the light and led him to a

shelf on the wall beside her new bed. There, carefully arranged and religiously dusted, sat her collection of ceramic and porcelain daisies.

"See?"

He saw, and he knew. It was true. She had always loved him, just as he had always loved her. Theirs was a love that neither time nor distance could destroy, and now, because Laura required freedom and he needed permanence, they stood to lose it forever.

Steve gently touched the creamy white petal of a daisy. It was porcelain, smooth and silky against his flesh. If he closed his eyes he could pretend they were standing in a field of daisies. He could imagine himself making love to Laura among the crushed petals, with the sun bright above them and the hum of bees sounding in their ears. He swallowed and blinked. Men didn't cry. Not over a bunch of glass daisies.

When they went back downstairs, Laura poured them each a glass of wine, then she sat down across from Steve.

"How about a compromise?" she asked. "As I said earlier, Val will be here tomorrow, and for the next several weeks I'm going to be spending most of my time with her. I promised her I'd be her Lamaze coach, and there's a lot to do to get ready for the baby."

Steve nodded and waited for her to go on.

"We can see each other, of course, but maybe not as much as we were. Maybe if we both have a little time to think things through without the push-pull we feel when we're together, we'll be able to make the right decision. I don't want to lose you, Steve," she added softly, "but I won't marry you out of desperation."

"You're asking for a cooling-off time?"

"In a way. I don't know what else to do."

"What's the alternative?"

"There isn't any," Laura said gently.

He kissed her when he left, and he held her just a moment longer than necessary, and when he released her he felt oddly bereft.

"I'll try it your way," he promised, "but I'm not going to pretend to like it, and damn it, when Val goes into labor you better call me!"

Laura started to laugh, and she had a strong feeling that somehow, someway, everything was going to work out. "I promise," she said. "If I didn't, Val would probably disown me."

"At least one of the women in your family has some sense," Steve growled. "Let me know when it's convenient for me to stop by and see Val. I have a little gift for her."

"You are sweet," Laura said. Then she kissed

him on the cheek and gave him a little shove towards the door.

"This is it, Mom, the home stretch. Driving home today I got the weirdest feeling. I suddenly got so scared I had to pull over to the side of the road. I'm going to have a baby, Mom, a real, live baby. It's not going to be like the Betsy-Wetsy doll I could put down when I got tired of it, and I'm going to have to do this all alone."

Laura smiled and gave her daughter a hug. "Not quite, honey," she said. "I'll be right beside you, and somewhere up there," she paused and pointed upwards, "Daddy is watching over you."

Valerie managed a watery smile. "And let's not forget Aunt Blanche," she joked.

"You just wait until you see what Aunt Blanche has done for you. By the way, we're invited there for dinner tomorrow. I accepted for us."

Valerie looked horrified. Her hands instinctively went to her swollen belly. "You didn't! Mom, how could you? I know you keep telling me Aunt Blanche has changed, but how can I face her and Uncle Jim looking like this? I mean . . . well, you know how rigid she's always been."

"Val, are you ashamed of the decision you made?"

"Well, no, but . . ."

"Then we'll go to dinner tomorrow night with your Aunt and Uncle. You'll hold your head high and act like your normal sweet self, and everything will be fine. You'll see. You can't hide out here for the duration of this pregnancy, you know."

"But . . ."

"Honey, no buts please. This dinner is important to Blanche. She wants to show you the bassinet, and the rocking horse Jim made for the baby."

"All right, I'll go, but are you sure she understands? She doesn't think I'm . . ."

"She thinks, as I do, that you're a very brave young woman, and she's looking forward to the baby's arrival as much as you and I are."

Val shook her head dubiously. "If you say so, Mom, but this sure doesn't sound like the Aunt Blanche I know."

And at six o'clock the next evening they stood on Blanche's front porch and rang the doorbell.

Valerie was dressed in a pale blue maternity dress. Her shiny auburn hair hung to her shoulders and she looked beautiful and very scared.

"It's okay," Laura assured her just as the door opened.

Blanche looked at them, then her eyes focused just on Valerie and she held out her arms.

Her eyes wide and disbelieving, Val stumbled forward and let herself be embraced. Over Blanche's shoulder, Laura made a circle with her thumb and forefinger.

"Oh my," Blanche said, when she finally released Valerie. "I feel almost as though I'm a grandmother too. I just can't believe that in a few weeks we'll have a brand-new baby in the family. But come on in. Jim helped me set the table, and he's getting us a little something to drink. Not for you, of course, little mama, but I'm sure he can find you some fruit juice."

"That will be great," Val said, following her aunt into the living room.

"Look, Jim, here they are. Laura and Valerie. Did you fix our drinks?"

"Right here," Jim said. "Hello, Laura. Good to see you, Valerie. You're looking round these days."

Laura had always thought that Jim had untapped potential, and now she was sure of it.

He displayed an open friendliness that was endearing.

"This is lovely, Blanche, but I'm surprised you want to entertain, as busy as you've been lately."

"Oh that! You know, Laura, I've discovered that the busier you are, the more you can get done. These days I accomplish so much more than I used to."

"That's wonderful, but I'm afraid my going out to work has left me woefully disorganized."

Jim gave Valerie a tall glass of pineapple juice, and then he handed Laura a glass with a fancy cream drink. "My specialty," he said proudly. "Try it."

Laura did and it was delightfully cool and frothy. "What is this called?"

Blanche giggled. "It's his very own creation. He dreamed it up years ago, when we were on our honeymoon, but it's been ages since he's made it." She giggled again and put her hand to her mouth. "It's called *passion*."

Laura nearly choked on a mouthful of passion. "Oh my, that went down the wrong way, but it certainly is delicious."

Valerie was trying hard not to laugh, and when Blanche turned away, Laura gave her a light kick on her foot.

"Behave," Laura whispered urgently. "If you get me started laughing, I'll never stop."

Val nodded. "I sure am glad I came," she murmured. "I wouldn't miss this for the world."

Dinner was a gourmet delight. Besides sewing, cooking was something else Blanche had always done well. There was tenderloin of pork, pounded thin and sprinkled with garlic and lime and then coated with cracker meal and lightly fried. A sinfully rich fettuccini dish and tender broccoli cuts completed the meal, and when they were convinced they could eat no more, Blanche served dessert, a fruit-covered cheesecake.

"Good heavens, if I ate like this very often I'd weigh three hundred pounds," Laura complained, pushing back from the table. "Blanche, you must have spent all day in the kitchen."

Beaming proudly, Blanche poured coffee for everyone but Valerie. She got a tall glass of ice-cold milk.

"Now, while you finish your dessert, Jim and I will show you what we've been doing, Valerie."

The two of them left the room, and Laura and Valerie exchanged a look. Val shook her head. "Amazing," she said. "Absolutely amazing."

Val lifted a forkful of cheesecake to her lips and nearly dropped it when Blanche and Jim returned.

"Oh, wow! Oh, gosh! Is all this for me?"

It was almost like a baby shower. Blanche had filled the beautifully decorated bassinet with lots of packages, and behind her, Jim proudly carried a solid wood rocking horse, complete with a mane and a tail. It was plain that it had been crafted with love and care, and the wood had been painstakingly polished.

"Oh, Valerie, isn't this wonderful?"

Tears stung Laura's eyes, and she saw that her daughter was experiencing the same overwhelming emotions.

"Do you like the way I decorated the bassinet?" Blanche asked anxiously. "I hope you like yellow. Laura suggested it, for either a boy or a girl, you know."

"Aunt Blanche, how can I ever thank you? You too, Uncle Jim. The bassinet is beautiful and the rocking horse is a treasure. I can't believe you did all this for me." Then she did cry, the tears raining down her cheeks unchecked.

"Oh, sweetie, don't cry," Blanche begged. "This is a happy time. We did this because we wanted to make you happy. We don't want to see you cry."

"But these are happy tears, Aunt Blanche," Valerie sobbed. "To think that you cared enough to do this for me . . . it makes me so happy!"

They ohed and ahed over the bibs and booties and rattles and other little things Blanche had bought for the baby, and finally, when Val began to droop with weariness, Laura knew it was time to go home.

She gave Blanche and Jim a hug and tried to convey her thanks, but they both insisted that they'd had all the fun.

"If we can't be grandparents ourselves, maybe Val will share her little one with us," Jim said, his voice wistful. "This has been the best evening we've had in a long, long time."

"Well, don't worry, there will be more," Laura promised.

"So, now do you believe me?" Laura asked Val as she drove them home. "Didn't I tell you it was a miracle?"

There was no answer, and Laura took her eyes off the road for an instant, to glance at her daughter. Then she smiled, and turned her attention back to the road. Val was asleep, a smile curving her lips, and one of the baby bibs Blanche had given her was folded under her cheek.

* * *

Laura followed Val's waddling form into the large gymnasium. There were pregnant women everywhere, and many of them had male partners. But there were others, like Val, with older women with them. Mothers, Laura thought, who had to fill in for absentee fathers. Well, so be it. She'd vowed to help Valerie in any way she could. Val was determined to have a natural delivery. She didn't want to take any drugs that might hurt the baby.

"Ladies? May I have your attention?"

One of the pregnant women Laura had assumed was a student moved to the front of the room. She smiled and nodded to everyone.

"Yes, I'm pregnant," she said, "As if you couldn't tell, and I'm your instructor, and everything I'm going to tell and show you tonight has been personally tested. This is my second pregnancy. I have a three-year-old son who was born using the Lamaze method, and I wouldn't consider having a baby any other way. Now, how about if everyone finds a spot and gets comfortable on the floor. Did you all bring your pillows the way you were instructed?"

Valerie looked down at the floor and shook her head. "I don't know if I can do that," she said dubiously.

Laura cut her eyes towards a woman much larger than Val who was already seated on the floor, with the pillow behind her, and a man who was probably her husband, behind that. "If she can, you can," Laura hissed. "Now snap to!"

For the next hour they all practiced breathing exercises. Laura learned how to gently rub Valerie's belly to ease her contractions. She was also shown where and how to massage Val's back during the actual labor. And then they were shown a film showing a real birth.

"Wow," Valerie said, as they left the gym later, "I didn't know it was like that. Did you?"

"Frankly no. In my day we were put to sleep, at least at the end. Of course a lot of babies were delivered by forceps because the mothers were asleep and couldn't help, but that's how it was done. And I would never have dreamed of asking your father to go in the delivery room with me."

"So you've never seen a baby born before, right?"

Laura shook her head. "Never."

"Well, what do you really think? Will it make you queasy to stay with me?"

"No way," Laura said. "It's going to be an experience I'll always remember."

Twenty-three

Steve chuckled as Valerie heaved herself off the sofa. Laura had invited him and Sheila for dinner, and the three of them had enjoyed a great time teasing Valerie about her figure, or lack of one. Privately, Steve thought Laura's daughter was adorable, even prettier now than the first time he'd seen her. It was as if she had bloomed with her pregnancy, as though as the baby inside her grew, so did her radiance.

But it was fun to tease her and see her mock anger.

"Don't worry, Val," he said, grinning as she waddled across the room to get a pillow, "this is only temporary. One of these days you'll be slim and trim again."

Valerie waddled back across the room to her favorite chair, pillow in hand. "I'm beginning to doubt that day will ever come. I'll probably be like an elephant and be pregnant for nine years."

"I think it's only seven years," Sheila said solemnly.

"Seven years! Good grief! Can you imagine?"

"Frankly no," Steve said. "I've always had the greatest respect and admiration for pregnant ladies. I know this is an old saying, but I'll bet it's true. If men had to have the babies, there probably wouldn't be any."

Laura couldn't resist. "Why, Steve Walker, are you a c-h-i-c-k-e-n?" She bent her elbows and flapped her arms, and her eyes sparkled mischievously.

"Watch it," Steve said, his tone low and menacing. "You know what happened the last time you did that."

Realizing she'd probably pushed her luck a little too far, Laura blushed. She remembered all right, only too well!

"Uh-oh, I think we're in the middle of a private joke, Sheila," Val teased. "Care to enlighten us, Mother dear?"

"No, I wouldn't, and it would be very prudent of you to mind your own business, young lady. Just because you're pregnant doesn't mean you can take liberties around here, you know."

"Aw gee, I can't have any fun," Val pouted, sticking her lower lip out. "Come on, Sheila, help me up out of this chair. I think it's time we went to my room and had another makeup lesson. We'll give these two spoilsports a little privacy."

Grinning widely, Sheila gave Val her hand and helped her heave herself out of the chair.

"A few more pounds and we'll need a forklift around here," Val grumbled, but they all knew she didn't mean it. If ever a woman was glorying in a pregnancy, it was Valerie. But Laura still couldn't help wishing the circumstances had been different.

"At last!" Laura said, sitting down next to Steve. She handed him a glass of brandy, and held her own glass to her nose and sniffed appreciatively. Then she sipped. "Ah, I needed that. Coping with my brat of a daughter does try my patience."

Steve laughed. "She's a doll, and you know it. Despite the fact that Vicki and I got off to a rough start, I have to admit that you've done a good job with all your children, Laura. You should be very proud."

Laura put her glass down and leaned her head on Steve's shoulder. "I am," she said softly, "but it wasn't all my doing. Paul was an exemplary father. I suppose that's why I worry about Valerie raising her child all alone. I truly believe children need both parents."

"Ideally, yes, but I think one good, loving parent is enough. And from what you've told me of the baby's father, he sounded like a real loser."

"Let's not talk about that now," Laura said. She snuggled a little closer. "Let's just enjoy being together."

Steve nodded silently, and tightened his arm around Laura's shoulders. Her silky auburn hair tickled his chin, and the fresh scent of her shampoo teased his nostrils. "Ah, Laura," he said softly. "Being here with you like this makes everything all right."

He felt her nod, but she didn't speak, and he wished he knew what she was thinking and feeling. Cuddled against him the way she was, she seemed content. But was it just a transitory thing? In some ways he felt he knew Laura, but in others she was a total mystery. As a young girl she'd been more dependent and clingy, but now, as a mature woman, she was brimming with self-confidence. And he liked that about her. He really did, but he couldn't help wishing she would need him just a little.

They stayed that way for a long time, not speaking, each of them lost in private thoughts, and then they heard the girls coming and Laura reluctantly sat up and fluffed her hair.

"Our peaceful interlude is over," she said, smiling ruefully, "and it's probably time we said good night. We both have to go to work tomorrow."

Val came over to stand in front of them. "Are you really going to take me for a ride in a '55 T-bird one of these days, Steve?" she asked.

Steve stood up and grinned. "With pleasure, but I think it will have to be after your little munchkin arrives, because right now I don't think you'd fit."

"I haven't had a ride yet, and I'm not pregnant," Laura complained. "Why does she rate?"

"Pregnant ladies deserve special treats," Steve said soberly, "but I suppose that since you're the pregnant lady's mother we could make an exception. When do you want to come by?"

"Tomorrow," Laura said quickly, "before you change your mind. But what if it's rented?"

"We have two now, and it's unlikely they'll both be out at the same time."

"Okay. I'll call you after lunch and tell you what time I can get away. Is that all right?"

"Perfect," Steve said. Then he bent his head and kissed her, right in front of two very interested bystanders.

"Wow!" Sheila said.

"Way to go!" Val cheered.

"One of the '55 T-birds is totaled?"

Steve couldn't believe what he was hearing, and it was eerie. Just last night he'd promised Laura a ride and now one of their prized classics had been reduced to rubble. "What about the driver? He's not . . ."

Rich hastily shook his head. "He's alive, but pretty badly banged up. I don't know all the details yet, but they did tell me the bird was totaled."

"Good God!" Steve stood up and began to pace and he raked his fingers through his dark hair. "I knew something like this could happen, and probably would someday, but I wasn't expecting it quite so soon. Well, at least we're fully insured. That's something."

"Uh, that might be a problem," Rich said, flushing. "I'm not sure Casey sent in the premium. She meant to, but . . ."

"What! Hell's bells, man, do you know what this could mean? If that driver is badly hurt and . . . shit! I can't believe this! What has that wife of yours got for brains anyway, sawdust?"

Rich's face grew redder, and he looked like he didn't know whether to cry or throw a punch. "Now wait a minute, Steve! I won't let you talk about Casey that way. She doesn't know much about running a business, but she's learning and she was trying to help, and . . ."

"Oh, she's helped all right," Steve growled. "She may just have helped us into a bankruptcy court!" He rubbed his temples. "Maybe this is just a nightmare," he mumbled.

"Look, I didn't say she hadn't paid the premium. I just said I wasn't sure. She . . . she's checking into it right now."

"Well, we both better pray that she did pay the premium, coz, because if we are uninsured we're in big, big trouble!"

Casey called a few minutes later and Steve could almost feel the tears dripping through the telephone. He swallowed his fury and tried to talk calmly.

"What did you find out, Casey?"

"Nothing," his cousin's wife said, sobbing. "The girl who handles our account is out sick today, and the woman filling in doesn't know anything about it, so I have to call back tomorrow and that means we have to worry all night and . . ."

"Casey, calm down and stop crying, please. That isn't going to help anything." Steve sighed heavily. It was going to be a hell of a night. "Try again first thing in the morning, will you, and meanwhile, say a prayer that the driver wasn't too badly injured."

Steve hung up the phone. Rich looked as sick as Steve felt. "Look, there's no sense getting all stirred up until we know something for sure, and maybe we'll get lucky."

"Yeah, maybe," Rich muttered. "Look, Steve, if it . . . goes bad, I'll find some way to repay the money you invested, if it takes me the rest of my life. I swear it!"

"Hey, come on. Knock it off. It's not going to come to that. We're probably getting all wound up over nothing."

"Yeah, maybe," Rich said again.

Laura called an hour later, sounding perky and bright. "I'll be through here in an hour. Can I have my ride then?"

"Sure," Steve said flatly, "if you don't mind riding on the back of a tow truck. One of the Birds was wrecked this morning, totally. There's not much left but tires and a steering wheel."

"Oh no! Really?

"Look, Laura, I like to kid around, but I wouldn't joke about something like this." His voice was sharper than intended, but he wasn't feeling very mellow.

"No, of course not. I just . . . was anyone injured?" she asked, sounding worried.

"The driver was pretty banged up. We don't know the details yet, but it looks like we could be in big trouble. Rich isn't sure his wife paid our insurance premium on time, and if she didn't . . ."

Steve left the rest of his sentence hanging, but Laura got the message. "Oh good heavens, and you were doing so well!"

Steve laughed shortly. *Were* is the key word all right. By tomorrow it may all be over."

"May I stop by on my way home?" Laura asked softly, "Just to offer moral support?"

For a moment Steve was tempted. Laura seemed to have a knack for making him feel better. And he knew she was genuinely concerned.

But his head was throbbing and he was being eaten up with heartburn, and he knew he wasn't fit company for anyone. The best thing he could do was go home and wallow in self-pity alone. Maybe he'd even get a little drunk. Then, in the morning he'd deal with reality.

"Thanks, Laura," he said, his voice sounding gruff and aloof, "but I think you'd be well advised to keep your distance from me tonight."

"Oh? You're sure?"

"I said so, didn't I?" He hated himself for cutting her off this way, but he hated himself more for needing her so much. What he really wanted was to bury his head in her lap and pretend it was just a bad dream, but he couldn't do that. Laura didn't want him to need her that much. Over and over she'd indicated that she wanted to preserve a little distance between them, that she needed freedom and space. He was afraid to hem her in, afraid to let her see how badly he wanted and needed her.

"Just go on home and spend time with your daughter, Laura," he said, "and don't worry about me. I'll survive."

Men! They were like little children sometimes, wanting to be coddled, and ashamed to admit it. She'd heard the need in Steve's voice, and she'd be damned if his gruffness was going to keep her away when she was needed. She'd let him down before, and she didn't want to do it again.

"I'm out of here, George," she called, gathering her purse and briefcase. "See you tomorrow."

"Okay. Have a good evening."

Laura doubted that was possible. She put her car in gear and pulled out into the traffic, feeling thoroughly discouraged. If what Steve had said was true the rental agency could be out of business before it really got off the ground, and Steve had finally confided in her that he'd invested a sizable portion of his savings in the business. And of course there was much more at stake than financial ruin. There was an injured man lying in a hospital somewhere, and Laura couldn't even imagine the guilt Rich's wife would feel if the business went under because of her.

When she parked her car outside the lot, there was no sign of either Steve or Rich. For a moment Laura wondered if she should just go away. After all, Steve and Rich were family, and maybe they were inside discussing personal, private matters. Maybe she'd just be in the way. Then she remembered how lost and dejected Steve had sounded, and her spine stiffened. The worst that could happen was that the men would tell her to get lost.

But when she went inside, she saw that Steve was alone in his office. Her heart turned over as she took in the terrible despair in his dark eyes, but she wasn't prepared for the quick, raw anger that replaced it when he saw her.

"Didn't I tell you to go home?" he snapped, getting out of his chair. "What are you, deaf?"

"Steve, stop it," Laura said sharply, her own anger starting to rise. "There is no reason in the world for you to act this way. I know you're upset, and I understand, but it's not fair of you to take it out on me and . . ."

"Laura, I told you not to come over," Steve said, speaking in a low, measured tone. "I warned you that I wasn't fit company for anyone. I'm going to go home in a few minutes and have a few . . . no, maybe I'll make it several good, stiff drinks, and I'm going to feel sorry for myself, and I don't give a damn whether anyone likes it or not!"

Laura nodded. "Good for you. I think that's exactly what you should do. I'll join you."

"No," Steve said flatly. "No. I don't want you!"

Laura backed out of the office, her hand over her mouth as if to stifle a scream of outrage. Steve almost went after her, but he didn't, and Laura drove the rest of the way home with tears streaming down her face.

"Mom, you know he didn't mean it. He was probably just upset."

Valerie looked almost as unhappy as Laura felt. She'd grown very fond of Steve, and she thought he was perfect for her mother.

443

"I know, hon," Laura said. "And I'm not mad. I guess my feelings just got hurt. I've never seen that side of Steve."

"Well, everyone has a breaking point, Mom, and from what you've told me, Steve's had his share of troubles in the past few months. Personally, I think he's entitled."

Laura set a plate of fried chicken on the table and sat down, but she'd completely lost her appetite. She knew that what Val said was true, and it certainly wasn't the first time she'd borne the brunt of a man's anger. Paul had been a fairly complacent man, and normally slow to anger, but there had been a few times in their marriage when he'd whipped himself into a fury.

"Men," Laura said. "Sometimes I think I should have been a nun and taken the vows of silence."

Val helped herself to a crispy chicken thigh and a good-sized helping of mashed potatoes. "Tell you what, Mom," she said, eyeing the bowl of fresh strawberries next to Laura's plate. "You worry and I'll eat, and tomorrow morning everything will look different. Want to bet?"

Laura managed a weak laugh, and decided maybe she'd eat something after all. She speared a chicken breast and helped herself to potatoes and corn. "You're absolutely right, hon," she said. "Now let's eat. We have to practice your Lamaze later."

* * *

Steve tied one on. And the next morning he had a whopper of a headache to prove it. On top of that he had a sour stomach and a guilty conscience for treating Laura the way he had. She had only wanted to help, and he'd pushed her away.

Groaning, Steve buried his head in his hands and hoped for a quick demise. He felt half-dead already.

And then the phone rang.

Casey was almost incoherent and he had to ask her to repeat herself twice before he understood what she had said.

"We're clear? You're absolutely sure the premium is paid to date?"

Casey's nearly hysterical laughter vibrated through the phone and made Steve's head throb harder. "Yes! Everything is okay, and I just called the hospital and the driver of the T-bird is in satisfactory condition. Isn't that great?"

"Super," Steve muttered, wishing Casey was close enough so that he could close his hands around her throat and squeeze. Then he immediately felt ashamed of himself. Casey was okay. She was hardworking and willing, and he was positive she hadn't meant to scare ten years off his life.

"Yeah, that's great, Casey," he said, trying to

sound more positive. "Look, can you tell Rich I'll be a little late coming in?"

"Sure. He won't care. He's so happy, nothing would bother him today!"

Steve stood under a stinging shower for a long time. When he got out he swallowed three aspirins and drank two cups of strong, black coffee, and only then did he start to feel human.

"Whoever invented alcohol should be beheaded," he muttered as he dressed. He debated about calling Laura before he went to work, but quickly decided against it. It would probably be best if he let a little time go by before he tried to talk to her. And maybe he needed to do a little soul-searching first.

As he drove to work, Steve remembered the night Laura had snapped at him for wanting to spend time with her when she'd had a long, hard day. After what had happened yesterday, he understood where she'd been coming from. "Nobody's perfect, Steve, old boy," he reminded himself, "and everyone has a bad day now and then. It's not the end of the world. You forgave Laura for biting your head off, now it's her turn to understand your foul mood."

And he was pretty sure she would. Laura was a sane, sensible woman, and not a flibbertigibbet who turned on the waterworks every time somebody gave her a look.

* * *

Laura spent a busy day showing several properties, and as she worked, her anger at Steve melted down. After all, everyone was entitled to be grouchy once in a while, weren't they? And after what had happened . . . well, she wouldn't have blamed him if he'd thrown a full-scale, five-alarm tantrum. She felt her lips curve in a smile as she wondered if he'd made good his threat to have several good, stiff drinks? If he had, then he probably had an old-fashioned hangover this morning, and he wouldn't be in a much better mood than he had been before.

She shook her head. Men! Sometimes they were just like little boys, and they could be as stubborn as mules. Steve had needed TLC and comforting last night just about as much as anyone she'd ever seen, but he'd been too proud to admit it. Well, maybe she'd let him stew for a while, thinking she was mad, and then, when she was sure he'd suffered enough, she would grant him forgiveness.

She and Val had another Lamaze class that night, and the telephone was ringing off the hook when they got home.

"Bet I know who that is," Val said teasingly. "Go easy on him, Mom."

"Maybe, and maybe not," Laura said, picking up the phone.

"Roses are red, violets are blue. You love daisies, and I love you!" Steve sang.

"What? Oh, you nut! So you think you can sing your way back into my good graces, do you? Well, let me tell you . . ."

"No, let me tell you," Steve interrupted. "I saw my life going down the tube last night, not to mention a sizable portion of my life savings. I was mourning the loss of a beautiful classic, not to mention that I was scared witless that the driver might die. I'm not making excuses, Laura, because I know I acted like a jackass, but I am sorry. Will you forgive me?"

"Well . . ."

"I promise to take you for a ride in the T-bird that is still intact," Steve coaxed.

"Oh, all right. I guess I'll let you get by this time. Did you have a beastly hangover this morning, I hope?"

Steve groaned. "Please don't mention that word. My head is still spinning. How did Valerie's Lamaze class go tonight?"

"Great. The sound effects in that classroom are something to behold. Twenty-two women all breathing and panting. It's sure a lot different from the way things were done in my day."

Steve chuckled. "Laura, you make it sound as though you had your children in the covered-wagon days."

"That's how I feel sometimes. Honestly, with all the modern miracles they have today . . .

sonograms and monitors. It's incredible."

"It sure is, and if it hadn't been for some of these modern miracles, my little granddaughter probably wouldn't be alive. Wait until you see the pictures I got today. She's growing like a weed."

Laura laughed. "Bring them over tomorrow when you come for dinner."

"Tomorrow? For dinner? Hey, you really have forgiven me, haven't you?"

"Don't push it, Walker," Laura said. "I'm giving you a second chance, but you're not a cat, you know. You don't have seven more to go."

"Yes ma'am," Steve said hastily. "I will be at your house tomorrow with bells on my toes. What can I bring?"

"Your appetite, and a good disposition," Laura said.

"So, it's all settled, Mom. I'm spending the night with Aunt Blanche and Uncle Jim, and you and Steve can go out on the town and paint it purple. Just imagine riding around Miami in a '55 T-bird with a handsome hunk and . . ."

"You think Steve is a handsome hunk?" Laura asked curiously. Normally girls Val's age thought anyone over thirty-five was ready for retirement.

"Well, for a senior citizen he's not bad," Val said slowly, cocking her head to one side consideringly. "That gray at his temples is kind of distinguished and I really like his eyes. I guess I can see why you have the hots for him, Mom."

"Valerie Susan Kinsey, if you say that one more time . . ."

Val threw up her hands and laughed. "Easy, Mom! You can't hit a pregnant lady, you know. Anyway, you know it's true. Why not admit it?"

"Because it's . . . well it's not dignified to talk like that, especially for someone my age. Good heavens, I'm about to become a grandmother for the fourth time!"

"Umm, a swinging granny if ever I saw one," Val taunted.

She was helping Laura fold laundry and now she held up a lacy blue bra and matching panties. "Umm-hmm, definitely a swinging granny!"

"Cut it out!" Laura cried. "You're making me blush. Daughters aren't supposed to harass their mothers this way!"

"But it's so much fun," Val said, "especially when you get all red and nervous, Mom. What's the matter? Does your sexuality embarrass you?"

"Oh Lord," Laura groaned. "What did I ever do to deserve this?"

"You just stayed young and sexy, Mom. What can I tell you?"

When Steve came by to pick her up, Val had

already gone to Blanche's, and Laura was glad. After the lively discussion on sexuality she'd had with her daughter, Laura was feeling extremely self-conscious. But the minute Steve took her in his arms, all the uneasiness vanished.

He kissed her quite thoroughly, then put her away from him and grinned. "I love Valerie," he said, "but I'm glad she's not home right now."

Laura leaned into him and sighed. They'd planned to go out to dinner and then someplace to dance, but right now she'd have been perfectly happy to stay right where she was. "Me too," she said.

"Come on," Steve said, "let's get out of here before I decide to carry you into the bedroom and ravish you."

"Sounds tempting," Laura said. "Do we have to go out?"

Steve hesitated a minute, then nodded. "Yes, we do. You've had a busy time of it lately, and so have I. We need to have a change of scenery, to wine and dine and dance, and afterwards maybe you'll let me stay over."

Laura smiled, a sultry smile that was filled with rich promise. "I wouldn't have it any other way."

Twenty-four

"Where in the world are we going?" Laura demanded, after they had been driving for more than twenty minutes.

Steve turned and gave her a wink. "We're going to Fort Lauderdale for a special dinner cruise. I thought it would be nice to do something a little different."

"A cruise? Why, Steve Walker, are you plotting to get me out on the water under a big Florida moon and romance me?"

Steve wagged his eyebrows, and his grin widened. "Got any objections, lady?"

Laura settled into a comfortable position, and rested her hand on Steve's knee. "Not a one," she said.

The evening turned out to be even nicer than Laura could have imagined. The leisurely cruise down the intercoastal was so relaxing.

She felt her tensions slipping away as she rested her head on Steve's shoulder and enjoyed the feel of his arm around her waist.

"This was a stroke of genius," she said, looking up at him, her gray eyes sparkling with pleasure. "This is much nicer than being cooped up in some noisy restaurant."

"I thought you'd like it. We'll be going to a little private island, and we'll feast on barbecued ribs, chicken, fresh corn and apple pie. And then there's some sort of show and dancing. And speaking of appetite, you look good enough to eat. Is this a new dress?"

He smoothed his hand over the soft, semisheer fabric and Laura shivered. It still amazed her that at her age she could be so turned on by a man. Of course Steve was a special man, and from the first time she'd ever laid eyes on him he'd made her heart flutter. That incredible male charm had not diminished with the years.

She raised her head and let her lips feather across his ear. "Are we allowed to neck on this ship?"

Steve whispered back. "Let's find out."

With a touch so gentle it reminded Laura of the caress of butterflies' wings, Steve tipped her face up and brought his mouth down to cover hers. Then the gentleness turned to longing, and then to hunger as Laura opened herself to him. And when a moment later, she forced herself to pull away, it was with a deep regret.

"You still pack a wallop, Walker," she said, her voice a husky whisper in the night. "We'll continue this later."

By the time the cruise ship docked at the private island, Laura was famished. "I could eat a whole rack of ribs," she threatened. "I hope they have plenty of food."

Steve took her hand and helped her disembark. Huge tents had been set up and inside were wooden picnic tables stretching from end to end. The smell of food made his mouth water. "Ditto," he said. "Come on, let's grab a seat."

To accommodate everyone they were forced to sit close and tight. It was a little awkward moving elbows and trying not to poke your neighbor, but it was also great fun. Laura couldn't remember the last time she'd done anything like this. The music was loud, the noisy chatter of all the people was deafening, and she loved it, even her greasy fingers and the moustache of butter from the corn on the cob.

"Can we do this again sometime?" she asked eagerly. "I can't remember when I last had this much fun."

"Good," Steve said. "We both needed this. I'll

tell you, I feel like a kid again."

"Well, save some of that energy, young fellow," Laura said, "because when we finish eating, I want to dance."

"Your wish is my command, fair Laura," Steve joked. "Just let me polish off this apple pie and I'm all yours."

They'd set up a dance floor under the moon and the stars, and a loudspeaker piped in music. Some of the songs were a little too fast for Laura, especially after such a hearty meal, but finally they played a slow song, and she tugged Steve outside.

He opened his arms and she moved into them, and then they were close, swaying gently to the music, their bodies lightly touching. A soft breeze ruffled the palm fronds over head, and the night enfolded them. As they danced they were alone, the only two people on the island. Everyone and everything faded away.

"I'm going to hate to see this evening end," Steve whispered against Laura's hair. Her scent filled his nostrils. The clean, soapy smell, the soft floral fragrance of her shampoo. He breathed deeply, drawing her in, and his arms tightened.

Laura moved against Steve, loving the hard, lean feel of him against her softness. For a little while she was young again, free and far removed from the every day stresses of life. The air was soft and caressing against her skin, Steve's arms were warm and protecting, and above them, the moon sent shards of golden light to illuminate them.

When the music ended, they boarded the ship for the return trip. "Happy?" Steve asked, as they settled in their seats.

"Delirious," Laura answered.

Buttons greeted them with all the fervor of an animal that has been denied human companionship for an unbearably long time.

"You faker," Laura scolded lovingly. "You act like I've been gone for months!"

"I'll walk him," Steve volunteered, "if you'll fix us a nightcap."

So Steve walked Buttons and Laura got out two glasses and a decanter of brandy. The perfect end to a perfect evening, she thought, then felt herself blush as she realized that the best part of the evening was still to come. Steve was planning to spend the night, and she wanted him to, more than she'd wanted anything in a long time. She didn't want to sleep alone tonight. After such a beautiful and romantic evening, it would have been sacrilegious to pull on an old flannel nightgown and crawl into bed alone.

Laura's cheeks felt warm as she thought of the new nightgown she'd bought especially for this night. And then Steve came in. He walked up behind her and pulled her back against him, and she felt his hunger against her, hard and strong. "Brandy first?" she asked huskily.

Steve released her, trailing his hand across her hip, leaving no doubt in her mind of what was about to happen. He took the glass she handed him and raised it to his lips. A swallow later he set the glass down and pulled her back into his arms.

She tasted brandy when their lips met, and her tongue flicked out to capture the deliciousness.

Steve groaned, and then they were walk-sliding towards the bedroom, unable to wait any longer to be together.

Laura flipped the light switch, and Steve saw the lacy black nightgown lying across the bed. "Beautiful," he said thickly, "but I don't think you're going to need it."

And she didn't. It went back in the drawer for another time.

Valerie came home the next afternoon, looking smug and self-satisfied as she noted the radiant look on her mother's face.

"Have a nice time, Mom?" she asked innocently.

"Very nice, thank you," Laura said primly, thankful that Steve had left before Val got home. She was sure her daughter knew what was going on, but she still felt a little uncomfortable when she thought of any of her children speculating on the intimate aspects of her life.

"Do we have Lamaze tonight?" she asked, hoping to change the subject.

"Yes. Are you sure you're up to it? You didn't get much sleep last night, did you?"

Laura's eyes narrowed. "Didn't I hear you say that I gave a pretty good backrub?"

"You do," Val said. "You're a great labor coach."

"Well, if you want to keep me around until the big day, I suggest you button that fresh lip of yours and keep your suspicions to yourself."

Val giggled, and for a moment Laura saw a ten-year-old, and not her twenty-two-year-old daughter, who was about to become a mother. "Yes, ma'am," Val said. "Consider it a done deal."

But by that evening after dinner, Laura was suffering from one of her rare migraine headaches, and she knew there was no way she could go to Lamaze class with Valerie.

"Do you think Sheila would fill in for me?"

Val shook her head. "She would, but she has a heavy date tonight. She called last night to tell me about it. It sounds like this guy is really special to her, so I wouldn't want her to cancel out."

"Well, how about Aunt Blanche?"

"No go," Val said. "She and Uncle Jim went shopping and out to dinner. She's probably not even home yet. Hey, how about Steve? Do you think he'd do it?"

"Oh, Val, I don't think so. I mean . . . well, that would be taking advantage of his good nature, I think. This kind of thing wasn't around when his son was born, you know. He'd probably be embarrassed with all those preggies."

"Come on, Mom! Steve embarrassed by a bunch of big bellies? I'll bet he'd love it."

"Well, call him and ask then, but just let me close my eyes and lie here for a while, honey. This is the worst migraine I've had in a long time."

"Okay. I'll close the door so Buttons won't bother you," Val said. "I'm sorry you feel bad, Mom." Then, as she went out the door, she muttered. "Probably too much sex."

Laura groaned. Between her throbbing head and her daughter's teasing she was ready to scream, but instead she closed her eyes and waited for her pain medication to take effect.

It was late when she heard Val quietly open the door. She heard her whispering to someone, then realized it was Steve when she heard a deep, masculine voice respond. Laura opened her eyes cautiously, waiting for the pain to strike, but it didn't. "Oh, thank goodness," she murmured. "It's gone."

"Feeling better?" Steve asked softly. "May I turn on the light? Val said that when you get a migraine you're sensitive to light."

"It's all right," Laura answered. "The headache is gone now. Fortunately, I don't get these very often."

Steve turned on the light, and Laura blinked. He wore a pair of well-washed jeans and a blue T-shirt. He looked comfortable and relaxed, and incredibly sexy for a man of his age.

"Did you . . . you didn't go to Lamaze class with her, did you?" Laura asked, cutting her eyes towards Val.

"Sure did," Steve said cheerfully, "and it was very informative indeed. Boy, some of those ladies sure are fat!"

Val laughed. "You should have seen him, Mom. He must have a belly fetish. He was fascinated by all the big tummies."

"It looked like a sea of beach balls," Steve

teased, "especially when they were all lying down."

"I can't believe you actually had the nerve to ask him," Laura said, turning to Val.

"Hey, I got a kick out of it, honest. It was a heck of a lot more interesting than watching reruns of 'Family Ties' on television."

"Well, if you enjoyed it, that's all that matters. How did it go otherwise? Are you getting the hang of all that breathing, Val?"

"Yeah. I think I got it," Val said, "and believe it or not, Mom, Steve really was a big help. For a novice he did all right."

"Thank you, thank you," Steve said. "And no applause is necessary. Well, I better get going. I just wanted to see how you were feeling. As long as you're okay, I'll get out of here."

"Uh, I gotta visit the bathroom," Val said quickly. "See you later, Steve."

Steve smiled at Laura and moved closer to the bed. "I think she did that so I could kiss you good night. What do you think?"

"I think there's a distinct possibility you're right, so why don't you just shut up and do it?"

At breakfast the next morning Val could talk of nothing but how wonderful Steve had been at Lamaze.

"Honest, Mom, you would have thought he was my real dad. He was so kind and considerate, and the instructor asked if he was my father."

"Oh? And what did Steve say?"

Val picked up a crisp strip of bacon and looked at it with pure lust. Then she shook her head and put it back on the plate and helped herself to a slice of whole-wheat bread instead. "He said he wasn't, but that he'd always wanted a daughter just like me."

Laura's heart skipped a beat, or at least that's what it felt like. A kernel of worry nagged at her. What if things didn't work out for her and Steve? Was Val going to be devastated by yet another loss? She should have seen it coming. As a general rule Val didn't attach herself to people at first glance. Normally she held back a little, and got to know people before she let them get close, but not so with Steve. There'd been an instant rapport between them. Val had taken to Steve like a kitten to milk. And Steve genuinely cared for her too. Everything that was happening was what she'd hoped to avoid. Steve getting to close, insinuating himself into her family so that none of them would want to be without him. She felt like she was being backed into a corner, and it was scary.

"Well, I have to get to work," she said, pushing back her chair. "What are your plans for the day, honey?"

For a moment Valerie looked a little unsure, then she shrugged. "I know you probably won't approve, but Steve said he wants to buy me a crib for the baby . . . you know, for after it outgrows the bassinet. I told him it wasn't necessary, but he insisted, so finally I said okay." Val flipped her hair back over her shoulder almost defiantly. "He's picking me up at two o'clock, and we're going to that infant furniture store in the new mall."

"Oh, Val! It's not that I don't approve. It's just that I don't think it's a good idea for you to get too close to Steve. I don't know what's going to happen between the two of us yet and . . ."

"Look, Mom, I respect your right to run your life anyway you want to. If things don't work out for you and Steve, I'll be sorry, but that won't stop me from having him as a friend. I already told Steve that, and he said he feels the same."

"You . . . talked about me behind my back?" Laura asked, shocked and angry. "What right did you have to do that?"

Val looked unhappy, but she held her ground. "You don't own Steve, Mom, and if you decide not to see him anymore, well, that doesn't mean I'll have to do the same. He's been really nice to me. He treats me almost like Daddy used to, and I like him a lot."

Laura felt like she'd been betrayed, but then she realized that it just her ego acting up. If she wasn't going to have Steve she didn't want anyone else to have him either. She felt incredibly selfish and childish.

"You're right," she said. "I'm sorry. You go on to the mall and have a good time, and don't pick out the most expensive crib in the store!"

"Don't worry. I'll be good."

Driving to work, Laura told herself to get a grip and stop acting like a self-centered pig. Everything Valerie said was right. If she and Steve couldn't work things out, that didn't mean her daughter had to snub him. But it was more than that . . . something nagged at Laura . . . something she couldn't quite put her finger on. She pulled into the parking lot of the real estate office and shook her head to clear out the distracting, worrisome thoughts. It was time to go to work. She'd have to find time to delve into her psyche later.

"What did your mom say about us shopping for a crib?" Steve asked. He took his eyes off the road just for a minute and glanced at Valerie. This was what he'd missed by not being around during Joyce's pregnancy, seeing the little daily changes, watching the mother-to-be bloom before his eyes.

"Fishing, huh?" Val asked teasingly. "Well, she reacted just the way you thought she would. At first she was dead set against it, then she got mad thinking that you and I were talking about her behind her back. I set her straight on that. I told her that no matter what happens between you two, I still want you to be my friend. You will, won't you, even if you and Mom can't work things out?"

Steve swallowed, but nearly choked. What was it about this young woman that touched him so much? It wasn't just because she looked so much like her mother had when she was young. There was just something sweet and nice about Valerie, something that made him want to take care of her, something that made him wish that he'd had a daughter just like her.

"Hey, don't even ask. Whatever goes down between me and your mom has nothing to do with our friendship. And just for the record, I'm not a quitter. I intend to do everything I can to make things work out between us."

Val laughed. "That's what I'm betting on, Steve." Then an odd look crossed her face.

From the corner of his eye Steve saw her wince. "Hey, kiddo, you okay? You're not having a pain or anything, are you?"

"No. It's the baby. She's moving. It feels so strange, odd, yet wonderful too. Want to feel?"

Steve was awed. There was just no other way to describe it. That Val would honor him by sharing such a private, intimate moment . . . he could only nod wordlessly.

He found a thin spot in the traffic and pulled over to the side of the road, then he let Val guide his hand to her belly.

"There. Feel it? I don't know if it's a hand or a foot. Can you feel it?"

Nodding, Steve let his hand rest against the hard mound of Val's belly. He'd felt this when Marcie carried Steve, but it had been a long time. He'd forgotten the wonder of it.

"Wow!" he said, shaking his head. "What is it you kids say? Awesome?"

"Yeah," Val said reverently. "It's awesome!"

It took hours to find the right crib, but Steve had made up his mind to be patient. He'd never had a daughter, but his wife had been a marathon shopper, so he knew how women could be when they were looking for a particular item, and a baby's crib was special, as Val repeatedly reminded him. It had to be just right.

She finally settled on a style the saleslady called "Jenny Lind." Steve thought it looked kind of old-fashioned, but it was what Val wanted, so he just kept quiet and signed the charge slip. Then he and Valerie went to the drive-in window of a fast-food restaurant and picked up burgers and fries and milkshakes for supper.

"Steve, thanks for today," Valerie said, as they drove home. "It was one of the nicest days I've had in a long time, and not just because of the crib. It was . . ." she hesitated and her eyes watered. "It was almost like having Dad again."

"I think that's one of the nicest things anyone has ever said to me," Steve said, "but I can't take your dad's place, honey, and I wouldn't even try."

"I know. I don't expect that. It's just that you're kind like he was, and I know he would have liked you."

"Well, I sure like his daughter," Steve said, "and I'm glad we had this time together."

"Cheeseburgers, fries and a chocolate milkshake?" Laura pretended to be horrified, but both Steve and Val knew she was delighted. Her secret lust for junk food was not much of a secret.

"Bring on the paper plates and napkins,"

Steve said. "No dishes tonight."

"You're my kind of guy," Laura joked, brushing by him on her way to the cabinet for paper goods. "So, how did the shopping trip go? Did you find the perfect crib?"

"Wait until you see it, Mom. It's a Jenny Lind. It's gorgeous."

"Now Val, I thought you were going to be . . ."

"Hey, this is her first baby, and after that Lamaze class the other night, I feel like I've got a stake in this kid. I told her to pick out what she liked. Personally, I thought it was kind of old-fashioned, but it was what she liked so . . ."

Laura smiled. "Jenny Lind's are supposed to look old-fashioned, Steve," she explained. "Anyway, I'm glad that's taken care of. I guess now all we have to do is lay in a supply of disposable diapers and wait for the little king or queen to make its appearance."

"The baby is a girl," Val said. She took a big bite out of her cheeseburger and sighed with pleasure. "Ah, junk food, one of the real pleasures of life."

Laura twirled a french fry in catsup, then popped it in her mouth. "Amen to that," she said. "How do you know what sex the baby is? I thought you weren't going to let the doctor tell you?"

"I didn't. I just know. I talk to her at night when I go to bed, and I just know."

"Does that mean I can knit pink booties and buy a frilly little pink dress?" Laura asked, her eyes bright with happiness. It was so wonderful to be able to sit and talk like this . . . so nice to feel so content and comfortable.

Val grinned and noisily sucked on her straw. "Feel free, Mom," she said happily. "Now, how about if you two help me pick out a name?"

So they sat around for the rest of the night thinking of names. Steve very seriously suggested Louise or Marilyn, but both Val and Laura vetoed them.

"Louise is old-fashioned," Val said, "and Marilyn . . . well, that makes me think of a blonde bombshell, and that's not the image I want my daughter to project. I was thinking more along the lines of Meredith or Leslie, or maybe Sharon. What do you think, Mom?"

"I think we should buy a book with names tomorrow and start with the *A's* and go straight through until something hits us."

"Good idea," Val said, yawning, "and on that note, I think I'll say good-night. All the intense shopping wore us out." She tenderly traced circles on her extended belly. Steve and Laura smiled.

"Good night, hon," Laura said. "See you in

the morning."

"Night, Val," Steve said. "Thanks for a great day."

"No, I thank you," Valerie said, then she leaned down and kissed Steve on the cheek.

"Well, you have definitely made a conquest, Steve Walker," Laura said, when Val left the room.

"It goes both ways. Do you mind?"

"No . . . oh, I may as well come clean. I guess I did at first, and to tell you the truth I still haven't figured out why. I should be glad my daughter likes you, and a part of me is, but I think I'm a little jealous. Isn't that crazy?"

Steve slid over next to Laura on the sofa. He put his arm around her shoulder and squeezed. "Wow!" he said, grinning widely. "Two beautiful women fighting over me! I didn't know I still had it in me."

Laura laughed and poked him in the ribs with her elbow. "You won't if you don't behave," she threatened.

Then suddenly Laura sobered. "I want to add my thanks to Val's, Steve. This is a very nice thing you've done."

"I don't think you understand, Laura. I didn't do this just to be nice. I care about Valerie and the baby she's carrying. In some ways

470

she's become like the daughter I never had. I'm not sure why I feel so close to her. I know part of it is because she's your daughter, but there's more. She fills a hole inside me that I didn't even know I had. Do I sound crazy?"

Laura was so moved and filled with tenderness that she could barely speak. Her voice came out in a rough croak. "Oh, Steve! Do you have any idea how it makes me feel to hear you say that? For me to know that you love my daughter?"

Steve smiled. "It's true," he said. "I really do love that kid." His grin widened. "And the mama ain't bad either!"

Twenty-five

Steve downed two glasses of bourbon when he went home, but he still couldn't sleep. He wasn't much of a drinker, and one drink usually knocked him out. Right after Marcie's death, he'd gotten into the habit of a drink before bed to help him sleep. But after a couple of months he knew he had to find other ways to cope with his loss. So he'd taken up jogging, and he'd learned to play golf. And usually, when he went home after a good workout, he was able to make it through the night. The nights were the worst. During the day, when the sun was bright, he could usually cope.

Now, he flipped over in bed for the hundredth time and sighed heavily. Val's baby would be coming any time now, and after that, once her daughter was on her feet again, Laura would be free to think about her own life.

What would she decide? Would he be in or out?

He was trying to do what Laura had asked and work through his feelings while they waited for Val's baby to arrive, but the more he tried to think, the more confused he got.

Even his cousin Rich thought he was slightly balmy to be so hung up on getting married. "Hey, what for?" Rich had asked the other day. "I mean, it ain't like you're gonna have a bunch of kids that need a legal name, you know? If the lady loves you and you're enjoying each other, what more do you need? Hell, marriage is just a piece of paper, anyway."

But it wasn't. It represented safety and security to Steve. There was something about the great institution of marriage that gave him a sense of stability. He remembered telling Laura he didn't handle loss well. That was certainly all too true. But marriage didn't carry a warranty against loss.

And once he had walked out on Laura. Now he was afraid she might do the same to him. He'd lost Marcie, and he'd nearly lost his son as well, and he couldn't stand the thought of losing Laura.

Steve sat up in the darkness as a new thought occurred to him. He'd once likened Laura to a bird, ready to take flight at the slightest movement. If that were true, what would happen if he tried to clip her wings? Would he end up destroying all the good feelings between them?

It looks like you have a choice, old man, he told himself. Accept what Laura is willing to give you, or walk away. He reached for the nearly empty glass of bourbon on his nightstand and quickly downed it. The choice was now narrowed to one, because he knew he wasn't going to walk away. Not unless Laura told him too.

"Mom, I think this is it!"

Val's voice was a mixture of excitement and terror, and Laura felt her own heartbeat speed up. "Okay, hon. Just stay calm and sit tight. I'll be home in half an hour or less. This is your first baby so you have plenty of time. After the next contraction, call Dr. Reynolds and tell him what's going on."

"Okay, but hurry, will you? I'm scared."

Laura hung up the phone and looked around the office wildly. George and Sheila were both out with prospective buyers, and they'd left her to hold the fort. Well, there was nothing for it but to switch on the answering machine and leave them a note. She had to get home to her daughter!

But George came in as she was rushing out

the door, and one look at her face told him what was going on.

"Hey, good luck!" he yelled after her.

Laura was not surprised when she got home to find that Steve was already there, walking around the living room with Val and helping her time the contractions.

"They're less than five minutes apart now," he said, "and Val said her doctor told her to come to the hospital right away."

"Then let's get going," Laura said, looking around for the suitcase Val had packed weeks earlier. "Did you remember to put the lollipops in your bag, Val?" she asked.

Looking pale and scared and much younger than her twenty-two years, Valerie nodded. "Everything is in there. Mom, can we go now? The contractions are starting to get stronger."

Steve carried the suitcase and Laura held her daughter's arm. By prearrangement, Steve got behind the wheel of Laura's car, and she climbed in back with her daughter.

"Oh, Mom, it hurts," Val said, moaning, "and I can't remember how I'm supposed to breathe!"

"Yes you can, sweetheart, and just keep thinking of that sweet little girl you're about to deliver. Won't we have fun dressing her all up in ribbons and lace?"

Steve concentrated on his driving. All he

wanted to do was get Laura and Val to the hospital before the baby popped out. Laura had repeatedly assured him that wasn't the way it would happen. Babies were rarely born in the back seats of cars. But it was possible. Steve had seen it on television many times. Babies born in cars, on elevators . . . in a bedroom at home, without benefit of doctors and nurses, or sterile surroundings. Oh Lord, he wanted better than that for Val! He wanted her to have a beautiful, easy time of it, and to deliver a perfect, healthy baby.

"Steve, you can slow down a little," Laura said quietly from the back seat.

He could hear Val moaning softly from time to time, and the soft murmur of Laura's voice as she coached her, but why was Laura telling him to slow down? Had something terrible happened? "What's wrong?" he cried.

"Nothing, but there will be something wrong if you run us off the road. Everything is under control, Steve. Relax, okay?"

He wished he could see her face to determine if she was really telling him the truth. But of course she was telling the truth. Why would she lie?

Finally the hospital loomed in front of them like a magical castle. "Here we are," he announced proudly. "Safe and sound. See?"

"Can you run inside and ask for a wheelchair?" Laura asked. "I'm afraid Val may have a little trouble walking."

"Oh, yeah, sure . . . right away. Wait here. I'll be right back!"

It happened quickly. One minute the attendants were helping Val into the wheelchair, and then she was whisked away, and they were left in the admitting office to fill out some papers.

"She's the labor coach," Steve told a bored-looking nurse. "Valerie's having Lamaze."

The nurse nodded and kept on writing.

"Shouldn't she go up there, wherever she is? Where did they take Val anyway?"

"Your daughter is probably being prepped, sir, and as soon as I get the necessary information you and your wife can go on up to the labor room."

"Oh no, I'm not . . . what I mean is . . ."

"He doesn't want to go into the labor room. It will just be me," Laura said, as she handed the nurse her insurance card.

"Whatever," the nurse murmured, "although why men are so squeamish, I'll never know. That's your grandchild being born, you know. I'd think you would want to be there."

"But it's not . . ."

Laura smiled and laid her hand on Steve's arm and shook her head. The nurse wasn't really interested in them, or in their family relationships. She was just making conversation.

For a minute Steve looked confused, then his face cleared. "Will they really let me go in the labor and delivery room?" he whispered to Laura.

"Well, I suppose if you really wanted to, but . . . it's not your responsibility, Steve, and I'm sure Val doesn't expect it."

"Oh." Steve felt like a deflated balloon. He hadn't even thought about going into the labor and delivery room with Laura and Val, but suddenly he realized that there was nowhere else he'd rather be, and maybe Val didn't expect it, but that didn't mean she wouldn't want him, and if she did . . .

"You go up and ask her," he told Laura firmly, "and if she wants me, I'm coming up!"

"But . . ."

"Just ask her, Laura. This isn't about you or me. All that matters right now is what Val wants, and if she wants me, I'm going!"

"Okay. Sure. If that's how you feel."

"That's how I feel, and you don't have to understand it. You just have to accept it." And after Laura left, Steve paced up and down the tiled hallway. He was proud of himself for standing his ground where his relationship with Val was concerned. Laura wanted him to accept her feelings — well, she could damn well do the same!

Val did want him, and when Steve heard

that, there was no stopping him. In record time, he donned the green scrub suit they gave him, and then they let him go in and see Val.

Her beautiful hair was plastered to her skull and she was pale, but smiling.

"Hey, you look pretty neat, Steve. Maybe you can get a part-time job here as an orderly."

"Don't get fresh, kid. I'm not much on hospitals, and if it weren't for you, I wouldn't be in this one. Now let's hurry up and get this show on the road, okay?"

Laura watched the interchange between the man she loved and her daughter with surprise and pleasure. She'd known Val and Steve genuinely liked one another, but this was above and beyond mere friendship. Unexpectedly, her eyes filled with tears. Was there more she didn't know about this man, who had come out of her past and stormed his way into her future? A smile curved her lips as she gently massaged Val's distended abdomen. Steve looked every inch the worried, nervous grandpa. Her smile widened. What a welcome this baby was going to get!

"Come on, honey, breathe. Slow and easy. That's it . . . let it out, that's right. Good. Now rest a minute. Good girl. You're doing great."

"How do mothers get so brave?" Steve whispered, his breath warm against her ear, "And beautiful."

"It's built in," Laura said, "but you're not doing so bad for a c-h-i . . ."

"Don't say it, Laura," Steve warned, trying not to laugh. There was poor Val, laboring away to bring her child into the world and he and Laura were horsing around. And yet, wasn't that what families did? And wasn't this caring and sharing more important than any piece of paper?

"Here comes Dr. Reynolds, Val," Laura said. "I'll bet it's almost time for you to go to the delivery room."

"Almost," Dr. Reynolds said, after a brief exam. "About ten or fifteen more minutes should do it. How's everyone holding up here? Are both of you coming into the delivery room with her?" he asked Laura and Steve?"

"May I?" Steve asked.

Dr. Reynolds shrugged. "Don't ask me. Ask our little mama here. What do you say, Val?"

"Please, Steve . . . if you wouldn't mind. I want you to come."

Steve reached out and grabbed Laura's hand, and he squeezed so tight she yelped. "Sorry," he muttered, and then he leaned down and whispered something to Val.

"You bet," Val said. She smiled and then the next contraction hit.

The delivery room was lit up like a parking lot, Steve thought. He helped the orderlies wheel Val in, and then he stood back out of the way as they transferred her to the delivery table.

"This is it," Laura said, clasping his hand. "We're going to be grandparents."

The words just slipped out naturally, but she looked at Steve, worried that he would think she was assuming too much.

But he was shaking his head and grinning widely. "It feels like it, doesn't it? This feels right."

Laura nodded, afraid to speak in case she might start to cry. Everyone's emotions were high right now. The birth of Val's baby was only minutes away, and the tension and excitement in the room was palpable.

"Ohhhh, Mom!"

"Right here, baby." Laura quickly moved into position beside her daughter and helped her into a semisitting position. "There, does that help a little?"

"Yes . . . oh, wow! That last one was a whopper! Am I almost there?"

"Almost, honey, and from where I'm standing you've been a real trooper. If I were your commanding officer I'd issue you a purple heart," Steve said proudly.

"Thanks, Steve, but right now I don't feel very brave. I just want to finish. Owwwww! Here comes another one!"

At Laura's nod, Steve slipped behind her and helped brace Val as she pushed. That freed Laura to massage Val's belly and ease the contractions a little.

"Whoa!"

"We're almost there, Val," Dr. Reynolds said, from his position at the foot of the tale. "I can see the baby's head, and a couple more good pushes should do it. With the next contraction I want you to push as hard as you possibly can."

The last two contractions drained all the color from Steve's face. He did what Laura told him to, but he moved automatically. When Val's face contorted in pain he experienced a helplessness he'd never known before. And then, suddenly, Val gave one last scream of agony. A moment of silence and then another cry, this time the lusty howl of a newborn.

"It's a girl," Dr. Reynolds announced loudly. "A beautiful, healthy little girl!"

"Oh, Val! Hear that, honey? You got your little girl! Just what you wanted!"

Steve stood there, dazed. The experience he'd just gone through was unlike anything he'd ever known before. There'd been nothing like this with his daughter-in-law because Joyce had been delivered by cesarean and it was an emergency situation. And when Marcie gave birth to Steve, fathers were left to cool their heels in a waiting room. But this, this working together to help bring a child into the world was incredible.

"Congratulations, grandma," he told Laura. He moved to give her a chaste kiss on the cheek, but instead she pulled his head down and kissed him very thoroughly. When she broke the contact she whispered, "We couldn't have done it without you, Steve. Val and I both thank you."

"Hey, what about me? Isn't anyone going to kiss and congratulate me?" Val asked. "And where's my baby? I want to see my daughter."

"See? What did I tell you? Even in the delivery room she's giving orders and being fresh." Laura felt tired and teary-eyed. She watched while a nurse held the newly delivered baby girl up so her mama could see her. The tears overflowed when Val reached out and touched the tiny fist.

"Oh, Mom . . . Steve, isn't she beautiful?"

"Whew! That was something, wasn't it? Here I am, fifty-two years old and this was the first time I ever saw an actual birth. Isn't that amazing?" Laura slid wearily into the seat next to Steve.

"I don't think I could go through this too often," Steve said, putting the key in the ignition and starting the car. "I feel like I've been through a wringer."

"Me too. Let's go home and have a glass of wine to celebrate."

Laura said she felt so sweaty she just had to shower, and somehow, without even knowing he had the energy, Steve found himself in the shower with her. He could feel his strength coming back as he soaped Laura's back. "I can't believe I'm doing this," he said, chuckling. "A few minutes ago I was totally, absolutely drained and now . . ."

"You're going to be drained in a different way if you keep moving your hands that way, Mr. Walker. Have you no shame?" She was breathless, and where Steve touched her, her flesh flamed.

"Not where you're concerned," Steve murmured huskily, deliberately sliding his hands up to cup Laura's full, ripe breasts. The water pelted them, renewing them, and he felt himself growing hard against her.

"Ah, honey, you make me feel so good."

Laura nodded, then lifted her arms and wrapped them around Steve's neck. She felt him reach behind her to turn off the water, and then he was toweling her dry with a big, fluffy terry towel. And somehow they made it to her bed before the skyrockets burst all around and over them.

"Well, that was definitely a nice way to end a very exciting day," Steve said, with a self-satisfied grin. He was perched on a stool at the kitchen counter, watching Laura scramble eggs and make toast. He sniffed appreciatively as the coffee perked.

"I could eat a whole cow," he said. Then he narrowed his eyes. "You're good at building a man's appetite, Laura, but I guess you know that."

"I've only started to practice," she said. Then she giggled. "Good grief, Steve, do you realize I'm a grandmother four times over and that is the very first time I ever made love in a shower?"

"No kidding? But . . ." Steve stopped himself in time. Laura's intimate relationship with her late husband was none of his business, and he wasn't going to ask any questions, but he couldn't help feeling proud that he'd taught Laura something new.

When the food was ready they ate hungrily, not talking until the plates were empty.

"That was either a gourmet meal, or I was in imminent danger of starving. Boy, I never knew eggs could taste so good!"

Laura smiled dreamily, resting her chin on her hand. "The baby is precious, isn't she? I wonder what name Val will decide on? I like Ashley."

Steve frowned. "Wasn't that the name of one of the characters in *Gone With the Wind?* A guy?"

"Yes," Laura said, laughing, "but it's a girl's name too. Anyway, that will be up to Valerie."

"Is she still adamant about not notifying the father?" Steve asked.

"Absolutely. As far as she's concerned it's a closed issue. She doesn't want anything to do with Robert, and frankly, I don't blame her."

"But legally he should contribute to the child's support."

"And then there would be custody rights and all sorts of complications, and the man made it abundantly plain that he wanted nothing to do with his child, Steve."

Laura refilled their coffee cups.

Stirring cream into his coffee, Steve grinned ruefully. "Like mother, like daughter," he said. "I guess I'm just not used to independent women, Laura. My mother was a housewife and a mom. She was totally dependent on my dad. I guess that wasn't really good for her, but it's what I saw when I was growing up. And Marcie was pretty dependent on me too. Oh, she worked for a while when Steve got older, but she was never really on her own, like you are."

"Well, she didn't have to be, and maybe I wouldn't be now, if Paul was still alive. But I

486

didn't have any choice about being on my own, Steve, and once I got used to it, I discovered it wasn't so bad."

"And we're back to that," Steve said. "Your independence."

Laura's eyes darkened to the color of a summer storm, and her voice was flat when she answered. "Not tonight, Steve, please."

"I didn't mean . . ."

Laura shook her head. "I don't want to talk about it. I'm tired. My daughter has just had a baby and I . . . just don't want to argue with you."

"I don't want to argue either, Laura, and I've tried to do everything you asked me to, but this damned independence of yours is getting out of hand. Just about all I've heard since we got together has been what you want, what you need. Your freedom, your space . . . well, damn it, what about me? Did you ever think that I have needs too? I've done everything I know how to show you that I love you, and that I'm willing to compromise. Hell, I can't believe you actually let me be a part of Val's delivery tonight. What was that, a temporary lapse or something?"

"You're not being fair!" Laura cried. "I've been searching my soul just like you have, trying to understand why I'm scared to commit again, but you, with your macho pride, you never thought about that, did you? Did you ever once think that I might be scared . . . that I might be afraid of losing myself again . . . me, Laura, and not just Paul's wife and Val and Vicki and Greg's mommy!"

"Laura, what are you saying? What do you mean, you lost yourself?"

"You really don't understand, do you?" she said, and she began to sob. "You don't know . . . you just don't know . . ."

"Tell me, please," Steve begged softly, reaching out to smooth her hair. It killed him to see her cry this way, and to know that he had caused it. "Please tell me, Laura," he repeated. "I want to understand."

She looked up, her lovely face ravaged by tears. And now she looked every one of her fifty-two years, but to Steve she was still beautiful.

"Don't you know that after Paul died I didn't even know who I was? I couldn't make decisions on my own for months. I'd call Greg and ask his advice, or I'd ask Blanche to ask Jim. I had no confidence in myself or my abilities, and in the beginning I thought my life was over too. I had become so dependent on Paul that I didn't know how to live on my own. Then, as I worked my way through the grief I began to see that I was a person in my own right. I got brave one day and went to the bank and spoke to a couple of officers there. They helped me understand some of the financial arrangements Paul had made for me. And that was the beginning. I started to develop confidence in my own abilities. And that's about where you came in." Laura's face softened and Steve gently wiped a tear from her cheek.

"You helped me the rest of the way, Steve, even though you probably didn't mean to. You bolstered my confidence as a woman. In a way, I guess you created a monster."

"No," Steve said gently, "not a monster. Never a monster. A beautiful, brave woman. The woman I want to love and be loved by. And that's all, Laura. That's what I wanted to tell you earlier. I'll take whatever you're willing to give me, and I won't push for marriage, unless you decide it's what you want too." He meant it, or at least he hoped he did, because this was the way it had to be.

Laura stared, open-mouthed, and then she started to cry all over again.

It was just that so much had happened in the past few hours. Val's labor, the baby . . . and Steve, beside her all the way, and she had liked having him there. Unlike what she'd told him, she knew she could have done it alone if she'd had to, but how much nicer it had been this way, how wonderful it had been to reach up and kiss Steve when it was all over. How sweet to come home with him and make wonderful, passionate love in the shower. How lovely to share a simple supper with him and talk about baby names.

"I'm not a crier," she said. "I don't want you to think that I make a habit of sobbing in my dinner."

Steve dabbed a stray tear from her cheek with his thumb. "I know, but tonight you're entitled. This has been an emotional day. Would it surprise you to know that I feel like crying too?"

"You? Why?"

"Because tonight you gave me something more important than any piece of paper in the world. Being in that delivery room with you and Val made me realize that I've been hung up on the wrong things. Like I told you before, I'm not a good loser, and I guess I thought that if we were married, I'd be safe. As chauvinistic as this sounds, I have to admit that I wanted you to belong to me, Laura. I wanted a piece of paper saying you were mine, a bill of sale, so to speak. Pretty macho and old-fashioned, isn't it?"

Laura's tears had dried and she managed a small smile.

"A bill of sale?

Steve grinned. "You know what I mean.

Marriage represented security and stability to me, but I'm beginning to realize that the only real security is right in here." He tapped his chest and Laura nodded. Then, to his astonishment, she yawned.

"Let's go to bed, grandpa," she said. "We'll continue this fascinating discussion tomorrow. I don't know about you, but I'm exhausted."

Steve stood up and held out his hand. "I didn't bring my toothbrush," he said ruefully.

"I brought you a brand-new one," Laura said smugly, "as well as a robe and a pair of pajamas."

"Well, all right!" Steve said.

Twenty-six

"I'm taking the day off in honor of my new granddaughter," Laura said at breakfast the next morning. Since she wasn't going to work, she had splurged and made them a magnificent meal. Hotcakes and sausage, eggs, and home-fries. They were both so hungry they polished their plates.

"Wonder what it was that gave us such voracious appetites?" Steve teased, "Going through Val's labor and delivery or what came after?"

Laura flushed, remembering the erotic scene in the shower. Talk about Dr. Ruth and sex after fifty! It couldn't get any better, could it? "Behave yourself, Steve Walker," she said, as they cleared the table and loaded the dishwasher. "Want to go to the hospital with me, or do you have to work?"

"I'd love to go to the hospital, but I really do

have to go to work, at least for a few hours. Give Val a kiss for me, and that baby too. Tell her I'll see them tonight."

"Perfect," Laura said. "I'm just going to pop in real quick this morning, and then I have a million errands to run. I have to buy disposable diapers, shirts and little sleep suits, and I better lay in a supply of formula too. Oh, and we'll need some more receiving blankets, and then of course I have to buy the baby a little outfit to come home in. That's a family tradition. The grandma always buys the baby's coming-home outfit."

Steve couldn't resist hugging Laura. She was so happy, so proud and radiant. "You don't look old enough to be anyone's grandma," he said.

Laura laughed and hugged Steve back. "I love your flattery, even when I know it's just a tiny bit exaggerated. Keep it coming."

"With pleasure." Steve said. "Well, I better get out of here. I hope no one realizes these are the same clothes I wore yesterday."

"Maybe you'll have to start keeping some extra outfits over here," Laura said. "But not while Val's here," she added hastily.

Steve laughed. "I think she knows what's going on, Laura."

"I know, but I just wouldn't feel right with her and the baby here in the house."

"Then we'll have to bring you to my place," Steve said, "because I warn you, Laura, much as I love Val, I'm not planning to become celibate, not when I know what it's like between us. I'm not that noble."

"Good, because I'm not either, and I already decided that we'd be spending lots of quiet evenings at your place while Val is here."

Steve nodded. "Now that we've arranged our sex lives, I'm out of here, and tonight, after we visit Val, we'll go someplace quiet for dinner, and finish the discussion we started last night. Deal?"

"Deal."

Laura stood at the front window and watched Steve drive away, and suddenly she had a brilliant inspiration. She smiled to herself as she worked the details out in her mind. Despite what he said, Steve seemed to need some kind of written assurance that their relationship was more than a temporary fling. Well, she wasn't ready for wedding bells, at least not yet, but she had to admit that the possibility was not as scary as it had once been. Maturity had shaped Steve into an intelligent, considerate man. And last night, when she had sobbed out her fears, he had seemed to understand. So, maybe marriage shouldn't be totally ruled out, maybe the decision could just be put on hold until she had a chance to try her wings a little more. But there was something she could do about the piece of paper Steve seemed to prize so much.

"I have a million errands to run, honey, so I really just popped in to see how you and that precious little baby are doing. Have you decided on a name yet?" Laura stood next to Val's hospital bed, and smiled down at the baby, who lay sleeping in a bassinet next to her mother.

Val shook her head. "I'm still thinking. I want her name to be special."

"And how do you feel this morning, honey? Did you get a good night's sleep?"

"Not really. I was too excited to sleep. How about you?"

"Well, I . . ."

"Oh, I get it," Val said, a teasing glint making her eyes sparkle. "Did you and Steve have a little private celebration?"

"Never mind all that," Laura snapped. "I want to know what kind of diapers you want. Any preference?"

"Nope, just get the kind that don't leak," Val said. "Hey, isn't Steve coming by to see us?"

"Tonight. We'll come by together after he gets off work, but he had to go to the agency for a few hours."

"Okay. Wasn't he terrific last night, Mom? I'm really glad he stood by us the way he did."

"That's the kind of man he is," Laura said.

"I know, and I'm glad you finally realized it too," Val said.

"Now don't . . ."

"Okay, okay," Val said, holding up her hands. "I'll lay off, I promise. But I really hope you hang on to him, Mom. He's a prize."

"We'll see," Laura said evasively, "now I have to go. Is there anything you'd like me to bring you tonight?"

"Yes. I forgot to pack my paperbacks," Val said. "There's a stack of them in my room."

"Okay. I'll get them as soon as I go home."

"Thanks, and Mom? Be sure to grab at least one or two juicy romances with happy endings. I still believe in that, you know."

"Good for you," Laura said as she leaned down and kissed Val good-bye.

By the time she got home laden down with packages, it was four o'clock. There would just be time for a shower and change of clothes before Steve came by to take her to the hospital.

Dropping all the infant paraphernalia on the floor in Val's room, Laura went to the bedside table to grab a couple of paperbacks. She smiled. Her daughter definitely had eclectic tastes. There were two murder mysteries, a gothic romance, a western, a couple of biographies, and several fat romance novels. "Oh, my," Laura said, getting a good look at one of the covers. It was certainly . . . well, steamy was the best word Laura could come up with, and that was what she felt coming out of her ears as she peeked inside and read the first few sentences. "Oh my!"

She scooped up a couple, without checking to see if they had happy endings or not. Then she laughed. Judging from the covers, there were plenty of happy times in between!

By the time Steve got home she was ready. She was wearing a pale green pantsuit with a cream silk blouse. She had shampooed and styled her auburn hair, and diamond studs glistened in her ears.

Steve had apparently stopped off at his place to shower and change, and he looked crisp and clean in tan cords and a cream shirt. And Laura thought he smelled delicious.

"Umm," she said, nestling against him after a hello kiss. "You smell like a citrus tree on a warm summer day."

"And you," Steve said, "smell like heaven. Did you have lunch? I thought we'd go to dinner after we visit Val and the baby."

"That's fine," Laura said. "Just let me get my purse and we'll go."

In her bedroom, Laura picked up the bag containing the baby's little outfit and a thin, flat package wrapped in foil and tied with a blue ribbon. She had a moment of doubt, then she smiled and tucked the package under her arm. Steve would understand what she was trying to say.

When they walked into Val's room, Laura stopped, looking around in amazement. "What in the world is all this?"

There was a gigantic pink plush bear sitting in one corner of the room, and next to it a deluxe playpen, and on the table beside Val's bed was an enormous bouquet of pink and white flowers all arranged in a baby bootie container.

"Steve . . ."

"Hey, I had fun. And the baby will need a playpen. It's the only way Val will be able to keep the baby safe when she's busy."

"But it's too much! You already bought that wonderful crib."

"I told you. I had fun. I did the same thing when little Sandra Lee was born."

"But she's your granddaughter," Laura argued.

"And so is this little one," Steve said, his jaw jutting stubbornly. "Right, Val? It may only be an honorary title, but it means a lot to me.

And don't forget, I was one of the first people to see this little doll baby."

Laura subsided then, shaking her head and smiling as Steve leaned over the bassinet and made dumb faces at the baby, who stared up at him with wide, unblinking blue eyes.

"You're overruled, Mom, so you may as well give it up," Valerie said.

"Okay." Laura handed the bag she'd brought to Valerie. "Here's the coming-home outfit. See if you like it."

Val opened the bag. There was a tiny little dress with matching ruffled panties, a minute pair of pink socks, also with ruffles, a soft pale pink shawl, and the smallest white shoes any of them had ever seen.

"Oh Mom! This is adorable! She's going to look so sweet. I'm going to save all of this to show her when she grows up."

"She's a lucky little girl," Steve said. "She's only hours old and already she's surrounded with love."

A fleeting look of pain crossed Val's face, and Laura knew she was thinking of Robert. She quickly covered Val's hand with her own. "Someday, there will be a wonderful man who will love you and the baby the way you deserve to be loved."

"I know," Val said, blinking back tears. "I just wish this guy here had a son who wasn't already married!"

Steve grinned and shrugged. "Sorry, kiddo."

They left before visiting hours were over. Val seemed really tired, and the baby was sleeping peacefully, so they decided to cut out and give the new mother a chance to rest.

"Where are we headed now?" Laura asked as they walked to the parking lot. She felt wonderful, and she knew she would feel even better once she and Steve finished the discussion they'd started the other evening. And she couldn't wait to see his reaction to her little gift.

"I have a little Italian restaurant in mind," Steve said. "Feel like eating pasta?"

"Mm, sounds wonderful. I'm starved. How far is this place?"

"Not far," Steve said, grinning.

And in minutes they were pulling into the restaurant parking lot.

"What's that?" Steve asked, as Laura tucked the flat package under her arm.

"Later," Laura said mysteriously. "Come on. Let's go eat. I'm hungry."

The restaurant was small, dark and cozy. "How will I know what I'm eating?" Laura whispered to Steve, after straining her eyes to read the menu. "I know dim lights are supposed to be romantic, but isn't this a little much?"

"I kind of like it," Steve said. "I can steal a kiss whenever I want, and no one will be the wiser." He proceeded to lean over and very effectively prove his point.

"Maybe the lights aren't too dim," Laura murmured softly. "I'll just judge everything by taste."

Steve ordered a robust red wine to compliment their dinners, and then he sat back and smiled at Laura. "For some reason I feel like you and I are starting all over again, like everything that went before was just a dress rehearsal, you know?"

"I guess it just proves that even at our age, we're still learning and growing. I know I've changed since a few months ago."

"So have I, but I still want to marry you, Laura. Is there a chance?"

"Not now. I won't say never, because life has taught me that's foolish, but for right now I have to be me, Laura."

"You can't be Laura and my wife at the same time?" He was doing what he'd promised himself he wouldn't do, and he hated himself for it, but he couldn't stop. "I want to understand, Laura. Believe me, I'm really trying, but if we truly love each other . . ."

He felt sick. After everything, the beautiful

lovemaking they'd shared, those unforgettable moments together with Val in the delivery room, the first look at the baby they'd promised to share . . . after all of that, and the memories of their youth, it still wasn't going to work.

Laura bit her lip, then held out the package she'd been guarding. "Here. This is for you."

"What is it?"

"Open it and see, Steve. I hope it will explain how I feel about you."

Laura waited nervously while Steve unwrapped the package, and then she lowered her eyes as he lifted the sheet of paper out and began to read. What if he misunderstood? What if he thought she was mocking his need for security in their relationship? What if, after everything else, it still wasn't enough?

Finally, when she thought she would scream if he didn't say something, she heard him clear his throat. She raised her head and looked at him.

His eyes were shining with tears, and he had an odd, almost stunned look on his face.

"It's . . . not a joke," she said softly. "I just wanted you to know that I do understand how you feel, and I understand your needs, even if I can't fulfill them right now."

"Laura, this is the most beautiful thing I've ever seen. Did you write it yourself?"

"Yes, and I meant every word. I love you,

Steve, and I honor and respect you, and I will be your loving companion for as long as we both desire." Laura smiled wistfully. "More than that I cannot honestly promise."

"It's more than I hoped for, Laura. I thought . . . well, all along I guess I've been waiting for you to tell me to get lost, but instead it sounds as though you want to keep me."

"I do." Laura said teasingly. "I like the way you kiss."

"Mm, and I like the way you take a shower."

"But it's more than that, isn't it?"

"Oh yes, much, much more. And I suppose I'm greedy. I want it all. I want us to live together and share all aspects of our lives, but you're not ready for that, are you?" Finally, he was starting to understand. He didn't like it, but he did understand. "All right, so how do we do this? I guess I'm hopelessly old-fashioned. I don't know how to have an . . . affair."

"That's not what we'll be having. Do you really think I'm the affair type?"

Steve held up his hand. "Hold it. I'm getting confused. You don't want to marry me, and you're not the type for an affair, so where does that leave us?"

"Loving companions?" Laura asked.

"Isn't that splitting hairs?"

Laura shook her head vigorously, and Steve found it hard to believe that she was a fifty-two-year-old grandmother of four. With just a little imagination he could see her as she'd been at seventeen, young, eager and unafraid of anything life had to offer. In a way, she was still like that. Life couldn't get her down. She simply wouldn't let it. And that was one of the reasons why he wanted her so badly. He needed some of that fearlessness, some of that eternal optimism.

"I don't like the word affair. It makes me think of married men sneaking around behind their wives' backs."

"Nevertheless, if we continue to see each other and sleep together . . . unless you intend to abstain?"

"Not on your life," Laura said. "Look, Steve, I think I've paid my dues. I was a good and faithful wife, a loving mother, Lord, I'm still mothering and I guess I will until the day I die, but now I think this time is for me . . . for us. A marriage license won't make me love or respect you any more than I do right now, and I suppose that's what I was trying to convey with that special paper. We don't need anyone's blessing, Steve. We just need to know in our hearts that this is right for us."

Steve nodded and covered her hand with his just as the waiter arrived with their wine and a huge bouquet of daisies.

"Daisies!" Laura cried. "How did you manage this?"

"This is an important night. We had to have daisies."

The waiter placed the vase of daisies in the center of the table, and then poured them each a glass of wine. Then he bowed discretely and left them alone.

Laura could hear the soft strains of a love song playing in the background, and the daisies seemed to be nodding their heads at her, telling her that everything was just the way it was supposed to be.

She started to laugh, and it caught on a sob. "This is like a . . . dream. You, the daisies . . . the way we feel about each other. Am I dreaming? Do you really understand?"

Steve kept her hand tightly clasped in his, and with his free hand he reached in his pocket and pulled out a small box. "This is for you."

Laura stared at the tiny box. A ring. It had to be a ring. Had Steve misunderstood everything she'd tried to tell him?

"Steve, I can't . . ."

"Just open it, Laura. It's not what you think."

She opened the box, and it wasn't a ring after all. Inside, nestled on a square of green velvet was a tiny gold charm. It was in the shape of a daisy and her initials and Steve's were carved on the back.

"A daisy?"

"Daisies for Laura," Steve said. "Will you wear it?"

"Yes! Oh yes, I'll wear it!"

"And I will keep this special piece of paper in my wallet so I'll always have it close by," Steve said.

"And you do understand?"

"I understand how you feel, yes. I don't necessarily agree, and I'm not promising that I won't continue to propose to you at regular intervals. I'm a persistent guy, Laura, and I'm too old to change my ways."

"I still want to get my own apartment," Laura said. "Can you handle that? We can spend some of our nights together, but I want my own place to go home to when I need to be alone."

"No problem," Steve said. "I understand now that this is just something you have to do, but maybe after you've done it things will start to look different."

"Maybe." Laura sipped her wine and gave Steve a misty smile.

Anything was possible, and she wasn't completely ruling out marriage, because maybe in a few months or a year she would feel differently and want the security that marriage could provide. But for now she needed to stand on her own. She needed to pay her own bills, make her own decisions, and have her own space. She needed time to get to know Laura before it was too late.

"Will you help me pick out furniture for my apartment the way I helped you?" Laura asked. She wanted it all settled, even the smallest, most unimportant details. She reached out and pulled a daisy from the vase.

"Yes."

"And will you be patient with me when I'm cranky or have a migraine headache?"

"Of course."

"And you won't be hurt if sometimes I just want to be left alone?"

"Well . . ."

"What about spoiling Val's baby? Are you going to hassle me about that?"

Steve burst out laughing. "How can I when I'll be doing it too?"

Laura cocked her head as she reflected. "I'd like to go to Arizona after Val gets on her feet. I'd like to meet your granddaughter. And I can't help wondering if we'll be able to mesh all our children. You never know when one of them might come home."

"We'll deal with that when and if it happens. Anything else, my lady Laura?" And now she was his lady, and unless he screwed up really bad, she would be his lady for the rest of their lives. Because Laura was a keeper, and he was working on being secure enough to let her have the freedom she needed to soar high and free. And in the end, he'd be the winner because love freely given, always came home to roost.

Epilogue

"Mom, I'm only going to be a few hundred miles away," Val said for the fourth time that day.

Laura was helping her pack between tearful episodes. "I know, and I'm sorry for being such a twit. It's just that I got used to having you and Ashley around, and now I won't get to see you very often."

"Well, Steve has promised to drive up with you any time you want to come," Val said. "And tell the truth, Mom, aren't you kind of excited about moving into that cute little apartment you rented? Wow! I'll bet Steve will have some great ideas for christening the place."

"I am anxious to get settled in my new place," Laura said, ignoring Val's teasing smile, "but it will be strange to leave this house for good."

"It's served its purpose, Mom," Valerie said. "All of your kids grew up here, Daddy spent his last days here, and it gave Ashley her start. Now it's time for some other family to enjoy it."

Laura nodded. "That's how I feel too, but even though you know something is right, sometimes it's hard to say good-bye."

"Then don't say good-bye," Steve said, coming in from outside where he'd been loading Val's little car with baby paraphernalia.

"Right. I'm not going to say good-bye," Val said. "I'm just going to put my daughter in her car seat, wave to my two favorite people and drive off into the sunset to my new life." Val's brave smile trembled for a moment. "You know I have to do this, Mom. I have to be my own woman. It would be real easy to lean on you and Steve, but that wouldn't be good for me or Ashley."

"Then, go on, get out of here," Laura said, lifting her hand in a wave. And then she leaned over and kissed her tiny granddaughter one last time.

She stood arm in arm with Steve as her baby, and her baby's baby drove away.

Then, as the little car passed out of sight, Steve drew her into the warm circle of his love. With his forefinger he lifted the tiny golden daisy from where it hung around her neck, and

510

he smiled, the smile that could still make Laura's heart dance in her chest.

"Now, Daisy Lady," he said, "this time is for us."